RISING

HORIZON

BEATONE HAJONG

Become
Shakespeare
.com

First Published in 2018 by

Becomeshakespeare.com

Wordit Content De sign & Editing Services Pvt Ltd
Unit - 26, Building A -1, Nr Wadala RTO,
Wadala (East), Mumbai 400037, India
T: +91 8080226699

Wordit Art Fund helps deserving authors publish their work by
providing monetary support. To apply for funding,
please visit us at
www.BecomeShakespeare.com

ISBN - 978-93-87649-26-2

Acknowledgement

Alright, I'll be honest. It's sometimes very hard for me to write acknowledgments. When I think back to my earlier Novels which I've written, I still see those names whom I associate with. I would begin just like those. Firstly, I wouldn't be able to write without the support of my parents, my two sisters; Bloomy Hajong and Ebica Hajong and of course my small brother, Econ Hajong. I would also want to extend my gratitude to all my family, relatives, my grandmother etc.

And then my friends, who've shown and supported me with the kind of work I had been doing. Their blessing meant me a lot. Each Novel that I took up to write, the inspirations were people and the surroundings. In many ways, I could say part of those stories that I wrote were inspired from my own life too. I have some important friends to mention, Samadhan Koli, Chettupalli Anil Kumar, Debashish Bhoi, Gokul Prasana, Amandeep Kaur Saini, Isha Mittal, Harjinder Bangar, Uday Sharma, Musiba John, Rishab Malviya, Abhinandan Singhania, Pragya Sandhu and Himanshu Yadav, Himanshu Singh Rajawat, Prince Bhasin, Neha Tomar and Nivransh Dev Gupta. These people are amazing and I couldn't be more grateful to them for their love and support.

Like always, the first gratitude would go to the readers who've supported me all through the way. Without you all, I wouldn't have been able to write. To the publisher, who believed in me to represent my work. It's their hard work and constant support that made it to possible path. Without further ado, I would take the chance to pay my thankful heart to all.

About the author

Beatone Hajong,is an Engineering Graduate. Currently, he's in the final Year of MBA Program in Lovely Professional University. By far, he's passionate about Writing and Music. He also has a great interest in Sports, especially Football. Loves to travel, meet new people, learn new cultures, learn new languages. He also loves to taste different kinds of food. Loves beaches more than hills.

He published two novel earlier in his credit, A Turn in the Road and Side by Side.

You can reach him through social media, on facebook, Instgram, LinkedIn. This is his first book of the Horizon series.

Contents

Chapter one

Eight Years Ago

Santa Cruz County, Arizona

I was eleven, when my Mother told me a legendary story. Each night before she could make me go to bed, I used to listen from her. The stories would stay with me for weeks. Often, I would demand to repeat all those. So, each week she would find something new to tell. There was never a day she would skip. So, you can consider my growing years was way different then one would think. I grew up listening to stories and tales. But there was something that I couldn't know much about my her. She was extremely artistic like soul. She had great affinity toward water. I never knew the reason behind. Every story she narrated, had relation with water. However, it tempted me all the time to hear from her. Often, she would take me to beach for a walk. My dad was way far from all these stuffs. He knew what my mother was, back then I was just a small kid who hailed to be loved and pampered with affection. Dad was a Chief of Police, had nothing much more to patrol around the place with the siren car. When I reached out to grow up, I was sent to school, however I couldn't grab much about the school learning. Instead, I was over driven with my mother's stories. Gradually, I felt addicted to her. Although she never meant to hurt me, I would agree with her disagree involving stories related to water. Within days, I got fascinated with the connection being relating to water. She once told me that I was different from all. I was born with extraordinary power. Dad would say nothing about all these. The only response that could be received from him would be an affectionate love. He loved my mother more than he loved himself. Thereby, there could be nothing that would go wrong between them. There was the secret reason behind, why they loved me like a golden star. I was born with supernatural power. At that time of my age, I wasn't mature enough to know about that. Neither, I felt like knowing it. Only the saying came from mother about my extra ability. But, as the days began to swift away, I gradually blanketed about all the things that mom had been telling me since my growing years.

It's the heat summer. I barely had the idea that I had an assignment to complete. Onto my next room, I was busy planning up my next school day. Somehow, I could realize that I had passed another year at Arizona. I loved the weather, the people, and the town where I lived in. But, what kept me intensely related to this place was the hot summer. The weekend was packed with the ultimate joy of fun for kids like me. My twelfth birthday fell on Sunday. So, I knew, I'd have my full day in my hand. I didn't have to go to school to ruin my birthday. I hoped something better I'd receive from mom. My mom was out of home that noon, and I was wondering about my forth coming birthday presents. Minute later, I heard the sound of a car approaching closer. I shifted to look out of the window. Mom stopped and clunked out of the front door. She turned to look at my window, and flashed a smile at me which in turn I hoped to be the dedicated love showed toward me. Instead, I was falsified with my expectation. She wasn't right, she looked pale, fearful and frustrated at the same time. I felt suspicious if dad had to something to do with her mood. I ought to know, if that was the case. But, I knew mom wouldn't let me know with my demand between them. She was seen seated at the living hall. Stepping down through the staircase, I silently joined beside her. Of course, she looked exhausted. That was understandable.

"Hey mom" I muttered.

She grabbed me close to her and gave a room by her side. She spoke nothing, gazed at me warmly. I found it quite strange and awkward to say. She hissed her breath out wanting to expel with words what she had inside her thoughts. I waited to listen from her. She wouldn't narrate a tale to me now. I didn't hope that.

"You need to be strong" she glanced at me, and then turned her face in the direction of the window.

I wasn't sure what she meant by that but I considered it as an advice for me and let it stay with the words. Just then, dad's siren was audible. He galloped in triggering the bell outside. Mom paid no heed of attention about his arrival. I hurried to open the door for Adam Cameron, my dad. He smiled and held my hand to walk in that followed with a kiss on my forehead. He walked into the same room where mom was seated. He exhaled a shallow breath before he could take his seat.

"What's the matter" he intent to know.

She ignored to look at his side, instead her face still faced in the direction of the window. Through the window, the clear view of the beach was accessible. I wondered, what she was looking for through that side. After prolonged silence, she uttered wanting dad alone in private conversation. Dad shook his head agreeing with the urgent need between them. He left me seated. I watched them as they walked out of the room outside at the backyard. I wanted to follow out with them but it wasn't wise hence I waited for them in the same room for their return. But, as the time began to run away it shrunk to get late. It's almost dark now, and the twilight beyond the horizon was sinking down below. I watched it calmly through the same window. Their voice began to hover louder. I could feel the intense argument that evolved between them. I tended to fear, planning to confirm what went wrong between them. I stepped out of the room directing toward backyard. Their heated argument continued, it was all relating to me, both denying in accepting their faults on each other. I heard all their sayings, just by the line door that accessed the pass to backyard, I stood silent. Mom felt the disturbance and turned to look. She saw me and stopped their talking. I felt nervous and fearful. I ran upstairs to my room where I fell on my bed with intensified sadness and depression. I cried. Tears fell endlessly. I still do remember the last time I cried, when dad took me for the first time to school. That was long years back. I locked myself for an hour inside the room. Neither, they both showed to me. It's almost half past nine and I waited with a hope that I'd receive some consoling love from any one of them. I was almost dried up with the tears out of my eyes. Still laid on bed with the scene of argument that floated before me. That's the first time I saw both against each other. My eyes almost went down to sleep when then a knock came up at my door. Mom called me once, and I realized it was her voice. I stood on my feet shuffled toward the door and opened for her. She immediately embraced me with love, I felt little satisfied for she still loves me. She took me to my bed and sat beside. She brought the dinner plate along with her.

"I'm so sorry my sweet love" she said.

She handed me the plate and I continued to eat listening to her.

"We love you and there's nothing wrong that I want to happen for you" she continued.

I could just nod my head listening to her. When I was over with the dinner, she had asked me to hear her very carefully. I was just wondering, if she'd narrate me another tale to make me go to bed. But this time, it was all for real to know. She made me lay down on bed. She roomed herself next to me. The ceiling looked dull and the corners were covered with the mask of spider webs all around since last summer. It's been almost a year I had never touched those corners of my room in cleaning up. She dimmed the bulb and added by my side. She covered the blanket on me.

"Your dad is a good man. He loves you to core. But, there's something you need to know. You're grown up now my dear. You are grown to understand and keep secret in your life".

"What's secret" I demanded.

She looked at me, and smiled for seconds. Her palm ran on my forehead. It's moonless night outside. But the breezy night could be felt severely rushing through the window panes.

"Listen to me very carefully" she urged.

I shifted little closer to her wanting her to stay always by my side.

"You're very different from the rest. You should always know that *Anna*. Never be so close to anything or with anyone that could hurt you. Trust me, you'll know it later as you grow up" she continued.

It sounded strange to me, what different I was? It made me believe I wasn't a human. But, I was for I could see myself. And the other half of my heart was already shattered into million pieces that mom told me that she'd leave us the next day. I didn't believe her at first but she sounded serious. I had to accept for what she told me. I'd stay back with dad for the rest my life. She hadn't mentioned where she'd go, where she'd live. The reasons why she'd leave us, except the fact that Adam knew everything about it. I demanded to know but unclearly mentioned nothing about all. Instead, she urged me to be strong and promising, she'd return back to us with time. Dora Cameron, my mother always stayed away from the social culture amongst the people from the town. All though sometimes, she'd behave strangely, it wasn't that acceptable. However, things have changed now. Within these years, she got many new friends from the town. The last thing I wanted to know was the small secret she had to tell. It's almost midnight by now. And the suggestions she gave seemed to fade away by the time I was falling asleep. I demanded to know, what she had about the secret to tell.

"You're not like the other human, you're a mermaid my dear" she revealed me.

I felt the thrust of being numb. I was awestruck with the fact, hearing I was never a human, but a mermaid with a fish tail. She lately told me that I'd be able to transform into mermaid anytime, provided I find any water bodies around. I didn't believe the story; I took it as myth. I felt, I was having a nightmare with mom. If it ever comes to be true? I wondered what I shall do? I imagined to kill myself. How could I have a dual life? I'd be dead corpse being alive. People wouldn't believe me. By the time I woke up the next day, mom wasn't next to me. She was seen at the front porch preparing to leave. Dad stood helping her. After the last night incident, it seemed they got much closer than ever before. I watched them very closely through the window. When everything was done, she prepared to go. I wasn't sure where she was going. She started her engine. Dad stood with solemn feeling of being deserted from her. He couldn't stop her neither he could ask her to stay few more days. All I could know was that I'd live the rest of my life with dad. She looked at me for the last time. She turned to look at my window. I was staring at her like ages have passed away. Her eyes spoke much more than I could realize. It read more than she could show me. She couldn't help herself to stop by at least for the sake of her daughter. I watched her with deepened shades of sorrow being away from her. She gave very shallow smile before she left, and to that it had lot more emotions that anyone could identify seeing her face. I ran down to see her or to get a hug. But, by the time I was there at the front gate, dad was standing alone watching her car gone. We watched together as she vanished from the sight. Dad held my hand and we walked back to house. I began to feel the loneliness without her. Dad never says all those stuffs. For men it's always hard to show love for women.

When the weekend arrived, I had to celebrate the birthday along with dad and few of my friends. I began to miss mom within a week of her absence. More day past, things were getting a little strange. My health shrunk down. Dad always proved his advice upon me to eat up whatever came before. He wanted me to look healthy. I grew slim and slender within a week. I tried hard but I couldn't stay upon it. Perhaps, it had something with mom to do. I began to comfort myself doing pretty crazy stuffs. I knew, I had to overcome the fact that mom was gone. Indeed, dad wanted the same. The only hope for me was the promise that she made before she left us. I'd only hope to wait for her return without any precise knowledge about her time. The summer had to rush away and to these days I'd the summer finals to get over with. I stopped going to the beach since mom had left us. But, on one occasion I intended to revisit once again. For my friends strolled down the last week to spend their weekend. I visit alone now. Dad rarely gets his time to spend the weekend with me. But I never minded about that. He does try his best. When he gets a little time off, he'd always be ready to take me anywhere I wished to go. I began to build my habits to stay alone without any remembrance about past. However, it seemed inevitable not to recall mom. Sometimes, dad said mom was very different from all of us. She loved us all. And now, I miss her a lot. My dad didn't leave his job as the Chief of Police. He still loved to do and serve people protecting the town. People knew him across the county, he seemed quite famous person. Adam had always been a good dad to me. Although it sounded disrespectful to call him, Adam, but I wouldn't with an intention. He's my dad and I do care about him. My years wouldn't have been so good to live if he wasn't there after mom was gone. He once told me, he'd love to shift from Arizona, although he didn't confirm yet. I tried to know from dad the reason why mom left us alone, it wasn't appreciable I realized a lot later as I could reason by now. He never told me about that, instead he'd ask me to go to visit the beach.

On Sunny Summer Sunday, dad was off with his duty. He was going through some newspapers with the television telecasting the NBA finals. I was never interested into sports. So, for me it was blank before my eyes. I grabbed a seat beside him with the bowl of cornflakes mixed with milk in my hand.

"Hey, dad" I wished him.

He asked me to sit near him. I joined watching the NBA, with least interest. He rarely spoke about mom with me, although inside he too missed her every day. I planned to confirm if we were really leaving Arizona.

"Dad, are you sure you wouldn't miss this place?" I said.

"I'd but, we got to move on with the journey of our lives. Your mom wanted us to do that".

I couldn't say more than that, but had to end up embracing him. That following night we had shared the dinner together. That was long time after, we both had gone out to dine. However, dad wasn't sure yet where he would want to shift. Perhaps, he had in his mind or maybe he was not quite sure whether he actually wanted to go from Arizona. Only he could flash that feeling that he needed to shift from here. The reason, he told wasn't that clear. All he could tell it was for my good. Even if I liked the place and the heat, I was severely tempted by the thought we would be going to new place very soon. Remained behind would be nothing but to carry the memory we had here. Adam told he would finalize by next Sunday. He would talk to the authority about the re-establishment.

Nearly weeks have passed until dad decided the place. For the last few days, he was on search in getting a new house. He never yet disclosed to me where we were going? But on the day, he left his Job as Chief of Police, I had seen the paper kept on the table with the slightest hint about the place. Dad wasn't at home then. He was hired for the last patrolling of the day or could say it was his last duty here at Arizona. I was glad to know that we were moving to California. When dad returned he seemed quite exhausted. He wasn't the part of the department from that evening. I waited for him. The dinner was prepared. After mom had left us, he was everything to me. Somehow, I managed to complete the semester that year. In course of time, I was almost over with the dreadful past of missing mom. I could only move on with the truth that she had promised about her return. Dad was no more that busy with his days. Within weeks of time, we prepared to move out of town. Many of my friends knew about it. Some demanded to know about the reasons. I could only hastily wonder with the truth behind leaving the imprint that had in my mind. I would miss Arizona of course, the height of summer here, the rusty winds, the Sunlight that mirrored out of the mountains. I never gave much thought about the place anymore instead, I heaped to move out as quick as possible. By the end of summer, we were basically out of Arizona.

Dad sold the house at Arizona, received some handsome amounts to pull the journey to *Sonoma County*, California, a small place with small population. The placed seemed quite ecstatic with greenery surrounded with trees and rivers that flowed out through the way to enter the county. Of course, the place was very close to one of the beach that ran across the longest shore over the State of California. It caught me easily to get accustomed with the place. The weather had a lot to do with me. I wondered if the place was just like Arizona. But it appeared to be opposite. I could bear the heat easily. The presence of sluggish green nature avoided the area being getting burnt in the heated summer. When we reached the nearest place to it, we hired a car to drive to our house. We drove twenty kilometers to reach the exact location. Dad showed me the house we bought. Thankfully, I could appreciate him well. With scenic and exotic location, I failed to believe that actually we were going to live here. I had only wished if mom would have been here with us.

By the beginning of autumn, we were actually living there at the Sonoma County. A small driving distance, away from home the beach was located. I had the thought once to go for a visit to look up at the new place. The oak trees surrounded our home with the long tendrils of various species of plants covering the backyard. Though it looked like we were staying in a forest, however it had the vigorous mesmerizing and intensified place. I began to fall in love with the surrounding. We were way out of the main land. So, it obvious we could hardly see people around us. The day we reached, it was pouring rain heavily. I had great affinity toward cold weather. The only difference was I got adapted to heat staying at Arizona. Here things would change up easily I could follow that perspective. Dad got back his job as the Chief of Police. He usually gets into people very quickly unlike my mom, and to me they always told, I was different. The only truth that I could grasped, in my memory was the last word she told me before she left. Yet then, I wasn't experiencing about the fact that I was born as mermaid in life. Dad knew all the things that he had to know. As usual, he got the same rank in his profession. He began to take his duty in serious way. Within few weeks of stay, he got to admit me to a school. He wanted to complete my graduation year. However, I rarely gave a thought to it, no matter even if the surroundings seemed very seductively mesmerizing environment. I had to make new friends and meet new people. In all my qualities, I was very weak in making friends or meeting up new people.

Right now, I had to concentrate only on my new life to build up with the nature's environment and new people. Dad informed me he'd get me admitted, so he had asked me to be prepared to go to school. I had no idea about the new school, how would be like or else I would be sucked to death. I prepared mentally myself even though knowing I would be scared the first time. Dad returned from his duty when the sun was almost down under horizon. He was supposed to bring me new stationeries for the next day. He got it right and remembered about it. He handed me and walked on to get refreshed. I prepared the dinner for him. When the darkness crawled in, the weather had changed almost. The thundering began to sound and the flash of lightening apparently reached to the surface. We sat for dinner. He talked about his duty, although the interest wasn't in me in hearing about. I left the table when we were done with the dinner. The drizzle began to fall. It turned cold within no minutes. Before I could step upstairs, Dad had something to tell.

"I've a surprise for you"

I stopped momentarily. I would want to know, what could he give me now? I brightened my face with slightest glow, looking toward him.

"Thank you" I said, maybe I was pleased hearing that.

The rain was just a mist as I walked into my room, but I was happier that I had something to do the next day rather sitting idle at home. I looked around to make sure the room was well settled. That's when I noticed, an album I carried with the memory of my mother. Before I could sleep the night, I flipped few pages to look at those old pictures. I inhaled a deep breath stilled with the album in my hand on bed staring intently outside. The rain hadn't stopped yet, and the weather chilled at its lowest degree.

Chapter Two

Present Day,

Sonoma County, California

I knew it would begin with the end. And the end would look like an empty vessel tumbling before my eyes. I've been choked and wandered about these many years. So, that was my story eight years ago. That was me, just me. Now the things have changed. I'm still into graduating. Adam, my dad and I had lived for these passing years without remembering mom. But, the last night before I had gone to sleep, I had the reminiscing picture of her. It was inevitable to recall her back. Maybe I had a dream about her, she missed her daughter I could feel that. But mom, she was strong, and I still wonder the lack of reasons where she had gone these many years. Neither, did dad know about it precisely. Long ago the time had passed. I know one thing, mom loved dad more than anyone else in this world.

When I opened my eyes in the morning something was different. It's been raining since last night and the frost stuck up in the air unraveling the mist of cold weather. It was the light. It was still the green gray light of a cloudy day in the forest, but it was clearer somehow. I realized there was no fog veiling my window. I walked out of my bed and watched out through the window.

A fine layer of hailstones from the last night covered the porch. All the rain from last night had frozen into solid. I had enough trouble not falling down when the ground was dry. I glanced at my truck. It needed to be dry out from the water. The rain stopped since hours. It might be safer for me to go to school.

Adam, left for work before I got downstairs. In a lot of ways, living with Adam was like having my own place. I threw down a quick bowl of cereal and glass of orange juice from the refrigerator as breakfast. I wiped the rain waters from the truck which took few minutes to dry out. Dad actually gifted me the truck the day I went to school for the first time. No matter how old the truck was, it had something more than that in driving it to school. It's nothing more than a Chevy as class. I informed dad before I got out school. He would come for lunch from his work. I kept it prepared for him. I would see him only at the end of the day. I drove to school. It took time for me to make new friends. I still met none who could be with me to share my company. For a while, I had to try hard to find a parking space. I found it quite cool enough to have a Chevy truck driving to school. Along the rows there were many in numbers which indeed are the costliest car parked alongside. The day was dimmed and calm, breeze blew in constant fierce. However, it had the touch of coldness in it. I clunk the door and carried my bag in one of my shoulder. As my step headed forward toward the entrance, a young lad appreciated about my ride.

"Nice ride" he said.

"Thank you" I said. I could only try to be friendly.

I headed on to the inquiry section about my class. The lady seated urged me to stay calm for the line seemed to be quite longer than I expected. I had to wait for ten minutes until my turned had arrived. I could find, I was the last person standing in a queue, behind me none. The lady gasped once and threw an unpleasant smile though to her it seemed quite fine. I just widened my lips in response to her.

"Annabell Cameron" she spoke my name.

I nodded my head waiting to hear where she would send me.

"How long have you been here?".

"Quite a few weeks" I said hastily.

She looked at me once with that same intent and sent to math section. I did really hated math. I didn't even realize when I first walked in, the class had already started. I stood at the front door and my mood in call of fear tone. The teacher saw me at once and asked me to come inside. He saw my I-card hanging through my neck. He watched very closely to know my name.

"Annabell Cameron, I would accept you to enter the class on being late. Since it's your first day to Math class" he said.

He sounded humble and quite graceful enough as human. There was only one seat left to be filled. Everyone looked at me in strange fashion. Did I smelt bad? I had the cliché on me. Somehow, I walked to my seat. Next to me a guy sat. Dazzling to look at, I ignored the first moment, for I felt embarrassed of being late to class. I thought everyone came to know my name by now. The guy next to me seemed pretty silent and wondered to look at. More than I could pay attention to class, I felt slightest disturbance. I never knew the reason behind. Maybe, the guy had something to do on that occasion. Somehow, I maintained to stay steady paying on my attention as hard as I could apply. In course of the class, he would peek at me, his eyes toward in a sudden glance. Things weren't in state of normalcy. Though his pretty face stitched to silence yet there was mind conversation that went through. His intentions weren't caught in my mind, trying to avoid me as possibly as he could. Apparently, things were done with strange feel of embarrassment. When the bell rang, he walked out quickly avoiding the rest. I found it quite strange at his behavior. I've never met yet who could try to be so friendly with me. But on that occasional day, Peter Pho encountered me at the cafeteria. I wasn't known to him. Neither, I actually knew him well. With the pack of lunch, I was seated at one table, few tables away from the guy at the Math class. I couldn't concentrate on eating rather my sight would want to peek at that guy. I've never seen so beautiful and glorious face. But that person, he was something different from the rest. His pale white skin and the shimmering face which had the glow like that of a shinning piece of diamond were the real cause to pull attention. His table seemed empty except that he occupied one side of it. His golden blue eyes and the reddish lips pressed close invited me more into him. He pricked his eye toward me, watching me at close gaze. Just then I was interrupted.

"You're Annabell Cameron, aren't you?" said Peter.

I nodded, watching him pull the chair for himself. Peter actually had the Asian features though his ancestor perhaps had clan back there.

"Hi, I'm Peter Pho".

He offered me the piece of sandwich. But looking onto my plate, I've had enough. I had the ardent interest in knowing about that guy. He was still there at the same place. His turned his face away from me and I felt how hard he tried to keep away from people. I felt awkward. Maybe reason was me that led him feel indiscipline about the day. He walked out, not bothering much. He even didn't turn his face on our side instead he headed out to the front porch of the school building.

"Who was he?" I keened to know.

"That's Alyward Pyne".

"Is he always like that?"

"Actually not…. he never shows his few of his extraordinary

qualities he has. He's always in demand, especially girl's attention".

"What you mean by extraordinary qualities?" I urged to know.

"Well, he has something that ordinary people don't possess. Why don't you change the subject?".

I didn't want much more to know or to gather knowledge that seemed uninterested either. For the rest of the day, I haven't seen him. Though the fact I wanted him. Peter waved me a last goodbye before we left the school. I walked out through the front area toward the parking lot. The numbers of car decreased in its row leaving behind mine and few. Few cars away, Alyward stood leaning behind his car. I handled sharply with control to look at him. Though my eye never pointed directly at him but mirrored by my hair that fell between us. He willfully gazed at me with strong consent of softness on his face. The tenderness on his face encapsulated my thought, overdriven what was he up to, waiting for none. The hindrance fell off, claiming it to be hard, I ignored the rest of the moment in quick session. I opened my front door and took in to control the steering of my Chevy truck. But, before I could empty out the place, he was already out of his away. I stopped for just seconds at the space where he parked his car. He vanished so fast. The parking lot stood all empty. I drove back with positive opinion. Back at home dad would arrive. The sky clouds turned dark. Adam was already there. It began to drizzle the moment I reached home. Dad was seated watching television.

"You're early today" I purred.

He turned toward me and responded nodding his head.

"How was your day?"

"It's the same" I shrugged, and went upstairs into my room.

I thought about him, or faintly I could recall his name as told by Peter. My math class went worse that day being seated alongside gorgeous, beautiful human. His every corner of his eyes dazzled me along. He wasn't very hard to escape out. Neither, I could stay away from him. The fact that he had on his face was much more smoldering to look at with such beauty that he possessed. His white glowing pale looking face and the physical features with great shape has much more to do. In all, Alyward Pyne was perfect for anyone.

I went downstairs to add up with dad for dinner. He prepared the night. He seemed calm and well composed although he looked tired. The dinner was quiet, no words from any one of us. However, he wished goodnight before I left for my room. Dad slept at ground floor. He had his bedroom at one side of the building, while he gave me the upper floor to be mine. I wasn't in mood that I would be studying the night. In more percent of my mind it was Alyward who had been occupying inside my brain. That's the first Math class I had attended in whole semester. My admission took quite longer, for I had arrived here in the middle of the semester. That night I couldn't even surf the internet, my modem has crossed its dated limit. It was sadly outdated now. I had to go to bed early though I didn't want to.

The next morning when I stepped downstairs, dad was already gone. He baked bacon and cheese for me for the breakfast. I least liked bacon for breakfast instead, I looked for the orange juice in the fridge as usual. Chewed few loafs of bread with cheese. I left the bacon inside the fridge for dinner. I had to prepare with my bags for school. My feet dragged as I climbed upstairs to my room. The day bloomed in bright sunlight unlike the other day. The wet weather was gone, with the pleasant view across the woods. I had to clean up my truck which was covered with fallen leaves. It took quite a long time to clear all the mess. I was ready to leave.

Peter was the first person I met at the front porch. He had few of his friends along with him, all unknown to me. He began to introduce one by one. Among them a girl, seemed quite acquainted with me. She introduced me personally as we walked on through the aisle to look for our classroom. Her face was readable, believed she wanted to be a good friend of mine. Without much delay and hesitant I would be, as I thought.

"Hi...I'm Jessy Cole".

"Annabell Cameron"

"I know" she said.

I wasn't that good enough in remembering people's name. To my conclusion, I wondered how could people know me, when I just arrived few weeks earlier. I had walked through the detention room in searching about the morning period I had. In the inquiry, I was noticed about my class. Before lunch I had to attend the Math class. The lady at the inquiry room chattered about me. Not bad though, she was quite humble today. She mentioned me the way to Math class. I knew my way although I had to appreciate her chivalry. Jessy left to her biology section. I hated the subject Math. I wasn't late, in time that day. The weather outside turned heated with the burning glow of rays from breathing sun. Inside all seemed settled down, few in junks of piles of chattering out. I firmly stood at the entrance. Maybe I was nervous or scared to push myself in. I saw him seated at the same place. With the other left empty next to him. My feet shrugged hesitantly if I would want to sit beside him. He looked at me through the edge of his eyes and that same face flashed the silent hood of smile. He turned his face once away from me. His pale white skin and the lightening blue eyes still pulled the attention. His gestures implemented to be the other way. I moved to walk into my seat. My footsteps silent until I took my seat beside him. He glared at me once again in some intent way through his eyes. I saw his face, I could tell. In course of time, I finally felt quite settling with him. Though he seemed to be quiet the only show he had could be his imminent behavior that he had that uniquely made him different. I shadowed my face with my hair fallen between us. I would lie the rest people that I was watching him very close at every moment. Frequently, his eyes turned on mine as the class proceeded. He looked very tempting and non-repelling. I bit my lips again on my next glance at him. When the bell rang out, he hadn't shifted his feet not an inch, in others words he waited for me to walk out of my seat. That was unusual of him.

"I'm sorry for being rude to you" his voice was almost a whisper.

I quietly made my face that would pull me into feeling of ecstatic moment.

"Its fine" I corrected.

We walked out together through the corridor heading toward the cafeteria.

"I didn't get a chance to introduce the other day. I'm Alyward Pyne" he sounded tempting.

In response, I showed him the touch of concern. At the Cafeteria, Jessy along with the rest waited for me at their table.

"What brought you here from Arizona?" he muttered.

I wasn't even expecting that, how he knew from where I belonged. We grabbed the plates in our hand and collected the food items on our plates. But, before I could join the rest I had the intuition that he should slightly know about me.

"It's a long story" I just added.

Peter waved his hand calling out for me. I stood with a choice where I should head ahead, to them or staying in his company.

He maintained to understand the need, and in a gentle notion Alyward directed his way. I fell the urgent vacant that very moment. I watched him walk toward his lone table. I peeked at him before I shuffled to the rest. Peter seemed to be very much into me. In any case, he tried to do whatever possible way he could impress me. But, I still couldn't count his chivalry over me. He's good guy but not the choice I had in my mind. With genuine consideration, I wanted him only to be my friend. The last few days, he had been very much in contact to me. I would appreciate his care and tender conduct toward me. On the other hand, Alyward seemed to be mystified filled with secrets and untold qualities. He glanced at me from his table. I made my hair fall between us walling the scene of his face. I cornered my eyes secretly through him through the spaces between hairs. I bit my lips once again with the facet smile that came quickly. He glimpsed to know the slightest moment we had. He smiled away his pale glowing face. He seemed to have completed his lunch, ready to move out.

"Anna, where are you?" Jessy shook my body.

"We've great weekend this week. We're going to the beach" Peter declared.

"Are you coming with us?" Jessy asked.

I never knew within few weeks; I could have the set of friends. I was just added another girl in the group. I turned my face to look at the table, as I lifted my head to look for, Alyward wasn't there.

"Hi Annabell" Lexie inclined her voice.

"Just Anna" I amended.

"I'm Lexie" she introduced herself.

I nodded my head in response to her. I had the lunch plate yet to be completed. The rest were moving out from the cafeteria while these set of groups were yet to end up their dinning.

"Are you coming with us?" Lexie demanded again.

Everyone looked at my face, startled with hopes in their face arguing inside that I should come along with them. I froze for seconds, before I could set my final convey to them. Maybe I was wrapped in Alyward's thoughts. I wanted to know him very closely. Indeed, he was quite the different type, gorgeous, much handsomer like any of the movie actors. Within few days of being together, I was driven to get obsessed by him.

"I shall try" I finally added.

Peter sighed at my words, wanting that I should be sure. He wanted me, but to my condition I was probably confused with myself. I needed some time to spend myself. I disjoint myself from the group as my lunch was over. It wasn't much easy to leave them. They were the first people who turned out to be my friends willingly. I just hoped they forgive me for today on my unacceptable conduct. I left them heading toward the main building. Instead, I wondered to search for Alyward if he was available. Whether it's the cafeteria or the parking lot, I was tapped with his constant gaze each day. I never wanted to speak the truth, in precise way I loved to look at him.

At the parking lot Alyward stood in support at the back of his car. His hand placed on the roof, and watching him closely I could realize his eyes cornered to peek at me. It didn't move neither he did blink even once. My car was four cars away from him. I walked on to grab the front door. He stood still watching at me, with the slightest imperfection through his gaze. I managed to show in return. It was quick contact. He was so tempting plus attractive. Maybe I wasn't able to comprehend to look away. I couldn't resist him. I clunk the door and got myself settled inside immediately. My hands were on the steering wheel. I led my way through the same path, but he wasn't there. He was gone. The parking lot stood empty. I was the last person to drive out from the porch. I braked my car for seconds to look the perfect place where he usually kept his car. Examining what possibly could make him so fast. He wasn't a vampire though. He doesn't look like. I drove back with that cumulative thought in my mind. I was hurry running back home. Dad didn't reach yet. I waited for him to add up the dinner with him. I could hear his car honking outside, as I turned off the television. I was off to get him inside. It's almost dark outside and the howling of wolfs could be heard in the long forest area.

"Your mom called" he said as he saw me.

I never believed him at first. It's been eight years away that she willfully wanted to talk to us. Should I be over joy or should I get angry at her? I was soaked in multistate feeling. We walked in to the sitting hall. I kept the dinner prepared for both. I was keened to know where she was. I could only pull my interest if mom will ever be back again.

"Where's she now?"

"She's away from us, she told me she was at Cruz Bay, Virgin Island. I gave her your number. She wanted to talk to you".

I stood watching dad helping himself settling up the things. My feet stiff enough to make a move under the circumstances. I hated to appreciate that mom even called us. After all these hard years, how could she couldn't even think of us. I knew, how dad had come up to live his life with me. I know, he's been the best man I've ever known in my life.

"She said, she would be calling you tonight" Dad suppressed his voice low.

He prepared the table for dinner as I watched him settling up the whole. I joined with him to dine.

"How's your school going?"

"It's great" I shrugged.

"Did you get new friends?".

Alyward came up in my mind instantly. When he talked about new friends, I knew I had the others with me. I nodded my head.

"Why mom is at Cruz Bay?" I breathed in.

"She has got some work to complete".

It always freaked me out about her for none told me the right cause what she was exactly up to. It frustrated me more than getting angry at her. Neither dad willed to say anything about her. I had to confront myself with nothing known or filling up myself with the least importance in her life.

"Are you ok?" dad concerned before I could leave upstairs.

"I'm fine" I nodded.

I got the outdated modem fixed the last week. Adam fixed for me. I rarely realized how much he cared for me. Though he never showed it but, his actions toward me, it's appealing of love. He always anticipated to stay his life simpler than I would imagined it to be. I was browsing through the homework to be completed from the internet. Just then, I got the phone rung up. I gave pause thought before I picked it. After three continued ring, I held the receiver in my hand. From the other end the voice called out my name.

"Hey, Anna it's me, your mom".

I heard her first and then browsed up through my mind what's the next she would say. I waited breathing softly.

"Are you there, dear?" she said again.

"Yes mom" my voice fell shallow.

"I know dear, I've left you alone, but look I've something important here. I just hope you forgive me" she paused.

"I missed you" my voice in honest emotions.

"I missed you too honey. Your dad told me about your new school. How are the guys, did you make new friends?" she never stopped inquiring.

"Nothing much special here" I ended my talk short.

"Listen, I promise you I'd be back to you all very soon. And I'll tell you everything when time comes".

"Right" I said not willing to continue with the conversation.

"I know dear, you hate mom very much, she's bad. She's ignorant".

It brimmed my eyes and I could realize the moistening eyes that turned wet quickly. I could no longer stay on phone with her. I immediately plunged the receiver back to its position. I was off to bed after surfing little more internet. Every moment it had the notion of mom's call indulged in my mind. Further long, I couldn't wait to stay longer instead the night fell asleep as I settled myself to bed.

I had the dawn falling on me the next day. Dad was out in the yard cleaning up his car. He opened up the bonnet to look up the fault in the engine. I walked downstairs to ask him if he could find anything fault in my truck. I had the least knowledge about vehicles.

"Morning dad".

"I checked up your truck, the next week I shall have your tires changed" he said.

I opted to look the fault. The wheel tires were almost worn out. On any rainy day, it was sure the wheels would no longer stay gripping onto the road. Perhaps, it would likely to skid with the loose of control. Fortunately, the day turned to be sunny for the rest of the month. And I would have safe drive until I get the new tires fitted on my wheels.

"Aren't you not going today?" I asked.

Adam closed the bonnet checking the fault. His hands engraved with oil greased. He looked at me. I was next to him watching him working out on the engine.

"I will" he breathed out.

We walked in together back to house. He had the breakfast kept on the table. I still had an hour to leave for school. He was almost prepared quickly to leave for his work. When dad is in uniform, he always looked the worst kind but I never implemented to comment on that. For that was his job. He had few pieces of bread and jam as his breakfast and readied himself to leave the house. The whole day he's under the constant effort of duty.

"See you in the evening" he said, as he walked out of the house.

I watched him start the siren car, and he drove out of the gate. I had the other picture if mom was there our life would have been different. Dad didn't need to do so much for us. He'd have his life quite free and relaxed. I confined myself to engage in preparing for school. My graduation years weren't that good enough to be talked. I still had more to come out from the remaining part of my year. But very soon, I would love to see myself as pass out graduate. I drank a glass of juice before I left for school. I drove through the heated sunny road. And the constant fear that hit me was the tires. Somehow, I kept driving slow avoiding the risk of skidding in any part of the road where the potion would be wet by water. Of course, the tires have lost all its cut grip.

At the parking lot, Alyward stood at the back of his car supporting his hand on top roof. He sensed me before I arrived at the place. I couldn't read on what he was up to. May be by default, he was waiting for me. I passed him watching his eyes toward me. He flashed a quick shimmering smile which was melting. I hold onto the line to park my car. I couldn't park at the same place as each day. I had lot more distance apart from him today. Yet then, he was visible to watch. He was still there watching me. I felt little discomfort about the moment. I ignored, instead I walked along the way toward the main building. He followed me then. He met me again at the corridor.

"Anna, I think we shouldn't be friend".

"You realized now" I explained.

"It's not that easy".

"Are you convincing me? well you don't need. I can follow my own way" I frowned.

"I know, I reacted badly to you".

I stumbled my feet as we walked through the corridor. Alyward managed to hold me from falling.

"At least watch when you walk" he warned.

"You don't need to explain much; you can go your own way" I insisted him.

I followed toward my English class. He took the other way. That following day, I had skipped my math class. Coincidently, Alyward didn't attend the class too. What so ever way he was, I couldn't repel myself from his magnetic personality, his tender voice, his hypnotic eyes. I wanted nothing more than to be with him every now and then. Even if I wanted I couldn't stop to think of him. Alyward was out in the parking lot, his hand placed on the roof top. His eyes magnetically corned toward me. The space between us was all empty. The rest of the vehicles were out. I was gripped in his gaze and constant scenario. I could do nothing but to reflect myself to him. After all, if he was something sinister, he'd done nothing to hurt me so far. He flashed his last smile before he vanished quickly from the area. I was again the last person to leave the place. I stared in his way and left for home.

Dad was early that evening. He was seated with the television on. The newspapers were on the table. Before I could lead myself to my room I added with him for a while. He asked me about my day. Nothing new as usual, he got the same answer. I left for my room spending the minutes with him. I went upstairs to change myself and settled my bag and books. After an hour of time, dad called me down. He had the dinner prepared in the table. We sat together.

"So, how was your mom?"

"Fine" I gasped and handled the fork.

The rest of our dinner was quite silent. Only gestures applied much to our conversation. Dad was indeed not much talkative, a silent grown man perceiving to take the responsibility. I went upstairs bade him goodnight. He did the rest of the cleaning stuff that night. Back in my room, I settled all my old books which were of no use anymore for that year. I sat on the internet to browse. I had never given much thought about my future. It all depended on my graduation grades. I turned to look at the window side. The night felt quiet and silent. Even the breeze wasn't that strong enough to blow away through its path. By now, dad must have gone to bed. My feet dragged to close the window. I could hear the howl of wolfs reaching closer to the forest area. I decided I might as well go to bed early that night. Adam continued to watch me anxiously. He wasn't asleep yet. And it was getting on my nerves then. I stopped on my way and grabbed the bottle of cough syrup from the table. It's been two days I was literally suffering of cough. The syrup did help me and I felt it eased, and I drifted to sleep. Before I was completely into bed, Alyward somehow remained stagnant in my mind. That was the first night I dreamt about him.

Chapter Three

It's the weekend. I still remembered the request my friends made me to come along with them to the beach. I exactly had no memory whether I agreed with them. But, that early morning Jessy called me up, asked about my truck. There was nothing to make an excuse but then dad was supposed to fix my tires that day. I had explained her. Somehow, I could convince the truth to her. She agreed to that. They would pick me up here at home. Lexie called me for the second time. I was inside the bathing room, preparing for myself. I quickly received, my body wrapped with the towel. She made sure that I should be prepared in early hand. The quick conversation ended soon. I threw the phone straight to the couch and ran into the bath room again. I pulled the showered and poured the streams of cold water on me. From down stairs, dad called out. He had the breakfast prepared. He left for sure. To signal him, I raised my voice about his concern. I heard the sound of the car passing out through the gate as I watched dad going for his work. Wrapped in towel, I was still there watching him through the window. He saw me and waved his hand.

I walked to the closet finding the best suitable dress for me. I had rare idea about clothing, basically I had never given enough thought about my clothing wears. That looked the best I chose for me. I've never been on swim suit but going to beach means I should have one. I was ready by then thinking onto my thought. I moved down stairs. The breakfast table had the choice of meal that I loved. For some reason, I felt dad won my heart for another next time. I knew, it was the food that I loved. I was seated up with the breakfast plate. With a wonder of thought in my mind, I could only have Alyward come along with us, might things would be different for me. I didn't have the means to reach him. Over the weeks, I only had the chance to see him at school. Maybe that's one reason that I never missed school. I had the phone in my hand but not likely his number. It sounded quite frustrating why I was into him in offset manner. I had just met him or saw him at school. I would likely to know what his problem was. Engrossed up with the verse of Alyward, I was suddenly interrupted by a loud noise. I felt the shook in my mind. The loud noise was knocking at my door, the car horn honking outside. It was Lexie at my door.

"Are you ready?" she spoke.

I nodded gently, my face flashed a smile seeing her. Jessy and Peter were in the car. Of course, Peter was driving. I picked my belongings and walked out from the house locking the door. My truck was parked outside. I had the quick glance at it. Something new was imprinted on. The tires were changed. Dad changed all the wheel tires this early morning. That gentle smile and affection roused within me. I couldn't thank him that moment instead I shall have when he would be back home to offer my thanks. I walked on along with Lexie. The open hood car really looked delicious for a ride. Lexie and I took the back seat. Peter released the gear and we were out of the place in no sooner time.

"How far is the beach?" I claimed to know.

I wasn't mean to ask any particular person. But probably, I expected from the one who was just seated next to me, Lexie.

Instead, I received the answer from Peter. Though he seemed quite gentle to me, I just had the thought he should be what he was.

"It's seven miles away sweet heart" Peter blurted.

Addressing me as *sweet heart* was never something I would want. And all through this summer, Peter was always onto me, in every way or every possible space he could get, he took the opportunity trying to impress me. He's a good friend of mine. Lexie looked at me and made a jubilant face, her eyes raised up. I passed a crooked look wondering the reason why she would make that face although the reason seemed clear to me.

"Oh!!! C'mon….Peter is a good friend" I purred.

She blinked her eyes and that same facial expression appeared on her face. Up from the front seat Jessy interrupted, she wanted to take part in our ideal conversation. Peter talked once. He knew, we were talking about him. But, he never paid heed to what we were. Miles the distance we had covered. The beach was seen as we turned the road. It's a clear day, and the breeze began to flow in all direction as we were nearing the shore. Peter had to park the car in a safe place. It's never the busiest beach in the world. However, people do love to hang around. I was empty. I didn't have the swim suit like the rest. Jessy and Lexie were on with their sexy suit, Peter on the other hand in shorts. I was as usual.

"Won't you get in the water?" Peter questioned.

"I'm fine to watch you people".

"I've an extra pair, you can fit on that" Jessy handed me a pair of bikini swim suit.

I wasn't in state or in a mood to get myself wet. I declined to fit on such type of clothe. I walked with them through the shore, until they had halt to a place to get into the water. The beach almost looked as barren land. Few meters away few couples were there. And the long length beach shore stood deserted. Peter and Jessy were already in the water.

"Why the beach is deserted?" I asked Lexie who stood next to me.

She was yet to get with them. She gripped her feet stiff in the ground, fixed her bikini once again. She was on orange cream bra and panty, dazzling to look at with portion of her cleavage being exposed. I never had such a figure like her. We marked to stop before she got herself into water.

"There's a legendary story, Anna" she muttered, as I saw her being joining the rest.

I waited at the same place. Few minutes later, I had the ceramic thought to tour the surroundings for a while. I did actually forget what my mom told me eight years ago. I walked along the shore moving toward the east. Jessy called my name loudly. I waved at them with the slightest fraction of smile that evolved out. Peter on the other hand stared me for long, and his shorts were almost below his hip level, I could sternly watch at that. They began to play with water. I reached quite far away from them. The shore never ended soon. And the heat of the noon poured out in disrupted manner. My feet slid to move toward the water. At the edge of it, I felt cold as feet began to get wet. I realized it wasn't something I should feel. It shook my body. Within fraction of seconds something was happening to me. There was no one near to me. My feet changed its color. I was scared and nervous. I felt like every heroic movie my DNA was being changed. I could feel the testimony of being someone unknown. My feet almost transformed by now. The deep blue color with the shine of diamond scales appeared. And I couldn't move my feet at all. Fixed at the same place, felt the glue of water. I screamed for sure, I was terrified, petrified. Somehow, I could pull myself away from the water. I ran immediately with the hold of fear inside me. *What was that happening to me*? I failed to know. That wasn't the complete change for sure. Something else were more there. I reached the car. Peter saw me breathing heavily with fear. My face almost soaked terribly, frightful expression. He called me out seeing me running away. I looked myself at the rear-view mirror of the car. My face turned pale white. It's almost bloodless. And my hair had the silky golden shine. But it did vanish very quickly. I took it by surprise. My pale odd white face reproduced to regain my originality. I couldn't believe to myself. Such of transformation doesn't exist. But, *why only me*? It rumbled my head with the tonic sense of terrific syndrome of fear inside me. The rest ran up to catch me.

"What's wrong Anna?" Lexie hummed to know.

"Nothing"

"You look distracted. Are you ok?" Peter concerned.

"I think we should go back" I demanded.

They weren't eager to leave early but I couldn't hold on to stand anymore. My feet still felt the chilled cold water. It made me weak inside.

"Alright, we'll drop you home" Peter looked at me.

They fastened themselves quickly, we drove back as early as possible. The twilight behind followed us, as I glared at the setting sun across the ocean. By the time I was home, it was almost dark way. Peter stopped the car at the front gate.

"Thanks for the ride. I'm sorry, I ruined your day" in apologetic manner.

"It's fair enough" Lexie replied.

"See you tomorrow at school" Jessy spoke.

I stood listening to them, as Peter brightened the dimmed headlights.

41

"Goodnight Anna" Peter wished.

I nodded in simplicity. My eyes began to burn as I glared at the headlights of the car. They drove out of the place. Dad was waiting inside. The only light that could be seen lit was the living room. He, as usual watched the repeat of NBA matches. The main door wasn't close. He left open, I didn't have to wait for him to open up.

"Hey! dad"

"How was your day? Well, I kept your dinner on the table".

"Thanks dad" I spoke less, instead I began to feel drowsy and headed upstairs.

He didn't pay much attention to me. That's one thing I loved about him. I wanted the privacy to be maintained. I marched to the bathroom looking through the glass mirror. My pale white face did leave a mark on me. That following night I couldn't save myself. My whole body dehydrated out of strength. I didn't even bother to take the dinner left for me at the table. Dad felt asleep on the couch watching the NBA. I went to bed early, couldn't even follow my daily routine to surf the internet.

When the dawn broke out, dad was already prepared to leave. I was with him in the porch. He settled his car and waited to leave. He slid the window, his hand on the steering wheel. I hoped to recall to thank him about the tires.

"Thanks dad".

He nodded "See you in the evening".

He left the plate of scramble eggs and toast on table. In the Jug, there was the juice of orange as usual for me. I had in take the breakfast heavy. As from the last night, I had covered up my diet. I prepared myself as early as possible. For some reason, I wanted to catch up Lexie as soon as possible at school. When the time arrived, I turned my truck and left. I had a smooth drive with new tires along the way. As I passed the space of parking lot, I found the place vacant. Alyward wasn't there. I passed glaring through the glass. And my car almost halted at his place. Behind me, there were many searching for a space to park. Horns blew from back, I had to take immediately the safest side to allow them. Finally, I got a space where I could stand my truck. I looked the vacant place. His absence distracted my mind shortly. I wouldn't want that to happen. For sure, my day wouldn't be so good to pay attention to any teacher. I walked ahead, inside, my thought asked about the reason of being absent. I first looked for Lexie, I avoided the math class. During lunch, I could catch up Lexie at cafeteria.

"Hey! Anna....how are you today?" Jessy glanced at me.

"I'm good".

I joined their table and sat by Peter's side. Lexie was late to join. I inquired about her. She completed her biology period. Minutes later she showed up. She sat next to Jessy. She had the lunch box in her hand.

"Well, Anna have something to ask you" Jessy muttered.

She looked at me, her face blossomed with the same smile. She looked quite provocative. I guess, she was quite interested to know about the thing I would want to know.

"What's that?" she asked me.

"It's private".

Jessy made face, it was quite sarcastic to understand. Lexie looked at her, she raised her eyes with the pleasant smile in friendly manner. Peter and Jessy left for the rest of the period to attend. Lexie and I stayed back. We strolled down toward the backyard where the school park located.

"What's that you want to know?".

"You told me, remember about the legendary story at the beach. I just want to know, what was that?" my tone sounded effusive.

"What you going to do knowing that?".

"Listen I need to know. You can help me out".

"How that's gonna help you, Anna?".

I had given her the words with time, I would let her know the details about it. After prolonged persuasion she had agreed to tell me all of it.

"I just heard from my mom. The beach once used to be the peaceful area in the town. Many people have seen unexpected things there. It used to be place for mermaids. It was many thousand years ago. The mermaids had a leader in their team. They say there was a group of sea pirates, who would land there. If it happened, they would hide under water. But unfortunately, one day a pirate saw one of the mermaid, since then it became their camp. The mermaids began to fear; they couldn't live in peace. They were often disturbed by them. But the greedy pirates prepared themselves to destroy them. There was a bloodshed war between the pirates and the mermaids. Lots of blood split all over the ocean. Their queen leader was slaughtered. The mermaids lost the war, those who remained fled to save their life. Somehow few could escape. People say they are seen along the Cruz bay now, Virgin Island. I heard the pirates group still lives. They say they have some evil powers that kept them still alive".

I was attentively listening to her. She stopped after that. Though I didn't hint her to continue, I managed to get the idea by now.

"I need to go; I have a lecture".

Lexie walked on through the cemented path. When she was

about to disappear from my sight, I could gather the courage to ask her.

"Hey!!!!!! Do you know Alyward Pyne?".

She turned back and smiled out. She stopped her feet for fractions.

"He's out of town" she smiled again.

"Thanks".

I found myself seated at the same place again. Inside of me, I had the eager urge to know where Alyward could go. I waited till the sun descended toward the west. I met none at the parking lot. The rest of my friends had left for home. My truck was kept parked lone. When I reached home, dad wasn't there. He never called me. I tried for more than hundred times I believe but, none came answered. I prepared the dinner for him, likewise I had left for him on the table. I was into my room very early that night. As usual I was surfing the internet. I heard the hissing sound of a car. I grabbed my feet to look out of the window. It was him. He looked very unsettling and dejected with some hint of disputes. He was a silent man, and I knew the only kind of person who would love his daughter more than anyone else in this world. I wanted to know where he was but, looking into his present condition I avoided. In fact, I wouldn't want him to trouble the night. Instead, I continued to surf the internet thinking that he would be alright by next morning.

When I woke up the next day something was different with me. I had the feeling of getting stronger and confident. Although, for me it was unusual. I felt better and enigmatic inside. Something secret held into me. Dad was in the hall seated idle with the newspapers on his hand.

"Hey!! dad".

"Hey!! honey…I had your breakfast prepared, it's on the table".

Adam wasn't on duty. But, he never said the reason why. Moreover, I avoided in his business. I left for school. Alyward wasn't there. Somehow, I had been managing to stay alive with my inner confrontations. My math class now turned to be rude for me. On my side, I had the seat vacant of him. Even at lunch I couldn't much be free with the rest. Often, Peter tried his best to console with his tactics. But it didn't work for me. I never disclosed about my inner lining. It's only me what I had been going through inside. Lexie on suspicious note would try to ask me. I don't know, she always brought out the topic about Alyward Pyne with me. I wouldn't deny that to hear. Indeed, something I wanted to know about the guy more. Something strange began to take place. I wasn't hoping for it. The only new thing that was involving me was his absence. *Why I was into him*? I couldn't figure it out. Each day turned pale though I had the company with me.

At night I felt the lone breeze through my window. I never felt like going to school anymore. But dad would always push me into my truck at least for a week. I've decided with strong determination not to think about him anymore. But that very same night, I had a dream about him. It felt so real. That was my second dream I had dreamt about Alyward. The week was gone, and I was in state where I couldn't lead myself. I tried to be friendlier with the rest. Perhaps, I began to like the irritating behavior of Peter. At least, he does try to make me laugh through his nuisance pranks. His company and the rest somehow comfort me. Another week ended without his appearance in school. Things stood unsettled inside my head confirming adequately not to remember Alyward. But, he was someone that I couldn't repel away. I was bordered with the line where I couldn't move forward than to get stuck in his dreams each night. I waited till the third week of the month. Lexie had told me the last week that he came back in town. I planned to confirm him anyway. And next day back at school, he didn't show up. And the next day another no show. More days passed, things were getting little strange. The illusion of false faith began to convert upon me.

The month was over, and I had no seen not even his slightest glance at all. The rest of my friends almost forgot about him. It was me who had him to think about his bothering absence. I felt abandon though I had the others with me. It was the beginning of new month by next day. Dad and I got out for dinner the night. Before I would see the next morning, I fixed my closet with new sets of clothes for the coming month. I wanted to visit the beach again by weekend. But this time all alone. I still have the story in my mind that Lexie narrated. It's worthwhile that I should not think about him anymore. I felt quite perturbation knowing that I could feel something different within me.

The next day, I had a new beginning. Dad was early as usual. I had done my homework and all the rest of school stuffs. I left thinking I would meet up Lexie the first. But the unexpected began to take shape with some expectation. As I reached the parking lot, Alyward's car was kept parked at his place. He was still inside I could see him through the glass. I slowed down my car and crossed the bump. I watched him close as he got out of the door. He saw me, I felt it. I ignore to halt there. I placed my car at the right place. His hand rested on the top roof as always and glared at me with keen notion. I followed toward the main building, he followed me behind. I reached my locker. He didn't stop instead, he was standing right behind me.

"I'm sorry I didn't show up for half a month" Alyward sounded effusive.

"Why do you even bother about that?"

"I know it's hard to tell, but Anna we can't be friends".

"You should have figured it out very early" I left for my class.

He watched me going. During lunch, he didn't show up at the cafeteria. I searched for him. At math class, he was already there. I entered and sat by his side. I exhaled my breath out. He looked very seductive and appealing. I couldn't stop to turn my face at him for once. His eye had the intensity toward me.

"What?" I demanded.

"What's there in the beach?"

I was wonderstruck with the idea that how he had come to know where I was supposed to go. I never intended to know much about it.

"How do you know about it?" I questioned him.

We were interrupted by Nash Billy, our math teacher. The question came for Alyward. To me it seemed the complication that it had in the problem. Alyward made it quite simpler and he could get the right answer. I only calculated how he could solve the complication in the problem. When the period was over, we were returning back to the parking lot. I bade goodbye to Lexie and Jessy. Peter saw me with him. He wasn't that happy enough to know that I was with Alyward the whole day.

"You didn't answer my question" Alyward demanded.

"Do you wanna come with me?"

I hoped the right answer from him. I waited for fraction of seconds until he agreed to find the time with me the weekend. I followed toward my car. He waited for me to go out. He came behind me. At the junction, he bifurcated his way toward home. I drove straight through the lane that led me back to home. That night Lexie called me up. She was quite sure about me and Alyward. I had to conceal about it until I was sure with myself if it ever happens. I had talked long hours surfing the internet. Dad was asleep. It's almost the midnight, when a wolf howled. Dad got out quickly with the gun in his hand. It seemed the creature was at our front gate. Dad blanked fire at the spot but went in vain. However, after that it was peaceful night to get back to sleep. I ran down to catch up dad.

"Are you Ok?"

"Yeah!!!!!!… There was a wolf howling outside the gate"

"I heard the sound…. get a sleep dad…goodnight" I said.

He went back to his bed. I was still on phone with Lexie. I had to re tell her about the incident. She never believed that I stay in wolf prone area.

In the mist of morning dew, I woke early. Dad had a visitor downstairs. I watched them through the window. He once told me the truck which he brought was his friend's truck. And then the young handsome lad stood by his side must be the son of dad's friend. I stepped downstairs wanting to join them.

"Hey!!!!dear".

"Morning dad".

"Remember I told you about my friend. He's Burney Gaige and his son Tyler Gaige. And this is my daughter Annabell Cameron".

"Hi Anna" Tyler sounded friendlier.

Dad and Burney left with their stuff to spend the time inside. Tyler gave the company to me. He was free to talk unlike the shy guy. They stay few blocks away from us.

"So, did you like the truck?"

I wasn't much listening to him that instant. Although we were near to my truck. He looked at me.

"Are you ok?" Tyler concerned.

"Oh!!! Yeah!!! I'm sorry….Yes, I did like the vehicle" I stammered.

He flashed a smile that was quite innocent to observe. We walked out of the gate. Few meters ahead there was a small canteen. The vicinity was peaceful to look at. Dad sometime would order the breakfast from the canteen.

"You must be enjoying your school?" Tyler spoke, as he pushed the door.

We sat at a table. I was supposed to leave for school. It wouldn't be polite enough to leave the guest empty, so I decided not to go for that day. I had received two call from my phone. Lexie was the first one. After half an hour it was Jessy again. I just had a glass of squash that came from a mango pulp. Tyler took a cup of cold coffee for himself. Within short meeting he seemed to be comfortable. I found him quite interesting to talk. We headed back on our way. Dad was still inside. We shuffled in. I had never seen that they both would love to watch NBA matches. I stood right behind the sofa. They weren't aware we were inside. Burney turned back and saw us.

"You're back" he looked at us.

"Dad, I need to go to school".

"Sure".

"Would you mind if I drop you?" Tyler sounded polite.

"No thanks…I'll drive alone".

I went upstairs, prepared in quickly and followed downstairs. I had the truck key in my right hand. I bade both goodbye. Tyler accompanied me till the truck. I took hold of my seat inside. He kept watching at me keenly. I triggered the key and I was on with the engine.

"Well, see you later?" Tyler voice sounded husky.

I gently had the smile on my face. My eyes followed to blink with the right signal on him.

"Yup!!" I muttered.

And then I left. He waved at me. I could see that from the rear-view mirror as his image turned to diminish away. At the parking lot, Alyward waited for me. He caught my sight as I approached the car site. He asked for the reason of being late. Somehow, I managed to overshadow the story that morning. We proceeded toward the math section. He looked greenish in appearance. At first note, I failed to notice that.

"Why you look greenish?" I inquired to know.

He invested his breath silently and glared at me with strong misinterpretation. I was perturbed by his sudden change in his appearance.

"It's the florescent effect" he stammered confusedly.

I didn't know what he meant by that. I nodded just in casual state wanting to know nothing more than what he replied. He grabbed his seat quietly. I took by his side.

"Are you ok?" I concerned once again.

He glanced at me in quick succession and nodded his head. Nash Billy entered the class and began to teach. When the period got over, the rest period we avoided. Peter saw me with Alyward. His intentions were pretty much clear. He hated me seeing with him. He passed me through the corridor without even looking at me. I didn't want to feel him that way. Jessy and Lexie met us. Alyward stood steps away from them. I didn't know the reason, why that so? But with short conversation they had left for lunch.

"Why were you steps away from them? Do you hate them?" I was quite serious.

"No...I'm actually bit not that social or I love being in solitude" he mumbled.

"But with me you seem to be wide open".

We headed toward the parking area. He wanted to show me something few miles away. I couldn't stop but to agree with him. When the sun slanted toward the west, he took me where he wanted, a place that I couldn't imagine in real. The twilight felt upon me. And the breeze blew that touched my inner core. Surrounded with mountains and the lake between had the fragrance of being in paradise. I almost lost my inner sense seeing the beauty of such existence. Alyward caught my hand, as we walked on through the green meadow. The green grass shone silvery and the reflection of it flourished out into the whole area. We sat just on the edge of the lake. Up above the singing birds chirped as they returned back to their nest. My feet slightly could feel the touch of water from the lake as I dipped my feet under it. It shook up for once again, as I felt drenched inside of me. I immediately pulled out my feet. Alyward who was next to me, concerned about the sudden shock. I made sure that he shouldn't come to know what I was going through. He stared at me with strong intense eyes. That greenish color eyes still had the fluorescent in him.

"Huh!!!" I groaned.

"What?"

"This isn't real. This kind of place doesn't exist".

"It exists in my world" he sounded very sweet.

I looked at him and he stared in my direction. We've spent for more than an hour. Dad called me each moment. I knew, he would be upset with my response. Alyward, though didn't touch me on that very moment of time. He dropped me back at home. I waved my final hand to him. Dad was out in the veranda, saw me with him for the first time.

"Who was that?" he questioned.

"That's Alyward Pyne".

"Well, we're waiting for dinner".

I had the least idea about Burney and Tyler who would be invited for dinner at our home. They were inside. As I moved in,

Burney greeted me. I sighed and shrugged in mixed emotions for I didn't expect the thing to happen. Dad joined them in the dinner table. Tyler looked at me and passed a short smile.

"Hey!!" he waved.

I nodded my head with lips slightly to show I was surprise. I assured them to catch up shortly as I went upstairs to change myself. I could never speak the lie to Adam. That veracity still existed in me since when my mom had told to cultivate the good habit. I reached down quickly to get on with them. Dad had already served in my plate. Tyler was just next to me. There was no sort of talk that could involve me around between them. I ate silently listening to Burney and Dad. Tyler in between would insert his idea as the conversation continued.

"Are you alright?" Dad asked.

"Yeah!!! I'm good".

After the dinner, I had spent few minutes with Tyler, asking many of the few personal questions that he could tell me. We sat together outside with the cool breeze that blew in. It's the log of wood that the other day dad had pulled down to construct the garage. The sky was lighted with stars above.

"What you do?"

I know, it was one of the uncomfortable question that Tyler had to reply. He smiled before he could convince me.

"I help dad" he said.

"Really"

He smiled again, and to my concern I couldn't make sure was he telling the truth. Tyler Gaige had the physical appearance with strong arm and shoulder. In fact, he was muscular with lot of strength in his body. To be precise, he was more gorgeous to look at. His eyes were deep green with the kind of spike of his black hair. The fact, that he had reddish white skin that killed every passerby who'd look at him. Tyler wanted me to visit him by the weekend. I gave him my word that I shall see him. They left when the night turned dull. Tyler waved his hand. We strolled inside as their car headed out of the gate. Dad was walking alongside me.

"How you find Tyler?"

I wasn't expecting that, I shrugged and shocked. I halted in the porch looked at him with glimpse of surprise. Dad smiled at me and walked on. I followed behind him.

"Dad, he's just a friend. We just met".

"Ok!!! What about the other guy?"

"Dad could you stop asking…. well goodnight" I walked upstairs into my room.

He was talking about Alyward Pyne. I avoided much to talk about him right now. As usual, I surf the internet before I got to bed. I only wondered that Tyler Gaige never seemed to be rude kind of human being. He was polite and calm. But, his Dad was even more kind. I could finally see Adam well composed with the place. That's the kind of friend he chose seemed rather faithful to be with.

Most of the time at home, I spent in lone hour. Though I got the friends at school but they weren't that close who would stay next to me. Now, that I had the option to spend even my valuable time with Tyler. Days wouldn't be that hard to let the time go. I began to like the company of Tyler back at home. But at school it's more of Alyward. Things began to change in my life. But I still had the fear to figure out about my sudden feeling of numbness with water. I wanted to convey myself to check about it with thorough experience. However, I didn't want anyone to know about it including dad. But, I guess he knew it in an early hand. My mom told whatever she knew to him that I was uniquely different girl in the society. People wouldn't believe if I say that instead the feel of humiliation would rise inside of me. When the weekend arrived as per the word I kept, I drove with my truck to Tyler. The following past week I had much spent my days with Alyward. Many began to take notice of us at the premise. However, things were stable not to put into any misconception about our relation. I wasn't sure what was going on between us. Whatever it was it had something more to do with our feelings.

Tyler was out in the front courtyard of their house. They lived in a big mansion. They had the garage just next to their entrance. I stopped the truck. He noticed me and left his work incomplete and walked toward me. He was into repairing of his bike. Lot many spare parts of cars and bikes could be seen.

"Hey!! Anna" he was more appealing to look at.

His physic appeared bare. He had the t-shirt wore as he approached toward me. My door clunk as I stepped out of my car. He hugged me and lifted an inch through the air.

"I never expected you'd show up".

I smiled on that as we walked toward the garage.

"So, you help your dad as mechanic" I squinted.

He laughed and glanced at me "That's the kind of work I do".

I added to smile again with the slightest hint of being cool with him. He gave me a place to sit. I watched him fixing the clutch wire. We talked more as we heard one another. His father arrived shortly. He saw me and shuffled toward us.

"Hey dad" Tyler granted.

"So, you enjoying" he said looking toward me.

"Yup!!!" I nodded.

"Take care of her huh!!" he looked toward Tyler.

Burney left us then. Tyler resumed back to fix the wire. We began chatting again. I had never learned to bike yet. I had the interest since I was a small kid. It almost took more than an hour to fix the whole parts. By the time Tyler could bring it out in the sunlight the day almost came to an end. The setting sun descended toward west. I had dined with them the night. Tyler had helped me to drop back home. Dad waited for me but this time I had informed him. The next day I had to resume back to school.

Alyward waited for me at the lunch table. But before I could take his side, Jessy and Lexie met me up at the library. Peter wasn't seen for the last few days. I had come to know from them. The reason wasn't that clear. Lexie somehow tried to connect him within the week. But from the opposite side there was no response. They decided they would visit Peter the evening. I wanted to come along with them but Alyward wouldn't leave me alone. I had to persuade them for excusing me out.

"Are you into Alyward?" Jessy yearned to know.

"No…I can't say anything about that" I muttered.

I left them with the small hint of goodbye for the day. At cafeteria, Alyward's complex had the effect on everyone else surrounding him. Each glaring eyes that came from every girl around had the tempting look to get his glance for once from him. As I entered the door, he stood from his chair. I followed my way toward him. He helped me to pull out the chair for me. I joined him. The people gazed at us, almost in sudden mist of shocking scene. There was nothing new about it. Alyward sat by my side. He offered me with the lunch box. He looked at me with gentle kind of expression and flashed a hilarious smile at me. I wondered what's that for rather I attempted to question him.

"What's wrong?" I bit my lips.

He smiled again and his bluish eyes captivating. He stared at me with the intense question that floated on his face.

"Anna, there's something you should know about me" his voice sounded seductive.

I bit my lower lips again nodding my head. I wanted Jessy and Lexie to come over and meet him. Rather, my intention was to make them a good friend with Alyward. They arrived at the cafeteria shortly. I was still with him listening to his words that engaged me more toward him. Lexie waved her hand at me. They took another table.

"Excuse me for a while".

Alyward nodded his head "Sure".

I walked to them, Jessy saw me coming toward them.

"Why don't you join us?" I urged them.

"Will he be fine with us?" Jessy suspiciously.

"He is a nice guy".

"Alright" Lexie agreed.

Alyward looked at me keenly as we approached to him.

"Hi Alyward" Jessy gestured.

"You can join us" his voice too soft.

Since that day onward, they both were quite comfortable with him. And for Alyward, he was always someone whom every one notices. He waited for me to leave the parking lot, when everyone else was gone he asked if I could give a little time for the weekend with him. He wanted to take me to his home and meet his family. But I stood in dilemma whether I should give my priority to him or Tyler. I had promised I'd see Tyler this weekend. He'd help me to ride bike. Somehow, I persuaded him about my awkwardness. He agreed to listen. I didn't want both to hurt in any way. Instead, I had the preplanned thought to visit the beach all by myself the weekend.

Dad had the dinner prepared for me. As I reached home, the first thing that he promised me that he would take me to nearby town for his anniversary celebration. It's been almost long years that I had rarely remembered about my mom and dad's anniversary. Dad was still in connection to mom. I've often seen him talking to mom over phone. But, he never spoke about it since the first time I had talked to her. Their anniversary was week away. I claimed to know, if mom would come along with us, though I wasn't expecting her for now. I got ready myself and moved downstairs to dine with Dad.

"How's your school time going on?" he asked.

He never stopped asking me question. In more to say, he was more curious to know about Alyward. I had to utter all I had during whole time of our dinner. He was a good man though. As soon as I was over with the dinner, I left dad wishing him goodnight for the rest of the night hour. I sat on my study table and began to serve the internet. Tyler called me out. He reminded me about the visit to him. I know, it wouldn't be fair enough if I go, for I had declined, Alyward for the weekend.

"Hey!!.. Are you ready for biking?" said Tyler over phone.

"Kind of" I giggled.

"See you on this weekend".

I had to urge myself to know, how I shall disagree with my present situation. I wanted Tyler to understand on his own, about my disability about the weekend. We talked for minutes. He wasn't stopping. I couldn't lie even to him neither I could dishonor his expectation.

"Tyler…I'm so sorry I won't be able to show up this weekend. I promise the next weekend I'll be there" I had to gather my strong courage to deliver that.

"Are you ok? That's fair enough" he agreed gently.

I completed few of my written works before I went to bed. The next day, I had the plan ready to out myself to the beach.

Dad went for his work. I was left alone at home. It's the frozen dew that fell on the porch. Fortunately, I had the cover on my truck. I delivered a message to dad before I left home to the beach.

Hey!!! dad… I shall see you in the evening. I'll be going to beach with few of my friends. I may be late to reach home by evening. Love you.

He replied me instantly. I read it before I stepped out with my truck.

Stay safe dear.

I followed through the way. I had to drive miles. None of my friends knew about it nor did I want others to know. The beach wasn't that crowded. I could faintly see any people around. I stopped the truck and looked around searching for anyone. But then I found none. I parked at the road end. I began to walk along the sandy shore. I felt the thrilling chillness in the water it had. I couldn't be more protective than being myself at risk. I moved forward toward the water. Much deeper inside, I began to feel the threatening coldness on my body. I could see my legs under water. It began to form something which I usually felt the first time I was here. It existed right before my eyes, and by the time I could analyzed myself, I was fallen onto to the ground. Unconsciously for few minutes, I could hear nothing but the roar of sea waves that wet me. When I opened my eyes, I found myself to be someone that I wasn't. I could feel my feet embedded together into one form. I couldn't move smoothly but crawled through the shore. My skin was milky white, and my hair with the golden reddish in color. I looked more beautiful and seductive too with those faded blue eyes. But below my hip I had the regeneration of fish tail. I was nude from the upper half. And the clothes I was on torn out. I found myself to be a mermaid. I had the cover of diamond scales covered on my body. Though it shone bright I could feel quite strange about it. I could only take the help of my hand to move. I looked at myself thoroughly, gazed at my fish tail for long time. The empty beach gave me the privacy to know what I was exactly. My milky white face looked glorious and my lips turned reddish. I was lying flat on the shore with my hands covering my breast. Somehow, I crawled into the water. I never knew how to swim much. I went deeper into the ocean water. I began to swim along the shallow, but with few of my trials, I realized I could breathe smoothly inside water. That was unusual for me. I dived deep and moved into deeper section where usually large sharks are found. I could swim freely with my will. I gradually lost the fear. As I reached the ocean floor, I looked up, and I knew how far I was from the real world. Looking at myself, I felt uncommon amongst them. The cluster of fishes whirled around me. And deep below, the ocean floor covered with the reefs and corals. I came across the dolphins where I just saw them in television or pictures. I swum all around and I found none of my kind. I could barely see the sun. I felt something new after all these years. Above me the crest and trough hit hard into the shore. I floated on the surface and looked around at the vast ocean. It's endless and my eye sight couldn't grab till the end of it. I swum again under water but this time I maintained the depth. I began liking for who I was. It's the whole new world that anyone could feel. So fortunate I was that the blessing stayed back with me. Gradually, my ability to tackle waves and speed increased. I had spent long hours under water. What amazed me was that I could breathe smoothly. I had grown that ability too. Faintly, I remembered mom had warned me to keep it secret except that dad knew all about it.

I walked out of the water from the deep, and though my feet weren't there to make me stand. I crawled out into the shore. I used my hand to help myself to get onto the dry area. I watched myself again and it's amazing. I touched my tail and

I could feel the shine of diamond shape scales over me. And my whole body turned into milky white, except from hip I had the greenish color spread along. The golden reddish hair shone brighter in sunlight. When it's wet, it had the glamour of effective fragrance around. I was nude and laid on the shore to dry myself. The beach was still empty, only the rush of gusty winds passed by. The sun almost doomed in toward the sinking horizon. I watched closely at the last rays of the twilight. When I tried to move I still haven't realized I was completely dry and my feet were back. I was no more the mermaid. I was the same Annabell Cameron. And the only thing that mattered me that moment was, I was naked without cloth. I hurried myself to my truck and searched for the spare shorts and top in my bag. Luckily, I had them. I looked for my phone, there I found the number of missed call that came from Alyward and Tyler. It's almost dark by the time I was prepared to return back home. On the way, dad called me out. I consoled him about my safety, there was nothing to worry. He waited for me. When he heard the sound of my truck, he hurriedly arrived at the gate.

"I'm ok dad" I said as I walked alongside him.

"Well, I had the dinner prepared. Fortunately, it wouldn't be a waste" he smiled.

I accompanied him. He served me the glass of juice and took his chair. He glanced at me before he had the word inside him to ask me.

"So, how was your day?"

"It was awesome terrific and wonderful" I shrugged, my eyebrow raised higher.

"Why are you shrugging?"

"I'm tired dad" I said casually.

"Go get a rest".

"Goodnight dad" I left the table and went upstairs.

I changed myself into my night wearing that I usually use. I began to surf the internet. I had searched many stories and researched about mermaid that night. I couldn't believe I was among one of such kind. It's little strange to be. I gathered all information I could from the internet. I went through thoroughly. I texted Alyward about the missed call. The same was forwarded to Tyler. Hopefully, they weren't that harsh on me I expected that. Eventually my day ended with the last work to complete on my home work. That was another night I had dreamt Alyward Pyne. He seemed more indulged on me. In fear, my sense talked that he knew who I was. I couldn't keep the secret hold onto me. So true it pictured in my mind, I couldn't escape out of it. In sudden notion of jerk, I woke up in fear. My face slightly frightful and soaked in confusions. But that was a dream I realized. I still had the silence secret about me of being a mermaid.

Tyler called me early before the dawn broke out. He expected me from the other end. I had to make him wait for minutes before I could give him my final answer.

"Hey!! Anna" from the other end. Tyler very captivating voice.

"I'm so sorry, I couldn't receive your call the other day" I said.

"That's no problem. I had the bike prepared for you".

"That's awesome. I'll see you soon this weekend" I assured him.

We hung up the call having few words of conversation. I began to prepare for my school. Dad was still there. I went downstairs to help him in the kitchen. He already had prepared his breakfast for himself. To be more precise, he was just about to make mine too. I didn't want him to take the burden about me.

"I'll have my own" I released him.

"Really, can you cook?" he made sure about that.

"Of course, dad you can relax" I smiled.

Somehow, I fried an egg and the juice from the fridge would add me enough to make my breakfast complete. Dad bade me bye as he left with his police car. Alyward texted me and made sure if I would be available as early as possible. I did all my stuffs ready as fast as I could. I had to wash my truck. The dirt could still be seen. On the other side, there was the slightest fault that imprinted on it. I never saw the dent that formed on the sides. I realized it came from the last day hit that trailed on my truck. The wooden branch that fell on it imprinted the effect to much higher degree. There was only one whom I could rely to get it done. Tyler wouldn't say no to mend my truck. So, I decided this weekend I shall have two things to be done, a bike learning and to mend my truck.

At the parking lot, Alyward waited for me as usual. He immediately grabbed by my side and added up to walk along with me. Heading toward the main building, we were toward entrance of the library hall. His face in some satanic confusion ruptured with the mismatch feeling of having something awkward in his mind.

"What's there in the beach?" he asked me.

I fermented myself being stiff at my position to walk. I wondered with the shallow feel of grievances, confusion *how did he know about it*? I stopped my feet, he looked at me. In wondered and fear of regret he questioned.

"How did you know that?" I firmly inquired.

He glared at me intensely. Something awkward to say, more of a kind he ignored inside, I could feel that. Yet then, I approached if he would somehow let me hint the way he could know all things.

"You didn't answer my question" he demanded.

"Were you following me?"

"Whatever" he left me alone following his way toward outside.

That wasn't something I wanted to happen, and the conflict between us still evolved. Jessy caught me by the corridor. She seemed relax, something new thing might have happen to her, as I presumed.

"Are you Okay?" she muttered.

I nodded my head and walked along to join her. We were in the open porch out in the sunny light of the day. From the rear end, Peter came toward us. He looked at me for once, with the thought he had to talk to me. I haven't seen him for the last week.

"Hey!!" he said plainly.

"Where were you all these days?" Jessy intended to know.

From behind Lexie came up with the friendly sound she murmured.

"Why did you abandon us?" Lexie said with zest of smiley.

"I got busy. I missed you all, I swear" Peter gestured being cool.

I looked around for Alyward being concealed in my own world. Much of my attention weren't with the rest. They headed toward the cafeteria as the schedule of the day arrived to end. But, he never showed. My voice quiet and I felt the humiliated being submerged with the kind of emotional feeling that began to feel toward him.

"Why are you quiet?" Lexie asked.

We were seated on our regular table at the mid of the cafeteria.

"He isn't here" Peter blurted.

I didn't appreciate the way he said that. I could see the envious look in his eyes. Though Peter had been good friend of mine all through the summer, yet I had always maintained the slightest distance away from him.

"Let's talk something different" Jessy sounded interesting.

They began with something; I wasn't a part of it. I played to listen to them without much involvement about the topic. The fact, that I knew was, I could be different from all here. Indeed, I was. I had the little secret in me. Too timid to face the world all alone, that could be one random drawback that I carried. Not because I'm a girl but that my inclination toward Alyward had changed my inner vibes of emotions and feelings. Maybe, I was falling for him, I rarely realized that. Still not sure whether it's the right thing to do or my way would be diverted toward misery.

I walked down through the stairs toward the parking lot. From behind the sweetest voice called my name. It's appealing and non-repelling voice I knew. That must be him, I turned to look back. Indeed, he was right in front of me. He looked very deep into me, I wasn't so prolific that moment to look at his face. Even though my face faced him, my eyes were sighting somewhere else.

"Look, I'm sorry about the morning" he barely apologizes to any people.

"Where were you the entire day?" my tone quite aggressively insisting.

"In the library" he spoke softly.

We walked together toward, he followed silently neither I had the corner of my mind to indulge him.

"Anna, I want you to give me another chance to show myself who I'm exactly" being very effusive.

I turned to look at him, my inner vibes of sudden feeling erupted, much of it spoke through my eyes. I stood numb before him wanting nothing more to stare at his glorious face. I nodded my head with the real response he waited for, I bit my lips with the thought I had for him. I shuffled toward my car. He was still at the same place with the elated gloom on his face. I focused to stare at him before I got inside the car. He constantly followed until I left the place. He then took his own way to home.

I could barely wall myself to stop thinking about him anymore. I knew, I was in love with him. Thus, that part kept us going, no matter how bad situation we came across. Until now, I've never indulged much to know about him. That one uniqueness distinguished him from the rest. I opted to find out, what made him so attractive from every way. He's even emotional and has feelings to understand. The week passed and things started to get adequately settled between us. Each day, we saw each together more than ever before. But this time, it was from me who had given the whole effort to keep up the vital relation between us. The weekend was about to arrive and I had given my word to Tyler to fetch him with my car. I had the dent of my truck to be repaired. So, the day arrived I had done the same as promised to him.

This time I mentioned dad about my visit to Tyler Gaige. As usual Tyler was at the garage. I blew the horn to aware him about my presence. He immediately followed toward me with only shorts on. He hugged me as I stepped out of the truck and lifted me few inches from the ground.

"I was expecting you" he squinted.

The day burnt sunny as the sun rose from the deep east side. We walked in, he pointed out the bike that he repaired the last week.

"Wow!!! It's just incredible. It just looks like a brand new".

"Yeah!!! I gave it a rigorous polish. It's yours now".

I smiled, "I'm so grateful Tyler, you're gonna make me learn a bike".

"Not a big deal" he giggled.

"Oh!!! I was wondering if you could help me in fixing the dent of my truck".

"Of course, show me" Tyler said willfully.

Before he made me ride a bike, we've spent few hours in framing the dent.

"How did it happen?"

"I don't know. I just found it last week" I said casually.

When the noon headed to end, his father arrived. As usual, he found good with Tyler. Burney had been a good friend of my dad since we came to Sonoma. And that we two families had been in close relation since the last few years. But all through these passed years, I rarely had the chance to know about Tyler although I had heard about him from my dad. It's recent time that his visit made us even more closer to each other apart from the fact that our both dads had been good friend since the beginning of our presence. When the evening focused, we were riding toward the west along a long-stretched meadow land with the thin strips of road passing through the mid. I held my hand tightly on Tyler's shoulder as he rode the bike somewhere miles away from home. He stopped. I looked around sighting the panoramic beauty of the place with the glorious nature that indulged on.

"Wow!!! I can't imagine place like this would exist" my voice wondered.

He smiled as I peeked at him.

"So, are you ready?"

"Ready for what?"

"To handle the bike" Tyler sounded jubilant.

"Oh!!!! yeah…" I stammered.

I was on the bike, and I knew I was shivering down through my spines. It's the first time I had been trying to learn how to ride a bike. And that Tyler was there to guide me with the instructions. Of course, riding bike would sound awkward for any girl, that's another section of male dominating vehicle. I pressed the button that started the engine. Tyler looked at me carefully. I felt quite nervous or precise to say I was scared for the first time.

"Hold your breath" he muttered.

"Oh!!! C'mon stop making me nervous".

He laughed "Hold the clutch, and change the gear and then slowly release the clutch again" he instructed.

"I've never found the complication in my math class than learning to ride a bike" almost pathetic I sounded. I inhaled a deep breath and retook my position again.

"Are you okay?"

"Yup" gaining my confidence.

I operated as directed by Tyler. As I rolled the accelerator, I found myself riding away from him.

"Just be careful with you gears" he shouted.

In return, I waved him back with the positive action. Somehow, I could ride in first gear. I covered few meters away from him. He was seen away from me when I stopped my bike. Seeing me, he shuffled on toward me. Tyler reached toward me. He patted at my back giving the sign of good ride for the first day. He took care of the bike then. We walked on back though the same route.

"That was a good ride" he complimented.

"Was it really?"

It's almost the sunken day. We headed back to his home. Tyler safely parked the bike inside the garage. He provoked me to have the dinner with them. So, for now I had agreed to participate with them at least for the moment. I haven't mentioned to dad about that and I knew for sure he would have my share of dinner prepared at home. The meal was quite deliciously prepared. Burney offered me with the plate of prawn which he had prepared by himself. I had never been much into people dinner's table. Tyler sat by my side, so there was the slightest feel of comfort zone. His dad faced us and continued to chat about our day's activities. After spending few moments of my time, I was to head back to home. Burney had suggested Tyler to drop me. But, that wasn't required as I had my truck with me. I assured them I would be safe back to home or in other words I had precisely made them a surety call as I reached home.

Dad wasn't asleep. He waited for me watching the sports channel as usual. I joined him instantly to give his loneliness a company.

"Are you okay?" I yearned to know.

He gave me a hug and kissed me on my forehead.

"I kept your dinner on the table. And your mom called me this evening, she wanted to talk to you" he said.

I nodded and gestured calmly without paying much heed of interest about mom's call. He looked at me quite in deserted glance.

"You should go to bed dad. Goodnight" I insisted him.

I went upstairs. I had the little thought about my Mom. Though it's been almost long eight years that passed away, yet she never had tried to show up other than to make call to her daughter and husband. That night, I went blank to bed without surfing the internet. I tried calling Alyward but went unanswered. The only option I had was to leave a message for him.

The next day I felt different. I felt quite stronger and confident. In fact, my appearances were changed. I had that look that glimpse on my face when I was turned into a mermaid. I could just observe at myself standing before mirror. Thought it wasn't supposed to happen that way but it was real before my eyes. It's natural but to the onlookers they would probably consider those beauties to be extra make up on my face. My golden reddish hair and milky white skin returned back. Those who looked at me couldn't divert away their gaze. Those attentions would be grabbed due to my faded blue eyes that seductively pulled attention toward me. I was noticeably looking beautiful with those gifts upon me. I was still examining at myself for I couldn't believe to have look like this once in my life time.

"Oh!! my god....I'm a mermaid" I hissed.

I managed to settle myself with the school stuffs before I thought to leave. Dad was gone before I could make him show what exactly I looked like. Of course, he saw mom that way, I made the assumption long back about my mother. Alyward called me on the way. As usual, he waited for me at the parking lot. He walked toward me as I opened up to step out.

"You look beautiful with the change" his tempting voice again touched my ears.

"Thanks"

He held my hand as we walked through the way toward the main section. Others who looked at us stood awestruck with the kind of still face staring at us as we passed them. There was some kind of strange feeling that I felt. Even more was that it differentiated us from the rest. I submerged more into him. My hands tightly fitted to grab his arm. He covered me like the shield of protection. As we reached the main entrance, we were encountered by Jessy and Lexie. Seeing me they weren't to believe if it was me in real.

"What have you done?" Lexie intrigued to know.

"You just look awesome" Jessy with gesturing compliment.

Alyward looked on at them and passed shallow smile that pretended to be fake though. However, it wasn't that unpleasant to look at. I had to go along with the rest. He had to take the other side of the way for his class. Until the lunch, we had to wait the hours to meet up again. I followed along with the rest. He waited till I could be visible. The math period was cancelled for that day. It was notified to us that Nash Billy wouldn't be available for a week. In the mid noon, I received a call that came from Tyler. I wasn't expecting though. He talked about the next weekend about my bike learning. He sounded quite intrigued and interesting with the new activities that he brought up. I had spent few of my minutes in talking to him. Alyward waited for us in the cafeteria. He was seen alone occupying one table. His exciting faced glowed up as we entered the place. The three chairs were left empty.

"I guess; we shouldn't add up for today at least in your private matters" Lexie being humble.

"He wouldn't mind, I'm sure about that" I looked at him.

He smiled looking at me. His golden blue eyes looked very inviting. We were still in the dilemma whether they both add up with us. Finally, the final said came from Jessy, disagreeing to come with me to the same table. I couldn't stop them. They were gone to the next side of the cafeteria. Lately, few minutes later they were joined by Peter Pho who followed giving the slightest stare at me. I was at the same place stood still when that happened. I joined Alyward Pyne. He rolled his tempting eye at me for seconds and I was solemnly into him.

"What went wrong?' he questioned.

"Nothing" I mumbled.

He went to get the lunch plate for both. I watched him very

closely. Things began to indulge me more with the rise of imagination that struck my brain. He was indeed a lot different from the rest. I tried to find the solutions to my questions. *Why is he not liked by anyone else in the premise*? He wasn't weird though. I understood him well. When he returned holding the plates, he already knew I indulged thinking something else.

"You don't have to think about me much" he said.

I felt flattered, how could he do that. *How could he know I was thinking about him*? It wasn't something usual I thought.

"How did you know that?"

"I guessed" he replied.

"So, you can read minds".

"Anna" his effusive voice "I can read each and everyone's mind here except for you. You nothing, that's really frustrating".

"No, you don't need to read me" I calmly reserved myself.

I had fallen more for him. He looked very innocent with the kind of expression lighted on his face that cured my inner agony. I wanted to be close to him all the time.

"You don't know exactly what I'm" his voice very captivating.

"Yes, I do know" maybe I agreed blindly trusting him more than ever before.

"Will you come with me?" he asked.

He wanted me to take to his home. I agreed to come along with him at the end of school hours.

Chapter Four

It was almost dark when I stepped into his home. Of course, he looked rich, yet then the simplicity portrayed with more humbleness in his living style. He switched on the light as I stepped forward to enter the house.

"You don't need to be scared. It's just me".

"You live alone here?" I cared to know.

"Yeah!!!! for years".

That was the first time, I had learnt to know the deeper side of his life. He lost his parents at the age of ten. But, he was left with a gift which he never revealed to others. I looked around the rooms of his house. He took me upstairs to his personal room. The walls were covered with the beautiful paints, photographs of his childhood.

"That's you" I said pointing at his old photograph.

"Yeah!!! I was seven then" he smiled.

I browsed more from the wall. As I stared around the room, there was something that I couldn't grab to know about him. He led me downstairs and gave me the room to sit on a sofa. From the refrigerator, he brought a glass of soft drink. He offered me in a glass. He added by my side with his own glass. He stared at me with the suspected fear in his eyes. I intended to know what could be wrong. But more than that, I felt pity about the fact that he had been living lonely life. My subconscious slammed at me wanting to know about his mom and dad. He disagreed to speak about them. He could find the strength to remember all of his childhood spent with his parents. There was only one frame with his parents that I had seen in his bed room.

"Anna, I want you to know one truth about me" he mumbled.

"Yeah!!!".

"You won't believe me" he sounded very touchy.

"I do believe in you".

"I've a power in me" he said.

I gazed at his face something that looked startled to find out what he actually meant by that. My expressions in flee of supporting factor to agree with him.

"Show me" maybe I sounded quite casual.

"I can look into the future" he sounded serious.

"You mean to say, you're a clairvoyant. You talk to dead people".

"Sort of but I don't talk to dead people" his eyes in mysterious form.

At first, I didn't believe in him but when he showed me with the real evidence I stood numb. He even told me about my next day's schedule. I wondered how he could do that. But, what's the most basic question that rose was from where he got the power to look into the future. It's kind of strange to me now. I wanted to go home immediately. He urged me if he could drop me back but I declined his chivalry.

"Are you okay?" he concerned.

I nodded, as he came up to my truck. The darkness arrived soon and I had the call received from my dad. I explained him about my visit to Alyward.

"I think I should go now" I demanded.

He gently nodded his head and arrived at the conclusion to depart from me. He stood silently saying nothing, while I was still with the strange feeling that I began to feel toward him. That's was quite weird. But the fact was that I had the crucial doubt arrived on my mind about my reality. Perhaps, he saw the future to find out me who I was exactly. Maybe he knew, I was a mermaid in the beach which was why he always asked about the beach. I bade him goodnight for the rest of the remaining hours.

"See you tomorrow" he said.

I nodded positively and moved out from his place heading toward home. On my way, I had another call from dad. He sounded worried about me. I couldn't persuade him about that, I drove as fast as I could. When I reached, I found dad outside impatient. He lit the torch, as the howling of wolves could be heard from the nearby forest zone. I parked my truck and stepped out of the car.

"I was worried about you" dad paid attention on me.

"I'm fine, dad" I breathed out.

He walked behind me, the dinner kept ready on the table. He hadn't taken yet. He asked me to join him. But before that I wanted to take a look at my room. I got refreshed before I came downstairs. Adam was seated on his chair waiting for me.

"What mom told you about the last time" I keened to know.

"She hasn't called you, right?" dad looked at me.

"Yup!!" I nodded.

We proceeded with the dinner. In moments, he glanced at me in like something was wrong on my face. I rubbed my forehead without any known fact, thinking that something went wrong with my face that's why dad was glancing at me with suspicious notion.

"How was Alyward?" he questioned.

I never expected that from him. *Would he stop talking about Alyward Pyne*, that's what my subconscious spoke to me. Questions like those shook me. And now that Alyward knows to see future, he must have been seeing us what we are doing.

"He was good" I ended up shortly.

When I finished my dinner, I left dad as soon as possible. Tyler left me a message. I read it as I opened to surf the internet. The thought that haunted me was the truth about Alyward. Much of my dealings weren't that easy to know what kind of guy he was. He knew each and everything in and around him. I never gave up the thought that he could certainly come out to be powerful human being. I thought over and over again the night. It amazed me more than I'd be surprised. On what conclusion I would arrive on his appearance. It hustled me more than I could think about. Beyond that I had to accept, in whatever way he was, I clarified myself.

I missed the school next day instead, I gave a sudden surprise visit to Tyler. He wasn't expecting that early morning. Out in the front yard, he had the coffee cup in his hand. He watched me precisely as I parked the truck at front gate. I walked toward him. He followed to approach near to me.

"Good morning pretty lady" he wished.

"Yeah! morning".

"Skipped school" he began.

We walked through the green grass that covered their lawn. I was mentally disturbed by the fact Alyward could follow me anywhere. I figured out, he must have been watching us even now. But the real truth was that I was in love with him, a *clairvoyant*. I explained my reasons and worries to Tyler. I'd hope, he would understand. I spent the rest of the day's hour with him. When the evening arrived, for an hour, he taught me to learn the bike. By now, I was quite smooth in riding. Tyler sat behind me as we drove to the same road that led us to the meadow field.

"That's a quite lot of improvement" he muttered.

"That's your hard work on this girl" I grinned.

He laughed, and placed his hand on my shoulder. I wanted to take a walk through the meadow ground. I stopped looking at the farthest stretching end of the land.

"I wish I had a bike" I said.

"You can have it…. there are lots spare parts lying in the garage"

We headed to walk on along the soft grass. It's cold and wet. I felt the chillness arrived on my spines. The sun ahead was sliding down below the horizon. We waited for the sun to set before our return. It was serenely dark when we turned back. That was the second night, I had my dinner with them. But this time, I was enough comfortable to be around. His dad also joined us for the dinner time. Burney, informed dad about my presence in their house. The night felt really calm and quiet by the time I returned home. Dad wasn't asleep, he had the remote in his hand, changing up channels he looked for. As usual, I saw him in the same room lying on a couch.

"Good night dad" I said nothing more.

I went upstairs, he didn't response back. I ignored to surf the internet the night. But I had something tumbled up in my mind wanting to know about clairvoyant. I began to look out for it browsing the sites instead of going bed early. Finally, I could gather some information about it. I only had the preplanned thought how should I see him the other day. Of course, he would know whatever else I had done. He knew only to see the present and the future, but not the past. It couldn't be called as the disease to him but with some extra power he was born with. He told me he had been doing this since his childhood. I went to bed collecting those little things I wanted to know.

Dad called me up the early morning. He prepared the breakfast for me like every morning and left for his duty. I stood in dilemma holding the phone, not well confirmed to make a dial to Alyward. I gazed out through the window seeing dad driving to work. The weather was slightly doomed with shallow light that passed through the pores of leaves. It drizzled the last night and I could feel the wet things around. Fortunately, my dad covered my truck before he went to bed the last night. I could see the layers of cloud above darkened as I walked out for school. When I reached the parking lot, I saw the glimmering face of Alyward. He waited for me. I parked to my place and caught him up. His eyes shone like the sprinkling diamond on the surface. That's the kind of transition could be seen in him. It's not the effect of lens, he's not defected with eye problem that was for sure. He held my hand as we walked to the entrance. He showed much of his effusive concern about me. Those could be read through his eyes.

"You're a good rider" he praised.

I knew, on what he was talking about. I lessen my interest on that par rather gestured him shrugging my shoulder.

"That guy…you should stay away from him" he said in suspicious notion.

We halted immediately, the pause was sudden and it screwed our minds for seconds. He was talking about Tyler Gaige. *What's problem with him, I bothered to know.*

"He's a nice guy" I retaliated.

"You know nothing about him" he imposed again.

"I know him for long time. He wouldn't do anything to harm me".

We divided our way as we neared to our class room. He had taken the other section of the period. He promised me, he would see during lunch. For some reasons, the math class was cut down. So, for at least a week we wouldn't sit together solving equations. At lunch, he waited for me. While I approached he added his step from behind following the route to cafeteria.

"Tell me Anna, what made you so fascinating about him" he never stopped to question about Tyler.

"We should stop talking about him, end of the discussions" I demanded.

"Alright" he said, not willfully.

He grabbed the chair and sat. The rest of my crew wasn't seen. I added by his side. He looked at me sharply, his eye blinked, with the notion that hid something from it.

"Your eyes" I mumbled.

"It's natural" he stammered.

Gradually, the cafeteria was filling up. As usual we were on the same place. People looked at us, many with concuss intention. It was to be avoided. I had accepted him the way he was. He wasn't the kind of person who would hurt the person he would love. Of course, he wasn't a disabled man but had something extraordinary to be precise.

"So, it's like every *Clairvoyant guy*, do go transition every weekend" I was engrossing.

"No…. It's only on me, it's not in everyone's quality. I'm fortunate, I got the qualities in me" he stared smoothly at me.

From the entrance door, I had seen the glimpse of Jessy and Lexie entering the cafeteria. They paid least amount of attention toward us. I looked at them for a while. They glanced at me with no much interest on us. Only my expression felt upon them wanting them to be more with me. It wasn't the kind of friendship I wanted to last for short term but they could only be the one who would at least support me. It was something more to do with him, I could feel their intentions. Peter wasn't present too. I ignored the rest to think about it. It wasn't the best of summer I was going through. Though the fact that Alyward would always be there by my side. On the other hand, Tyler was the only new companion who gave me much more than I could think about him. Besides, Tyler always helped me in repairing my truck and learning bike. Most of my lone hour would be spent at his garage. Tyler, a muscular guy suited him with the heavy metal works he does at his garage.

Before we parted, Alyward asked me for the weekend. I gracefully willed my instinct to give him the time. When I returned home, dad was already prepared with the dinner. Burney Gaige was already there with him, that companied them was the bottle of beer on the table. I felt exhausted of tiredness enveloped me, I couldn't wait much with them downstairs. I didn't see the presence of Tyler. Urged to know from his father, he said about his local friends that invited Tyler for a birthday party. I went upstairs and dropped to fell on my bed for a while to untie myself from the restless school hours. I heard the call of dad to join them for dinner. It's been weeks, I haven't changed myself into my real appearance of being a mermaid. I wanted to see myself all over again, and for that I needed to visit the beach again. I strolled downstairs to join up for dinner. My plate was already made with the following recipes that dad had prepared for the night. I couldn't say much about the friendship of dad with Burney. It made them look like they were childhood friends. I sat up with them, and the last thing I had to explain was my day at school. When I was over, I moved upstairs, got engaged myself with the internet. For at least twenty minutes, I talked to Alyward before I went finally to bed.

When the weekend arrived, on early Sunday morning he came to pick me up. Dad saw him at the gate with his car. He proceeded toward him. Alyward stood waiting for me.

"You must be Alyward" dad keened to know.

"Yes Sir" he sounded polite.

"Well, come in".

By the time he was actually in my house, I was at the ground floor. I smiled at him. His gesture even more soft to noticed. And the kindness in his look he bore melted inside of me.

"Do you like spaghetti?" dad offered him a plate.

"No, thanks, I'm done with breakfast" his voice very humble.

"Can we go now dad?" I looked at him serenely.

He nodded looking at me, and the next he turned to look at Alyward.

"Do take of her".

"Yes Sir".

As we walked out of the door, dad waved at us. He brought a jacket for me. He helped me to put on before I got in the car. He was pretty playful, crunched up to put the hood over my head.

"It isn't that cold" I forged.

We drove from the way, almost miles covered. The weather began to change, as in the mid section of our expedition we halted at a restaurant. Bakersfield was far from the county side, almost the whole day may take to reach. The clouds began to hover above, almost the dark side of the lighted day was about to fall. By the time, we initiated to move ahead it was drizzling, and I knew the focus to keep on, it meant to rain heavily, and most of my prediction came true. The fallen drops of rain came heavy on our roofs and the cold winds thrust upon us that hit our skin, crumpled to frozen ice like case. By the time, we actually reached Bakersfield it didn't stop raining.

"What's there in Bakersfield" I meant to know.

"I often used to come here. I've a very old friend who runs a restaurant".

I nodded looking at him nothing to know what to say ahead. I looked outside through the glass, and most part of the glass being covered by mist. I wiped out with my jacket and cleared my eyes to look outside.

"So, you knew the weather would change?"

"I guess, I just saw the future" he added.

He stopped the car. Ahead lay the restaurant, he helped to open the door at my side and held my hand. I walked along with him proceeding toward the place. The climate turned damp, wet with the slippery feel on the road. The sky masked with black clouds above with those of the chill rusty winds that blew from north. It turned out to be a rainy day often with the laziness that cramped upon my shoulder. He pushed the glass door. The first thing I noticed was the lighted candle at the service side. Each table was placed with a candle lamp, as the day masked with the dark clouds of course the light faded away. That glowed on our table was the new candle that had been placed. I actually began to feel cold with the sudden changed in the weather. However, Alyward's offered jacket kept me warm.

"It's wonderful" I mumbled.

There were few on our sides, they looked at us. But the genuine attention that felt was on him. He wasn't the common sight for all instead, something different he had in his personality. The waiter arrived as we waited for seconds for him. Alyward provided with the required dinner set of recipes to be taken.

"How often you used to come here?" that was required question.

"Quite a lot" his eyes looked mesmerizing to divert my attention.

I couldn't look at his face for it reflected very much about him that once I would be engrossed, it seldom left me void thinking about him the whole night. Most of the time, I avoided to look at him, that was necessary to do. He'd understand the reason behind but never would mutter about it. He stared at my face with effusive content that intently made me involved with him.

"Anna" almost undeniable "It's always been something I wanted to share about" he stopped.

"Yeah!"

He sighed and stared on the table.

"Is there something wrong?" I concerned.

"I know, I was bad to you for the last few weeks, and I had no idea what I was doing but, I don't have the strength to stay away from you anymore".

"You don't"

His constant stare toward me made me feel passive about us. That was the first time, he actually told me what he had kept for long time. His hand softly touched mine. The candle still glowed, however the weather hasn't changed yet. We were served with the recipes. There was the silence for moment, holding on to our mind what could be ahead between us. With him, I always felt protective no matter what consequences could arrive. Not because he was clairvoyant guy but inside his heart he was a real man to love me. When we finished with our dinner, we headed back to home driving the long way. It rained continued the whole highway. The weather was quite patchy, as we entered the county area it was again the same, not single drops of water that fell. He came home to drop me. Dad was out in the veranda waiting for me. He walked with me up to my front door.

"You too had good time" dad asked.

"Yeah right" I said casually.

"Goodnight sir" Alyward released my hand.

"Goodnight young man".

I stood, watched him go toward the car. Dad entered inside the room. He didn't prepare the dinner for me. He claimed the idea about that before I left. I went upstairs, looked at my phone. The missed call buzzed up with many number of times. Most that came were from Tyler. I redialed but went unanswered. Lastly, my option could only to send him a text. That was probably the night I actually could assure, I was very much in love with Alyward. I avoided surfing the internet. Instead, I grabbed a book to read to call back my sleep. I began to get involve with the novel in my hand. But with each line his face appeared on the page. I felt asleep within no time that wasn't in my sense to know. The next morning would entirely be different to me, even before I could think it had to be. By midnight it literally felt cold, I squeezed myself inside the blanket. The pictures about the day's visit screened before me. My senses were yet to control by myself. It's almost the deep section of my sleep where I couldn't even bother to hear the howling of wolves around. My state was felt very dark and my restless day brought me the end with peaceful story to dream the night.

Chapter Five

Beyond the window I reached out, found myself at the beach. For prolonged time I had no company. Regarding my transformed form, I was indulged by then with the thought. I walked in toward the shore and as the waves touched by, I was involved in transforming myself into mermaid. My lower portion now in fish tail, and I looked gorgeously mesmerizing. My upper half unfolded to be naked. But this time, I had the costume to cover myself. I crawled toward the water and swam into the deep. The vast ocean stretched across far off land, and as my hands and legs moved I speeded up more to explore the sea world. Many times, I had encountered those clusters of fish twirled around me. I enjoyed the game with the aquatic creatures. Even the color of water was matched to my sense to accept with the purity of being a half aquatic creature. No one knows yet, except my dad, who haven't seen me in real yet then he knew by now. As I was visiting far across the vast ocean with the twirled of joy inside me, an unexpected journey led me into the real life of being a mermaid. It's not the illusion heading toward me. Of course, under water I could see clearly as I had the features of being an aquatic creature. When I rose out to the surface of the water, I was actually missing the mainland. I've left it far away behind. I felt terrified and looked around, but found none. In the middle of the ocean, I was the only mermaid that was visible around.

Not even a human ship could be noticed. I dived again and began to search my way back. From ahead a figure approached to me. I could see clearly, quite visible to recognize. Both swam toward each other. I felt it was someone I knew very well. And to my disbelief fact, it was my mom who came to me. I looked exactly like her. To agree with, she was more beautiful than me as mermaid. We looked at each other, very close. The surprising thing was still there in me or more was that I couldn't forgive myself seeing her. I felt quite effusive with my mind that she had in her. And we both on the lonely ocean floated together just to bring us together.

"Anna, my child" she said.

"Mom" I swam toward her.

"My daughter, how have you been?" her question touched me.

"I've waited long years for your return, please come back".

"I can't, tell your dad, I love him".

"Don't do this again" I pleaded.

"I promise, I'll come back to you all as when my time ends" she said.

That wasn't quite understandable to me what she meant by that. All she had warned me to stay safe and protected. Before she parted away, she meant something very crucially important which I grabbed consciously. I never knew what the danger could come to me but she promised to protect from any harm. I looked at her as she swam away. Gradually the rays faded away and she disappeared in the middle of the ocean. I swam onto the surface of the water, and looked around again. The land was visible to me. But the imprint of my mom stayed behind me. The last thing she did to me was a kiss on my forehead. She never mentioned where she was heading at the end. Her world changed and I knew the change would come to me as well. I had to follow mom, find her and bring back home. I made promise to myself. It made me felt she was in trouble. I began to feel the cold in me. I squeezed more to get myself warm. And the memory that mom had left imprinted on my mind. It wasn't something that I could forget. It's been long years that I actually had seen her. So true, it was that the love between daughter and mother flourished out in no time. I just heard her voice once in phone that was at the beginning of time. The realization came until I found myself wakened up seated with the exhausted face on my bed. I grabbed the bottle of water to cool myself and regain my mental and emotional stability. That was the first night, I dreamt to see mom. The novel was on my bed. I closed the chapters and placed back from where I grabbed it.

Dad washed up the truck early morning. He was brushing the front glass. I went downstairs to add up myself to his company. The climate was cool enough to influence the silence of the morning. He saw me coming toward him.

"Are you okay?"

"Yup!!!. I'll do it myself" I grabbed the brush from him.

He allowed me for that little portion to clean.

"Would you want to join me to Burney's house?" dad asked me as he walked through the stairs.

I nodded not being sure enough, but I wanted to meet up Tyler. So, for no reason I just wanted to come with dad. He prepared the breakfast by the time I had wholly completed with the cleaning stuff. Dad received a call from Burney before we left. He wanted to drive the truck through the way. He didn't allow me. When we neared to the place, Burney was already outside waiting for us. Tyler wasn't seen with him neither the garage was open. The lock at the door was visibly passed as dad stopped the car. We walked in through the long length cemented path way. Both shook their hand and hugged themselves. I was looking around here and there in search of Tyler in the surroundings.

"Well, he's gone to market to fetch the dinner. He'll be back soon" Burney told me.

I nodded with a hidden charm within me. They both went inside while, I stayed back at the lawn. I walked on through the green grasses that were smoothly spread across the open space. Just then Tyler's bike sounded, it reached closer. He saw me and shouted out my name. He spotted me and stopped his bike.

'Hey Anna"

"Heyyy!!" I said.

"I didn't expect you would come"

"My dad is here too" I added.

"Really, that's great".

He parked his bike and, walked on with me. The entrance door was open. Dad and Burney were inside. We joined them. Tyler unloaded all the kitchen stuff he got.

"Would you help me out to prepare the dinner?" his voice sounded too polite.

"Sure" I added.

That was the first time I actually tried to do some cooking stuff, otherwise it was always my dad who would prepare for me. I could hear dad's voice. Faintly their talk wasn't clear enough on what they were discussing about.

"What's going on at school?" he eagerly asked.

"Nothing so special"

"Are you sure about that?"

"Any doubt?" I said.

He smiled and got back to handle the frying pan. The dinner was almost ready.

"Hey guys, the dinner is ready" Tyler informed dad.

I got the dinner table ready. They came by and sat to their respective chairs. Dad looked at me and passed a short smile. Burney, on the other hand took a glimpse at the recipes. Tyler began to serve. I was seated next to his chair. He joined us then. Everyone had their glass filled with wine. The aroma of red wine tempted my lips to taste. It was after long period of time I had actually tasted. Tyler passed a silence glance at me before he attempted to take his first sip. Our talk began with the topic about the oncoming celebration of Burney's birthday. Tyler wanted to celebrate his dad's birthday at our home. I actually wanted the thing to happen that way. Dad agreed. There was no need to persuade for his friend. The birthday was week away. When we finished with the dinner, Tyler burnt the bonfire at the front yard. We all gathered surrounding the fire place. Burney wanted to share a story. I was quite relaxed. It's been almost years; I would be listening to story. The excitement rolled on my face hoping that it would be something different for the night. Burney began his words. My ears caught his first word. Dad looked at me, that same expression flashed on his face when mom used to tell me her stories. Tyler looked disinterested about the time. His attention wasn't much to hear the story. However, he was putting an effort to do the same. The night fell very calm. The fire kept us warm. It was almost mid night listening to his story. We were supposed to leave home. Tyler wanted to drop us back. We left back for home. Dad was driving the truck. I was half asleep when we reached. Just the wish of goodnight, I uttered the last word and went upstairs. I ignored to complete the homework, the next day I had to show it out before my teacher.

I haven't talked to Alyward for days. I missed my school life for at least a week. I never knew the reason, why he reached far away from being in touch. However, the week was spent with great ease. I never felt bore to have most of the time for myself. The loneliness was always killed with the presence of Tyler. I never wanted to know the reason why I had skipped school for a week. I had the urge to know if Alyward has seen me in the future. If that was the case, he knew everything by now. That would be an awkward question if I ask him about me. He's a Clairvoyant and, I know about it.

As usual, he was leaning at the back of his car. His deep eye focused at me as I drifted my feet toward him. He looked very vibrant, something fishy in his mind. And my thoughts failed to understand. The closer I went, the more secure I felt.

"How was the week?" he sounded soft.

"It was good".

We walked on toward the entrance. Jessy and Lexie were at the porch waiting for Peter.

"Hey guys" I said.

"Where were you?" it came from Jessy.

"I was spending the week with my dad".

Alyward stood little away from us. And every time I spoke to them, his eyes cornered toward to me. No one neglected to look at him. Even Jessy's eye pointed sharply at him. I didn't want him to feel awkward about the situation hence my conversation with them ended shortly. I joined him as we walked along the length of corridor looking for Math section. That was the first class of Nash Billy after his returned. We took the same place. He looked at me very calmly with the slightest touch of his rare smile. His eye froze on me. I couldn't turn my face away from him.

"Why are you looking at me like that?" I mumbled

He kept silent and signaled with his shimmering smile at me. That was more than acceptable behavior that he produced.

He turned his face, facing toward the white board. Nash Billy entered the class while, I was still soaked with the scene that left on my mind. I bit my lips and turned my face away to look forward. It wasn't that easy to sit by his side. Each time the closer he was, the better I felt. It's after a week that he was actually before my eyes. I least bothered to know the reasons why he actually stayed untouched to me for a week. But, anytime he'd be close it seemed I would forget the worries that I bore in my life. Nash Billy ended the class early. We proceeded toward the cafeteria.

"What's his name?" the questioned came from him.

We walked through the cemented porch. Cafeteria never went empty without people. The packed session would only be seen more during lunch.

"Whose?"

"You know exactly about whom I'm talking about" he said.

It shuddered me for a while. It seemed he was very much eager to know about Tyler Gaige. We sat on the table, the lunch pack was delivered to us.

"He's Tyler Gaige" I finally revealed his name.

Alyward nodded his head with the pleasant notion in coming to know his name. His sharp mind could be one reason that made him exceptionally unique. Few tables away from us, Jessy and Lexie were spotted. Seconds later they were joined by Peter. He neglected to look at us. Even the rest wasn't that easy with me. Maybe I was drifting away from them but, that wasn't the case that I would want. Even though Alyward was good to them, they had the resistible feel toward him. Yet then he never ought to concern much about people's likeness toward him.

"Do you have any other friends" I was quite sensitized to ask that.

He looked around and looked down on the table. When he raised his eyes to stare at me, his face soaked into the mist of sudden vibes that couldn't be express. I watched him very closely. His dry throat sipped a glass of water.

"No......" he said plainly.

That softest voice that came pricked inside of me giving the feeling that he needed someone.

He hissed and breathed out while he was browsing to tell *"Anna, the final thing in my life is that I want you to stay by my side"*.

I held his hand, as I lifted my inner feel to touch with the moment. When we finished the lunch, we skipped the rest of the periods. The rest looked at us giving concuss focus on us. He drove back to his house. I added with him following his SUV. That was the second time, I visited his home. Lot of changes he made by that week. He changed his bedroom. Even on the walls the paintings were removed. I urged to know about them, he made a separate room for them. He had his whole house painted newly. It looked shimmering from outside more than that it attracted any passersby. He had his floor replaced with new tiles that probably had the color of crystal glass that reflected every bit of rays that fell on it. As I wondered around the house, his kitchen was noticeable along the line of his bedroom. He added his company to explore all corner of his house. It was truly impressive to appreciate his caliber. As I went through his kitchen stuffs, he got two bottles of soft drinks from his refrigerator. He offered me with great ease. I smiled peeking at him as I received from him. Most part of his house under the glow of white caramel paint that was splendidly painted on the walls. It seemed to be ridiculous in imagining, to live all alone in that big house. But, he had been doing the same for years. He never revealed about his resident, although, it was me the first he actually trusted. Then he took me to another room, where he spent most of his leisure time. Maybe it looked like more like a work place for him. The tables, the chairs, the sofas with carved design on it were few of his things. He had racks of books surrounded by and lots of collection of disc. I looked around and the view through the window was unimaginable. Far across the meadow, the mounted lake between the mountains could be widely seen with its scenic sense of beauty that had in the nature. Over to that the more addition was the air that blew in to the room. The weather damped in, slightly the mixture of black clouds was visible above. The signal to rain was approaching closer. And I knew, it was something more than I hadn't expected from him. I was still gazing out through the window. It captivated me since years. The precise thing was I couldn't move out of the place. He then played a sweet soft music.

"It's beautiful" I said.

Right behind he stood calm as I turned back, my height reached just below his chin. So close that his breath added to mine. He held me and pulled in the middle. I felt nervous standing close toward him. He kept his hand on my hip.

"I can't dance" I stammered shyly.

He smiled reading me. He made me turned around his tip of his finger. I had twisted for thrice. He then stopped, the shyness floated on my face. He gently made me sit on the bed. He picked his guitar from the corner. Abandon the rest of the world and his glorious melodic voice tuned out with a song. I was amazed to hear him singing. When he ended the lines his face still carved on upon me with the intimate desire to kiss me. I felt his breathe very close to me. I was nervously stiff. Though I wasn't sure what I was doing, I found it inappropriate at that moment of time. I turned my face away. The moment of abashed ambience hovered in. The slightest feel of abatement sense pricked me. Perhaps, my act was aberrant to him. However, he controlled his emotions and feelings over me.

Outside the darkness was revealed through the window. I needed to return back home. The thundering clouds roared with their cry. The sign was more of a strong storm that was arriving from north. Alyward offered me with the dinner. Likewise, we both had dined together. We spent few more time together. I had the desire to know how he could do such things.

"How do you do that?"

"I don't know. It just came with me" he said.

"That means you can tell me what my dad is exactly doing right now".

"He's waiting for you in the veranda" Alyward answered with surety.

I had to go with his words yet whether to believe him or just to accept what his truth. I prepared to leave back home. He wanted to escort me back. The dark clouds began to fall as small droplets of water. The drizzle started as he took the seat to drive. I had given him the key of my truck. We drove along the long length empty road. I wanted to have him my truck for his return. The silence along the way put me to deep sleep. By the time we neared, my eyes half opened. He smiled glancing thoroughly at me. I looked out through the glass. It was raining. From the main gate I saw dad, he was rightly standing in the veranda. I turned to look at him. He was right what he had told me. I believed him.

"Goodnight" I said and opened the door.

He waited watching me until I was in the veranda. I was wet by my hair. He turned the truck and moved out. Dad willfully came up to help me out. He had a towel in his hand. I rubbed my hair to dry myself. He asked me; if I wanted to have dinner. I ignored my desire for I wanted him not to work this late night. He knew, I wouldn't instead, went upstairs and got involved to surf the internet. Alyward texted me as soon as he reached back. In the same I replied him. I looked for some home work to complete. I was struck by the scene that pictured on my mind. I felt regretful for not allowing him to kiss me. Perhaps, I was scared to do that. However, he did not force too, that gentle sense in him was extremely appreciable. I pondered for that same thing for a while until I found myself in deep sleep.

I heard the crackling noise from outside, as I struggled out to look out of the window. I was still under the soul of being in drowsy state. Though the last night, I was early to bed but the morning weather actually signed for a lazy day. I went downstairs to look for dad. He was at the front yard. The other person faced his back toward me. He had the axe in his hand helping out dad to cut the piece of wood into pieces. I walked toward them.

"Dad what you doing?" I demanded to know.

"Well, I'm renovating the garage. Tyler is helping me out".

"Hey!!" said Tyler.

The voice came after long pause. He turned around and saw me. I wasn't expecting him though. He hugged me and wished me about the morning.

"How come you're here?" I tried to know.

"Well, your dad wanted me to help him out".

"You can bring the log Tyler" dad said as he walked inside the garage.

He nodded and smiled toward me. He picked up the heavy weighted log. His strength was visible. I stood firm watching him do that. Strange but he was able to hold the weight.

Though Tyler was muscular but as compared to the log size he was more of strength.

"What?" he asked as he placed the wood on his shoulder.

"Nothing" I said with the casual intention of my tone.

He walked toward the garage. I kept watching him. His strength was unimaginable. It looked he could easily bash ten of people all alone. He looked back at me, his face outcasted the rare of his expression. In response to that I smile a little. He walked inside the garage where dad was waiting for him. I followed in to prepare myself for school. His aberrant behavior caused me to think what made him so strong. I was quite hurry to prepare myself. Tyler was out with the axe piecing into pieces. His strength was of no comparison.

"How you do that?" I pricked my doubt.

"Do what?"

"I mean, you're so strong" I mumbled.

He laughed for seconds, and then laid the axe on the ground. It seemed, he thought for a while what he needed to say. I was ready to leave.

"I work out that's it" he said precisely not true though.

I nodded on that par and bade them goodbye for the day. Dad waved his hand before I was out of the gate. Tyler smiled out at me as I turned the steering to change my direction. Tyler was strange that morning. That nature bloomed before me for the first time. Even though I had tried to know, he never revealed. By the time I was at the parking lot, I almost forgot about him. That extra ability of strength wasn't there in Alyward. Most of the time, it's his soft nature of his mind that worked. Slightly things were changing, I began to realize, the fact that it wasn't revealing to all. My focus on other greatly enhanced since before. I felt much better and with great power within me and though it limited me with only the aquatic world.

Probably, that was the only way I could survive being who I was actually inside. Just known to me, I precisely knew how I should be dealing my life ahead. With one condition that mom wasn't the part of our family anymore. The motive still stayed young within me to search for her. The thoughts browsed upon me not aware I was already at the parking lot. Up there in front, I saw the darkest phase of the day. It shook me up and I tumbled my feet over the brake and the accelerator. My truck skidded ahead for meters and crashed on to another van. The glass on my side crackled into pieces. And the cut appeared on my forehead in no time. The horn continued to blow as my head laid unconsciously on the steering. Alyward wasn't near, his presence wasn't felt. The situation turned rough and untidy. I felt my breath losing away. My eyes blinded hazy. People gathered within no time at the accident site. Within fraction of moment, I was carried off on a stretcher toward the ambulance.

When my eyes opened, dad was just next to me. I was given the treatment. My forehead was given one round of stitched. It hurt badly. Tyler stood straight to my view at the end of the bed.

"Hey!!! How you feeling?" he came and sat by my side.

"I'm bringing the lunch" dad walked out of the room.

"Feeling better" I snorted.

Tyler looked very much obsessed with the situation that occurred to me. Indeed, in his eyes, I could read his ardent feel that he wanted to stay back with me in the hospital. I appreciated the care of love he showed. Dad returned back with the lunch boxes.

"Here you go" he handed the boxes to him.

He left us spending few of his time urging Tyler to take care of me. He promised he would come in the morning. The day edged to end and I could view the twilight fading away from the sky. Tyler was given a separate bed for the night. My instinct wanted him to stay in the same room. Fortunately, the grant was done. We had our dinner together. The stitches on my forehead ached very much. The bruises slightly dried out with the application of few suggested medicines. Before the night began with the silent call, the doctor had checked me once. Tyler supported thoroughly with the last check up for the day.

"Are you okay with the cold?" Tyler sounded very caring.

"Yup".

He got me the quilt and the blankets. He got another for himself. Dad once made the call to him. I missed surfing the internet for the night. But more I missed Alyward. He never showed up. And the thought hinged on me that he could see what was going in my life. Presence of Tyler wouldn't be the safest path he could do to come to look for me. It guided me, accepting the fact that they both should never face one another at least before me. But someday it has to end and that end I shall free either one of them from their mind. That's the first night I slept in the hospital without my stuffs that I generally do have. When morning broke out dad was already there. Tyler went to fetch the breakfast. My limit of patience did not bother me at all. I lost the tolerance to stay back in the hospital. I needed to go home. I felt quite upright with my health by now. But on doctor's advice, I was supposed to get discharged only by evening hour. I had to wait the rest of the remaining hours somehow to make sure that I had the best thing to do. I expected something that would come by now from Alyward. But there was no show of him. I rarely could entice to do something out of my own way. Tyler returned with the content of breakfast. All three of us had the same. My inner confrontations couldn't be able to handle with ease, the reason was the feel of absence about Alyward. He couldn't come I followed to read that. But somehow, Tyler should be away at least from me for few hours. The situation entrapped me being confined within these few people but not the one my heart wanted.

Dad and Tyler went to meet the doctor who treated me. My expectations ended right from the other end of the door. Aylward stood calmly before he entered. He threw that same sensing smile as he walked toward me. He stood very close to me. I woke to position myself on bed.

"I'm so sorry" he blindly apologized.

"No…I'm fine".

He looked on my forehead and touched the stitched part.

"Does it pain?" the questioned allured me.

"No" I said softly.

"I thought I needed to see and I couldn't hold to wait more".

"I expected you" I smiled slowly.

Just then dad and Tyler entered the room. The scenario turned vital with sense of heated thought between minds. The fact, that dad knew about him. In otherwise, on the other hand Tyler acted cool though the plutonic condition in his heart attempted to be unsettling.

"Hey! This is Alyward" I introduced him to Tyler.

"I'm Tyler"

Both shook hand with one another, tried to be friendly. It's the first time they met each other, greeted each other and nothing more between them but still with the moment to hold on. My intuition urged me to clear their inner firing heart between both regarding me.

"Well, Alyward is a good friend of mine" I spoke looking toward Tyler.

"That's cool" Tyler not quite appealing.

Alyward stood next to my dad and maybe he realized, he should leave the place to provide the privacy.

"I think I should leave" he said.

"Hey!! I want you to come this weekend to my house. We're celebrating Tyler's dad birthday" I invited him.

"Be there" Tyler said.

He nodded and smiled as he walked out of the door. By the end of the day, I was given the agreement to be discharged. Dad waited for me at home. Tyler picked me to drop me home. He hasn't gone home at least for few days. So, he declined to stay back the night in our house. Just the dinner we shared together. He left within no time. Burney called dad twice at the dinner table. Hence, the urgency was revealed. After the dinner was finished I went upstairs leaving behind dad. As usual, he switched on the television to watch the highlights. Up there I received the call from Alyward. We've spent at least for twenty minutes talking to each other. But before going to bed, the thought about mom arrived abruptly. It's been almost more than a week I've not gone to beach neither I saw myself in my original form as mermaid. I loved to see my other half of my life as the aquatic creature. But, this weekend the celebration of birthday was packed. I had to make a plan before that. Somehow, I could sort out within week's days. I never saw another dream about mom since the last.

When I opened my eyes, the bruises on my forehead was gone. The pain vanished away. And everything around began to take the best shape of life. Besides, being a mermaid, I realized a lot later, I had the power to heal myself. I immediately ran downstairs and picked up the key of my truck. Dad was outside at the front yard. He saw me being in hurry.

"What's wrong?" he asked.

"I'll be back by evening" I just answered to that.

I drove toward the beach as fast as possible. I wanted to feel my power within. Regenerate myself into the greatest part of being another life. I parked my truck at an empty space. The beach was usually empty during early morning. I plunged into the water and dived as deep as I could. Gradually with every part of my body, I was transformed as the mermaid. I saw myself as the beautiful creature of god. I tried to learn to control my flow and the waves of water that ran all across the deep water. I had learned to follow the language of sea. But more than that, I grew the skill to control the rest of the sea creatures. Lots of unknown creatures began to follow me. Only few I could make out what they were exactly called from school books. After spending most of my day's hour in the sea, I finally found something worth to be taken. A male dolphin followed me each and every where as I swam across the water. That cute creature turned to be the best of friend in my sea world. I've chosen the name for him. I learned to communicate with them, and the same was for them too. Somehow the power to control huge currents of water took birth within me. I tried searching mom but went in vain. The reason wasn't clear to me. She wouldn't be available here anymore. The day was beginning to wind up moving toward the west. I had to say goodbye to my newly fellow friend, *Jimmy* who happened to be the dolphin. So, close we grew within hours that I felt I've known him for years. He wasn't like a pet to me but someone who had more to survive along with me.

I turned back into my original at the shore. The twilight across the line just edged below the horizon. I walked toward my truck. My bruises on my forehead were gone. And the pain wiped away. I actually felt strengthened enough to stand on my own feet strongly. I glanced at my phone, there was ten missed calls from dad. But avoided to reply as I was returning back home. The darkness began to slide in through the lone road. As I drove through the dense forest area, the slightest fear of being in loneliness engulfed me. There was the thought of Alyward running on my mind. I could hear his voice speaking inside of me, urging to be fearless as the road turned ever darker ahead. The shiver on my spines hindered me with the clueless way heading back toward home. The phone rang suddenly, petrified with the jerk of sound that came from the phone. I managed to see, it was dad. I breathed in. The mixed feeling stayed within me, till I found myself very close to home gate. Jimmy was one that struck up my mind before I entered home. I parked the truck safely inside the garage. The light was lit up in the living hall. The chattering was enabled to hear outside. Perhaps, to my conclusion there was someone with dad. I walked on to the veranda just stood waiting to get the door opened up. Just then from behind Tyler gulfed upon me.

"Hey Anna"

 In the dark the visibility wasn't too clear to recognize at once shot. It frightened me terribly. I stood numb for seconds, I wanted to scream out, but I could hold the fear within me. I turned back in an instance.

"Oh!! gush Tyler.... that wasn't funny" I said with breath exhausting out.

"I'm sorry" he giggled.

Dad opened the door and put in his interest about the incident.

"Are you okay?"

"Yes dad, I'm fine" I said.

Tyler walked in along with me. Burney was inside. Seeing me he called out, I smiled for while and ought to join for little talk. With the short conversation I went upstairs.

"Hey!! Can I come up with you?" Tyler scrabbled.

"Alright come on" I agreed.

We went upstairs. Tyler was the first person to enter into my bedroom. Even dad wouldn't try to but I trusted him with no offence. As I opened the door, he stood astonished inside glaring with thorough stare at my room. I had the pictures of my kid hanged on the walls.

"You were so different" he said breathing out.

He walked close to the picture with my mom. He watched them so close that it felt his intention like he knew mom for so long many years. My room finally brightened with higher watt of bulb.

"Who's she?" he scarcely asked that.

"That's my mom" I added with him.

"You look just like her" he added more.

He grabbed the chair and sat right front to me. He looked devastatingly hot and sexy. And I still pondered about his strength. I had nothing to begin with about any of the conversation that would carry between us. I know the friendship would be the better option than to think other way out. But right now, choices were still there with no more precise thought to lead on with life. However, things weren't that easy for Alyward and the only truth is known to me.

"So, the guy at the hospital, do you both hang out" he asked being easy.

I smiled, not with the intention. He looked at me silently with some sudden feelings inside, his face calm and sober to apprehend.

"Nothing much, he's just a good friend of mine" I replied, maybe I wasn't ready to disclose the truth inside of me.

I knew, that I began to love him more than anyone else could. And the only reason that kept it right was that we were silent about our relation.

"So, is he going to show up on dad's birthday?"

"Maybe" I ended shortly.

Tyler flamed to look uncomfortable with the passed time. He was just moving to- and- fro seated on the chair. And I could still see those verves that protruded out in his arms. I realized he was short temper guy who had the least strength to hold onto to anger and agony. The envious feeling was watchable in his eyes. I understood things weren't going to be easy in Alyward's presence. He tried to calm himself that was notable.

"Are you okay?"

That was another sign of something strange in him. Apart from his muscular strength, he rarely improvised what he has got. Maybe the awareness wasn't still in him. He nodded on my question. Unsettled up with his inner mixed feelings, he agreed to leave me without any further explanation or any conversation.

"I'll see you at dinner" he said and walked out of the room blatantly.

I watched him going with the slightest hint of frustration mind that he held. His conduct put me with confusions. I said none, with the thought to catch them up downstairs. When the dinner was prepared, dad called me down. I followed through the stairs. Tyler was seen seated with his face casted with the silent grief of tortured feeling inside. He didn't bother to look at me. I joined by his side. Burney too looked him perhaps, it made me feel he was aware about Tyler's unnatural appearance he flashed.

"Are you okay son?" Burney claimed to know.

"Yeah..I'm good" he nodded and looked toward me.

I smiled out though not perfect to be praised but one could follow I was flashing the same. He turned his face away so quick that it began to bother me much than he expected.

"What's wrong?" I urged to know.

"Is everything fine?" dad put on his concern.

That same bounded expression appeared on Burney's face. He tried to talk to him, somehow things went right until the dinner was over. I needed to confirm what was going through his mind. Tyler was out in the front yard, perhaps he was waiting for his dad. The sky was brightly lit with the moon. Of course, that was the first night of moon.

"Can I talk to you for a minute?" I hindered at first.

We both spent few moments watching at the clear moonlit night.

"I know, I was awkward at the dining table. I'm sorry about that" he plainly said.

"Why were you so biased?" I questioned.

"Sometime, I just can't handle my emotions" he said, staring toward me.

Burney shuffled out from the room. They were supposed to leave home. Dad walked to add the company until the car.

"Hey! Will you go with me to the beach this weekend?"

"Sure…do remind me once" Tyler prompted.

They left us. Dad saw at me for like seconds and went inside. I was the last to enter the house after deliberately watching the mesmerizing moonlit night so far. When I entered, dad was on with the television. I wished him the last word of the day and followed upstairs. For another twenty minutes, I got engaged in thinking about Alyward. I avoided surfing the internet for that night. My struggle to find mom was still under frame. I could never speak about that to dad. He wouldn't allow me if I do so. I went to bed with the half thought on my mind. When the next morning bloomed out, I found myself awake with the natural effect of golden rays falling upon me. The slit through the window allowed the shimmering glow of light that fell directly on my face. My eyes failed to open on the first attempt yet at the next I was wholly on my feet. I watched the clock ticking ahead while I wasn't yet ready to move down. When things got ready, I held my bag and ate few of fruits that were on the breakfast table. Dad was gone to fill his duty time. I left for school locking the door.

Alyward was seen at the same place with his hand placed on the roof of his car. I parked next to him. His stare toward me always had the pleasant issue to compose with ease. He came around on my side and very closely stood with his hand on my waist. No one was near to watch us. I felt the warmth of his soul and his breath even calm and softer. The softest touch he had blew me off with the soulful feeling of anxiousness and free of grief and pain. When his lips met mine, the world felt closer between us. He kissed me for the first time. The bell rang loud. It woke us up with soulful touch of love that we went through. He held my hand as we walked on through the open porch of school entrance. There I met Jessy and Lexie, who were heading for English class. They flashed a smile on us but went nothing with words. He had to move toward the next class. We walked through different corridors for the morning period to be completed, with the words of promise to meet during lunch.

Before the weekend ended, as per the words of promise we had celebrated Burney's birthday in our house. As per my expectations there was nothing that aligned to happen between Tyler and Alyward. It seemed to look like they have turned the best of buds within that hour of meeting. It's the second time they faced each other over any non-tense issues. Tyler behaved humbly with all respect with him. On the other hand, Alyward looked seemingly attractive on his black blazer coat he wore on that occasional night. There were many friends from Tyler's side. Even those came from Burney's colleague were the part of the birthday bash. It almost lasted till midnight hour. I had my most time spent with Alyward. He was partially new to our house. Although, he never got the real chance to be with me earlier. That very evening the porch wasn't empty. I urged him to walk along with me to backyard. Tyler saw us but retaliated none. I could picture that envious glare at us. He then left to company his friends.

"He doesn't want me with you" Alyward muttered.

I couldn't disagree to that for he had the ability to read minds. Moreover, his power to observe the future intensely summons me to trust all his words blindly.

"He's a nice guy…I don't know what he has been into" I said without surety.

The sky above had fallen dark as the crest of cloudy nights blanketed the lights of moonlit night. The backyard was silent and the only being was us. He looked deeply into my eyes and that stare had the effect that he threw in his glance. His lips met mine and the kiss lasted for minutes. It began to drizzle and the sound of thunder clouds reached the surface. We ran through the yard. People gathered inside, there Tyler stood holding a glass of beer along with his other company. I wanted to know if he would like one glass of it. But, his humble nature ignored to taste the alcoholic drink. Seeing us, Tyler walked toward our side. I was just next to Alyward, stood silent watching him approach toward us.

"You must be having a great time" Tyler's voice sounded coarse.

"Happy birthday to your dad" it came from Alyward.

"May I serve you a beer?" Tyler forwarded a glass of beer.

I watched at him silently, he accepted the offer.

"Have a great time" Tyler left us.

He taunted me though his intention wasn't to make me feel unpleasant. In course of such revive moment, I could just hold on what I was being. There was the kindest smile that flashed out of me as Tyler looked at me for the last time before he finally walked away. Alyward, who seemed so rare with such drink struggled hard to even finish his first glass.

"Are you okay?"

"I actually never felt this way before in my entire life. It's the first time, I actually felt courageous to stand among people with a glass of drink of alcohol in my hand, and I can't stop in sharing my feelings with you".

His voice sounded coarse, dripped with the effect that blew his sense. Just one glass effectively gave him the aura of being in alcoholic state. But he looked cute and smart in his sense, even more attractive when he's intoxicated. I slithered with the inexpressible bill of smile that widely made me happy to watch him as the person of being in honest humbleness, followed with the justified notion of being down to earth.

"Give me your hand, let's walk inside" I asked him.

His eyes reddened with the effect that triggered he would tumble in any case on his steps.

"I'm in sense, I can handle myself. It's not the first time I drank" he boastfully uttered.

Yet then I wanted to hold him, he grabbed me as our feet followed. Dad was inside with the rest of the people. Tyler wasn't seen among any of them. Perhaps, he was gone I assumed. Alyward slightly felt the need of my hand. He appreciated my concern. Dad was among with other people inside. He saw us going upstairs in my room.

"Is he alright?" dad voiced at us.

"Yep..he's good" I reverted.

As we entered the room, he strictly fell on the bed. I watched him being very exhausted.

"Are you okay?"

He nodded and closed his eyes. I walked toward the window. He watched me shuffling away. I wasn't sure if Tyler had abandoned the party. I searched for him outside where the crowd stood open in the front yard. He wasn't seen. I returned back to bed by then Alyward was asleep. By midnight all were gone. Dad once came to knock at me. I assured him everything was fine, knowing that Alyward was with me. His unconscious fall of sleep made quite indulged to gaze as much silently as I could very closely. The peaceful appearance reflected on his face with the perpetual shine of shimmering face. I've never seen such pretty boy ever in my life. His lips always tempted me over and over to kiss him. When the night fell deep in the sky I added by his side to join the moment being in one bed. I nearly had no freaking memory to recall mom that night. Having him with me was the best feeling that I could treasure.

The next morning was cloudy yet visible enough to watch outside through the window glass. As I opened my eyes, next to me was an empty sheet of cover on bed. I wondered where he was gone. I stepped up to look out through the window if Alyward was early to wake up. But then he wasn't available, nowhere around my yard or anywhere. That could be considered an unusual sense of behavior about him. Not to be well confined with me, he had left as early as possible and, while my sense wasn't able to feel about his disappearance from the room. I received a message shortly. He was perspicacious enough to realize that things would change for me that morning. It relieved me for second thoughts again. I texted back, if he could show me up at school. That came back with positive response from him.

Dad prepared the breakfast and kept it on the table. He was gone for his day's duty. The time almost knocked for me to leave the house, Alyward texted me another time calling me in hurry. I picked up the key and moved out to haul my truck. I drove across the way. In the mid-way, I was intercepted by Tyler who went unnoticed of me. He had his car being driven toward the beach. He failed to look at me as his speed seemed faster. That was first time I saw him going toward beach. I had to bifurcate my way to school, knowing that Alyward had been waiting for me. Tyler passed by without any concern or perhaps he didn't see me at all. That shook me with certain rise of doubts within my mind. He wasn't looking the way actually he would. More than his normal facial expression it suggested he was in extreme pain or frustration which he wasn't been able to slick out of it. He was handling very roughly his car. It all came into my notice within that fraction of time that he crossed me at high speed. All the way, I thought what must have been troubling him. Even the last night, he wasn't the way one expected to be. I reached the parking lot of my school. I saw Alyward's car but not him. I pulled out of my seat and searched for little moment. I wondered where he was gone leaving his car behind.

"Hey" a voice interrupted me from behind.

Alyward placed his hand on my shoulder. It shook me off, and my spines turned with fear for seconds.

"You scared me" I muzzled.

We walked through the cemented pattern way toward the main section of the building.

"There's something I need to say you" he sounded quite serious.

"Right, what's that?"

The sound of our steps hummed in the corridor, mentioning

the only hearable was the heel of mine that clapped on the ground. Yet the story didn't reveal from him. When we reached the next turned, there his voiced predominantly sounded over protective toward me.

"You should avoid going to beach for at least a week".

I heckled the thought in my mind. That wasn't possible for me to stay bounded within my house. I cleared to know, what could be the reason. He seemed very antagonist in telling what he had in his mind.

"Look, last night I had seen the future while sleeping on your bed" quite serious.

"Tell me what did you see?" I demanded softly.

"It's happening. And it can cause you a serious damage" he unfurled once again.

My intention to know further halted just in like stuck up with glue on my feet. He fleeted his feet and drifted away shuffling toward his section. Just the one call of urged to meet me up during lunch he assigned for me. I was immediately slammed with the recall of my memory that this early morning, it was Tyler who was seen moving toward beach. I'd never given the thought if it had something to do with him. But by then, Alyward wasn't there with me to let me more know about the tedious situation. Somehow, I completed the first period of the day but never found within the school building.

Chapter Six

At the beach the ambience turned dark with the arrival of Tyler. His extreme hold of anger and agony in some way began to deal him majestically with ferocious manner. He wasn't the man he carried, turned more violent and rough with the ongoing moment. Those who saw him fled away with fear and those who didn't he frightened at them. The horizon was rising higher as the sun began to glow over. Tyler's strength doubled, looked more huge and tougher than ever before. That wasn't his normal appearance. By far, it was something he had supernaturally. The beach was almost empty. No one stood by the side, watching him with the supernatural effect of human kind. The empty beach gave him the peaceful effect of what he was up to. He cautioned himself setting into a position. He stood stiffly with the outgrowing of his strength near the edge of the shore. When he raised both of his hands forward it lit like the glitters. He was under the effect of glowing bulged of shimmering light. His hands had the power to do anything he would want. He walked deeper into the sea water. And his strength entirely visible enough, that he could do anything with that. He began to draw some pattern with hands in the air. He began to feel his strength in controlling what he exactly had. Gradually, he began to pull or moved the sea water under his strength. His hand movement steered the way he wanted. He could create waves larger than any size of buildings in the town. He was raised higher and higher as much as he could from the ground. He lifted the water as high as possible. When he looked down, he actually realized he was floating in the air. Right before his eyes, he had the control over the sea water holding on with his strength. To magnify his strength, he sliced out a wave over which he surfed on and toured over the vast ocean. For him, it felt like a game. Surfing over the wave under his own control. He need not needed any artificial surf board. Even to addition he could ice the water. That too he played for a while icing over the whole ocean. Tyler never realized that he had such powers within him neither he was told about it by his father. Those super natural powers he had weren't something that came easily to him. He wanted to know the history behind from his father. When he returned back to home, he was actually that same Tyler Gaige. That following night, he never hinted to know much deeper about it. He seemed tired and fell on his bed early.

Alyward denied to reveal out what was the reason at school. I returned with empty minded. Something it wasn't inevitable for not letting me visit the beach. Dad was inside prepared with the dinner. He claimed nothing to know on my returned. I felt exhausted with the day.

"Are you okay?".

"I'm fine dad" I walked upstairs.

He mentioned me about the dinner in the table. It's been more than a week I've never sat to eat with him. But, he never minded about all those stuffs going on with my life. I found the phone idly kept on my table. Within fraction of seconds, it beeped with a message. The text came from Tyler. It arrived unexpectedly. Yet, I was concerned about him that day. He had something to tell me in person. We talked for a while through messages. But before the night felt deeper, the thought arrived if I could know the real reason why I wasn't allowed to know. But interrupting

Alyward in the middle of the night wasn't appropriate I thought once. Therefore, I ignored to call him instead, I went to bed early the night. It made me felt antisocial that being an aquatic creature I would be living a hell of my life and *Jimmy* who would perhaps wait for my return. It's only when I be there at the shore, I could call him to communicate else we were always untouched. The night turned cold as I felt asleep. Since the last time, I've never seen mom anymore coming in my dream. Though I wanted to meet her up, it wasn't possible because of Alyward's over protective concern on me. Besides, mom never showed up anymore, that was the last time I had met her in the ocean. Up there I had no idea where mom must have been. It's havoc the issue in me. Dad never spoke about her. Even if I tried to talk about mom, his word would fall silent except that he would try to console saying she was perfect where ever she is. It happened twice like that, since then I declined to talk about mom to him.

It's Sunday morning when I woke up to watch at the rising sun. Dad was out of his duty. So, he decided to wash up the truck and his car too. I thought to offer him my helping hand too. I walked downstairs.

"Hey dad" I called him.

He was spraying the water through the fountain pipe on his car.

"How was the sleep?"

"Fine and good"

"I shall get to your truck after this" he said.

"Its fine dad, I'll do it by my own" I smiled at him.

He glanced once toward me and continued to spray water. When he was finished, he handed me the pipe to spray the water to my truck. He too joined along with me. The glittering day emerged from the east.

"So, how you two are doing?"

The question caught me instantly. Realizing that dad was referring to Alyward. For instant, I shall not blurb about our relationship. It never had yet to do much about our relation.

"Good" that was too short I knew.

But dad had something to know more about. He solemnly accepted with the thought that I had nothing further to tell about our relation. That seemed quite arrogant as to my tally. Yet, satisfactorily it stayed silent for a while. Finally, we were done with the car wash.

"Are you expecting someone to arrive?" dad played another question.

"No..not sure exactly" I shrugged.

He smiled and walked inside the house. I left the truck to dry outside in the shining sunlight. But before I could get myself engaged with the other stuffs, I had the conclusion thought that there the chance that Alyward would show up. As I shuffled ahead to move inside my predictable idea appeared to come true. I heard the sound of a car arriving close to the gate. I stopped myself at that fixed instant of time. It was Alyward as I wanted it to be. He saw me and flashed his tiniest smile. I stood stable and steady watching him approached through the gate. To that guy, he was at his sexiest look to grab my attention. I was chuffed by the way he reached toward me. He kissed me without any hesitant. I escorted him inside. Dad saw us both, he was comfortable with the morning. Its holiday and we had no program to play the day. That's the only day where I would often visit the beach at any cost of time. But to my utter dismay it wasn't possible in presence of him. And I still had the faint remembrance about last night. Tyler suggested me, he'd like to meet me up at next weekend. Something very fishy he has to tell about himself. I wondered what was wrong to him. Dad prepared the table. Over the time, we were all seated in the dining table with the plates. The rise of morning break hour stood aloof as the cloudy frost of dusk began to gloom out into the air. There prevailed the slightest touch of breeze that blew from south. Perhaps, the winds were bringing the rain. With the tremendous effort of inside story, I prayed silently that the day shouldn't be spoilt just because of unwanted rain. This would really make the place disorder and would be difficult to go out. And as I took the spoon in my hand, it proved me wrong, the drizzle showered around. My shortest glance fell on Alyward. How actually I hated cold and rain, it was well known by him. I made my face at him, he out casted his sarcastic smile on me and faced toward dad, whom he was involved with. Gradually, the drizzle turned into huge fall of rain. My vision fell outside staring at the wet ground in constant manner.

"Anna," the voice interrupted me.

It came from Alyward seated next to me. Dad looked at me in an occasional suspicious way, wanting to know the hindrance that walled me. I was perfect just smuggled with the weird thought about Tyler's strange talk last night.

"What are you thinking at?" Alyward ingested plainly.

"Nothing" I simply said.

When the breakfast was over, Alyward came up with me into my room. Due to the heavy fall of rains, we weren't able to go outside for the day. Just with the glitch of temporary thought we began to spend the time at home itself. The music player was kept next to my book rack. He played a song for me. It was the same song that I heard the last week. No matter it wasn't the best of all I've heard yet. He sat on the edge of the bed by my side. Though silent for seconds, he picked something that he had long time in his mind. It sounded weird to me however it concerned me though.

"Don't you find Tyler little weird?" pathetically it reached my ears.

"You know nothing about him Aly"

I liked calling him *Aly* than being his usual name as Alyward. It sounded easier to me. He looked at me more in concuss fashioned granting nothing more to tell about Tyler. He stopped to talk. Maybe, I wasn't right to tell him that way. The music at the background ended soon. It was one of the shortest songs I've ever heard in my life. Just a minute sound it buzzed.

"Just avoid going to the beach for a week at least" he warned me again.

This was his second time he told me about that. I furled my mind demanding to know what could be danger if I went there. He ignored as much as he could. Underneath his mind, he was hiding something that he didn't want to let me know. He had seen the future beforehand compelling himself not to disclose even to me. That wasn't right thing he was doing to me. However, I kept calm trusting him with full confidence and heart. After long pause of silence he finally felt right to let me know what he exactly saw that night.

"You got to know something about Tyler, which you don't know" he said in serious way.

"What"

"He can be dangerous at times. Just be careful with him. I'd suggest you stay away from him".

That did not sense my mind with his words. Such was the thing that he wanted to keep it secret. Should I hold on to belief that story about Tyler? Yet, few things made sense, for Tyler was slightly different the last time I saw him. What could bring the drastic change in him that was questionable.

"What he is?" I followed more.

"I don't know exactly"

I nodded without much enthusiastic urge to know more about it. The rain stopped, however the cloud could be seen dark above. Significantly the day turned quite better to hang out. The reminiscing thought about mom struck up my mind. Besides, things weren't going right with her. Alyward stood up to change the track. I watched him going toward the table. Furthermore, he yet had no idea who I was actually. Even if he had the slightest suspicious thought on me he never showed out. The secret only renders upon me that I was a mermaid of my life.

He wanted me to take out. As the day fell slightly observable, he sought to take the chance to move before something else goes on. Dad was inside watching the highlight of NBA. The little concern to let him know approached within me. There was nothing needed to be pursued. Alyward wanted to drive his own car, so by his ardent cause of acceptance, I joined him in his car rather than pulling out my truck. The sign of cloudy atmosphere still hovered above the sky, though the clear sky could be visible, it had the fragrance of wet mud on the road. We passed across the cypress trees that were grown straight along the road way. Miles away from now, we had stopped at a restaurant, not exactly sure enough where we were heading onto. But somehow, the day slightly turned sunny. For little while, I could feel the warm ambience as we entered the restaurant. I ensured dad, Alyward would drop me back home by evening. When the waiter arrived to our table, there was the exclusive expression that raffled on his face. It wasn't that pleasant to watch at. When the order was finished, I demanded to know what made him that way.

"Are you okay?"

"Yup!" he shrugged.

For the slightest seconds of my mind, I realized we seemed to be numb without connection between us. Maybe there was nothing to talk about. The silence slithered in following the time to be as long as could lead us. I watched at the television that was being played. The restaurant had the new kind of paint on the walls. The Italian cuisines were the best that I had seen on the menu card. Until the waiter arrived again, we haven't spoken even a single word to each other. But this time he seemed normal on his behavior.

"Are you hungry?" it came very softly.

I grinned for shortly and nodded my head with a wish. Within few seconds of our wait, the waiter arrived with the recipes. When things are against you, it doesn't matter about that particular thing on you but right now it was something different I had been going through. I never had the courage to open up myself with the real truth before anyone. However, I always had the real perspective to let know him the truth of my life. But, as when the opportunity knocked before me it toppled me down with real fear dragging before my eyes. I looked out through the glass wall, a car splashed the dumped water on the road and passed by. It knocked me down for moment with the feel of some weird notion that held me up.

"Do you believe in fairytales?" I sounded coarse.

He stopped his spoon which was half way to his mouth. He dropped the spoon and stared at me with some silence on his face.

"Sometime, I do" he said.

I didn't get what he meant by *I do* to that question. Maybe, he doesn't hold that believe anymore. I further denied to proceed what I had in my mind. I actually got the answer from him, if the fact that I would reveal that I was a mermaid from a sea, he wouldn't have believed or he would simply mock at me in bizarre style. That wouldn't be tolerable for me. The anxiousness carried on me. It's been almost a week I haven't gone to beach. Or in otherwise I was missing my new dolphin friend *Jimmy*. Since the day he warned me about the beach, I had cautiously applied his concern safely. The day faced toward the west, and from the other end of the way, the visibility of rainbow color displayed in the open sky. It lasted for minutes.

We watched for few moments outside, but the undying signal from the above sky demanded the black clouds. In steady manner, the darkness above us crawled in. The sign of rain followed us. But the breeze allured the ambience with the ecstatic sense of humor and romance. It was something that I always wanted to happen with him. The church bell rang as we walked through the open space, the meadow was well gardened with varieties of flower kinds. Lots were seen, plotting out their joy of happiness in one go of their life. I could see the car and the restaurant. Having him alongside, made the time even greater. Nothing held inside timidly, I stayed with my mind shut, wondering the view around as he walked by my side. There was always something about him. Each time he looked fanatic and that kept me engrossing toward him. The setting sun was engulfed below the horizon and the orange faded rays began to fell on us. Even the shadow lengthened. And I knew, the time for us to drift apart was running closer to us. It took us to moment where we had our first meet, that same lingering shy glance at one another. We stepped ahead returning back to car. It's obvious there was no one who would be more into me to take care, as like him.

"I had a great time" I hummed at him.

He opened the front door of the car letting me in to the adjacent seat next to him. He silently smiled at me looking up in the sky for the next seconds. The dark clouds hovered very much into the place. Even the noise of thunder reached the earth surface. There was call from dad advising us to return as early as possible. Just then another blows of thunder burst and the phone went dead.

"We must hurry up before it gets too wild" he muttered as he buckled up his seat.

I managed to do the same. We drove across the same road that led us to way back to home. It began to grow colder as the wheel ran through the lone road. Due to the presence of stagnant water across the path, mirage would blink at each corner of the turn, and with every hump Alyward carefully balanced his steering. It began to drizzle. And to my spines the cold caught me. The worst part about the place was that, the county would turn cold at very rapid rate. And that was inevitable to escape at any chance of cause. I actually thought about Tyler the whole way about our meet on the next weekend. Though, I still firmly had no evidence what Alyward meant about him, I did not take the matter too serious in anyway. Maybe he could be right but for right now, it was just a hunched to me as like Alyward. The rain drops began to fall vigorously, my spines crapped with cold. He noticed me squeezing up and bothered expression floated on his face. His golden blue eyes caught the sight of jacket at back seat. He pulled with one of his hand.

"Wear this" he said.

I gently took from him, giving importance to his great concern.

"At least you could tell me you get cold when it rains" he said. That sounded quite possessive.

"I'm fine" I replied not bothering much.

The rain never stopped until we were at the front gate. Dad was outside with the umbrella. He saw us. Alyward stopped the wiper. That gave us the clear access to watch dad. He had another umbrella for me. The car stopped right before him. The decent peek came from him. He watched me with the effusive sense of holding immense love.

"When am I gonna see you again?" he said.

I stared at him holding the same feeling as like him. Dad kept watching at us. Though it wasn't the appropriate place for us, yet then our inner confrontations couldn't let us stop. He kissed me, as he stretched his body away from his seat. The rain poured heavily, and the thrust of wind hit the car with immense power at it. Somehow, dad was managing patiently to wait for me in the heavy rain.

"I should go now. I'll see you soon" I said him the last word.

He nodded willfully. Dad came to fetch as close as he could. He handed me the umbrella.

"Goodnight sir" Alyward wished dad.

The thunder and lightning shuttered on, and the dampness around covered the whole front yard. I watched him drive away with the umbrella opened up. Dad was already inside before I stepped in.

"Tyler called. He was asking about you" dad said.

"I made an appointment with him the next weekend" I said.

He nodded and followed his way toward his room. I walked upstairs. The misery of cold blew from all sides. The rains never took the name to stop. Rather by next hour, it was harsher with strong currents thrusting the walls. I went to sleep without much thinking about the weather.

The summer holidays began. For the last one week, I wasn't in touch with my friends, especially Jessy and Lexie. Neither they were in contact with me. I had tried to call one of them at least that morning hour. When I opened the door, it was almost bright outside with the frozen and dried rain water from last night. I had the call of Alyward kept in waiting mode. Lexie didn't response to mine call. The next option left with me was Jessy Cole. She was immediate to pick the call. From the other end, her voice suitably heard. Her first wish was about the summer holidays. Then I went on to ask about her curriculum about the remaining days. She told she'd leave for Nebraska within few days. She had her aunt staying there. While Lexie had already left to Wisconsin to her cousin's house the earlier. The intent never came up to know about Peter Pho. However, the news about him reached to me through. He had been busy in engaging himself in some sort of rock concert in Texas. With the few words of short talk, I hung up the phone. The message inbox blinked as I opened to see Alywards' message. Left was only me with none remaining behind though Tyler's company would settle up my day. I had learnt to ride bike by now. So, instead of using my vintage truck I preferred to ride motor cycles. All I had no concrete plan to spend the summer though *Jimmy* was always there for me waiting. It's the first day of holiday, and for me everything was the same except that I could watch television. I asked Alyward not to come. Not because he would care me so much but, I wanted him to be little free out of me. Sometime, I wanted to give him his own time for himself.

Tyler showed up after half of the day past. I was with dad spending the whole day watching with him the NBA repeat matches. Not a huge fan of NBA, as like him but, I liked when they scored in the basket.

"Hey Anna" he talked.

I opened the door for him. He looked literally fresh and the smell from him entirely catchable.

"After a long time" I said.

He joined along with us. Dad appreciated his presence. The fact, I was all alone for the whole summer, he wanted Tyler to give me the company for at least this summer.

"Do you want to go the beach?" Tyler persuaded.

"Right now, it's three" I said looking at the wall clock.

"Well, just be carefully" dad warned. His concern on us never ended.

Tyler had his bike. I preferred to ride with him for he was an excellent rider. I got ready hurriedly to catch up with him. He waited for me. He started the bike. I sat at the back. Dad watched us leave the place. The summer was always unpredictable here at Sonoma County. It had the different forecasting ingredients about the climatic condition about the place. Though the significant rain weren't shown up in the sky however the day turned cloudy. Black clouds spread up into high sky. Tyler speeded up the bike, passed across many cars behind. I held my hand onto his waist. The onlookers would surely spill the savage thought about us. For the ride wasn't quite decent to the passersby. The day began to turn damp. Slightest drops of water were felt on my jacket. How so ever it wasn't that heavy to make us wholly wet. The cold shattered me over again. But, coincidently I had the jacket worn on me. Tyler finally stopped his bike, just adjacent to the minivan. It carried some sort of junk foods. Tyler walked toward the van. I watched him, appealing to know what he was going to get. He bought two ice creams.

"Ice cream...ewe!!!!!" it slammed my thought.

The idea went bad as to me. But, so humbly he brought I couldn't deny him. It never went right with my combination. *Cold and ice cream..gush!!!* it was always a bad combination. He offered with the softest touch of it. I accepted and began to company him. We walked along the dunes that got slightly wet with the drizzles that continued. I applied my hood to cover my head. Tyler seemed quite comfortable with the weather. The remembrance struck me up. The idea that he wanted to put up few days back.

"You told you'd tell me something" I said deliberately.

"Do you really wanna know?".

"Well, I guess I would" I reverted enthusiastically.

"It's weird and strange. You won't believe me if I told you" he said.

"Try me" I said confidently.

He shook his head and looked at me once as he licked his ice cream. We didn't stop or halted instead, we followed through the wet sand dunes. The drizzle continued. The ambience was allured with the fresh air that blew from deep ocean. I proclaimed to stay careful, avoided as much as possible to get myself involve in touch of water. That would immediately cause me something to change that I wasn't ready to show or reveal to anyone until now.

"You know, it's been a week, I don't know something happened to me" he began.

I added as a silent listener. My ice cream was over. He still had few bites left. Rather his strange and weird story I began to find fantasizing. It was more like a super hero story than to hear a real story. When he paused to speak further, I cautiously took the initiative to know if he really felt that way. But in response to that, he was quite sure about it. He told he had some supernatural power. I do know he had the immense muscle strength. But, what Alyward had told me was yet to be proved right if that was the case with him. He continued with the strange words. Hearing to that somehow, I could hold to keep it in my mind though, no comment expelled from my side. Maybe Tyler was right what he was saying to me. It occurred to him only under certain circumstances. He was yet to know that situation. The matter appeared serious to me as I went on to listen to him. he wasn't an ordinary person; it began to make sense.

"What about your dad. Does he know about all these?" I asked him willingly.

"No…. I'll make sure that dad comes to know about these. I know, he's hiding something from me" Tyler's face pretty serious.

I wondered at his face, that read much more what he meant by that. We turned back our way returning toward the previous site. People gradually began to disperse as the setting sun was sinking below the horizon. The faint light fell on the shore and the end of twilight shrunk. The drizzle stopped for a while as we neared to the spot. My jacket got wet, however technically I was dry inside, same with him.

Dad prepared lasagna for dinner. In addition to that, he had the new recipe which he decided to cook. The presence of Indian Fish fry, was kept displayed on the dining table. That's the first time he was actually interested in fish. Tyler joined the dinner with us before he planned to leave home. I had tasted one of the best dinner till yet. To say, I ate the Italian dish like I never did. The likeness over lasagna a reason that never stopped me to like Italian dishes. When we finished the dinner, I escorted Tyler till the gate and thanked him for being there with me the whole day. I had no idea what would bring me the next morning. I even asked Alyward to stay away from me for a week. I needed some space of my own. He didn't make a call nor sent any messages. The thought arrived if I could take the chance to make a call to him but, I avoided. I could hear dad with the television sound downstairs. I planned carefully to make another decision to visit the beach the next day.

Of course, its summer and the vacations are not meant to spend idle. To generalize much with the condition here, people spend their vacation with friends and families travelling long toward east, west, north and south. But me, stuck up in one place. Dad never had any choice to let me go. The fact, he had no one where he could send me. I went to bed fagged over the awkward day that grabbed the night.

Dad was outside waited for his colleague. When he arrived, I heard the sound of the car. I wasn't ready to pull myself out of my bed. The cold in the morning caught me tight. I wasn't yet ready to lay my feet down onto the floor. But the anxious feel, to get way myself to the beach let me pull over the bed. I initiated to get myself served with the proper beginning of the day. I could hear dad talked with the man as I stepped down.

"Where are you ready for?" dad concerned to ask.

"Oh! I wanted to visit a friend of mine" that was of course not the accurate replied.

He nodded his head, not very much convinced though. The man looked at me. Not sure if I was Adam's daughter.

"Just return home by time" he said.

I smiled with the right signal on his real care on me. The morning gloomed out dry. Though the last night, there occurred to be slightest fall of drizzle. By morning it had dried up all. I pulled over the cover placed on the truck. Opened the door and got myself fixed. I started the engine, it sounded good. Everything was perfect. I drove through the gateway pulling the steering over the main road that led me to the beach. Dad saw me changing my direction. But, prompted none. Early morning the beach was always not full. That ardent feel of being with the company was a long waited for me since the time Alyward had warned me to avoid going to the beach. Finally, I breathed much better and smooth as I was nearing closer to the shore. I pulled the brake of the truck and waited no more than to jump out myself into the water. The water felt cold in the beginning but as I began to transform it reverted back to normal sense. I could finally feel myself as the one I waited long to see. The beautiful aquatic creature in me, took birth again and, the effusive feeling controlled my heart beat as I went deeper into the sea. I was finally no more the ordinary Annabell but, the mermaid queen of sea. I began in search of *Jimmy*. Somehow, I could follow the way it used to be there. I heard the squeaky sound. He was faintly visible right approaching toward me. I swam through the deep, as we neared each other. He followed my way and finally the dolphin was with me. *Jimmy* looked quite upset by me not because I didn't listen to his words but because for week I haven't shown to him. He gracefully asked me to follow him as I swam in his direction. He took deeper into the site where actually it's his territory. I actually never thought he would want me to meet all of his kinds. The cluster was seen clearly before my eyes. Hundreds of dolphins surrounded me with pride of joy and rejoice. *Jimmy* took me round and round, my tail looked playful while they followed me like the whirl of water that flourished in the deep. I swam for more than I could imagine that day. Finally, I was into their mob as one of them. And the urge played upon me to lead them. Finally, I had few of my armies now who would support me in all my circumstances. That was my inner world under water, and my inner nature of being the aquatic creature as mermaid. I never found any of my kind until now or it wasn't something I was expecting. Because I know, it was only me the kind of myself. The dolphins found me intriguing including *Jimmy,* neither do I could leave them. More like a family they had grown toward me. And the sea was all the land of their life. So, was to me when I turn into the queen of mermaid. They called me as the *queen of sea.* It was strange to accept that name but they were best of family I could consider. The salty water never tasted as it used to be. I could easily inhale and exhale breath as like the rest. I began to learn their way of communicating process in the mean while.

Much part of the sea I was familiar by now. Excluding the area where usually fishermen do drop their nets. I never met mom since that day onward, my expectation died down to see her anymore within the region of my choice. Instead, my more reliable choice had come among those clusters of dolphins. *Jimmy* accompanied me to another side, I enjoyed watching at those deep-sea creatures. The more efficient joy to see was those coral reefs under the sea bed. Being a mermaid,

I actually had no idea what I needed to do with such blessings. I considered my life a gift of nature, so for long time of my life there was no bad feeling about being a mermaid. Though the fact, I knew, I couldn't be the normal type human being.

The day's light almost doomed in through the horizon. Yet my anxious to stay behind kept me looming through the water. I swam onto the water surface after long hours of time. *Jimmy* came up to surface along with me. He squeaked at me. I rubbed on his head as he felt the tender love of affection. I never knew much about dolphin through study but, in actual shot of life I really had understood how those creatures were. I needed to return back home as soon as possible. With the last sign of goodbye, I had left out from the water and swam toward the shore. *Jimmy* fled through the water as he swam down, right toward his mob. I watched him going with the squeaky sound he made. As I left the shore with step following toward the truck, my legs began to reappear as usual. I was transformed to me again. The darkness slithered into the sky as I put on my clothes to fit on. The missed calls from dad were visible on my phone. I tried not to call him back as I was returning back. There was nothing from Alyward neither Tyler did inbox me anything about his next weekend.

Dad was busy in the kitchen when I reached home. I usually don't go into the kitchen. I had rarely tried cooking. To be honest with the truth, I was very bad at cooking stuffs. So, dad never called me in to join him. But that night, I wanted to know about his expertness inside. I wanted to know how he made the lasagna the last week. That fondness over the recipe stayed back with my target to search for mom. I wanted to bring up the topic about mom to him. But, somehow that hindrance between us over her appeared as he was busy with the frying pan. That intense feel to talk about mom was still alive in me. Often, I failed to understand, *does dad ever cared about mom?* If he cared about her, he wouldn't have let mom go just without any reasons leaving behind. Even though the fact, I knew I was actually mermaid's daughter, he never revealed about the truth I was actually one of her kind. But, he patiently waited for the right time, maybe for him the right time never yet arrived. I still remembered when mom left us, she had told him something, which I also couldn't even know, as it was a whisper into his ear. I opened the fridge and took out one energy drink and sat on the dining chair that was in the kitchen. Our kitchen was quite bigger than I expected. So, it had lot of empty spaces. And for people like us it was more than enough. Most of the time it's always empty during the day. Either dad would get his lunch done at his workplace and I, you know.

"Hey!! dad..I want to ask you something if you wouldn't mind?" I peered my myself carefully.

"Yes!....go ahead" he looked at me.

"You know mom is not with us, so why don't we just..." it ended blatantly.

He glanced at me, maybe quite serious in his opinion but to me it always looked him very nerdy. That nerdy expression always crapped him whenever mom would be the topic of our discussion.

"She promised me something. With time I shall let you know everything, Anna. So, just be patient. Your mom's fine, wherever she may be" he said.

I nodded and had that unsettling smile on my face.

"So, dinner is ready"

"Yup!!!....I'll handle the plates" I stood up to get them.

I never had any disgrace feeling toward him. He took care of mom and also me. Moreover, he always worked hard. The choice was right for mom to choose him as the man of her life.

After the dinner, I went upstairs without wasting much time with dad. I tried calling Alyward but responded none instead, I left a message for him. I texted him about the vacation, what he'd be doing for the rest of the summer holidays? *Is he here or gone somewhere*? I needed to meet up Tyler not because I had some necessary work but I enjoyed his bike riding. I left a message if he could show up the next morning. I received immediately proving me right. He was ready after all. I went to sleep after that text. That was another night, I dreamt about Alyward. It's been long time since we were together. The last time I had asked him not to show up. But, that what wasn't I meant. It could only be for him to let him be for himself for a certain time. And now even his call goes off without any acceptance. Somewhere down in his life, he would be watching me. As a clairvoyant guy, he wouldn't let his power go wasted for none sake. In every moment, I could feel and sense, he was watching me through his third eye. His care for me could only be seen through the melted heart that obviously captured me. For Alyward, it's been always not the way to show his feelings but in actual he had the other side of his life where he actually showed his feelings much more than what I could understand. I expected Tyler the next morning.

When I woke up, the time for the break of dawn was already gone. The first sight that fell outside my window was the sunny sunlight that came into my room. I shuffled toward to open up the window letting the morning glooming air to blow in. I saw the bike kept parked at the front yard. Tyler was here, inside with dad where he was actually giving the company to him in watching a movie which actually featured a sheriff role in it. I got myself prepared and stepped downstairs. He waved his hand and sounded the morning wish. My face still looked gloomy not fresh enough, I smiled at them. I sat by dad's side. On the table, there were few pieces of French fries and a piece of toast kept. I opted to grab it before anyone could. I watched with them the movie until the end. By that time, it was almost noon. Much of my time, I derived to serve myself internet. But the summer was too hot to sit all alone.

Tyler persuaded me to come along with him for hiking. I never had the trial of hiking over a long steeping mountains or slopes. Well, it made sense to me to come along with him. Dad was left alone at home. He had no duty for the rest of one week. But sometime, he'd go out into the town just for a lenient inspection around the places. When we reached the spot, Tyler just halted his bike just next to big poplar tree. The ambient felt quite silent with the hiss of freshly air that blew from North. He handed me a bag that carried few of eatables. He managed to pull out the camping canvas. The hill wasn't that heighted to climb up, just few meters to move up. I followed him. I insisted not to feel the tiredness within me. When we were at the top, we grooved for the safest place where we could nail the canvas to build the small camp house. Tyler initiated with the proceedings as I gave my helping hand in planting the tent. When everything was done, we halted and looked below down the steep slope of the hill. The small town of ours was visible enough from the spaces of clouds. He joined by my side. He looked at the clouds that floated very near to us.

"It's a beautiful town right" he spoke and glanced toward me.

I nodded "yes" and walked toward the tent. I felt hungry for the trouble to get me up on the top of the hill actually dehydrated me. He came and joined along with me. He took a can of drink which was quite freezing to hold. He offered me one. The fruits and the loaf of bread were there for both.

"You never told me much about him" Tyler intruded.

I wasn't quite sure in what he meant by that. After minutes of thoughts, I realized he actually meant to say about Alyward.

The situation, for moment kept me on hold with perturbations of mind conflict, what should I say to him.

"So, you both hanging out together" that sounded envious, though loyal.

"I don't know" I ended shortly.

"Why don't we talk something else" I said.

He took his second sip of his can and nodded his head forwarding right to change the topic. Then we were on something else with the breezy environment that fluently arrived.

"What you gonna do after graduating?"

"I want to do course on English creative writing" I answered.

"That's good!!" he smiled.

I had eaten almost all of the breads by now. There were few left for him. I could see the edge of the hill top few steps away from us. It intrigued to follow there. Without any second thoughts, I unhooked from the place and walked toward the site.

"Where are you going?" Tyler concerned.

He followed me with no time. I wished, if Alyward was here it was much a better place for both of us. As I reached the edge, right down below, the blue water was visible. It's the lake that I heard about as I reached to this new town. But, I've never been there. Tyler stood up by my side and added to my view.

"There's a history about this lake" Tyler added.

"What's the history?" I urged to know.

Tyler saw the anxiousness on my face regarding the lake to know about its past story. He made his face looking downward not that gentle though but acceptable. I said for another time, in urge to know about the history. It's the childhood phenomena about me that listening stories and tale I'd love to do.

"Oh!!! It's just like a fairy tales Anna...C'mon" he walked back to the tent.

I stared down for a while until I felt quite satisfied with my inner instinct. The water never moved, it's still and silent down there.

"So, you don't want to share it" I said plainly.

"Do you really want to know?"

"I guess so" I gestured.

He began, though at first the thing wasn't that easy to believe what he was narrating. I actually couldn't believe that it's so old lake, people rarely visits just because of the history behind that it left. And the real thing was that the history wasn't known to all.

"They say it was a place for sea creatures" Tyler looked at me.

That was serious, I claimed to myself.

"What sea creatures?" I plugged on him that intrigued me more.

"It was the hub of mermaids. They lived here for many years, until one-day tyrant pirates from the Caribbean destroyed them. They were killed and the war was on till all mermaids were down. They lost the war, while the victory was claimed by the pirates. They were left with none" he stopped.

That frightened me for a while, though I tried masking the fear on my face. I looked outside the tent. The day was almost settling down the horizon. The orange rays fell on the whole area, as the twilight shrunk below the hill top. We prepared to step down the hill. He packed all the things up tightly. The story still rumpled on my mind. But more than that, I could feel the non-existence of my life if that's the case. I don't know where mom could be right now. I needed her. It always slammed my subconscious in search of her.

"Were pirates too powerful?" I asked Tyler, as we reached the poplar tree below.

"They had some magic in them" he said peeking his eyes shortly toward me.

He pulled the bike out of the positioned and settled all the things. We got ready to return back. The day ended and the darkness crawled in the forest. The chirp of home going birds were the last that could be heard. By next hour, the howling of wolves be more precise to our ears.

"From where did they enter the place?"

"There's only one way here, the beach" Tyler said as he asked me to sit on the bike.

I sat behind him.

"You can hold my waist" said Tyler. That sounded friendly though. I placed my hand at his waist. He accelerated like the speed of light.

Dad waited for us. The dinner was prepared. Tyler added us for the dinner. But, before he left I wanted to thank him for showing up. If his presence wasn't there I'd have died out of bored feeling. I walked along with him till the gate.

"Hey!!! Tyler"

"Yeah…"

"Thanks for being here with me" I said.

"It's okay"

He started his bike and wished me goodnight before he speeded up like a rocket. Dad went back to bed early that night. So, inside I felt the silent more compressed as there was no sound of television. It does make me feel bad sometime because it's only two of us that lived in the house, and most of the time it's always silent. And when abruptly that silent encloses the house it's felt awkward. Since, the habit of hearing dad watching television was always there to accompany both of us.

I surf the internet gathering to know more about the history behind the lake. Most of the things were true that Tyler had told me. It shook my spines after reading the page. It made me feel how the mermaids have fought for their lives. Yet, they never gave up. They're still fighting for their justice over that long history. Recent news revealed up about within few weeks of research. The researchers spotted few of mermaids at Cruz Bay, the US Virgin Islands. It intrigued with the interest to know with the next page that I clicked on. Perhaps, that history was repeating all over again. The mermaids were preparing to avenge their long-term grudge over the pirates those from the Caribbean Islands. The hub was growing day by day, as many more were spotted within few weeks. I followed the daily news through the internet regarding them. It wasn't yet telecasted as the researchers were on a secret mission to search for the accurate evidence about the existence of mermaids.

I went to bed with that collection of information. But before I was wholly asleep I tried calling Alyward for the seventh time that night. The response wasn't receiving from the other end. I texted, leaving him the last message of the day. The suspicious arrival of thought bridge me regarding mom, it gave the specific intuition about her. I knew, she was there at Cruz Bay. However, for me it could be difficult to reach her. I had least idea about the Virgin Island. I just heard once from mom in a story that she narrated when I was a kid. Reaching there could be one hurdle for me. I could be new to the place and the trouble that would hover could be researchers out there. Either I had to take the route through the Atlantic Ocean or as pure human to reach the Island. In either of the two ways, the probable chance to find mom wasn't there at all. But believe stayed behind along with me pushing upward with hopes and

faith. Even more I was sure that, dad never spoke about Virgin
Island. That was more evidently proving that mom would be
there amongst those other mermaids there. The whole situation
never wrapped in one mind. Maybe, I needed some one's help
to do. Bearing alone wasn't that easy for me. But, the fact none
of my friends knows me, I'm a mermaid. Except that Alyward
perhaps, sensed it by now. Even though Tyler could be able
to recognize me in disguise he'd never reveal it to me. Things
between us always had gap. The inner truth never came up
though it was in ideal thought that we were in doubt about
each other's nature of life. On the other hand, Alyward's mind
could be understandable, revealing that he's a clairvoyant by
nature, acceptable enough to face his truth. But what bothered
me more was Tyler. He's the other kind who scarcely faces
the difficulties of life. He's strong and powerful that appeared
physically. Inside, he's something else that made him that.
But I never stressed much on him although we've spent lot
of time together. It never made me feel to know more about
him. He's just one of his kinds and, I felt comfortable enough
with his nature. I needed mom to see me what I've grown
up into. I'd be glad if mom could see me as the young girl
today. She never saw me like how I'm today as real human.
Neither did I saw her as mom. These long many years, it took
lot of time to forget the parting moment we had. I never knew
how dad could stay without thinking about her. Even if he did
that somewhere down he always thought about mom. I never
questioned about their relationship. What surprised me more
was how dad and mom got together, a human and a mermaid.
It was oblique to my mind. Yet then they had a good relation
with them. I knew, just one thing that mermaid never tend to
stay forever with their partners. When they are done with their
fulfillment they leave with a promise to return back. But most
cases they don't, once they go away, neither they intent to hurt
their partners. On the other hand, their loving natures keep

the other person waiting for years inducing within them the trust of true love. That's what mermaids are expert in. They know how to love people and even more they know how not to hurt their partners, although they may be doing that but not actually make the other realize about it, which to me is absolutely ridiculous for human mind to fail to understand that.

Chapter Seven

When I woke up, I found the window flapping. Though, the sun shone bright, the breezy wind outside tangled the environment with dampness that brought the moisture from the sea shore. For sometimes I watched outside, dad was at the gate, perhaps to wait for his colleague. It's the summer and the vacation were still yet to be over. It's been more than week, I never contacted with Jessy and Lexie yet. I tried but couldn't reach to their line. It always showed up busy whenever I called them. Dad was gone when his colleague arrived. He saw peeking through the window. He waved at me before he got into the car. The rest of the day, I wanted to spend it on the beach. So, I prepared for myself and travelled down with the truck toward the beach. My expectation didn't pull me higher. I expected few people to be present instead, it stood like a barren land. As I neared to the shore, the scene before my eyes were different to notice. I didn't expect Tyler would be there. I stopped my truck few meters away from his parked bike near the shadowed sand dunes. I looked around to find him but his visibility wasn't detected. I waited for a while inside the truck hoping that he would be seen somewhere down the shore. Far ahead that instant moment of time, I had figure of human being approaching toward the shore. He had bear body only with the shorts worn. Of course, when he was closer to sight at, Tyler looked something different. His muscular body gained weight and looked even more powerful with strength in him. He walked toward the water. The motion of his hand began to create the shape in the air. I watched wondering what he was trying to do. *Was it a black magic*? he was trying it, it mismatched in my mind. I kept silent as I gazed at the site. The motion of his hand gradually turned more powerful which for me was unbelievable. It shook me up for its the first of kind I was witnessing unusual thing ever in my life. Tyler began to control the ocean through his supernatural power. He lifted the water bed up into the air. The crater formation took place as he did that. He played with it for at least a minute until he lifted down. He looked stronger than ever before. I wondered how he inherited those unusual powers. I was still inside the truck stuck with the fear of spines. The nerves began to shiver, as he picked up a wave which he froze into an ice sheet. It appeared like a bridge over long distance covering the ocean. He shuffled on it and as he followed ahead into mid ocean, he applied his power to freeze into ice sheets to make his way. I wasn't dreaming, it was happening for real, I pinched myself. It was the real observation to my eyes. When he reached the height of the wave he turned back and looked down. He raised himself up to certain height from the water surface. It looked like he had been the *God of Sea*. He played with his powerful gifts lifting and splashing waves through the oceanic water. And to my surprise, he never needed any medication to heal himself. His source of healing was water resources. I watched him long until he was busy on his own to skate through the ice sheet that he created. It wasn't that easy for me to hold on longer at the site. I turned back my truck to be back at home. Whole through the way I still couldn't believe that Tyler was a kind of *Demi God*. It irritated my mind knowing that he was not the kind of person I thought to be. But much stronger and powerful in every sense. On the other hand, he concealed the real truth in him. That was something very shocking effect that glimpsed before my eye. Maybe, I wasn't in the whole complete world then driving back to home. I had escaped a treacherous accident on my way. Just by inch the other person managed to safe himself, as he pulled over his steering right down the left that led him stopped before he actually fell along with his car right below. I had seen the man screaming at me through my rear-view mirror instead, I least bothered him thanking god he was safe, else the crash site would've been definitely bathed with blood. Of whom we both would become the victim. It was a narrow escape and my stilled heart, beat for long time could ultimately breathe better.

When I was at my front door, dad wasn't inside. I saw him glancing at me from the garage. I decline to meet him instead, I went upstairs indulging at the suspicious thought that Tyler was unbelievable today. *Was he actually a monster*? Often it tricked me. No, he wasn't a monster either but to be more precise without surety he was a born *Demi God*. That almost ended believing something unusual has taken place. No, I wasn't to share it anyone not even with dad. The reason began to appear clear before me. That's why it was Alyward, who always stopped me from going to the beach. I needed to talk to him, but he wasn't responsive with any connection. It's been more than weeks; I haven't visited him neither he intended to see me.

As usual dad prepared the dinner, I joined with him. We had few conversations over the whole day. But, that moment of time I was actually drowned with the illusive picture that I had seen at the beach.

"Are you okay?" dad urged to know.

"I'm good" I pretended.

What I should demand to know from anyone, it blocked me for a while. I needed to find the solutions by myself. Of course, it would be wrong if I tell Tyler that I knew he was a *Demi*

God. For none knows, that I was a mermaid too from deep sea. Unfolded secrets wouldn't be right if it was dug out from the core. So, I chose to stay silent even if the real stories were known to me. I left a message to Alyward that night before sleeping. But more than that I couldn't let myself calm on my bed, it haunted me about Tyler's gigantic actions. I walked out of the bed in search of my water bottle. It was fallen on the floor not realizing its absence on the table, I searched for it. But as I took another step near to it, my feet trampled on it. It squeezed, the cap burst out with all the water spread on the floor. I felt wet on my foot. Somehow, I let the things go right cleaning all the stuffs within that night time. After that it was very hard for me to go to sleep back again. I tried to avoid thinking about the incident that was witnessed. *How would I feel if Tyler stands with me ever again*? Of course, for me, he would be different in my perceptions. But, I should never let him know regarding my knowledge about him.

I heard the sound of a car moving out of the gate. It was dad I assumed. The morning shuddered with the damp beginning. Of course, there was slight drizzle about last night. That added the more vibrant coldness with the pathetic scenario of Tyler's unusual act. I laid my feet on the floor the breezing cold caught my feet. The floor was dry by now. The empty bottle was kept on the table as I proceeded toward the window. I had seen Alyward had texted me back. I wanted to meet him up immediately.

"You were right about him" that's what I wrote to him.

The car was recognizable as I peeped out of the window. I granted someone's of dad had come to fetch him for the duty. I readied myself to step down. To my utter most imaginary surprise Tyler was seated with dad at the front veranda. It was unreal, he was right before me. Not the guy, I saw last day in the beach. My face crackled with sudden shock, not visible enough to notice but inside it was fiddling up. I swallowed the saliva that accumulated inside my mouth. Hard to believe it was the real Tyler I had seen last day in other form.

"What's wrong. Why are you taking me by surprise?" he spoke.

It so happened that I had just urged myself not to think about him but to my utter dismay he was right there. I shouldn't escape him nor I should put my ignorance upon him. He stepped up closer toward me. Dad was ready to leave out. Just few words he left for both of us and gone out of the gate.

"Nothing, you look different" I tried to be normal.

"What's your plan for today".

"I don't know what else are left for me" I said as we walked.

The day began to turn dry as the brightness began to hover around through the spaces of leaves that fell on the ground. The wet areas were almost dry within an hour. I feared on what I should begin to indulge with him. Neither the fact could be taken out nor the false could be proved. It needed to stay silent as long as it had the space to keep concealed within.

"Well you didn't tell me about him?"

"You know him well. You've met him twice" I said, hoping that he wouldn't further involve the topic.

I stopped talking about Alyward furthermore. He felt the silence for seconds realizing I wasn't interested to take on my personal matters to him. We had our lunch together. He helped me out in the kitchen. When the day was on its way toward ending, I received a message from Alyward following me to show up at his house. It was the best time I thought. With cross talk about the time, he assured me he would come to pick me up within no time. But, Tyler was still there with me. I needed to be away from Tyler at least for hours. Fortunately, he opted to leave back home. Something urgency inflicted in him. Burney had called him up within short notice.

"I shall have to go. Thanks for the dinner" he said.

He left me. The day was yet to fully complete with its ending. Dad hasn't returned yet. I waited for Alyward at the front yard. The two coincidently arrived at the same time. Dad saw him out of the car.

"What's young man what made you bring here?"

"I need to talk to your daughter sir" he being extremely polite by nature.

"C'mon in"

Alyward followed dad. I was out in the front porch. I couldn't stop the emotive call that bulged out from me. I immediately gushed into him and embraced him. He kissed me. It's been long time after we met each other.

"I missed you very much" he sounded too caring.

"I missed you too" I added the same.

"C'mon get in you both" dad called us.

Without waiting with dad, I immediately took his hand and we stepped upstairs. Alyward followed me. Dad spoke loudly saying he'd notice us when the dinner would be available. Inside, the room was dark I had to search for the switch board in that darkness that crumpled the room.

"You were right about him" I instantly began.

He intently looked at me with the flow in his eyes which actually weren't able to read much. He stepped closer to me and took my hand. I felt the warmness around his palm.

"Are you afraid?" he asked being very noble.

I stared at him seeing the purity in his eyes. It melted my inner core urging to trust as much as possible limit I could. I didn't doubt for a moment if he was there for me. And his presence mattered me lot, which indeed would instill me with confidence to face the world.

"No" I said.

"Then you shouldn't think about him" he sounded motivated.

Despite the fact, I could be careful about myself more than what I wanted him to be safer than me, cause the reason could be much more un-protective in case of him. He was just a plain human although he could see future being the clairvoyant. But that supernatural ability lacks in him unlike Tyler who could do any harm to any kind.

"Do you talk with death people?" I asked.

He laughed and smiled grazing his thought over me. His reddish lips always pulled the view of any one standing close to him. But, his smile often kept me stunned with the majority of my thoughts focusing at him. And that could ultimately put me under a spell bound cause.

"I told you once, I don't" he smiled out.

"I'm sorry…. about that. My memory isn't that strong" I said.

He sat on the edge of my bed. I added by his side. He glimpsed over me and his sharp jaw pointed toward me. It talked something around his mind.

"Read my mind" I urged at him.

"I can't" he said willfully.

"Try"

That smile which he always had on his face do froze me up. It never kept me engrossing what I want but every time he's with me it out sourced me with that kind of feeling that I always wanted to have. He tried to look deeply into my eyes engaging to try himself, if he could penetrate my mind. He threw that focus of unsettling expression.

"I can't penetrate your mind, Anna" he said sadly.

"You don't need to do that" I said with that strong feel for him.

"You just need to be careful about Tyler" he cared for me.

I nodded "What about you?"

"He can't reach me" he assured.

Dad called us from downstairs. He had the dinner prepared for all of us. We joined him.

"I'm grateful to you sir" Alyward pretty humble.

"You don't need to be son, take your seat" he patted at his back.

When we were done with the dinner, we headed outside toward the front yard. Dad got himself busy with the daily television as he does. We walked on through the cemented porch. The breeze outside allured the night with the glow of stars up lit in the night sky. That ardent feel engulfed us being close to one another as we sat on the green grass which dad had recently planted in the front yard. It's been almost two weeks since he did that and showed rapid improvement in its growth. He sat by my side and looked up into the starlit night sky.

"Where were you?" I questioned to know.

"I was out of town. Just took the chance to visit my parent's graveyard" he said very softly.

"What you'd want to do the rests of the summer"

"Spent the valuable time with someone who cares for me" he whispered.

I was dazzled to hear that and passed my brief smile to him. He innocently glanced at me that something magical felt like taking place. I could feel the sky above us watching closely, as he his lips met mine. It was dad when he called for us in. Alyward wanted to leave the night back to home. But my intensive persuasion made him stop by with me that night. We moved inside. I wondered if he wanted to join dad. Well, that's not what I would want him to do at least for that time.

Somehow, I could manipulate him to come along with me upstairs in the room. Dad was left alone with the television being watched.

"Don't you never watch television with your dad?" he asked.

"Well, he has his own program to watch, which for me not the interest one. I actually not try to disturbed him when he's at home"

He gently sat on my bed. I watched him with the corner of my eyes, as I moved toward the table to place the water bottle. He looked around the complete room trying to find if there was any change, I had done since the last time he was there. I joined by his side.

"What you did all through these days?" he peeked at me.

"I read a new book. I visited the beach despite of your warning".

"You seem to be brave" he muttered.

I giggled at that sarcastic urge from him. I handed him the book which I was actually busy with the whole summer. He held it by hand and looked at the title.

"What's the story" he asked not bothering much to read by himself.

"Read it, I believe you like reading books?"

He smiled giving a shallow pause over it moving his hand turning the pages. He began to take a good look over the words. Not going much deeper, he stopped.

"Not the kind of my type" he said.

He lingered around the room for a while and walked toward the window. When the window was opened, I felt the sudden rush of cold breeze blowing rustically inside. It touched my spines and shivered momentarily. He turned back and concerned.

"Are you okay?"

"I'm good" I shrugged.

He pulled the curtain, though that somehow stopped the wild breeze to much extent. The star lit sky was visible through the pores of the transparent curtain. He shifted his feet toward me and gently laid his body leaning against the head of the bed. He held and cuddled me toward him. I felt warm when that happened. I felt his breathe over his chest as my motionless head stayed stiff upon him. The night passed and the deep silent from the homeless night felt. The howling of wolves from nearby woods were the only elements that could pull one's attention. But to me, I got used to them. Alyward managed to stay abide by the disturbance that he felt. Hours left to open up the next day. I was finally asleep under his arm.

In the next hour of the day, I sensed the dawn had been out. I heard the slight sound of car moving out of the gate. Dad was too early to be out. In the next hour, when my eyes were actually open, I was still in his arm. The blooming warm rays penetrated through the window. It fell on his face. It shimmered him with the gentle glow of kindness and gorgeousness. He looked very defensive and admiring. I could go on and on watched him with that charming beauty that flashed on his face. His eye lids were too humble to open up in the sunshine. I gazed at him like I never had seen ever in my life. More than anything else, he looked very lively and filled with treasure in him. The one precious soul I felt with. I watched at him silently until he moved his eye lid to open up slowly focusing out. He glared brightly as his eye balls looked for object. The sudden fall of golden rays at him turned his pupil blind folded for seconds until he visualized I was just next to him. When he found me, he briefly felt my presence?

"Hey!!!! morning" he said.

I gestured with a smile at him.

"I think I should leave back".

I wanted to add up to join him. But not sure enough if I needed to go along with him. The inner instinct however felt suggesting and I could follow to go along with him. He prepared himself as he stepped downstairs. I informed dad that I'd be spending the rest of day with him. I locked the door as I headed toward Alyward's car. He stood waited for me. He was already inside taking the control. I took the seat just next to him.

"Shall we move?" he asked.

I nodded, focused the brief smile that figured on me. We drove through the empty road. Usually the way remained empty early morning, passed through the woods that ultimately led to his home. I don't remember how many times I've been to his house. Everything was the same nothing changed, that furnished floor with tiles, and the exact decoration that I had seen the last time I was here. He escorted me to his room. I still remember the last time he made me turned around his fingers. *I wondered what would he else try*? Not much figuring out to read him well, it always the tempting cause that he possessed. As usual he played the music player choosing one of his favorite of all time. I gently took the bed's edge to comfort myself.

"Don't be shy…. it's all yours" he said.

That actually made me felt little awkward. It crawled up on me, felt slightly mismatched with the situation at. Somehow, I submerged myself staying still, feeling the warmness within the room. And Alyward so close to me, stood with his breath being silently murmuring out.

"Oh! Aly..c'mon don't embarrass me" not serious in my notion.

He smiled and gestured through his face. He loved to hear calling me Aly, though he never said that.

"I'm gonna get you breakfast" he quickened downstairs.

After browsing through his room across the walls, I walked toward the window and looked outside, merging to loop myself in the view that was right before of my eyes. I couldn't escape the scene of beauty it had to indulge with. Nothing altered, still the same feeling fell on me hoping that would rise into everlasting story of love that I've been with him. I was soaked with the beauty of the nature when then he arrived with the breakfast. I didn't realize, he was standing behind me in addition to my view.

"Every morning I watch those birds chirping their morning rhyme" he murmured very softly into my ears.

It shook for moments, faltered by his presence so quick behind me. I turned back rolling my eyes on him. Within few seconds of fly by time, I felt indulged with him.

"You're so privilege to reside by this place" I muttered wondering looking outside.

"Well, the breakfast is here" he squinted.

The morning broke with the silent cause of shimmering beauties in it. And as the sun directed to move toward the rising spot the rays entered with pride of hopes into his room. It felt directly on his bed. The freshly born day gave enough to abide by to ensure the purity of our soul that we're lingered on. He gently took my hand and made me sit on his bed. He added by my side.

"You really take care of me so much" with firm dedication I spelt out.

He smiled at me with that same look which he carried since the break of dawn.

"Cause I know, you're the soul that I was born for" he said too effusively.

That effectively touched me more than I could feel. He handed me the plate that had the varieties of choices to fill up my pouch. I ensured nothing more than to obey his heart that immensely cared for me. There's no such thing that I'd received from anyone else the expectation wouldn't be much from other. The difference could be felt though I was pampered by my parents yet the feeling from someone you love wasn't that enough to express from inside. It had something essence in it that actually built inside, though inexpressible but could be felt with whole of nature's gift. I began considering to take the breakfast. He joined me. There was the silence for a moment to grasp the exotic view from the window as we continued to bite the toast.

"What else you know about him?" Alyward sounded catchy.

I gasped and looked at him. That was sudden in motion. Didn't expect, he'd probably try to know about Tyler. It hit my thought what else I should share to let him aware that Tyler was actually a *Demi God* by birth. Perhaps, he knows more than me about him. However, they haven't met each other very much. But I assumed, that he must have been known about his nature by now.

"You stopped me to go the beach. I thought you knew" I added.

"He's *Son of God*. A *Demi God*, that's what I saw" he said.

I nodded my head releasing the juice glass on the table. I wasn't so terrified hearing from him. I had seen him in real so.

"You didn't tell me beforehand".

"I was concern with your safety" he said being possessive.

That was well enough to be accepted. After we finished the breakfast, he quickly cleaned up the place. The time stood idle, the rest of the day was yet to pass by. I've never talked to any of my school mates. The summer holidays almost passing away and none ensured to call me neither Jessy nor Lexie. The day lighted up bright as the dew over the grass had dried up.

I had taken last chance before we moved out from the room to view the panoramic sight of the location. He came up and added himself behind me.

"Would you like to walk with me?" he sounded too soft.

"Yeah" I hissed out.

When we reached the plotted garden, he seemed to glow in the sunlight. That however kept me busy watching him rather than taking the moment to rejoice myself with the ambience.

"Why you looking at me like that?" he squinted.

We walked passed a couple seated on a bench. I happened to glance at them with the position that the girl was nearly kissed by her boy.

"Nothing" I muttered as we headed ahead.

He threw a sullen smile at me. We stopped, when we found an empty place to hang around. It's just the two, quite away from the rest of the people. I wanted to share the part what I had witnessed about Tyler. But for a mere thought of disambiguation, I denied to utter it out. The rest he knew by himself.

"Do you think Tyler will do any harm to me?"

"That depends with whom you're with" his voice quite docile.

"What if he sees me kissing you?"

"He saw us many times together. I believe, he wouldn't feel anything more than to envy upon us" he squished.

Sometimes it made me felt whether I was living the life I chose but that wasn't happening. In fact, often it troubled me with both. Deep inside, I had Alyward to hold me but I couldn't ignore Tyler too. In time of need, he showed up his presence. But love wasn't deceivable. Yet, not to focus on where I should finally end up. Those hiccups of tormenting drama were always played in the scene of my life. On the other side, it ached that mom wasn't there with us. The ultimatum still suggested me to find her. Unless the idea arrived to me I wasn't able to take a step on. The only possibility I could see was I needed help of someone who could support me all through the journey. But I never chose who could be that. It's so painful to stay with junks of disoriented feeling in life. These few of my inner fragile thoughts often haunted my life, which weren't breakable to escape. Back in the days of childhood the hope of love and experience were truly adorable. I was never brought up like any of the dream girl with the high cost of expectation to live life. Just the simple and liable enough to face ahead whatever the circumstances could put me through. And here I was with the guy after many years of waiting I could actually say I was in true love.

The silence lingered around for long time until Alyward snapped his voice pulling my attention toward him. We talked about life and future. We couldn't stop to involve Tyler in our discussions. When he stood up from his seated posture, he desired to walk ahead toward the lake. It was pretty much like a park that was made into with lake as the center of attraction. It wasn't too late before we headed back. Dad once made the call assuring about me. I ensured him, I'd be back home, need not to worry about me. Alyward with his careful responsibility drove me back home. We didn't dine together that following day. But I liked the place once where he had taken me. Away from the county side, faintly I remembered the place as Bakersfield.

Dad was outside waiting for me. Alyward didn't hinge on to come inside instead he drove me at the front gate. The breeze blew silently as the rustling noises of the branches of leaves could be heard swiftly. The darkness above hovered around, and the faintly light from the moon began to generate.

"When am I gonna see you again?" he said, unbuckling his seat belt.

"At the weekend" I said and got out of the car.

He shook his head and wished me goodnight before he speeded away. I watched the car until it damped away from my sight. I opened the gate and dad was right there.

"Hey dad!!!" I said.

"How was your day?".

"Nothing special!!! What's there for dinner?

"Well, I bought chicken wings for you".

That actually made me happy for moment. Something, I always opted to have. Before I joined dad for dinner, I roomed myself upstairs settling up the things. When I shuffled down dad was already seated in his chair. I preferably assumed he would ask me about Alyward. But that wasn't the case indeed. He was silent for the whole time. When it was over the only word he uttered was *goodnight*. In response to that I showed him the concern. I went to my room searching for the best thing that I could spend the night with. And then there was the book that I had left half reading. I tried calling Lexie but it wasn't reachable. It's been more than months that there was no news about Peter Pho too. Since the time he had seen me with Alyward, he slightly drifted away from me. Never knew what exactly he had in his mind about me. Though in every case I felt he'd try to flirt other than doing nothing. I had never seen him lasting for more than a month with any girl that he be. While I continued reading the book, it finally led to sleep. There were no messages nor any other stuff of call that came that night. However, things have changed now in everyone's life except that I was still the same. Tyler's image before me was way different than that I had the perception about him. It changed my attitude toward him. Fortunately, I've not revealed the witnessing part to him the last time he visited. I needed to reconsider myself in being what I was. So, for the next predetermined thought, I had planned that each end of the week, I needed to go to the beach not because I was a mermaid, but I needed to create an army to protect our kind. That could only be possible if *Jimmy* would help me out to show me the path.

Till yet I've concealed my reality to the world but now it was rising time that I show up to the destroyers. Often, the thought about the story of the lake haunted me. Though it was a long back history but, what concerned me more was about mom. And the reason, that she became a part of that combat which was why she's not with us today. Preparing herself to armor against those enemies of sea to reclaim back what it belonged to them. I was new into that world. Maybe that was one reason, she never told me anything about it. She wanted to keep me safe and protected with dad. I don't lament the case but I needed to do something which could benefit to her as well as to our kind. She wouldn't expect me to do such but she had to accept the truth.

When the next morning arrived, I had preplanned to visit the beach. The day wasn't bright enough to light the whole way. Dad was still at home. I was early to leave, even the dawn had to break. I never knew, when I had the strong attachment toward that beach. But that's one place where I could get all the answers that I've been looking for. Before I left home, I wrote a message which I had displayed on the dining table "*Dad need not worry about me, I left for the beach, perhaps I may not return today*". I knew, he wouldn't appreciate the fact that I had left him without notice. But right now, things in my life began to change and he had to agree in course of my journey, knowing the fact that I was a mermaid. He needed to leave me alone to be a free girl of sea, which he exactly knew. He hadn't come in search of me. Of course, he knew every place around the town. When I arrived at the beach the morning dawn was actually on the verge to glow its pretty face. I expected *Jimmy* on the surface not much deep enough. I got off the car and immediately I marched toward the shore pushing myself into the water. As I swam through the layers of freezing liquid, I was finally into my own image. I was the little mermaid wondering through the water entering the deeper section of the ocean. Deep under, I called for *Jimmy*. He showed up from the other end. That anxiousness face was revealing on me. It appealed for something that I desperately needed. He could realize on what situation I was. I never knew, we had a strong connection, the fact that related us so easily were that we both belong to the same category of fish species. Only the fact, that I was given something extra bless to me as half human else I was wholly into aquatic life. When he found me, he squeaked in search to know on what trouble I could be. We had developed our own understanding language between us. I somehow explained the real story and urged for his help. So different *Jimmy* was, that those dolphins at the show never would match to him. He didn't need training like the ones to put up dolphin shows at the amusement parks or water parks. I've heard from legend story that dolphins are the one who guide people in the sea when they are lost. Indeed, they are, the legends were true. The most beautiful creature that one could admire were they like. *Jimmy* guided me to their mob, the place where they had their others members. It's like their homes of hundreds of dolphins staying together. It was their territory. Something awesome experienced as I swam through their territory. He headed toward their main leader, who leads them. The reason was that he needed to persuade their leader. Their leader seemed stronger enough to handle their kinds, much larger in size and fit enough to control the territory.

"Is he your leader" I asked, as we swam closer.

Many of the other dolphins were watching me very close. It sounded ridiculous how could a mermaid and dolphins could unite together to form an alliance. Of course, our kinds, are far more superior then them. There could be made no comparison amongst us. Yet then, there was something that connected us. When *Jimmy* rightly front of their leader, he bowed his head before him. They had their own customs to be followed. I've never seen or heard that even the species of other world would follow certain customs amongst them. This actually had showed how cultured our earth had been. Being living on earth surface, we rarely had the knowledge to understand the inner world, which are very different from the rest. Each one of them had their own traditions. And we being as human seldom care to know the hidden beauty of our nature. When *Jimmy* has spoken about me to their leader, he intended me to meet him in personal. I wasn't that comfortable enough without the presence of *Jimmy*. So, I claimed his presence too. He took us to somewhere bit away from the rest. His appearance seldom said he'd be ready to help me out in any away. But, I had kept my hope to grant what I wanted.

"I understand what *Jimmy* had told about you but, I don't know how far we'll be able to do so since we're far more inferior then you all" the dolphin leader said.

"It doesn't matter sire" I addressed him.

Jimmy looked at him and then looked at me. I wasn't expecting much from them it was just like trial to me. If it ever happens to be true then I shall have my vengeance over those cruel pirates.

"Any way we can yet try our best to show you the way toward Virgin Island but beyond that we won't be able to take risk. I hope you understand" he said again.

I shook my head, as my tail made a swift flow of movement within the water. He promised, he would give his army of dolphins when in time of need. With those words of negotiation, we left back to the water surface. *Jimmy* accompanied till the surface. When I resurfaced my head out of the water it was almost the end of day. I needed to go back home. I bade goodbye to *Jimmy*, not sure for how long but it was until I had promised him I'd return with some agenda next time. The sun was sliding toward the end of the day as I took the chance to take its last glimpse. There was a text message from Alyward, that wrote saying to stay alert in the beach. I replied him within no seconds of time. I prepared to leave back home. I knew the fact that dad would stuck up with the write up that I had left for home. Instead, he'd be happy to see back home again rather than those fake words that I had left for him. The thing was that I just wanted to ensure the probability case of my return, for that morning I was originally determined to obey my own inner will of instinct.

Dad was outside with Tyler seated at the front porch with the fire lighted in the mid-section. I looked out of the window as I slowed down the truck at the gate. I saw Tyler walking up toward the gate as he helped to open up the way for me. I wasn't expecting him at that hour of time. I parked the car inside the garage and kept it secured from the rain. Tyler still managed to keep his gaze at me. I shuffled toward them. The fire was burning some kind of raw meat and the smell alluded into the air, it caught my nose in an instant.

"Hey!!!.." Tyler stood from his posture and hugged me without any hesitant.

He kept an empty place for me.

"Hey dad!!!" I said.

He looked at me once and then fiddled with the firewood. He wasn't that pretty to look at. Maybe he wasn't happy with my out casted behavior in the morning.

"What was that in the morning?" dad said.

Tyler looked confused for he wasn't aware what we were talking about.

"I just wanted to assure you not to get worry about me" I replied being modest.

He gestured through his eyes as he looked onto the fire that burnt the meat. Tyler turned the rod that tilted the part of flesh that was burnt. The other side still looked raw.

"What kind of flesh is this?" I mumbled to know.

"It's a reindeer" Tyler said.

"How did you get it?"

"Dad went for hunt the other day, they shared among their friends, and this happens to be a part of that".

There was nothing to talk about neither I could share certain things before dad. I realized that Tyler had changed a bit in every manner of his outlook. Though it wasn't that catchable under the influence of fire light but somehow it came into my notice.

"Well, I'm going get the bottle of wine" dad said.

Dad went inside the room, to get the bottle of wine. The meat was almost over with the burning process. As it got roasted the smell seemed much more acceptable enough to taste.

"Are you okay?" Tyler pretended to ask.

"Yeh!! I'm good" that was casual.

He returned with the bottle of wine in his hand. The one I actually like to taste a bit. As dad was pouring into our glass, the sound of the car arrived very close to our ears while Tyler was busy preparing the flesh of meat. He cut few slices and placed it on the plate. I turned to look at the gate. The car stopped before it. There was nothing to relate about the scenario with the others. Dad after pouring for himself instead, he took a sip of his wine with the piece of meat that he tasted. From the gate entered Burney Gaige, I wasn't expecting that Tyler's dad would be around here. He waved at us. Tyler stood immediately from his posture and walked on to escort his father.

"Hey dad!!!. I wasn't expecting you".

Burney put his hand on his son's shoulder as he walked closer to us. Dad stood to welcome him for the grand dinner of roasted meat and wine. I somehow showed my concern to him with the slightest act of embracing Burney. It over looked like a family picnic around that night hour. Even if I wanted to move upstairs into my room, I couldn't do that. I had to keep joining them till the end. And there was Tyler who actually gave me the company. I never actually protrude into my dad's business. Every time he's with his friends or colleagues I try to avoid the situation. But in presence of Tyler it gave me certain comfort to stay among them. As the minutes moved on, I couldn't bear to stay more.

"Please excuse me" I said, and roomed myself to disjoint the group.

Dad looked on me as I walked toward my room. I could read Tyler's face, he actually wanted to join me upstairs. Before I stepped further away from him, he actually notion.

"Do you mind if I join you?" he said.

That state of mind I had no stable idea what I wanted to do. Some privacy or a companion I failed to decide. But, thinking about being alone upstairs that would probably give me the bore feeling without anyone to converse with.

"You can" I said.

He came up with me. Not much argumentative with the situation, he least bothered to concern the reason. As Tyler stepped forward into my room, his first sight fell on the walls where actually I had pasted lot of photographs. It was all kind of mixed pictures including mine and lots of celebrity images.

"I love that woman" he said pointing toward an image.

I turned to look on what he made the comment. That was the picture of Angelina Jolie that he liked upon. He wasn't the same person that I knew. His behavior since before had slightly changed. That favorable attitude toward other wasn't readable. For a little while, I was drowned with the thought that if I began to reveal his hidden truth, he could no less than harm me here within a minute. That shape of *Demi God* instinct showed on him. Though for many it wouldn't be noticeable to recognize him as the *Demi God*. He turned to look at me. It shook my spine, it made me look like he was on aggressive counter. It shivered me with little danger. But that wasn't his intent. His look gave that vague impression on others. His deep green eye even looked for intensive that adhesively attracted people into his eyes. It wasn't like before. He gently sat on my bed. But, I was still standing on the floor. Though he never concerned or realized about what I was fiddling inside my mind.

"Are you okay?" he said lastly.

"Yeah!!!" I said. This time quite bold enough with my voice.

I joined by his side. Outside the hiss of air juggled. Through the window, dad's voice arrived inside front the porch. They were still there at the fire place. We began to talk, Tyler turned friendly enough to make the night co-operative. It never related about what we were indulged with. Instead, that following night we began to talk about movies and travelling. There was no sense of reminder that Alyward was the other side of my life. Though there was many call from him I forged to inculcate not to diverge my intention with the night that I was going through. Our conversation continued until there called a voice for him. It was his dad, who waited for him at the front porch. But before he left, his words imprinted on me with few of his inner claim of his mind that rumbled with confusion that evolved in my life since then.

"I want to say you something" he said, just standing close to the door.

"Yeah!!!".

"I think, I'm in love with you" he disclosed without any hesitant.

All my side couldn't intake the words of his truth. I forbade what I heard from him but that was what that reached my ear. He looked at me and then left for home. I shut the door and leaned my back with the thought that tremble me. It's not that I disliked Tyler but where I could land if love was to choose between two men. I'm in dilemma. I fell in love with Alyward, I feel very protective with him. The fact stood before me that Tyler wasn't a bad guy either. He's always been there for me in all my necessaries. Moreover, he had been a good friend since the time we arrived here. I placed a wall between my thoughts and my heart not to pressurize much about the beats of love that chose me in between two men. Without putting much effort to think about I went to bed. I never gave up the thought for how many days have passed by. The vacation was on its way to end. I needed to prepare myself all over again mentally to face the school life.

All through the week, I waited for Jessy and Lexie for their return. There was once the last meeting, I had encountered with Alyward before the start of the new session. Nothing revealed much about my inner self, knowing that I had been placed into dungeon of deciding situation between two guys which I couldn't firm to make it right. Neither, I could ignore Tyler nor the one I had actually fallen for. When I met Alyward before the summer holidays ended, he came up with the new kind of intensified way to spend the rest of the six months of session. He intended to pick me up every morning. I couldn't disagree to that. Somehow, I needed to be away from Tyler. It was necessary for right now. Encountering them both again could probably lead into some nuisance disaster in relation which I never wanted to happen at any cause. Since the time Tyler actually said to me of being in love, I had asked him not to take the route toward my way for moment of time. He wasn't happy to hear that yet he confronted himself with the strong hold of trust toward me. I couldn't hate him, neither he was the bad guy nor any devil in him. Just the form of *Demi God* he possessed. So, at least week we never saw each other. Dad frequently asked about him. In all his replies, there was nothing that gave him the clue about him. Just like one night during dinner, dad again questioned me about Tyler. It was just the night before my school was about to reopen.

"Did something happen between you and Tyler?"

"Nothing dad, we're fine" I masked the real thing.

"It doesn't" he meant.

I handled the tray of spaghetti and served for myself. Dad wasn't satisfied with my reply. He had that unkind glance at me before he poured wine in his glass. He offered me for little but with no concern words. I denied. He understood the agony of my inner peace.

"Maybe I can help you out?" he said again, demanding much more this time.

"I can manage myself dad" I said peeling my face with frustration.

He didn't move ahead more with other questions, instead he remained silent and began to eat his dinner. Tyler never showed after that night that actually mattered him the most. Moreover, he was actually helping dad in renovating the garage for the last few weeks. The work halted because of his absence, and dad wasn't able to continue without him. The intentions in me were never meant to hurt anyone but the circumstances brought to such situation that in every word I uttered it always looked like that, piercing the other.

Chapter Eight

Dad was actually trying to fix the wood wall in the garage. I watched him through the window, as the sun was rising ahead from the east. The frost dried up so easily that the heat began to smear in the nature. He didn't go for his duty that morning. Instead, he wanted to fix the garage completely by end of the day. Alyward would be here within few minutes of school time. It's the first day after long weeks of break that we shall be rejoining back to the place. I wanted to help out dad by seeing Tyler's absence. But the hindrance stopped me from doing so, yet again when I watched him working hard with those woods, I couldn't bear the kind of thing he was doing. It hurt me seeing him that way. It panicked me inside wanting to help him out. I didn't follow my inner assembling urge, instead I dialed for Tyler. From the other end the response applauded.

"Hey!!!.." he sounded extreme sober.

"Hey!!!!..uggg!!! dad needs your help" I said without briefing much.

"Sure...I'm coming there" he said.

"Yeah!!!" I hung up the phone.

The time ticked on as the minutes passed on. I needed to hurry up before Tyler sees me with Alyward. I made sure, he was here as fast as possible. I avoided taking up the breakfast instead the plan heap to grab it for the school. I ensured that dad gets his work done at least with the help of Tyler. I stepped out, dad looked at me. My bag was still in my hand not literally willing to hang it on my shoulder.

"Had your breakfast?"

"I packed it for lunch" I added.

"Your truck is ready" dad pointed at it.

"I'll be having Alyward to pick me by" I said.

"Alright" he said and continued to work on.

"Bye" I said.

He just glanced at me. Alyward was right there at the front gate. He saw me walking toward him as dad took notice of him. I skipped out of the porch and gently joined him. He turned the car to head on to school. Just then as he released the brake and forwarded with the speed, Tyler happened to cross by us. He didn't go noticing us. That slightly gave me the relief for moment. I sighed hissing out breathe. Just a narrow escape else the scene would bring something into it with the clash of omen between them.

"What's wrong" he concerned.

"Nothing" that was very effusively maintained.

Back at home, Tyler stopped his car. As he walked in through the gate, he saw dad working with the woods. He was trying to merge two together to form a side wall around the garage corner. That wasn't expecting, dad thought. On reaching close to him, Tyler muttered.

"I could help you out".

"So, she called you here" dad said.

"Yeah!!!"

"She's gone to school".

He shook his head with lamented expressible thought, in missing to meet me up the morning. Instead, he began to help out dad in completing his work. They were fine by the noon of their day.

Alyward parked his car just next to Nash Billy's car. So, for sure it was clear, we would have to attend his math class. That was reasonable enough at least for the beginning of the new session. So, Alyward wouldn't go missing at least from my sight for that day. As we proceeded toward the front porch of the school building, Jessy and Lexie were already there waited for someone. They had seen me but their action didn't response with nothing. Instead, I waved at them, which they retaliated the same. At the main entrance stood Lexie, Jessy was gone for her English class.

"How was your holiday?" I managed to ask her.

By my side, stood Alyward numb and quiet, just decent veiled look at her. She glanced at him in like for few seconds before she actually spoke to me.

"Great…. I had a wonderful time at Wisconsin" she said.

That was obvious I slammed over her replied. It didn't go like the way I wanted. Weeks after we met, I had the thought we would be a good sort friends like the olden days. But now, all are grown up, each one has their own life. Some trying to get engage with their loved ones, some falling in love for the first time. Many of the others are tensed with their exam preparations to get into professional college. But I was still that futile child wondering, looking at each one who passed by. Lexie left us with that short kind of words.

"Hey!! I'll see you soon" that came from my closest soul.

Alyward left for his English class. I had to move my feet that would particularly lead me to biology section. He kissed me on my forehead before he parted for that session of time. I marched ahead determining more that I shall confine myself within, rather than being to over friendly and kind to people who didn't even bother me. It actually meant to Lexie and Jessy who weren't the kind of people to me as they used to be like.

It's the first day of biology session. I occupied the seat that had the access through the window. That one thing that rumbled inside was the rhetorical kind of experience that I was facing. The face of *Demi God* and the love for *Clairvoyant* bounded with the unchallenged circumstances where I stood glued up with no sense of motions in life. In the meanwhile, the teacher began to teach his first lesson. I tried to maintain the attention toward him. But it was only known to me where I was exactly. Somehow, I had attended the class and ended patiently. The very moment it was over I was in search of Alyward. And there, he was seen at the front porch walking toward the other side of the campus. I voiced him out, and soon he turned to find for me. He stopped at that instant. I shuffled to walk with him.

"Where were you heading?"

"I was just looking for you" he answered.

We headed toward the cafeteria for the lunch. Though, it wasn't the time with a playful thought to skip the school for the rest of the day. There I had encountered with Peter who just walked out of the place. He said nothing but waded through the empty way. The stare toward me hinged on, as he passed by the rest. That actually mismatched me with the kind of look he threw. Alyward occupied a corner of the table. Peter was gone, that sensed me with the doubt what could go wrong more than being with an awkward guy like him. It faltered me in every way, I tried to look out but nothing made sense to cope up with the rest of the school. The lunch box was served before me. He found me engaged into something with my thought.

"What's troubling you?" he concerned.

"I don't know. People just changed their attitude toward me. Am in a position that I'm not supposed to be?"

"You don't need to worry about the rest, concern yourself" that came firmly from him.

I didn't put much thought into it since then. I tried to comfort myself, engulfing the ambience to feel relax as I began to take the lunch. Alyward looked at me as I reached the spoon half way to my mouth. I ensured to know. He gestured though his eyes much indulged into me. The day slanted toward noon, while we've just attended the first class of the new beginning of the session. When we got over with the lunch, a man in uniform arrived at the school cafeteria. He was dressed like a cop as it looked to me. Alyward turned to look at him, though his face wasn't revealing straight to us.

"Who could be that?"

"I don't know. Is there something wrong?" I said.

The man stood leaning his hand on the counter, in conversation with him. Something looked wrong and suspiciously, he looked on everybody. He spoke to the cashier and walked out of the place. There was the curious intention that emerged out on me. I'd want to know what the police man had said to him. After he left the place, we walked out of the cafeteria intending to spend the rest of the day with each other. Alyward asked me to join him to company to his home. I agreed to that idea, for we had planned not to attend the rest of the school curriculum. Just then a bell was rung up sounding from every corner of the school premise. The attention came from principal's office. The announcement came up restricting school teenage to visit the beach. It had been banned for at least a week. The reason never mentioned. The restriction was spread to the whole town. So, for few days the beach was banned for all. They said the policeman saw something anchored at the shore. It was a huge ship at the shore that arrived by last night. The first thought it hit me was about Tyler. But the doubt clearance wiped out when they actually mentioned about the ship. It gripped my mind as I stood hearing the announcement. *They had arrived here in search of the rest.* It imprinted on my mind to subordinate myself more protectively. The pirates are here, and for surety they'd begin their hunt. I still remember the story about the banned lake that Tyler once told me. The pirates wouldn't leave that place too.

"Are you okay?" Alyward shook my body.

We headed toward his car. He opened the door for me. I wasn't the fine kind of mere person that stood rumbling with the danger that approached. Somehow it kept troubling me though the fact, I wasn't showing it out to anyone. I felt sluggish and squeezed within myself. Instead of trying to plan in protecting of my kind, I was here with the love of my life. *Will that serve me what I want*? It crackled me often.

Alyward drove his car more swiftly than I expected. We passed through the rows of poplar trees that stood tall and, the shed that fell on the way descript the darkness to arrive within few hours. Whole through the way the silent enveloped on us, more like it was desensitizing moment that went through. He promised me to drop me back at sunset. As usual I had the chance to watch out through his bedroom window the panoramic beauty of the nature. After the rest of the hours, gradually I began to feel the kind of ecstatic energy that began to take birth on me. That he wouldn't deny in helping me out in all through my way. When the sun was crawled toward the end, he dropped me back home. Dad seemed worried about me because he knew I was a frequent visitor to the beach. At dinner, he actually began to talk to me regarding that issue.

"You must be knowing, what's going on in the town?" he said, as he poured the water into his glass.

I gestured shaking my head, indulging to take up the plate. He passed me the plate of potato fry.

"You must be careful" he said again.

He meant me not to go to the beach, but I couldn't give the word if I'd ever do that to follow him honestly. I'm on a mission, that's only known to me. Not for myself but to protect mom and bring her back to us. I said none but just listened him whole through the dinner process.

"Tyler was worried about you" dad said in sudden notion.

I was just about to get up from the chair. On half way he said that. For fraction of seconds, I showed my concern to that.

"I'll talk to him" I said, and moved upstairs.

Dad watched me going upstairs, he took his sip of wine. I called up Tyler that night. He did seem worried but I ensured not to do so. Rather, I asked him the favor if he could be available for me at the time of need. He promised me that, and knowing that he was in love with me, I didn't want him he should feel any guilty about anything nor he should feel betrayed in case we never meant to be. At least that feel for me shouldn't go in waste. We talked for an hour regarding the issue over the beach news. It wasn't him as I realized. The pirates arrived in the town. It smeared me with the real some fear that squeezed me inside. I needed to take immediate step toward my goal. For long hours, I couldn't sleep the night. If ever, the rest of the world comes to know my truth they wouldn't leave me without hunting. The secret nature of my life was still valid, except that dad knew who I was actually. But the rest of world blinded with the kind of life I appear before them. I gave a long thought until I felt tired with my mind. Then I actually fell asleep. The breeze came in through the open window. I had never dreamt about mom ever again. Somehow, the night passed by. Soaked with all those intense emotions of life, rather it made me stronger enough to face all by myself. The only one thing that played on my mind was to bring her back home safely. Looking onto the other side of life, it's dad who had been the most supportive person to me. Although, he never showed that nature of him yet it was understandable through his actions. I've never wanted to lose him like mom, who went away without any concern on me. Everything was misguided before me, and the aim lived alive to me in bringing thing all over again the same. That courage planted upon me to fix things back again, yearned with the darn interest to see those days back all over again as family. There was another thing to rejoice for me, it mattered all about Alyward, mentioning that he would love to be part of our family. The choice stayed open before me until I had to pick the right decision further with my mission to accomplish. The time slithered in with the real cause for me, it arrived with the notion of my life to face who I was actually. Something that I had never done in my life, it shall leave me for going onto long errand of life.

The morning horizon glanced through the open window. When I woke up, I found dad wasn't at home. The rumors of the news spread so rapid in the town about the anchored ship at the beach shore. I stepped downstairs in search of dad. His car wasn't there at the parking site, he was gone. I assumed he was early on duty that morning. With the mismatched thought about school I stood blunt, not firmly deciding if I wanted to go that day. At the beach site, dad along with other officials and cops, sighted the anchored ship. They were on thorough inspection about the anchored object, gathering information they could find out. They found none, instead the ship stood alone. All the presumed thought that calculated could invariably say, it was an alien ship. It wasn't an ordinary ship that looked like. So, they had to return with those small segments of evidence. Alyward called me up regarding my absence. He hasn't come to pick me up that morning. That was what I exactly wanted at least for that morning. Nevertheless, he showed me up at my house while returning back from school. I chose to spend the evening till dad's return. I prepared the dinner with help of him who gave his knowledge about recipes. The night began to fell, it almost more than hours that I was hoping dad to return soon. We waited seated on the ground at the front porch, glaring the night sky that lit with stars above. Alyward too close to me, as the ground turned to be friendly to us. His face almost reached into my eyes as we gather our inner vibes to join our inner emotions. The breeze allured the little environment we had. And that touched us more closely than ever it was. Under the brightly lit night sky, his eyes focused more deeply into mine and that spoke more than he could say. When his lips met mine, it was ever like the first kiss I felt. The joined of our heart lasted for longer time, and the kiss was much more than we ever had gone through.

The sound of the car arrived very close. To be sure it was dad, as I felt it. Alyward looked on me as he inched away from me. Dad's car arrived inside. He parked next to my truck. He saw us, before he got down of the car.

"Hey!! dad, how was your day?" I asked.

"Nothing new. Hey! Alyward" he said. They shook their hands.

We walked with him joining inside. He looked quite tired with the day. Alyward and I helped to get the dinner ready on the table. Dad came out after he was refreshed. He joined on the table.

"I'm sorry, I'm late. You guys must be hungry" dad said.

"That's fine sir" said Alyward, too soft to hear.

I began to serve the dinner for all of us. The bottle of wine stood untouched. Dad poured for himself first than passed to Alyward. He did the same to my glass. I sat by his side.

"You know what's going on in the town. The ship isn't like an ordinary ship" dad spoke holding his fork.

"Who could be them?" Alyward keened to know.

"Still no idea, maybe they could be pirates or someone else".

I heard them all, yet said nothing. Of course, there wouldn't be any doubt if I considered them to be the pirates. They've come here for hunt. The war never ended yet. They prepared to face the group of mermaids yet again. The thought that never caught me was *why they were against our kinds*. Even the past never told about it neither they imprinted any sign of clue regarding that. It all began long years back. Back then I wasn't even in my mother's womb. Dad warned us about the beach. After the dinner, we had spent few times watching a movie. Dad wasn't settled with the kind of mind he brought today at home. Startled by the scene of site he had seen at the beach. He agreed to go to bed early, thus we got the space around to watch a movie. Not much indulging what dad had told earlier about the beach story. Alyward wanted to go back when the movie was over. I escorted him till the gate. He was gone, I found myself back into my room. Dad was silent for that night. The summer was almost passing away and it's been long time I haven't visited Tyler. I slept the night without much intention of doing things right. I had skipped the school which for sure, I wouldn't have anything related to study.

Dad was out for his duty, which he left the half work the earlier day. With few of his men, he again dropped toward the beach.

This time the team could collect few of more information regarding the unknown ship. They returned back with few of the evidences that left by. The ship wasn't empty though, packed with materials, foods and ammunitions. However, it was yet not revealed whose ship it belonged. They must have been in the town by now. Dad and the rest returned back to their station. I left for school that morning, the reason that Alyward had come to pick me up. The news reached to my dad. At school, it was after the vacation we had attended Nash Billy's math class. He talked about the anchored ship. It was the most talked thing that had become in the town. The ship stood steady unmoved by any means. Almost the whole school talked about the story.

During lunch we encountered Lexie, but this time there was more appropriate gesture that came from her side. She wanted to join us. Jessy wasn't present that day. Her intention didn't outcast as she was generous and humble to show up. She sat up with us. At first, she looked on Alyward in friendly gesture, a smile was signaled to him. He in response did the same.

"Hey! *I'M SORRY* about the last week. I didn't really mean to ignore you people" she said. That sounded quite appreciating. She meant it, as she had apologized.

"It's okay…. you don't need to be sorry about it" I grinned, not much.

The lunch boxes were on the table. For a moment there was the quiet silence until she broke her voice to talk about the ship. Alyward, in small movement of his head shook off engaging to take part in the discussion. In the meanwhile, I stopped to verse as for me the lunch was more important at that time. I avoided the morning breakfast before I left for school. There was the craze of hunger inside of me. I sat idle hearing to them as I picked up my spoon in interval of their talk.

"Anna, your dad must be investigating about the mystery ship" she said.

Now that was a new thing to be heard from her. It's a mystery ship now while the truth is not yet revealed. Although, I need not to find, what that ship was meant for. There was nothing mystery about it, the fact that it had the vintage design that looked like a monster at its front part. Dad told about the shape the last night. I nodded my head on her filtered understanding. Alyward looked at me in like a second, that was just a blink of his eye that spoke the secret out from his heart right there. I was over with the lunch, it stood empty.

"Where's Jessy?" I actually felt like asking her.

"Oh! She's not well".

Alyward dropped me back at home after the school. He ignored to wait, for he had the reason of a work. Dad wasn't back at home. It seemed, he was really involving himself regarding that ship investigation. When I called him, he was in the restaurant bar with other colleagues. He asked to call for Tyler if I was scared with the darkness. Of course, I did the same and within an hour Tyler was with me. He was aware about the ship that stood by the shore. Yet then, he never premiered to discuss much about it. Rather we got engaged ourselves in preparing the dinner.

At the restaurant bar, dad in took few glasses of beer. Though I knew, he had the control over himself. A man came up and ordered the bar tender to make a glass for him. The voice grizzled, not acceptable to ear in other words it wasn't that polite to catch what he was saying to the bar tender. He looked very rough and un-smart fashioned. He had a hat worn on his head that had the symbol of a horse head. He smelled fishy and pungent odor even made him ignoring. When dad strolled to look at him carefully, he noticed he carried a dagger hanged on his hip, with the legs covered with high boots. Those were leather, as it looked very hard and strong. Thus, the appearance resembled much like a hunter. For a long time, there was no sort of conversation. When in between the strange man interrupted. He was already intoxicated. He looked at Adam, who was just next to him. The bar tender arrived at his side but this time he ignored.

"You must be the chief of police of this town" he said.

The smell of beer froze into the air as he spoke out. Dad turned to look back at the man.

"I'm Captain Nicholas Cook" he said, pretending much to be in sense.

"You should go home. You're over full"

"Right…. You know I used to be a captain. I lost my men in the fury storm that came through the pacific. It's been almost ten years" he stopped "Nice to meet you"

"Nice to meet you Nicholas" Adam said.

He walked out of the place shortly. Dad watched him limping out of the door. The man gave the rhetoric impression on him. Till the end of the door, dad watched him going out taking his route to home. Then he resumed back to join his mob. It was almost half past eleven, dad wasn't back to home yet. Tyler stayed back to accompany me. When I called dad for once, he was on his way. By 12:00 am he was at home. He smelled bad, and that liquor smell spread into the room.

"Are you okay?" Tyler gave his hand to hold him, as he opened up the door.

Dad pretended to stay firm on the ground though his body shook under the influence of alcoholic effect. He didn't watch at anybody instead, he followed toward his room. After spending few more minutes, Tyler urged to be back home. His dad was alone there. That last few minutes we were at the front porch, even though the breeze did actually touch us. It shivered my spines. I was very sensitive toward coldness. We walked as slow as possible till the main gate to escort him.

"There's something that I always wanted to share to you" he paused, staring at me.

We stopped in the mid-way. He came significantly closer to me. His face unreadable, yet focusing something hard to expel out of his mind. Perhaps, he wasn't prepared to say out. His deep greenish eyes moistened and the effusive tale of expression emerged out. He looked startled. Not sure to be what he wanted to, rather in fury of tormenting haunt of mind he resembled.

"Are you okay?"

"Yeah!!!...hey would you be available this weekend. I want to show you something at the beach, not the ship of course".

"Okay" I ensured.

He kissed me on my forehead before he walked out of the gate. He watched at me, before he galloped at rapid speed through his bike. That night I wasted none of my time since it was too late for me to go to bed.

When the morning rose out, dad was out in the open porch. I joined him a minute later. He looked at me and smiled, that was very affectionate applaud to show his love.

"I'm sorry about the last night" he said.

"Dad, what's wrong with you. For god sake I'm your daughter. You don't need to be" that came out as casual conversation.

We spent the morning hour together, helping him with few of his official documents to settle in the room. It was almost time for me to leave for school. But the intention stood firm without having much thought if I really wanted to go. Alyward would be soon here. Furthermore, that one thing that rumbled on my head was the ship at the shore. Even if I wanted to take its sight, for timing it wasn't possible to do so. For sure, dad's men would be available there. It's been more than a week I haven't seen myself under the water, and *Jimmy* must have been waiting for my return with the promise that I ensured. Their leader would be disappointed if I showed them the unwise act. They wouldn't be ready to help me out in reaching the Virgin Island.

"Does the ship look like a pirate ship?" I managed to ask.

"Well, I can't exactly say how pirate ship look like" dad muttered, as he dropped few piles of files on the table.

"You won't be going there?"

"Yeah!!!!…. I'll be there shortly" he said.

I nodded and sat by his side watching him flip the pages of files. I still remember the sweater that mom had knit for me when I was a kid, that was long time back at Arizona.

"You felling cold?" dad concerned.

I was on with that same sweater. It seemed, he too had the remembrance about that piece of cloth. He looked at me and smiled briefly.

"You planning to skip school huh!!?" he said again.

"Kind of" I said.

He said nothing instead, he walked to get a pen form another table. Within short moment of time, the sound of car was reaching into my ears. Dad pulled the curtain to take a notice of that. He looked for few seconds thoroughly.

"That must be your guy" he said as he came toward my side.

Alyward was here. He walked passed through the porch toward the front door. The calling bell rang for once and I opted to open for him. He looked confuse, for I wasn't in the attire that I was supposed to be.

"You aren't ready?" he said.

He came in and saw dad working.

"She decided to skip the school for today" dad spoke.

"Really, what's wrong" he said looking toward me.

"Nothing, it's just I want to spent the time with dad for today" I said.

Dad was supposed to leave. He got a call few minutes earlier, regarding the man he met last night at the bar restaurant. Immediately, he got himself ready in the uniform and left. Back at home, Alyward stayed back along with me.

When dad arrived at the beach he saw the old man, lying fainted on the dunes. The officials stood by his side. Dad examined carefully for seconds, sensing his pulses. He was alive.

"It's the same man I met the last night" he said.

Nicholas Cook, the captain was taken into custody for treatment. He was sent to the nearest hospital in the town. The thought of suspicious collision impelled on dad's mind. He began to disbelief the man. However, Nicholas Cook was kept under watch. By evening, dad visited the hospital where he was admitted. He wanted to inquire every detail about him. As the identity of Captain, it certainly gave the idea to relate if the ship belonged to him. There couldn't be seen any people, except that he identified himself as the captain, but *where his crew gone if he meant to be the captain*. Dad collected few of doubts from him. The information that came from Nicholas Cook sounded truth although in reality he was falsifying all of his stories. However, the record was kept about him. He denied that he had few men but certainly trying hard to prove to be all alone. His intentions never seemed clear. Something felt fishy beneath his reliability. Even he seemed to be telling the truth it wasn't that sounding enough to accept with honesty. Dad was done with him before he left for home.

Alyward was still there with me. He too had skipped the school just to stay back with me. But right before dad's arrival, he had left on certain occasion where he had another pal waiting for him at home. He bade me bye for the night. As he accelerated his car, from the other end dad arrived. Dad saw him, blew the horn. There was nothing interaction between them, none waited for each other to exchange words.

"Why did he leave?" dad asked.

"Oh! he had a friend waiting".

I prepared the dinner. Thanks to Alyward for being there, who helped me out in the kitchen. I had the dinner table prepared as dad refreshed himself and sat for dinner. He talked about the captain. For some reason, I was engrossed to listen him with interest. It sounded like a story to me, may be that was one reason. When we were over with the dinner, I got the call from Tyler. I remembered he had asked me to spend the weekend with him. We talked for minutes, certainly he sounded quite exciting about the coming weekend day. That was after long time of my days, that I had surfed internet. But what concerned me more, that made me feel was the insensitivity toward my life. I couldn't be under water for at least more than week. It troubled my dump mind, perhaps, I wasn't aware to find the lasting time for how long I could stay in human form. It began to heckle my thoughts and behavior that diverged from normal. I lost the resilient ability instead I began to feel dull and unhappy with pale outlook that sharply appeared on my face. I didn't recognize that but accidently I happen to glance at the mirror that night. There I discovered the real cause of being a non-human as mermaid. Staying as human was far more troubling. In time interval I had to convert myself into the other form as mermaid else things would turn disastrous. I realized a lot later the condition that I was facing. It needed to be checked, I reclaim to myself. The next morning would be my new chapter where I decided the pre-night to visit the beach. No matter, whatever the circumstances would come by, I needed to see myself under water. Moreover, I wouldn't want the rest to make them wait longer with my decision to finalize. I made sure that Alyward shouldn't be coming for me the next morning. I informed him through text.

Before the dawn was out, I drove to the beach. Dad was asleep then. When I reached the spot, they were right about the ship. It's not an ordinary ship that anchored. I took a round and looked carefully. It had the marvelous design that was ever created. Before getting too late, I undressed myself and dived into the water. Reaching the deeper side, I was finally transformed into mermaid, the actual me. It made me feel good. Everything began to recreate and regenerate within my body. I made the noise in search of *Jimmy.* Within short notice, he arrived flapping his fins. Seeing me, he was very delighted and joined with me. We swam toward deep following the path toward their territory. It was some kind of fest they were celebrating. In some kind of gesture through his fins, he welcomed me for being their part of their celebration. When we were in the occasion, their leader swam toward us and gave me the splendid welcome. I've never seen such custom of any sea creatures, it's the first time. Even the families of dolphins do have their own tradition that they fulfill. How cruel humans are? they even don't have the idea how pretty their world is, which in turn we sought to disturb their ecosystem. We need them. We can't hunt them for flesh to fulfill human needs. They are the beauty of this world. Dolphins seemed to be the most faithful sea creatures above all. And for now, it's me who knew much more than any ever human could know about them. Surrounded with their kinds, how happy they look at each other, and the only one of my kind amongst them. My whole day was spent amongst them. That following noon dad was at the shore. I had the vision about it when I surfaced out on the water. However, their sight wasn't able to recognize for I was distant away from the spot where the ship was anchored.

Nicholas Cook was under observation since the last few days. The ship stood isolated from the rest of the crew members. It's still the hidden property that it reached. Yet, the truth was being denied by the Captain. The conspiracy was planned not to reveal the reality. The town's security was kept alert, as the rumor was spread about sighting few of unwanted people for the first time in few places. We couldn't abandon the place no matter what the consequences would arrive in the future. And as the day's twilight was sighted, I got out of the water. By then the beach was empty. There was no sort of security guarding the place. I took the last opportunity to carefully examine the ship before I left for home. With no suspicious doubt on my mind, it's the ship that belonged to the captain that dad was talking about. But persuading dad would be tough until he gets the pure evidence regarding the case. He wasn't aware that they were here in search for the rest of the mermaid family. The war still prevailed. And the stories told by mom came out to be true. *Legends are real*, they weren't something created by human, they existed.

Chapter Nine

Tyler joined for dinner with his dad. He didn't show me up that following day. Burney served the water glass for himself, as he watched him.

"Dad, I want to know something?"

"Yeah!!!..go on"

"Am I different?" he looked at Burney quite intuitively.

"No…you're just like me" he added without further explanation.

"I don't think dad; you're hiding something from me" he seemed insisting.

Burney handled his spoon to take the bite of green salad. Tyler wasn't seemed convincing, he needed the right answers to know about their family background.

Burney sighed and breathed out for seconds looking toward his son. He nodded, agreeing he would say him what they belonged from. Tyler keened to know for he figured out something unusual which isn't seemed normal to him. He personally had that feel of guiltiness within.

"Yes!!! you're different, Son" that finally came from Burney.

Tyler startled and gazed in along the direction without any clue of sense. His dad maintained the cause for his regardless truth which often troubled Tyler.

"Who am I then?"

He stopped for a minute and looked out through the window at the darkness night. Tyler unconvinced with the situation yet, laid stable with the idea getting to know more about his background.

"We're half-blood son, not the purest form of human being" Burney said.

The answer hinged on, as he made the occasional interpretation without involving much into the dinner, Tyler's face wonderstruck with the reality that flashed out. He handled the spoon gently in order to intake his food.

"It doesn't make sense at all" he said.

Somehow, Burney was imposing the truth to convince upon him. The matter couldn't have concealed over the years that passed by. Someday, it was to be told. Maybe the right time was needed to let know the version of life that they were living with. It's isn't the open show game, that it could be known by everyone. None in the town knew about them, even though they had lived for years. When the dinner was over, both father and son sat outside in the backyard. There was fire lighted in the yard, as they sat encircling to it. The wind blew endlessly over the north. It touched the bare skin giving the sensation of chillness that had in the moisture.

"It's a long story son. We're the descendants of *Half Bloods*. I know, I kept the truth hidden for so long years. I needed the right time to deliver it to you".

Tyler looked at his father's face. The reflection of the fire fell on his face, as he felt the need to console himself with the little things of his life.

"It's strange" Tyler muttered.

"You want to know the history" Burney said.

Tyler shook his head pushing the fire wood little forward.

"Its five hundred years back then, the stories were told from generations to generations. We never knew whose descendant we belonged from. Until one day, an old man came to earth to reveal the truth. He was sent by *God*. But had the less knowledge, who could be the supreme power of him, that he was following his commands. In much like a son of god, he was considered. Many people didn't believe his tales then the only way to prove the right was to show them that he was unlike them so they were. God created the humans in many different forms, and in that we were one of kind" he stopped.

Tyler stayed silent, those words did little right to his mind, yet the thorough phase to unrealistic world never convinced him.

"Your grandfather was one of such kind. Long before my birth, there was a war between the humans and the gods. Those who believed the Old man story survived and those who didn't were cursed, but the curse was so intense it never went away. My father was against that Old man" Burney looked at Tyler.

The silent night gave the reverie to hear such legendary stories. The breeze hissed through its way. The fire made different patterns as it touched by the cold winds. Tyler showed the intention to hear further.

"Why was grand father against that Old man?"

"He never believed in *God*, he always told they never existed. If they would exist the world wouldn't have been so cruel, that's what he believed".

"What did the *God* do to him?" it came instantly from him.

"The *Gods* were angry on him. And one day to take revenge upon him god made a plan to destroy him".

"Destroy him" it shook him.

Burney stopped for a minute gazing at the night sky. There were no stars above, only the fire kept them in focus with the light that burnt out. It's almost the beginning of deep night while they were still instilled with the legendary phenomenal stories that expelled out.

"A god landed in the form of human. No one knew who was he?".

"Then what happened" Tyler utterly in depth to hear the rest.

"He took the form of your grandfather. One day, he came up to the house. Your grandfather was away out for an errand on his business. When your grandmother saw him returning so early, he made a new excuse regarding the cancellation of his errand. She never knew the reality behind that man. In disguise he was, that she mistaken him to be your grandfather".

"What happened to grandfather then?"

Burney stopped again and smiled looking toward him. Tyler looked very enthusiastic to proceed further with the rest of the story to hear about.

"They made love to each other. It was confirmed within weeks that she got pregnant by him. But your grandfather wasn't at home. Without any notice further, the man left the home. It wasn't quite understandable to her. Few days later, your real grandfather returned back. She took it by surprise. She couldn't believe what went within those few days. Who was that man with whom she had spent few moments of her life? She kept it concealed until one day it was disclosed somehow with rumor that came by. Knowing that, he left her within few days, it was the saddest part of her life. But she chose to stay strong and led her life ahead. People in the society neglected her, ignored her, and disrespected her in many ways. She couldn't endure. Then one day she had decided to flee to another village some miles away. There she gave birth to a baby boy. That was me".

"But dad, who was that old man, your father?"

"Later it was known, he actually came to punish your grandfather. Since then he never married any other woman nor got any one in his life. That's because he never believed in god and hated them disgracefully. That old man came to be known as the God of Sea".

"God of Sea...you mean Poseidon" Tyler found it intriguing.

He shook his head, as Tyler watched him carefully.

"Your grandmother died after I was born. And your mother too left her breath instantly after your birth. I inherited the power of *Poseidon* and so do you, and that's why you've unnatural power within you. I'm old now. I don't have the strength to generate the power within myself. But believe me, don't use your power for any unfair means or to harm lives".

That was the last line Burney had told him about the past. That was truly unbelievable to hear the reality that he brought to light before his son.

"It's time we should go to sleep" he said and left the place.

Tyler stayed behind for a while watching at the fire burnt. He gazed at the dark sky. After spending few more minutes all by himself, he finally ended his day.

Before the rise of the new day, I received the unexpected attendance from Tyler. He was with dad at the backyard garden. I heard them talking which intrigued me to take part with them. I got down myself to join in their reverie discussion. I realized, it's the end of week therefore his presence was felt. I actually had forgotten the word I had given to him. *He called me up to join him in visiting the beach.* I stood watching them behind, unaware about my presence. When dad happened to turn back, he muttered out my name. Seeing me, Tyler immediately caught his feet on the ground and headed toward me. He hugged me close and tightly. I felt it hard for his hands wholly covered me. Dad watched at us saying none.

"It's good to see you" I said.

"When shall we move out?"

"Wait…wait where are you planning to go?" dad put a question.

"The beach" Tyler said indefinitely.

"Look Son, it's not safe there for now. Why don't you hang in some other place?"

Tyler wasn't seemed convincing to that idea. Yet, he tried to persuade dad somehow giving the promise to protect me in case any misdeed happens to occur at the site. Dad painfully agreed to that but, he wasn't appreciative with the kind of gesture Tyler showed. However, he warned us to stay away from the ship. We left for the beach. That was after prolonged time I had his bike ride. When we reached the spot, the first thing that was visible was the site of the anchored ship. It outrageously engrossed our sight to hold onto that before we proceeded toward the main site.

"It's just amazing ship" Tyler muttered rolling his hand through its surface.

I watched him and followed as we reached the end part of the ship. He glanced at me as the morning broke brightly from the east. The sea was silent and felt the alluring vibes that influenced the area. We walked on through the wet sand dunes, Tyler just very close to me. The image of his focused on his face that resembled him to be the descendant of God's family. He looked at me and breathed in deeply.

"There's something you don't know about me" he began.

"What are you saying?"

"You may not believe me but it's the truth" he stopped going further.

I stood silent emerging the assurance that he wanted from me. I mentioned the suggestion in his way.

"I'm not a pure human blood" he said.

"Then who are you?"

"A *Half Blood*" he said.

That wondered me that flooded my face. However, I knew the truth since early time, as it was revealed to me long back. For me, it wasn't something new to hear it from the person itself.

"You've no idea the way I can control"

"Control what?" I urged.

He held my hand and stretched to walk on the next side where the waves seemed much rougher and coarse.

"Watch me" he signaled.

He began with the movement of his hands, gradually the waves were under his control, even the winds followed his commands. That was truly spectacular to watch in person. I've seen him from distance but on that day, it seemed unbelievable. The water surface was raised to high level almost at the height of a tower. It seemed, he was playing with water and the waves. Everything began to follow his commands. He could bring storm, disasters and silent the World of Ocean.

"Do you want to surf?" he muttered.

It smeared me with fear at first, for it seemed risk to walk on the surface of water so deep. Tyler began to spill his charm on the water surface. Gradually, he was able to control the whole of sea water. I watched him raising a wave which he lifted higher as much as he could. Later, I was amazed to observed his peculiar ability to freeze the wave. It resembled like the sheets of ice berg being floated in the air. It had the length stretching across the end point of the oceanic horizon. He was up at the top of the solid wave.

"Come on walkup" he said.

"It's too steep, I won't be able to climb the slippery solid wave" I said.

He stepped few inches reaching my hand. He pulled me up. Indeed, it was hard to walk on a solid ice berg structure. It wasn't even an ice berg but a wave which he solidified that stretched endlessly. Beneath us the sea water spread still that had crystal clear reflection.

"It's amazing" I muttered, as I followed him.

Far across the horizon shone out, that it looked the end of the world. Even the color of the ambient changed as the orange faded light prevailed out from the twilight bearing the end of the day. Indeed, his amazing power had something different in him. The real pure breeze of vast ocean was really charming to feel. It's never pure like this one that we experienced along the coast. But in the mid ocean over a solid wave, that looked like a bridge, it was enthralling. Besides, that one reason that kept me more intrigue was I could depict the way to move out of the place in search of Virgin Island. I mapped few paths watching over the vast ocean area. Tyler looked at me, his eyes deepened to watch at. Even that nervous me was the slipping nature of the solid wave, that formed the arc over the vast ocean. He caught my hand. I stood still, no movement, maybe I felt protective. His effusive expression slightly melted me inside.

"This is who I'm. A *demi god*" he said.

I looked at him, more in concern fashioned. That very movement, I discovered *Jimmy* on the water surface. That wasn't a danger to them. Somehow, I needed to ensure them. He saw me right at the top of the solid wave. It's magical.

Having the glance on me, he swam deep inside. Tyler added to my view. Seeing the dolphin, he turned his face toward me again.

"It's a beautiful creature" he said, about the dolphin.

"Tyler, you're gifted. You've an amazing gift with you".

He looked at me, desiring to feel the company of each other. When his lips met mine, I finally realized we kissed both each other. He kissed me for the first time. The state of my mind disabled to decide about our intimate relation. For it was never the same with him, as it's the first time, I knew Tyler in more appropriate sense. But back there Alyward would be watching us. He wouldn't forgive me if I did the wrong. He wouldn't trust me if I lied him about my other form of being a mermaid.

"I think we should go" I said.

I eased myself out of Tyler's hand. We followed through the way back down reaching the shore line. As we landed our feet on the sand, the wave melted immediately and all of a sudden it was no more. Before us that same vast ocean with an empty beach that laid silent. The day was over with the faintly light that fell from the stars.

Back in the hospital, a news went viral. Captain Nicholas Cook had managed to escape from the place even after heavy guard. The cops' unit began to search for him. It was already late by the time he vanished out. The investigation unit was set up immediately to look for the man. There was lot to know about him which was left unanswered. The ship from the shore was gone, as the rest of the unit reached the beach. Fortunately, no one took us to notice for we were on to the other half of the beach favorably away from the common place where the ship was anchored.

The rumor about Nicholas Cook reached to dad. We were still at the beach shore. The alluring scenario kept us engaged, but what was more intriguing was Tyler. I had surf through the sheets of ice that he created. It's obvious the experience to see him in real was far more different then I had thought. The day was on its' way to set toward west. It almost ended. Besides, that one thing that really mattered me was that he confessed himself so bravely, which wasn't expected. I had to agree with him in whatever he said till that day about his life. Hearing about the story from him, my perception really had changed toward him. Maybe I started to like more than ever before, I wasn't sure, was it. It blanked my mind to decide the right way. The twilight almost sunk below, yet it felt so good to be at that hour of time where the emptiness raveled on us preceding the next moment to rejoice for ourselves. We ought to return back home. The last sight of the beach was viewed. It impacted my memory like the capture of camera lens. Lately, I sat behind giving the company to Tyler on his bike.

Dad was gone when he heard the news about the Captain. That was unbelievable to hear even though under strong guards, he managed to flee out. The authority instantly called dad as the incident took place. Thereby, he didn't wait for us instead he galloped to the station in quest to investigate the rest of the case. When we were at the front gate, dad was already gone. There was slightest mix of mist in the atmosphere. The breeze cooled the temperature, while the bike stopped right at the front gate. From the other end the unexpected arrival of Alyward amazed me. It was undecided coincidence. He stopped the car and fluently stepped out following toward us. He looked very sensitive with the situation that flashed before him. Tyler eased himself upon his approach toward us. What could be more undying situation than their both meeting in such tormenting phenomena.

"Hey!!!!" it came solely from Alyward.

Tyler watched him as he eased out from his bike. There was the hindrance, both felt the ignorance over each other, ignoring to talk or to abide by each other. Tyler stood little away from us. His cornered eyes sighted us with deep feeling of envy.

"Anna…..I should go now" Tyler muttered.

 I eased out from Alyward marching toward him.

"When am I going to see you again?" I asked.

"Anytime you wish" he said, and readied with the bike.

On the other hand, Alyward, extensively possessive about me. He glared with the strange kind of expression on him. It demanded to be observed. Perhaps, they weren't the kind of human to unite among themselves. He was gone racing hard through the densely mist road. I resumed back to get back. Dad wasn't at home. His car wasn't seen even at the garage. Except that my truck was kept under the plastic cover. He walked on with me, the breeze from the silent north was pouring down few drops of moistened liquid. It signified the call of rain that following night. Within moment of time the dark sky showered its heavy rain. The cold squeezed me hard, complicating the night duration. But the only company that kept me warm was the presence of Alyward. That night we had prepared soup for dinner, in order to compensate the chilling cold that influenced the nature's night. We waited for dad. He was on urgent meeting with his colleague regarding the escape of Nicholas Cook.

The night almost felt deep, yet the intentions to stay awake instilled us. By the time, it was midnight the sound of his car could be heard. I glanced to look out of my window. The heavy rains didn't yet stop. In fact, it turned wilder with rough winds. It was pathetic to watch dad getting wet. I immediately ran with an umbrella for him. Behind me followed Alyward. Dad was almost wholly wet by the time I reached to him.

"You're still awake?" Adam said.

"I prepared the dinner for you" I said.

He saw Alyward. He handed him a towel to dry himself. Dad took the table to dine. We joined with him although we had already consumed our part. But just to company his loneliness.

"How was your day?" I asked him.

Dad drank a glass of water. He looked extremely exhausted. Alyward sat just next to him.

"It wasn't the best of day" he said.

"What about the captain?" Alyward quite keened.

"He's gone"

"And the ship" I added.

"He took it with him. It's vanished from the beach shore".

Dad looked at me in like seconds and handled his fork. He began to take his dinner after all those questioning session were done. We realized we shouldn't be discussion more about it. He almost lost his interest in answering to all those.

"Why so silent?" he muttered.

"Was the Captain dangerous to the town?" Alyward spoke.

"Not sure enough but indeed he had some intentions, which weren't able to unlock from him".

The rain hadn't stopped yet. After the dinner was over, dad went to his room. Alyward intended to leave back home. But dad ensured me he'd stay back because of the heavy rain falling outside. I was clear by now the captain and his crew moved forward toward Virgin Island. Here I was helplessly, stood under the drops of rain. Alyward prepared to leave even after my persuasion. He gave me his last kiss, as I watched him walk through the rain drops toward the car. He moved out of the place with the last sight of him. Dad was asleep by the time I had moved upstairs. It wasn't the best of days for all of us. Firstly, both Tyler and Alyward had encountered each other. Of course, that wasn't a pretty situation and then the fled of Nicholas Cook. Somehow, the night was too late for me to sleep back. I pondered more from the last day, which gave me the relaxation to let me fall asleep by the time it was almost about to break the dawn. There was no such ardent plan on the next morning, so I could peacefully go back to sleep. I canceled the plan to go to school.

Nicholas Cook and his crew were following the path toward the Virgin Island. It is then, they had shown the numbers of people they had. More than hundred people constitute their group. Each and everyone looked the same as all did the same job of pirates. Within those days in town, their people were scattered all around rarely revealed themselves. All they wanted was to find the best of ways to gather information about the mermaids. Somehow, they got the clue, and moved ahead toward the island. It scared me, mom was in trouble. And I had to protect our kinds. I couldn't take a good sleep the night. Often the remaining days haunted me. I had no clue what shall I do under that circumstances. On the other hand, dad was busy to investigate the situation. I avoided moving out of home. Neither the fact, I wanted to go to school at least for now. I couldn't figure out what should I do. If I was to do something, it wouldn't be by me all alone. I needed someone who could give me the support. Apart from *Jimmy*, now that I could hold onto Tyler who seemed much strong enough to help me out in accomplishing my mission. But, for that I needed to reveal out myself with the hidden truth of my life. It wouldn't be that easy for them to know, how would I do that, there was no way that showed me. In order to find the real answer, I moved out of that Sunday.

Jimmy waited for me. I dived deep into the water where he waited. He knew, I wasn't at the prettiest time of life. He squeaked at me, when he saw me approaching toward him. I managed to convey my detail thought about my trouble. We had spent the whole day under water. The truth to me was that I couldn't stay away from both. Both Tyler and Alyward had become the interior part of my life. When I returned home, dad was already with Tyler at front yard. They were burning the fire wood with the stuff to roast a piece of meat. When my stepped neared to them, Tyler had seen me. I wasn't in state to company at my first go.

"Anna...." Tyler called me.

Dad looked at me. His face read with the intention to join them. I marched with sloppy step. I breathed in and breathed out, as the breeze seemed to be freshened enough after the light shower of drizzle that fell.

"I was worried about you" dad muttered.

I shook my head showing the least interest to concern with them. However, it wasn't readable on my face. The suspicious face flashed as Tyler could read me. He turned the iron rod where the piece of meat seemed to be roasted.

"Are you okay?" he asked.

"I'm good" I slouched.

"So, you were at the beach?"

I looked at dad and shook my head. I needed urgent peace right then.

"I need some rest" I demanded.

I left them shortly. I headed upstairs, clenched my hand over one another. I received the call from Alyward. Through the window the cool breeze slicked in. The questions from him arrived non- stop about my week's absence at school. There was nothing reason I could validly put out. Rather, I made reasons of my choice about my ill health. He gracefully agreed to my wellbeing argument. I was always under the heap of fear about my mom. But dad never showed that little concern about her. I never knew, how he did that, after all she's his wife. If I were to be him maybe some action would have come up. Before I could go back to bed, I intended to take the last sight of them. They were still at the front yard. Tyler prepared to leave. That following night, he hadn't come to me, I couldn't figure out the reason of his ignorance. Perhaps, he followed my instinct about my desire to stay isolated for that moment of time. Before he marched away, he glanced at my window with his docile eye sight. I saw him watching at me, and that fragility in my mind broke down as soon as he left. Just the glimpse of him, perhaps that's what meant for me. Dad walked in. I heard the sound of his bike fading away. I went back to bed recalling out of my fractured memory the days I had spent at Arizona. When the morning broke out, dad called me loud out of the door. It sounded fishy to me. I immediately opened for him as if something fearful incident had taken place.

"What's wrong?" I urged to know.

My breath swallowed hesitantly. Even my voice sounded hasty. But instead, dad put on a smile without any known thing. I sighed at first instantly.

"Happy Halloween" he said.

My eye brow raised higher while it opened much wider than normal.

"Dad" I shook my head giving him same wish.

"I prepared your morning meal" he said and galloped downstairs.

Just then the phone buzzed out with a call. Alyward was online.

"Hey" he said from the other end, and wished me about the Halloween day.

It's 31st October, and I wasn't aware about it though. At early morning, it was dad and then there Alyward. Where shall I begin with the costume for the day. I had no accurate dressing sense indeed. Whatever came in front, I grabbed and wore it for myself. I gave the same wish to him.

"Hey, there's a costume party nearby would you like to come with me?" Alyward seemed persuasive.

"Okay" I agreed without second thought.

He'd be here by evening to pick me up. Dad was gone for the rest of his day's duty. Just the piece of toast was there on the table. Inside the fridge, I searched for the mango squash that I usually loved to consume. Tyler didn't show up yet nor by text or call. Somehow, I wanted to convey him the message about the costume party. I informed about Alyward's presence there. In fact, he'd be here to pick me up which I had told him. I knew, it wasn't the right thing to do so. Yet, I couldn't get the handle on it. I wasn't mean to bring the rivalry between them instead, I wanted them to be friend with each other. Even though after the text, there was no replied from his side. I did none thing to pass the morning hour till noon had arrived. Dad had come to fetch his lunch. For some reason, he felt it necessary to come home. The other night he had complained about the food that he usually took at the restaurant where he manages his lunch too.

"I packed your lunch box" I said.

I handed him the box. He had least minute of time to spend around home. He immediately left. I even forgot to ask about the captain if they had found any sort of clue. He just went as quick as possible. I wanted to let him know I wouldn't be available by evening. He heard a little of it as I cracked my voice loud, the moment he left the gate. He waved at me so I did the same. All I could do was to wait for the evening to arrive. Dad wouldn't be back home early; he had said to me. The dusk was almost fallen by now. I had no idea what I should be wearing for the event. I had never been to costume party ever before on Halloween night. Just then, I heard the sound of the car arriving closer to the gate. I watched cornering my sight through the window. Alyward came out of the car. There was certain relief I felt. He walked in through the gate. I went downstairs to welcome him. As I opened the door for him, he looked elegant on his suit and tie. The shimmering glow casted out on his face. His golden blue eyes looked very demanding to be watched. He stared at me like the glue stuck on his eyes. I preferred him that way but in awe, I couldn't even move myself to render the things that I needed to hurry on.

"Are you ready?" he finally muttered.

"Yeah!!!" I said.

He gave his hand to hold, I placed my palm softly onto it. As we walked out of the porch, I still could smell the fresh morning air of that evening. The twilight was sunken below the line of trees, and the ambient surrounded with cheers waiting for us. He made the way for me toward the car. His chivalry was appreciable to be honored. He helped me to open up the door and made me sit by his side. Before he got on with the driving, he glanced at me staring through the pores of my beauty that slashed out.

"You look beautiful" he said at last.

He released the car and we were out of the place within no time. I could see the people around. The crowd seemed enthralling with the vibes of rejoices over the whole damn plot. Lots of young guys and girls were the main seen of attraction. Alyward parked his car. He opened the door for me and forwarded his hand to grip. As we began to walk through the crowded path, many people were on different styles of dress. Indeed, the scene looked more occult with magical scenario. He happened to meet few of his friends. The drinks, the beer cans, the drugs were all the kinds of stuff that could be seen everywhere. Even the loud music was the part of it. People danced around, some even fooling, some even had no idea where they had come to. At many corners of the place, couples were no less than having public sex. Kisses and drugs were one of the major portions of the party. With more numbers of included teenagers, it was the roughest party I've ever attended. However, in literal sense it wasn't a bad time. As I moved on with the people I happen to come across Tyler's bike. It was placed few meters away from my distance. I didn't expect him. Alyward was with the others. I intended to find the guy where he could be. Or maybe, he could be with other chicks around. Or perhaps, he might have been consuming as many bottles of beer as he could. Finally, I was out of Alyward's sight. I hovered around the place in search of Tyler. It was the wildest party of all generations. More impressive was the location where it had a lake. Even that wasn't left empty though. As I shuffled through the edge of the lake a teenage couple was making love. The girl moaned every time the guy happened to put in. It almost gave me the impression of watching a porn movie that too live. Sex in the water, I could never believe that.

My steps followed ahead, the crowd never seemed to end. And there few yards ahead, Tyler was seen seated by the lake side. He had a beer can which I was right to think. I walked to get toward him, almost isolated from the rest. An empty vacant place accompanied by the lusty breeze that blew with cold content in it. I walked on silently so that he wouldn't be aware about my presence. I wanted to surprise him though.

"I wasn't expecting you" I said.

He shook for seconds and turned back to sight at me.

"How did you find me?" he asked.

I joined by his side and sat on the ground. The lake water shone out of the blue moon that shone above the clear night sky. I was quite comfortable to be with him. He gazed at the night sky while I added to his company. He wanted me to initiate with what I was here for.

"I just came across your bike and thought you must be near here" I said.

He smiled, too sluggish to observe. I knew the fact that he was under the effect of his beer. But most importantly what bothered me was his presence at that moment of time.

"So, you came with him?" that was immediate.

I shook trying to avoid the intense conflict within the mind.

"Why are you doing this to me?" he said again.

I stood dumbstruck with the kind of retrograde reply I got. He looked sleazy and influenced wholly with alcohol effect. He wasn't even sure what he was saying to me. Knowing that, he was not very much in sense yet trying to provoke himself to be steady enough. It's strange behavior. The lake was just right before. If ever something wrong happens with the mind, he might not be able to control himself. I understood that even before the situation could turn worst. I managed to pull him out of the place, little away from the lake side. Of course, it looked he wasn't much in his sense. After finding the safe place at least distant from the lake view, we opted to sit back onto the ground.

"What's wrong with you?" I asked being very much concerned.

"Are you asking me?" he mocked.

"I guess I'm" I said showing the seriousness.

"Nothing's wrong with me" he said, his voice louder.

The intention remained in me in wanting to calm him down. The conflict stayed within. However, it couldn't be solved so easily. It slammed me over and over again, thinking he didn't like me seeing with Alyward. It's never that I hated him but now that he revealed me his truth. I shouldn't be in judgmental state about both.

"I think you should go home" I said.

He looked at me like he never had seen me ever before. His deep green eyes turned red with the effect of his beer. In course of our talk, the interruption came up from behind. It indeed frightened me at first. I wasn't expecting Alyward in search of me.

"Where've you been?"

I turned to look back. It surprised me with fear, for there was Tyler in the company. I stood up and shuffled with the slowest step toward him.

"Hey!!!!…" I said.

He looked at me with unsettling mind and thought that read on his face. He saw Tyler that roused his extreme hatred toward him. Gradually, his face turned to be ferocious. Seeking something to word out toward him, and it intently came out from him.

"You better stay away from her" Alyward said.

That unacceptable comment induced the loss of mind. Tyler stood up and looked at him. Each facing, face to face. Very close that their eyes met aggressively.

"You know what, you can do nothing to me" Tyler ferociously came up.

I stood stiff with the fear to handle the situation. It was all because of me. I watched with anger on each other, in state to attack almost each other. But, the fragile heart inside me couldn't do to stop their heated arguments. Even the breeze stopped to blow. And more trembling, they both had been into fight. To wall between them I had to take the place, both to stop their fight. Both acted abrasively.

"Hold you both…enough" I said, as my both the hands stopped them.

I was angry at both. I didn't want to stay back in the party after that fight. It wasn't just comfortable by then. I watched both at them, too ferociously. And then I realized, Tyler had actually had moved out of the place. He went with the hold of upset mind. I wanted to stop him but there was no reason I could do. I called him once but, he least bothered and galloped away. Behind me stood Alyward, though not that satisfied with the situation. The party still continued with the rest.

"Take me home" I said.

My intentions weren't to spend any more of my time with him. Instead, I wanted to move back home and to spend the remaining hours of the night all by myself. He drove me back. All through the way we haven't spoken, not even a single word. The silence stayed all along. Dad was at home. I saw the light being glowed outside the porch. I avoided much to pay attention toward him. He stopped the car at my front gate. I got out as soon as possible. But he didn't. He realized, I wasn't that happy with him. Alyward stayed back in the car itself.

"I didn't appreciate you" I said that.

With that last parting word, I walked in. He was gone after I had stepped inside. When I turned to look back he wasn't there. He didn't say me anything. I wondered what was wrong with him. I walked and thought with every minute of space that I got. As I stepped in, dad was right before me. My expression wasn't that pretty to be felt. There was the gross and dull appearance that focused out of my face. Dad noticed that and with much concerning vibe asked me about it. He didn't ask me about the costume party. All he cared was about me. Somehow, after that sloppy discussion with him, I got the time to move upstairs toward my room. The night wasn't that too old to follow the next morning. It was still young to be aged. I settled up my things and coz inside the blanket, trying to read one of the Vampire Novel. The night wasn't passing too soon. When I had reached the hundredth page of the book, I began to feel cold. As the midnight arrived the cold wind from the north hit the window. I shuffled up to close. There was the influence of long silence that night. Even the howling of wolf wasn't heard from the nearby forest. I resumed back to bed holding to read from hundredth page. It was intriguing to continue. I've never been so fond of vampires before but I was struck with that book for that night. Many a times, I avoided thinking about the situation at the costume party. However, it always pictured before me even though the pages kept the interest upon it. I was almost at the end but couldn't end it at one go, as I had fallen asleep by then. I didn't realize if the night was to get over soon. It was almost the beginning of dawn when I had actually slept. There was no plan of going school the next day. Instead, when I arrived home last night, I received a call from Lexie who would be visiting to my home. I wanted both Jessy and her to come but since she would be busy with her school stuff she wouldn't be available.

When the next morning slithered in, I was still on bed with the coziness inside the blanket. Just then the thrust of hitting the door was heard. I immediately got out of the posture and looked for who could be that. Of course, it couldn't be dad to come along with such force hitting the door. When I opened the door, I saw the figure that looked very familiar to me. From her, came the sweetest smile that threw on me. I had to welcome her with huge hug. Lexie stepped inside. Seeing the unsettled bed, she was quite dazzled to look around the room.

"Oh! My God…your room is damn cool" she said, looking at the photographs.

There was one photograph with Alyward I realized, as she came across to that. She gazed at the wall impinging each and every corner of the room. When she was done with her exploration she finally came toward my bed. She sat on the edge corner.

"You're really something Anna" she said.

The impression about my room had an effect on her. I smiled on that reliable comment. Then again, the discussion bulged out about Alyward. It wasn't the best time to talk about him. I felt it. However, I managed to divert the talk. She understood that, as she too had been in relationship. I felt the need to know about Jessy and Peter. With Peter, the whole summer he wasn't in touch to us. Since the time he had seen me with Alyward, he mostly tried avoiding me. I was not in a position to understand the situation, how could he. It all fused up with no motive of life. But with Lexie's presence, it made me feel much better than any other days. At least I had some female friend around me. *Only a girl can understand another girl's feelings.* She had the same thought of skipping the school. So, the day wouldn't be going useless. Dad returned for his work. We prepared breakfast and enjoyed watching television. At noon, we had another plan to visit the beach. Knowing the fact, that beach is like the second home to me. I shouldn't be taking any chance to make her doubt about my real nature of life. I needed to control my emotions in order to protect my secrecy. By noon, we were at the beach, walked on through the heated dunes. And finally found a shed under a palm tree. I sighted at the spot where the ship went missing few days earlier. Fortunately, dad wasn't around. So, it gave us the relief access. We had few soft drinks carried with us. The temperature rose too high. While those drinks kept our thirst wet. We waited until the twilight took its shape to set below the horizon.

Before we reached back home, dad was already there. He had never seen Lexie before neither did she saw him. I introduced them both to each other. It was quite comfortable with a girl company for the first time else it always them. We helped dad to prepare the dinner together. There was lots of talk with her. Dad found her very interesting. For the first time, we had prepared chicken steak at home. The hidden talent about Lexie flourished out when her idea to cook the recipe rose. That was amazingly made. That was the first time, I found Lexie to be different then she usually was. I had wrong perception about her. The reason, she never showed her good side. *I never knew the reason why*. But I realized, she was the only one I could have best at my side.

We sat together for dinner. I blatantly looked at her.

"What's wrong?" she muttered.

"Nothing" I said. Maybe that was fishy, I felt.

I took a bite of the chicken steak. It tasted better than any restaurant stuff. Dad poured the wine in every glass of ours. And then the chatter continued subjecting various topics. I had never seen the other side of Lexie. Not only she was good at heart but in addition to that she was quite humorous to hook around. He made people laugh around. When that happened it almost made me felt like the sorrow around has fumed out from the congested life.

Chapter Ten

After the dinner, dad got himself busy with his files. I glanced at him through the window pane. His table cluttered with papers and files and books. On the other side, the television roared all alone with none of spectator watching. His room always seemed piled with heavy stuffs though those weren't the kind of metallic items. Lexie and I thought to take a round of the porch. The night always seemed much cooler than day. It's November, and for sure the winter will have something for this time of the year. I covered with thick fur to protect myself from the shivering coldness. Lexie borrowed. We decided to make fire. The breeze blew more effectively carrying the chill moisture around the air. Gradually, it turned ever colder than expected. We sat around the fire. Dad's light was still burning bright. He hasn't gone to sleep yet. Perhaps, he was the kind of man who bothered more about work than the rest of the things. I never understood him well. He spoke less and worked more. And I've been accustomed with that kind of nature of him. We sat around the fire.

"My dad liked you" I said.

She looked at me and grinned in friendly gesture.

"You've a wonderful dad. He's a good man. You're fortunate to have him" she said very effusively.

I shook my head realizing she had something done with her past. I pushed the firewood a bit. The sparks spread into the air. I didn't intend to put pressure in trying to know her past. Instead, I began to talk her in some other sort of things. There was nothing I could do to undo her past life. All that could be shown would be nothing more than a mere consolation words. The night was moving away. The silence felt deep. Even the howling of wolf had stopped. Perhaps, they have shifted their habitat somewhere else. As the winter knocked, it's for sure they will find a safer and warmer place. Just then dad arrived outside. He saw us with the fire. He shuffled toward us.

"You all are awake yet?" he said.

I roomed for him and sat beside me. I knew, dad wasn't that good at story. If it was mom, we would have something to hear from her. It's the section of midnight and with an abrupt notion dad began to narrate. It amazed me. But I liked that he involved us. I felt engrossing, as he began and couldn't wait to put my ear with silence. Lexie attended the same way to hear the narration. It wasn't something fairy tale but very honest and truthful from every way. We listened to him like a child. The night passed away with the clouds shifting their position with the blow of winds. The fire kept us warm and I realized the frost had wet my thick fur. It began to turn creepy with cold.

"I think; we should get back to the room" dad said.

That night, Lexie spent with us. She slept along with me. But as the night went deeper toward the next half of the day, the weather bitterly turned more severe with coldness. It wasn't something that we could escape. Even the fire couldn't keep us warm much longer. The abrupt change in the weather indicated the drastic occurrence of winter. Within few days, the leaves would wither away from their branches. I hated cold but nature's rule couldn't be un-followed.

The ship sailed through the heavy storms of Pacific Ocean. The journey just began. It wouldn't be an easy way for Nicholas

Cook to reach to the Island. They had to cross lots of oceans to accomplish their destination. The tip of South America still waited for them where they had to take a round to turn their ship toward Caribbean Sea. It's the middle of mid night, and the storm ferociously erupted in the middle of the ocean.

"Steer the wheel" Nicholas Cook shouted aloud.

The splash of heavy currents of water shook the ship. It had to fight against those rough waves that obstructed them. There was no sight nearby, it's the lonely ship sailing. But, pirates they know exactly how to deal under such conditions. They're experienced, they're professionals in whatever they do. Most important thing, they had been facing such danger for whole of their life. The water with heavy thrust hit the ship. Volumes of water contaminated in the deck, yet the ship stood strong fighting against those nature's omen. It took them under water, when the strongest wave engulfed them. But no person lost.

"It's the worst kind of thing I've seen Captain" said Zenna.

Zenna, the only woman in the whole crew. But, nonetheless she was no less than a man. She had a height an inch taller than Nicholas Cook. But what made her most appropriate was her fitness. She had that kind of figure, where anyone would love to say, what a piece of art by God. She held the rope that controlled the wind sheets. The storm instead of slowing down reached its highest peak.

"Pull the lever" shouted Jack Hammer.

He's the strongest in the ship. He came down to the deck and watched at the ferocious storm.

"You've no power to perish us" he shouted, added by his wicked laugh. The splash of water hit him. Standing at the tip of the ship, he dealt to enjoy the storm.

Nicholas Cook kept watching on all, as the rest of the crew in hand to protect the ship. Later, he added himself with Zenna.

"You look hot" he said.

Sometime, he's more of a kind of wicked nature. He gave his hand in handling the rope.

"Thanks Captain" it came loud from her.

"Steer the wheel hard you bastards, turn it to left" Zenna shouted in high pitch.

The huge wave arrived from right. It hit with strong force which tilted the ship. However, they weren't able to escape that one. It sank below water and rose again with high thrust. The water level in the deck began to rise and fall. Captain knew, they had to save their men along with the ship. Up there at the tip, another wave hit Jack Hammer but this time he wasn't able to withstand, he fell with heavy hard on the deck.

"You must be crazy Jack" Zenna shouted.

He stood on the deck, and turned to look back at them. He managed to hold the rope else he would have been blown away.

"Give me a kiss and I shall show you how wild I'm" he replied loud.

"Fuck you!" she said.

"Captain, the storm shall fear us" Jack added.

The storm continued for the whole night. By the break of dawn, the ocean stood calm and silent. All at once the clear sky above flourished. And the only object right in the middle of Pacific was the ship that stood floated on the surface. It was the frightening night for all of them. Restless for the whole night, that took the part in the war of storm. When Jack happened to open his eye first, the shadow of his body casted down in the dock. He was dropped down on the deck floor senseless until the winds stopped blowing last night. Every member of the ship stable enough at their own place wandering where they had been the last night. The vast ocean with endless directions stood open for their way.

"Hey look the storm feared us" Jack Hammer shouted.

That very moment, he woke up every one in the ship. It was the bright day and their hope roused higher with determining approach. Zenna looked around, broke from her sleep. The ship didn't move. The silent ocean showered the glimpse of their day.

"Captain wake up…. we're safe" she said.

He glanced at his compass and looked around to examine the position.

"Where are we?" he asked.

"We're in the middle of the ocean" Jack said from the tip end.

"Get the map" ordered Nicholas Cook.

Every one gathered around. From the deck end, Zenna arrived with the map. She unrolled on the wooden table. She read for a minute, carefully and finally pointed the spot they were. On the other hand, Nicholas Cook lengthened his binocular to look for the distant. There was no one around. Nicholas Cook got back to the deck, where the map was spread.

"Captain we're right here" Zenna pointed on the map.

"Let's sail, turn the wheel" he ordered.

Immediately the rest of the crew rushed to fix up the ship.

"Where are we heading?" Zenna followed him.

"To South America" he answered.

The ship made a movement as they fueled with gear to move toward Southern tip of South America. The ocean was clam and peace and they had the smooth sail in the direction.

Cruz Bay had become the hub of new generation mermaids. The Island *St. John* had a history over its past. Many researchers from American University had spotted the sight of mermaid several times. It always came in the news. And it got more popularized through You Tube. Yet there came no accurate evidence of it. Neither, there was any sample of such aquatic creature seen in the labs. Some believed mermaids are fictitious creature, those who saw they couldn't make people believe about it. We only existed through stories which had been the ladder for many centuries. But, the legends were always true. We, such creatures do exist.

It's Sunday and the buzz around the beach wouldn't be tolerable for her. Dora, my mother was seated on dunes that very day. She was accompanied by her new friend from the locality. Unlike any other Islands, *St. John* had something new to charm with. The beaches were splendidly excellent to spent time. Mom heard about the news of Nicholas Cook. While they were seated together, they were interrupted by a huge wave that felt on them. It wet them. But the effect of heat would barely let that wetness stay.

"I'm worried they've traced us" Dora said.

"We can end them, believe me" Keren sounded very confident.

Keren was one of such mermaid who was victimized often by pirates. She was fearless, her valor was truly commendable. After fighting for her life several times against the pirates, she had used to them. She had the knowledge how to deal them. In fact, she knew the warfare technique to be used against them.

"I know. But, I'm worried about Annabell".

"She will be safe wherever she may be. We won't let our kinds perish away" she said.

"I saw the news last night. A ship had been approaching toward this Island. I wonder how they came to know about it".

"It's pretty gross, it serious matter" Keren said.

Mom shook her head, and gazed at the far stretched distance across the Caribbean Sea. They walked out of the place and headed toward the restaurant. The breeze blew in with the moisture content in it.

"Tonight, there's a call from the king side" Keren muttered, as they resided inside.

They occupied a table and ordered for the breakfast. My mother wasn't still convinced if they would be able to defeat those rouge pirates. There could be many. They even didn't have the idea; they could come from all sides. Of course, there numbers exceed the mermaids. If they unite with the rest of the Caribbean Pirates, they will come out as victor of the war, which was why the doubt to win against them wouldn't be that easy. There's no doubt that they shall not come in full force. They will have many men along with them.

"Why the sudden call?" mom urged to know.

"It's regarding the battle" she said.

Mom shook her head and took a sip of her beverage. She glanced outside the shore. As the morning unleashed out of the sunken dawn people began to hover around the beach. It's the day's heat that pertain the rest to take up the routine to hook themselves up through the sand dunes. The rest of the remaining they were at the shore itself. They got back to the same place where they had taken the shelter for the day. The color of the sand reflected the glow of the golden rays that fell out from the universe. The fascinating part of the beach was the white sand.

When the dusk had fallen they finally moved out of the place. Keren and mom had been staying together since the time they had come into contact each other. The house was situated few miles away from the beach. Surrounded with lusty greenery with the presence of lake around the area constitute their heavenly abode of home. Keren had an old Mercedes which she had inherited from her mother. It's one of those antique piece, that still existed. Over the years, such design had stopped manufacturing. Thereby, there's only one in the town with such priority of the car's demand. But she never intended to sell it. It passed from generations to generations. Every at the weekend end they gather together. There where they execute their plan. Everything that take place they don't come in human form. Instead, they had their own womb where everything takes birth in their life. Normally, when they are in mermaid form, they swim far across the Caribbean somewhere mid in the ocean where they meet up together. It's not the same place they continue. Often after months of conducting, within the same place they locate themselves into another part. Usually their spot would be at the Atlantic Ocean. The ocean provided them much protection then the rest. It's extremely cold and hard for any humans to survive within that temperature below zero degree. But, mermaids loved the nature of that Ocean. It made them feel more safe and protective. Pirates never do patrol around that ocean cause, they know the consequences they had to face.

They both reached back home. It's the seven at evening. While the weather report said there could be a chance of storm arriving from the deep north of Atlantic. The island people shall have to be careful enough to protect themselves.

"I've never heard of the same happening in Caribbean Sea" said Mom, she screened on the television news.

She was added by Keren next to her with a bowl of cereal on her hand. Watching at the weather report, they both silently gazed at the television screen. Having prepared with the dinner, there could be only one thing that they waited for. The call from the rest. They communicated through telepathy. Keren waited for that call. When it was almost eight pasts, they sat out for dinner. As Keren withheld to drink a glass of water from her glass, she heard the vibrant sound reaching her head. Her mind played the attention to that as she was touched with the connection to the sound that blew in through the air. There the call came up that they had been waiting for hours.

"They're calling us" she said.

Dora stopped her spoon in the midway. But she pushed that slowly. She rested her hand on the table.

"We have to move as soon as possible" she muttered.

The wind outside turned rough, the pressure began to differ outside. Perhaps, it may bring rain.

"We must move out before it gets worst" Keren began to pack up her bag.

"When shall we return back to home?" Mom said after long pause.

"I don't know".

They prepared to leave. Keren started her antique Mercedes. She waited for mom to get inside. She speeded up like she was racing against her life. The only thing they were hinted was they had to move out of the place somewhere deep in the Caribbean Sea. They reached the spot where they had to dive into the water. She stopped her car which skidded to much extent in the spot. As if she was driving in a racing course.

"I've never seen this image of yours" Mom mumbled as she breathed out.

Keren smiled out and opened the door. She was then added by Dora. As they began to shuffle toward the deck of the port, they felt the grasping influence of the storm that was arriving. The port though stood empty and dark. No sign of human presence or any sound of animals from the nearby forest. For any normal human the fear would control them but, for mermaids when they're around water they always found the strength. The wind surrounded the area, even the thunderstorm began to throw its light on earth. The duo undressed and stood naked on the deck before they dived in.

"Let's jumped" Keren forwarded her hand to grab her.

Dora shook her head. They took the last look of the weather outside. It's cold, bitterly cold. They dived in. As they swam across the way, the deeper they swam under water they finally turned into their forms. Their naked body finally covered with the shinning scales on their body. They swam with their reliable speed to reach the rest of the mermaid crew. Mom had the blue color diamond scales tail. It had the prettiest fin on it, nevertheless those looked very fragile and soft. On the other hand, Keren had red color scales which reflected the light from the water. They came across many kinds of sea creatures. Creatures, I've never heard of before. It always intrigued me to look myself as one of them.

Mermaid, considered the finest mystery that ever existed. And I always felt proud of it though the fact was that we couldn't live a free live like the humans. We had to hide to protect ourselves. I wouldn't consider it as a taboo. But it's a blessing for all of our kind, it preserved our fear from the rest of the world. After miles away from the land they finally found the rest of the mermaid group. Deep under water they could never be reached by anyone. There number increased.

"I'm sorry we're late" Keren pleaded the rest.

The storm arrived with thrust hitting the ocean surface. But it least touched them deep inside. All submerged again to swim through the rough sea. Their leader waited at long distance somewhere in the mid ocean of Caribbean.

Duncan the only merman in the group led the team against the cruel army of pirates. Of course, the name that only flourished among pirates was Nicholas Cook. Dora and Keren reached the spot.

"I don't know where shall I begin? I can't be ferocious to you all" said Duncan.

"We apologized" Mom said.

"You must be knowing why we called you here?" Duncan said in serious notion.

Everyone followed to listen to him, as he began with the speech. The world under water seemed so differently created that one couldn't feel like living up in the human land. Duncan was the kind of merman who was selfless. He had every kind of caliber in him to lead the team. In addition to that, Keren seemed very useful to the group with her battle strategies. It's a long-term deal that we're about to carry for our lives. Until we feel safe to live freely, the war shall not end. Everyone gathered around Duncan. He was center of attention. Like any human podium there was he at the center. They created their own world under water. To reach the place it wouldn't be possible for any normal human. The meeting continued for about an hour. Every protective measures and guidance were given to all. It kept them fearless and enthusiastic to face any danger that would arrive. When they were over Keren was asked to meet Duncan in private.

"Wait for me" she said to mom.

The rest of the mermaids swam back to home. They were even faster than it seemed. When they reached the water surface they were transforming back to their human form. And as they walked on the shore, their tail disappeared and the legs began to imprint of the sand dunes. The storm was over by then. But, mom and Keren were still behind. Duncan was such a merman who rarely visits the human world. Once in a week, he showed himself up at the shore. But, many fail to recognize him in human form. Sometimes, he had to introduce himself to his kind, whenever they encounter him. That wasn't a problem though, it could be easily communicable through their telepathy conversation.

Mom and Keren arrived at the dock. Their clothes were kept at the same place where they had left. Still the night stood firm with darkness. No sign of moon or stars and the storm washed away the shore. Keren's car looked washed due to the fall of rain. Its midnight there wouldn't be anyone available on the road. The long way waited for them to reach back. The fearless mind shall have to be brave enough to face the darkness. However strong they prove but as soon as they go away from water bodies, strength would gradually be controlled by fear. With fear and terrified heart somehow, they made to home. The sign of relief appeared on both faces. Mom opened the front door.

"I just hope everything becomes fine" she said.

"Don't' worry you can relax now safely" Keren muttered.

"Good night" mom said and went upstairs to her room.

She actually tired calling me that following night but unfortunately our cordless phone went dead. More unfortunate was that my handset had no power. And dad, he seldom uses his phone except that one walky-talky that he always carried with him. Whenever he made a call to me it's always someone's number from his colleague.

Since Lexie had visited me the last time, I barely went out of home. Dad advised the week get going for any vacation. But I didn't heed my attention much onto that. Instead, I ignored his idea about vacation. I even didn't go to school. I stayed bore the whole week. Neither, I talked to anyone else. No one bothered, neither Alyward nor Tyler. The scar about the Halloween costume party still stayed afresh in three of us mind. I almost forgot by now about that incident but was it the same for them. It didn't show me positive vibes.

It's beginning of a new week. I wasn't in position to show myself at school. Yet dad had urged me to spend the time at least doing something valuable. He left the morning. Some clue he found last week about Nicholas Cook. Lately, he had come to know he was a pirate of that ship. Like always, I had the breakfast that was left on the table. I sip few glasses of juice which I felt too needy. I almost felt abandon by mom. Each night, I thought about her more than I could sleep. Maybe I was too concern about her. I never knew how to communicate with them. After prolonged sort of time hovering with those thoughts, there was the sudden buzz on my cell phone. For instantly it shook me, as I wasn't in world of reality. Lost somewhere in depth thought than I could exist. I received the call, and from the other end the voice sounded timid. It wasn't that easy to recognize the tone but as she began to speak out I found it was Lexie, who had been waiting for me at school. The thought that Alyward would arrive to pick me up wasn't the important as of now. We haven't talked to each other more than week. I strolled out of the door. The Chevy was kept right at the garage untouched for a month. I decided at least to pick up for a ride. Before I left, I had informed Lexie about my arrival.

Chapter Eleven

Winter at Sonoma County isn't really that good. It turns even worse when it drizzles. The unusual thing about the weather was that even in frost of cold, rain doesn't stop to fall. But that morning even though the night was bitterly cold, the morning could be freshly felt with little light that slithered in between the clouds. However, the winter breeze kept the ambience alluring. The dew hasn't dried yet. The road still looked damped and untidy. It's been after a month I had come with my truck. The place once used to be the junction of meeting. But on that very day, I haven't found Alyward's car. I parked my truck some cars away from the right end. I looked out of the window sighting for any companion. Fortunately, Lexie was just at the parking lot. She had seen my truck and shuffled rapidly toward me. I got out, and followed toward her.

"You made it late" she said.

"I know" I grinned.

"You look pretty" she giggled.

I said nothing but passed a slow witty smile. We walked through the green lawn area reaching toward the main entrance. She asked me about my period, I had to move toward the math section. We bade temporary parting time for that hour. As I stepped in to the class, I knew I had to be still with my feet. I was taken aback by Alyward's presence in the class. The seat next to him looked vacant. It waited for me. He didn't look at me, pretending he never saw me. But I could read on his face, he cornered his eyes to glimpse at me. I walked in silently to take the vacant seat. The discomfort was felt, as we had met after long time since the fight. There was silence until Nash Billy entered the class, all stood up to wish him morning. We haven't talk for the whole period. When the class got over, he instantly went out without bothering much about the rest. I never knew *why was he doing that*? And the fact that it was hard for me to talk to him that way. I wanted to discuss the matter with him, but he never showed the interest.

When everyone else was out I was the last person to step out of the class. The room was empty. But before I got out of the math section I heard a call inside my mind. I heard the voice and all of a sudden everything went blank in my mind. I began to feel someone was inside me. It wanted to talk to me. I heard the voice it muttered. It took controlled within and I was unable to think.

"Anna" I heard calling my name.

I tried to look around but there existed none. It all happened in my conscious. It frightened me giving the impression I was over taken by evil.

"I'm your mother. Now listen to me carefully. Before I finish talking to you, don't go outside, sit safely somewhere in your empty class".

I did as she suggested. I sat at one corner of the empty class. I felt very distracted that she was within my mind. How could she be able to talk to me that way. That was a miracle to me.

"I'm talking to you through telepathy alright. Listen to me, I know you're very upset with me. Since the last time I had met you in the ocean, we've never met again. But I'm bounded by many things sweetheart. I want to save you and your father" she continued.

My tears began to roll down through my pale cheek. Instead of listening to her, I couldn't bear and cried out.

"Stop crying, I'm always with you. I won't let anything happen to you both. I will always be around".

"Mom, please come back. We need you, dad needs you" I cried.

I heard mom slashing her tears out. Her effusive voice mingled in my conscious. She pretended to stay strong even though she wasn't revealing her rigorous pain. She stopped saying anymore.

"Mom…mom…. mom" I called her.

By then she was gone. She heard me calling her out but, she ignored to reply back. After seconds later, I felt light with my mind signifying mom had left me. I waited with that mournful heavy heart soaked in tears that helplessly fell out. I managed to settle myself up with my hair and cleared out my face. Then I walked out of the room. At corridor, I sighted Lexie who was on wait for me.

"Where were you?" she asked.

I was silent with fragility within my heart to respond anything. She caught my hand. We walked out toward the cafeteria. The ambience wasn't having the same feel as it used to be. The damp weather and the absence of sunlight made even more sluggish. And we walked through the open space, I came across Alyward. He crossed our path from the other side, went noticing us. I didn't feel any humiliation to that. He behaved the same way in the math class. I wondered what went wrong with him. I wanted to clear the misunderstanding that he had, but he never showed up. I watched him going away toward the parking lot. Lexie saw me gazing at him.

"Is anything wrong with him?".

"Oh…Nothing" I stammered.

We considered a table at corner of the hall. I wasn't even in state to take lunch but to compromise the companion, I somehow intended to take little. What kept rumbling inside, *mom*. It imprinted all the things she had told me. Few things I couldn't interpret though. I never had the power to communicate with her, it's only on her wish if she wanted. Maybe, I didn't inherit the power of telepathy. That's what caused me to think more about her safety.

When Lexie opened her lunch box the smell immediately caught my nose. It wasn't instantly acceptable. I sneezed out for more five times. But the legitimate thoughts kept me poured out of my mind.

"Are you okay?" she concerned on her term.

"Yeah!!!" I shook.

She then gave me the other box of lunch. I opened slowly so the next time I don't received that stingy smell. It wasn't that hard to do so. I grabbed the spoon and dug into it to heap my spoon with brown rice. For moment, I fiddle with it before I consumed. Lexie stared at me with some awkward glimpse. To her, it looked, I lost mental stability. My aberrant behavior even gave her more suspicious idea about it.

"What's wrong with you?" this time she was hard on me.

"I need to talk to him" I said.

"Okay go" she said, as if she wasn't caring about.

"I'm sorry I ruined your lunch".

She looked at me, pretending to be jolly though, I felt the ferocious touch of her. I gently got up the chair, something that intimately caught me inside. I wasn't in state what I really wanted to do. Her face glared at me more intensified with something that's happening unreal. To her, I was in perceived side where she couldn't make out. *My behavior,* I knew wasn't that appropriate with her. I walked out of the cafeteria lounge, giving her last concern glance to her. My first intention was to find Alyward. I rushed toward the parking lot where he headed earlier. But that morning, I haven't seen his car parked. Maybe, he came with his friends, I assumed. I walked on through the open space. The breeze faintly touched my skin, I felt the sudden cold. As I headed on, the empty spaces were seen, where the cars have gone missing before I arrived at the spot. Alyward's presence went missing. He was gone. I sighed with deep breath. Something, I wasn't expecting to happen. He wasn't even that easy inside the math class. So helplessly I stood by watching others. I had to return back to Lexie. Her expressions were unreadable seeing me again. She literally had nothing to say, might be she wasn't in mood to comment on my current status. When I sat before her, she raised her eyebrow once. That was her friendly gesture, I understood.

"I hope; you'll not walk away again".

I smile with shallow feeling inside. I shook my head gesturing the positive vibes to her. We completed the lunch together.

"Wasn't he there?" said Lexie, as we walked out through the open space.

We skipped the rest of the school. Instead, we headed to parking lot. She wanted me to come along with to her house. I agreed to her. We drove out of the school campus immediately. On the way, there was nothing more in my head than mom. The windy breeze slithered through the window. It began to melt the cold within me. I followed Lexie, aping the same way. That's the first time I'd be visiting her home. I've never seen Peter and Jessy for so long. I considered it to be their time. As all have their busy schedule to run their life. Several thoughts rumbled and jumbled before me. The fact no one yet knew me as mermaid, the other kind. I needed to admit it at least to someone who I could trust. Maybe I was still in search for that one person, other than my dad. After half an hour drive we finally reached her home. Lexie stays with her mom and dad. Her mother was there to welcome us. She introduced me to her mom. I did the same, she knew my name even before I had uttered for her.

"I know your name, Annabell Cameron" Lexie's mom said.

I smiled with the affectionate feel. The living room was extensively designed. Few minutes later, Lexie buzzed out from her room in changed dress.

"Come to my room" she called.

Her mom excused us both, and left us on our own. She had asked me to dine with them the night. Even though after my disagreement, I couldn't persuade her. Lately, I had to consume the dinner sitting along with them. Her dad's presence arrived a little late. Just before the dinner, he was there at right time. Her dad worked at the pharmaceutical store, a kind of panache guy. That was impressive to watch him. He joined with us. Gradually as we proceeded with the dinner I was quite comfortable to share with them. After the dinner we shared few talk. That was obvious a kind of family gathering amongst us. In the process of our chatting session and discussions, I received a call from dad. He looked worried. I ensured him not to worry. It was half past ten when I left back for home. Lexie's dad wanted to drop me. I appreciated his generosity. There was no need of that, I acted brave. However, Lexie and her dad escorted me till the gate. Her mom watched from the front door.

"Goodnight Anna" said Lexie's mom.

I shook my head "Goodnight all".

"I'd love to meet your dad" her father said.

"Sure, I'll let him know" I said.

I got inside the car and started the engine. They waved at me as I moved out of the place. When I reached home, dad was truly very worried about me although I had assured him about my safety.

"You shouldn't do such activity, it's not acceptable" dad said.

"You shouldn't worry about me. I'm sorry about that" I said and went straight to my room.

He sighed and looked at me as I walked up through the stairs. He dimmed the bulb and went to his room. He wasn't that happy to look at. The next morning would be the best day to talk to him, I thought. He spoke less whenever he seemed to be upset. But he never showed, something I admired about my dad. That's why mom loved him a lot.

The winter chilled wind whined through the forest. Though I hated cold but with passing days, I began to like the weather. And there was only one aim that stood with idea the next morning. I had to meet up Alyward. With firm thought about him the last night, I finally concluded to trust him. He was the only one who could make me talk with mom. I knew, he could do that apart from being a clairvoyant and mind reader, he must have something more in him, which he yet hasn't found out. When I woke up the next morning, I found myself late to get myself ready. I sensed dad had come once to call me up. When I watched out through the window the sun already bloomed out. Dad was out in the sun drying his washed car. From the garage, he got a range to fix the seat.

"Is there anything to mend in your truck?" dad looked up.

"I guess not".

He began to fix his seat. I felt the fresh morning. It brought smile on my face, no reason why. I got myself readied and stepped down.

"Dad, I'd be spending the day with Alyward Pyne. So, for god sake need not worry. I'll be safe with him" I said.

"Alright" he said.

He went inside after he fixed his seat.

"Did you take your breakfast?" dad came out.

I shook my head, before I got into my tuck.

"Just do take care, have a great day" he said again.

"Bye dad" I waved at him.

I drove through the road along the line of oak trees that stood tall. I slowed my truck. Alyward was seen out on his terrace. He had seen me coming. I stopped the truck right at his front gate. I walked in unlatching the gate. He walked down at the door. He opened before I rang the bell.

"Hey" he said.

"Hi".

He gestured letting me in. There was silence for fraction of seconds. To clip the awkward feeling, I looked around the walls. Right then, he was behind me.

"Anna, I'm sorry, I treated you bad the last day at school" he said, apologetic gesture.

"No...it's okay. I know things are quite messed up" I added.

"I know; I shouldn't have yelled at Tyler" he said.

He kept on saying about the incident on Halloween day. Repeatedly he asked sorry, knowing that he regretted about it. I wasn't here for embarrassing him. Indeed, it made me felt bad.

"I want a favor from you".

"Yeah" he said.

"But before that you got to listen to some truth about me".

He sharpened his eye toward me. That was more like a tampered look. It had the friendly gesture with it. He shook his head and comforted himself seated at the sofa. I added by his side.

"You know, I love you and keeping that honesty, I want to share something deep about me. Hope you won't break my trust" I began.

He shook his head and stared at me constantly. There was no blink in his eyes, even for a second.

"You go to accept the truth. I know I lied to you. But I had no other option then, you must believe me for what I'm about to tell you".

His gaze turned even more serious toward me. It looked like he was ready to face whatever would come out of my mouth. He nodded his head enabling me to speak ahead. I held his hand showing the warmth of love.

"I'm not a human" I admitted.

He was amazed to hear. Not expecting what it came out of me. Rather there was uncertainty on his face, confused with the situation struggling hard to believe even for minute detail.

"Then who you're?" he broke his long silence.

"I'm a mermaid" I revealed him.

He stood up from the sofa and juggled around for minute. Then he turned on to and fro every now and then. He wasn't able to look at me. Indeed, his eye diminished and melted the rays beyond his belief.

"How can I believe you?"

"Only if you come with me to the beach, I can show you who I'm exactly".

He paused for a second halting at a place. His breath ran faster than expected. Maybe, he wasn't expecting such miracle phenomena to happen.

"Why didn't you tell be before?" Alyward too concern about himself.

"I just waited for the right time"

When my reality was out before him, he wasn't able to decide which way to take. The honesty or the acceptance would be great barrier then, in multiple thoughts he got engaged himself. He sat down again on the sofa.

"How can I help you then?"

I shifted closer to him and bent on my knee. My hands placed safely on his knee.

"It wouldn't be easy for you, but, trust you can. I want you to see mom" I trembled with my voice.

He shook his head, and closed his eyes to look for her. I watched him doing that. Of course, that was strange to sight him that way. After minutes, he opened his eyes.

"She's fine at Cruz Bay" he muttered.

I shook my head with a relief. I needed to talk to her. And the only way to reach her could be the method of telepathy. I added by Alyward side. I never had that skill of telepathy communication.

"Aly…. You need to do one more final thing for me" I said, perhaps I was showing my love to take his name short.

He agreed shaking his head. He looked at me like he never did ever before. I felt that gaze with a spell bound of silence. For minutes, we stared at each other with the silence around. The feelings were erupting out all over again, to be in love.

"What shall I do?"

"It's little difficult but I know you can" I boosted him.

"I'll try" he agreed confidently.

"You need to enter into my mom's mind through telepathy. I want to talk to her".

He was stunned hearing that. He never did such thing before other than looking into the future. He found it impossible yet he never revealed it on his face.

"I never did telepathy" he added.

"I know, but I believe you can" I gave sign of an encouragement.

He shook his head. He gently placed, one of his palm on my head, to connect into my mind. When he closed his eyes, he was actually putting effort to penetrate into my mind. He tried for few seconds. When he found he was unable to do so, he removed his hand from my head.

"I can't penetrate your mind; you know that" he added sadly.

"Read my mind then"

"I can't" he said and tired hard for once again.

Even after trying for second time he wasn't able to penetrate. He looked frustrated and stood high, walked outside the room. I followed behind. I appeared before him. He stood stiff before me. His eyes sunken with swollen hope, yet I knew he could. The breeze outside added the flavor of being in an isolated ambience. And as the day evolved out, the weather began to change. The cloudy day glittered with the chill breeze adding to the environment. We stood firmly facing each other. He then grasped my hand pulled me closer to him. He gasped at me pertaining to attain what he wanted. He placed both of his hands on my head.

"You need to close your eyes" he suggested.

I did according to his guidance. After prolonged trail, he was able to take control on me. He literally entered in my mind. It's just the initial step to the process he did. I found hard in the beginning that his command over my mind. But as he processed further with his own will, I felt the little comfort to stand with my mind blank. The other thing he had to do was to connect with my mom, somewhere far from where we were at. It's the hardest thing he had to do then. Yet, he controlled on himself to process in contacting my mom.

When he found the connection to her mind, he hummed with pain that he was feeling in establishing the telepathy. I got the feel of her mind through the connection. I know the pain he was enduring, acting as the medium to transmit our thoughts. At Cruz Bay, mom was spending her valuable time with her friend Keren. The picture visualized before my eyes. And all of a sudden mom was captured in my thoughts. She got the link between our minds. She immediately galloped to a lonely place. Keren watched at her going, she keened to know where she was heading. The beach was packed with people all around and the spaces available could be less. So, she chose the safest side where the crowd wasn't seen.

"Dora where are you going?" asked Keren.

"I'll be back in a minute".

Alyward held steady with the pain on his brain. I too was in immense congestion of my mind that gave the blurred vision idea about what was going inside his mind.

"Mom…Are you there?" I called for her.

"How did you find me?"

"I'll tell you later all that, I just wanted to know if you're well with your life" I said quite effusive in my voice.

"You shouldn't have contacted me. You know how dangerous it could be" she added.

Our conversation lasted for long minutes. Not realizing what was happening to Alyward. Through his nose, the blood bled out. And the pain to withstand the telepathic conversation gradually increased.

"I can't hold any more" he said with pain.

I heard the panic voice of him. After all the conversations with mom, it was time to leave. We couldn't talk for longer, as it could be danger for her there. The Island isn't that safe for any kind of non- human creature. It's always hunted by pirates and black magic.

"I've to go for now" mom said.

"When am I going to see you again?"

"Very soon my dear"

She warned not to take any approach to reach the Island. But you know, I'm not that kind of girl who would set back due to fear. Although, I agreed to her, I would devoid if it's in my hand.

"Take care" she said.

"I miss you mom" I said.

"Goodbye".

The link was broken momentarily. And as Alwyard opened his eyes, he fell instantly on the ground. I saw him fall, his nose stained with blood.

"Alyward…are you okay?" I gave my hand.

He opened his eyes hearing my voice. His head was placed on my palm. He smiled though he still involved with the pain. He looked around the sky once and turned to face me.

"I'm good" he said at last.

I grinned not wide though. He got up from the floor and walked inside to aid him. The day just hatched with the bright light. Since morning, the dampness was prevailing. I aided him with medicine. He was well to do to look at by then. I prepared the lunch for both of us. He was at rest for an hour. When I arrived with the plates, he was already in state of falling asleep.

"Mr. Clairvoyant…. you must be hungry"

He opened his eyes and passed a glimpse at me. I placed the plates on the table. He sat leaning his back at the back support of the bed.

"I never knew I could do such strange thing" he added.

"I always knew, you had something more than what you are" I said handing him the lunch plate.

"When are you going to proof me right?"

"The beach isn't empty right now, by sunset I can perhaps show you my real image".

He shook his head and began to take his lunch. The rest of the day we watched televisions. He played his favorite songs for me. He took me to his room and I got the chance to look out through the window to view the splendid scene all over again. It wasn't the same the last time I had seen. But the winter had changed it, further with the essence of nature and fragrance that influenced the surroundings. I felt the ecstasy of being in his company.

"I'm glad that you've accepted me the way I'm" I said turning back to him.

The breeze blew smoothly through the window. It wasn't the kind of winter breeze that slicked in. I found it very bearable to me. And, what more added was the view outside the window. It couldn't be described with the words except that eyes knew how to appreciate it.

'You've always shown your courage, Anna" he said.

He held my hand and lifted it holding the tip of my forefinger. He made me turn around, the music slowly related to us. It was the softest tune that I've ever heard from him. It remembered me the first time I was with him. It made me felt like the first time. It's the kind of love that bore every pain to endure and enhance our life. When the music stopped, he too stopped to make me dance.

By then, the sun was sliding down the west. The first light of the twilight seemed to be the brightest before the end of the day. It's time, we move out toward the beach. He prepared to take his car. We drove through the long lengthy road of trees standing tall. By the time, we were at the shore the sun was almost below the horizon. He stopped his car right at the start of the beach shore. I got out first. We took a small walk until it was safe for me that nobody witnesses us.

"Are you ready?" I asked him.

I stood at the edge of the water. He looked at me with keened sight. I undressed before him. He didn't turn his face away seeing me naked. However, I could read his mind what he thought about that but I believed he was under control. His face read it was strange to witness such transformation.

'You wait here" I asked him.

I dived into the water, and as I swam deep, I finally transformed myself into my kind. I had to resurface to show him my real image. When I did that, I called him.

"Look at me" I said.

He was surprised, amazed, stood numb and shocked.

"Unbelievable" he said.

I swam toward the shore. He saw my whole body, covered with shining scales. He examined around me, and looked into my eyes. I was feetless, crawling on the dunes. He touched my tail and felt it vibrantly.

"You look amazing…. Anna" he complimented.

"This is who I'm" I added.

He smiled softly and sat on the dunes alongside me. The day ended and the night fell. He asked me about how I feel being a mermaid. That wasn't a long kind of story I had to make him hear. After spending for hours at the shore, we ultimately decided to turn back home. He carried me with his both hand. I was still in mermaid form.

"What makes you think that I look beautiful?" I asked, as he held me by his hands carrying to the car.

"Why are you defying yourself? you're rare" he added.

And as we walked, my feet gradually transformed back to human legs. I felt happy and safe than ever before. He got me inside the car. I dressed and joined him at the front seat. He took control of the steering and we drove out of the place back to home. Dad hasn't called me, I was expecting the same. Yet I found him waiting for me at the veranda.

"Hey!! dad, you're still awake?" I pretended to concern.

"The dinner waits for you" he said, quite jubilant.

"Yup...I'll join you within a minute" I said and headed to my room.

He waited for me when I stepped down. He poured water in my glass. The smell of steak was fantabulous.

"Wow!!... It's surprising.... you made it?" I said, seeing the chicken steak.

"I tried" he grinned.

We continued taking the dinner. There was the last bottle of wine left. Dad hasn't poured for himself. I was quite obsessed with that. I poured for myself. And while I poured for him, he wasn't in state to taste the red wine. However, to show the little sympathy upon me, he tasted.

"I'm not quite fond of red wine, however I'd love to taste for the sake of you" he said smiling toward me.

I cornered my eye at dad. He tasted his first sip, I watched him swallowing in. I sliced another piece of steak on my plate. Then with the flavor of red wine I grasped the taste of the combination.

"So, which wine goes with you then?" I asked him.

"Well, I usually love the white, the French" he pointed being more specific.

I shook my head, and continued with the slice of chicken steak.

"So, how's your days going at school?" dad never stopped asking.

I made my face disinterested. He smiled looking toward me.

"Not good huh!!" he added, giggled.

"Yeah kind of, same old stuff everyday" I said.

I concealed the truth about revealing myself to Alyward. Dad at no point would forgive me if I said him the reality. But, I wanted to keep it secret, that other than him, another person knows about my reality of being a mermaid. When we got over with the dinner, we like lovable daughter and father took slight walk outside to feel the breeze. The night was always the breezy part of the whole day. And that cold would catch easily. I always wrapped myself with thick fur.

"Dad you never talked about mom?" that came instantly to me.

He looked startled, subtle with the kind of question I forwarded. He stared at the sky for a minute flooded with some thoughts that definitely walled him with unrealistic measures. He then turned toward me with serious face, not scaring though but with zeal of emotions.

"It's not that I don't miss your mom. I know where she is, what she had been doing all through these years. You're too young to know all these right now. You know who you're and we are doing this to save you".

That effusively melted me inside. Not knowing what I had done with such silly things to know.

"Dad, I'm sorry" I said.

"It's okay, you're my daughter. You've the right to know about us" he added.

We walked in after those few sentimental conversations. I bade him goodnight, he walked inside his room. I planned to confirm if I could meet up Tyler the next day. But from the other side there came no response. Since the fight he hasn't shown up. When the morning broke out early, I drove myself to meet him up. Dad accompanied me till half way when then he bifurcated to his station. From the window of the car, I saw Tyler. He was as usual at the garage. But this time it was empty. He had all his bikes sold out the last week. Instead, he was in gallons of colors painting the walls. I blew the horn instantly. He saw me and left his work. I saw that same smile on his face. He speeded toward me. He was half undressed. I got out of the car. He caught me by and hugged lifting me an inch above the ground. After he released me, he gave another praise of look at me.

"I wasn't expecting you" he said.

We began to walk toward the garage. The morning ambience around the place felt refreshing. The birds chirped and made beautiful noise to break the sleepy willfully.

"Where were you all these days?" I asked.

He grinned and carried on to walk. He shook lightly his head and turned to face me.

"Well, I was on business" he added.

"I can see that, no more bikes in the garage".

"I wanted to turn the garage to some other workplace. I had to sell all the bikes" he said adjusting his hair.

He had almost completed half of a wall on one side. I looked around once again, it was really refreshing in such greenery surrounding.

"Where's your dad?"

"He must be inside. Would join with me?".

"Sure, I'd love to?" I felt overwhelmed.

He handed me a brush and the same color in a bucket. We began coloring the same side.

"Anna, I'm so sorry about the Halloween day" to soft to listen.

"Its fine, everything is alright" I added firmly.

He shook his head and began painting again. Within an hour we had completed the whole side of it. We sought to take little time to rest before we began for the next. His dad strolled out of the house, out in the sunshine. He saw my presence which he took by uttered expression, as he wasn't hoping for me.

"Good to see you" he said.

"It's nice to see to you too, Burney" I added.

"How's your dad".

"He's doing fine" I said being sure.

He chatted with me for like few minutes and then headed on toward the gate. Tyler didn't mutter at all. He just added his presence within us.

"He's not well" Tyler looked at his father.

Burney looked pale and gloomy. It's obvious, he wasn't well in health. That could be one reason he hasn't come for so long to meet dad. Tyler handed me a bottle of energy drink. I drank it in one go. My thirst was at highest point to dry my throat. His dad definitely looked weak and lean than before. We then resumed back with the paint to begin with next side of the wall.

"What you gonna start with this now?" I keened to know.

"I haven't yet decided".

I shook my head as I pulled the roller to rub against the wall. The day went away, and the arrival of mid noon exhausted us with the tired some work we were dealing with. Burney called us in for the lunch. After the lunch, we skipped the rest of the painting stuff, instead, we decided to take a walk through the open meadow few miles away. By the time, we got ourselves out of home the dusk had almost fallen. Tyler as usual rode his bike while I followed him with my truck. The sun merged toward the west. The meadow looked greenish with the soft content of grasses. He stopped at one point of the open ground. I just parked behind him. I got out of the truck and caught him in the company. Our movement made toward the empty space where the junction of two hills was accessible to glance at the panoramic view.

"Have you been here before?" he squinted.

The twilight rays fell on his face which he obstructed by placing his hand before his face.

"It's the first time. It's a beautiful place"

I felt the zeal of being in a silent peace watching at the view ahead. After shuffling for few steps, we stopped at one spot. We marked to sit on the ground with the view before us. I watched at the top of the hills, and the valley they made with the other one. Above us birds seemed to fly back to their homes. That was perfectly picturesque sight I observed.

"How does it feel being a son of god?" I talked.

He wriggled his body and turned toward me. His face signified nothing but shuddered with unexpected blow.

"There's nothing new" he shrugged.

The ambience turned shallow as the twilight began to dim in. We had spent an hour seated along the view. Tyler was worried about his dad's sickness. He, whole through the session talked mostly about his dad.

"He'll be fine" I consoled him.

He shook his head, and stood up on the ground. Then he stared at me forwarding his hand to me. I passed a brief smile and held his hand. He pulled me up. We walked back where his bike was parked. We sought to return back home.

"You could have the dinner with us" Tyler suggested.

"I don't want to make feel dad alone" I shrugged.

"C'mon it's just few hours together" he insisted.

I shook my head "Alright".

His dad waited for our return. At the time of dinner, I had received the call from dad. I provided him not to get worry about me. Gradually, the weather outside turned cold to cramped my feet. The dinner was served on the table. Tyler sat beside me. I missed Arizona, I missed the heat. It's never the same over here.

"You must be hungry Anna" Burney forwarded the plate of green salads.

Tyler took from his hand and served me on my plate.

"I wished to invite your dad someday" Burney said.

I shook my head pointing the positive gesture. Tyler glanced at me once before he moved his spoon to his mouth.

"How long you've been staying with your dad?" that was another from Burney.

"I guess it's turning to be two" I said casually, without much intervening to that.

"You're a strong girl" he added.

After the dinner was over, we sat together for an hour around a fire. The cold wasn't easy to avoid. It's crappy and harsh even to withhold with any kind of warm things. There was the constant breeze that thrust in with a chilled blow. I looked at Tyler while he was putting another wood into the fire place. His dad added by his side. I never knew, what shall we put into conversation. But, there was something that I needed to know or it was the desperate thing that I held with me.

"Why it's hard to be the other kind?" I sighed.

Burney looked at Tyler, by now he must have gotten the

idea, that I knew, he wasn't a pure human. He gestured with acceptance through his eyes. Tyler glanced at me and stayed silence, while Burney cleared his throat to speak out.

"So, you know who we are?" Burney added calmly.

"I'm sorry if it was an omen to know" I added.

"There's nothing omen to it, Anna" Tyler glimpsed at me.

"Apparently the truth is we are not human" his dad added.

"Are you scared?" Tyler squished.

"No" I shook my head.

I felt the conversation was growing a little serious. Although, it gave me the churn of courage I shouldn't be afraid of them. *No mistakes, I shouldn't falter. They are the gods who were right before me.*

"Well, Anna…it seems to be a long story how we are the gods. But I promise, I shall let you know. We *Demi Gods* don't lie about our existence but human do. Animals don't lie, they can't even show it for they lack to speak".

My attention to him was quite nervous. I shook my head with the touch of insight thought. It literally gave me the feel of being in a dominant rule, as I was the only person there with those *Demi gods*. They could do anything. My conscious hinged me out, and with abrupt kind of suddenness, I remembered about dad at home.

"I think I should leave" I said.

"Are you alright? Tyler drop her back to home" Burney said.

He walked with me till the car. I just had a thought that wasn't the right thing to ask perhaps.

"Well, Anna don't mind with dad. He's that way" he shrugged.

I nodded my head "I can go all by myself".

"Are you sure about that?"

"Yeah!!!" my voice crunched.

"So, when am I gonna see you again?"

"I can't exactly say. Well goodnight Tyler" I added.

I started my engine and released the clutch to move out of the place. He watched me from behind till the sight of me vanished. I thought about him as I was lonely through the way. On the other hand, dad would be very dissatisfied with my conduct. I still yet had no plan to compromise with. Reaching Virgin Island would be a bad thought for mom. But, if that was the case, I hadn't to listen to her. Protecting me wasn't the first priority, but considering the fact that I don't want to lose mom forever. I could protect myself. They knew very well. Other than dad, Alyward seemed to be that humble person who had the secret of mine. Considering him to be one of my own, I couldn't let him go. I was in position where my final decision never put me on. If I had to take Alyward along with me, I could give no guarantee about his life protection. I needed someone more powerful than him. And the only person that I see was Tyler. But they both will never stay together. I needed them to get together to join with me. The foremost reason could only be that I was the one between their disintegrated relation. But I was sure, I could keep up with the situation. The thoughts played within my mind and I never realized when I had stopped myself at the gate. Dad was outside, he walked toward me. I had the truck parked inside the garage.

"I actually feared you would never return" he said.

I briefly smiled out as I push the door. I joined with dad to walk in to the house. He covered himself with a jacket. I wasn't on the fur.

"So, how they treated you?"

"They were kind" I just added casually.

"I actually had prepared a soup. You know the cold, it will keep you warm".

From the kitchen, he brought out the bowl for me. I received from him and, walked upstairs to my room.

"Goodnight dad".

He smiled and gestured loving "No internet, just the soup and back to sleep".

I shook my head with loving concern. When I opened my door, it was the same as I had left the morning. There was no message or call form Alyward. Sometime, it would bother me more about him. I ignored to serve the internet as my dad had suggested. Instead, I grabbed a book from my shelf and lay myself on bed to read. As I began to continue from the portion, there was the sudden call of thoughts that roused in my mind. I began to think about mom's protection. I couldn't read more than a page that following night. I slept with a painful sorrow. The cold hindered me with sharp edges and followed me to hurt even internally. When the morning broke out, I was still on bed. I was startled to receive a call from Lexie. She sounded very excited and enchanting in her voice.

"Are you okay?" I asked.

"Of course," that sounded screaming.

"Something happened"

"You got to come to a school, we got to discuss about prom night"

"Prom night" I wasn't sure.

"Yeah!!!! It's happening next week. No one told you".

We ended shortly with our conversation. I wasn't in state of going to school but her talk about prom to somewhat intrigued me, though I'm not that girl who usually loves to hook around boys. Dad called me downstairs. I stepped out of the room, he was prepared with the breakfast.

"Good morning" he uttered.

I shook my head responding the same. I joined in the table. He poured for me the glass of mango squash.

"What's your plan today?" dad asked.

"Lexie has something important to tell me. So, I might move outward to school"

"That's excellent, you should see her" he said and walked out of the kitchen.

He wasn't going for work instead, he planned to stay back at home. By quarter past nine, I was completely readied myself. The truck was kept at the garage after the last night. Dad managed to wash it out. It looked fine and smooth shining out with the real color. Dad glimpsed at me before I left out.

"Keep it clean" he said from the window.

I shook my head and briefly smiled out. I got myself settled inside and started the engine. Just then, I got the call from Lexie. From the other end, she sounded very enthusiastic.

"Where are you right now?"

"I'm on my way" I added.

"I'm right at the parking lot" she said and dropped the phone.

I drove with the moderate speed, when I reached the school entry it was literally turned into a crowded street. From the far end, Lexie saw me and waved her hand. I flashed the narrow smile to her. I had to blow the horn much louder. Gradually, the crowd began to scattered around. I never knew the reason what was for. I occupied the safest place out from the crowd to park my truck. I got out immediately and headed toward Lexie. She opened her arm and embraced me with a warm welcome.

"I'm so super excited about the froth coming week" she said.

I shook my head, friendly gesture. She was excited but I wasn't feeling the same. Events like prom never excited me.

But to show the feeling of support I had join the share of happiness around with Lexie. It wasn't the day that I would like to attend classes. Back in the parking lot, I had seen the arrival of Alyward.

"There he is?" Lexie muttered.

He walked toward us, seeing me he flashed that short smile. I added the same to him. He kissed me. That was after a long time. Lexie was there with us giving her best company. We headed toward the auditorium hall where the meet would be conducted for the next week prom. At the entrance of the hall, Jessy was fiddling with other guys. She saw us arriving.

"Hey!!!" she felt amazed.

After prolonged time I had seen her. There was the heap of unwanted thoughts arrived between us for seconds. It couldn't be avoidable but then Alyward made it easy by uttering the first word.

"You look good" he said, glancing toward Jessy.

We walked in together and occupied the front row seat.

"So, are you coming to prom?" Jessy prompted.

"I don't' know" I said.

As we waited for the others, the dean arrived on the stage. He gave a long lecture about the whole idea about the prom event. Of course, he was too open to discuss about stuffs like sex, drugs, alcohol etc. everyone laughed when he began to discuss about such erotically sensitive stuffs. The gathering continued for an hour. When the session got over, we all moved toward the cafeteria. As we made our way, Alyward walked by my side. The rest moved ahead.

"There's someone wanting you" he whispered.

I looked at him, amazed, wondering around who could be. But, I had to believe in him for he could see the future ahead.

"I'll wait for you" he said and headed alone to a site where the shade was available.

Just then Tyler from behind came up. I wasn't hoping him to be there. We were little away from the people's sight. And then, there was Alyward watching us few yards away. The expression wasn't that easy to read on his face. It must have been hard for him to watch me with Tyler.

"Hey!!! Anna" said Tyler.

"Tyler" I mumbled.

He embraced me immediately.

"How...how come you are here?" I stammered.

He giggled and looked around. He saw him in the shade. He cornered his eye in envious manner, something that wasn't friendly gesture.

"Are you stalking me these days" I said again.

He laughed "No...I was passing the way and thought to see you up. You think me bad right" he smiled.

"No.... I was just kidding. Anyway what made you bring here?"

"I had to drop dad to one of friend's house".

"We should go" Alyward from the other end muttered.

I shook my head looking toward him. Then I looked at Tyler's face, the expression wasn't that cool to be notice. It's hard to say if they could like to talk to each other. But, that never happened yet.

"Tyler, I should leave now"

He shook his head showing the right gesture.

"Guess I'll see you around Anna" he said and walked off.

I shuffled toward Alyward in the shade and headed on to the cafeteria for the lunch.

Chapter Twelve

Life for me was kind of living with one soul of love. That love always came from dad's side. When I thought about mom, my fragility would break me inside wondering about the safety of her. If dad had some magical power with him there would be no reason he wouldn't go after her. But then, he was just plain human with none of majestic magical bless. However, I've never given much thought how I would die but to die in saving a soul perhaps for me the right way to go. And then the inclusion of Alyward, would matter me a lot. He was not only the person I love but, with some principles he had given himself to me. There left nothing between us to keep hidden. He knew me well and I knew him till the core. It's like, I'm dysfunctional without him. But loving the one you need the most always kept me enthusiastic with mysteries. Despite the fact, he had no such powers as Tyler I couldn't let him stay alone. In every story the guy appeared to be the dominant hero but in the case of mine, it's just the opposite. In other words, I was more worried about Alyward than about me. When it came to dad, he knew what I was. So, for him it's always the right thing to do without many complications. Maybe that's what my life. But as like, I felt lesser the complication more is the problems to arrive. Problem was about mom. She isn't at home for the last one year.

Creatures like us, always do have complications and fear. We're never settled at one place. Like lives of gypsies, we're scattered every year of time. But, being a mermaid, there the other half of my life I could see. Despite the fact, I was living as human there was no intention to spite anyone of my surroundings. It was just me and my dad living the life of normal human. Besides, the only thing that being a human could be felt was the generosity of living in a world created by god. But right then, things began to change just like the seasons. And I being an aquatic creature hated the cold. That was unusual trait. But it's not that I hated cold, but in human form it irritated me more. Whenever I took the chance to transform myself into mermaid, I embraced the cold ocean water. It gave me strength then.

That was another night I had dreamt about Alyward. Even though he seemed close to me, I profoundly found him quite away. He lived miles from me and that troubled me often. When I woke the next morning, I found the mist afloat in the air. There was no sign of rising sun from the east. The day covered with cold clouds and fog that clenched on the window panes. I walked aside to look out if there's any visibility outside but winter mist never gave the pores of access. Dad was on his hood outside the lawn finding the best place to create fire to withstand the cold. Now, the excuse stood right before me to skip the school routine. I walked downstairs to join dad in helping him burning the fire.

"So, you're early today" he said.

"I loved the weather" I sneezed.

"The cold caught you" he smiled.

"Yeah!!! Something like that".

We heaped the compilation of woods and the fire was prepared. As the day began to outshine the weather turned even worst.

The mist of fog never seemed to fade away from any side. For instant, it made me felt like we were living under a constant coverage of clouds and mist. I felt warm for a bit as the fire burnt vigorously. Dad brought two cup of hot coffee from inside.

"Perhaps, the coffee will keep us warmer and active" he suggested.

I smiled and took from him. There was the silence and whined of cold breeze that blew smoothly. It reminded me about Arizona, I've never seen such winter there. It's just so opposite side of a coin.

"Dad, I need to discuss something important to you".

He glanced at me and pressed his lips, urging me to complete what I had on my mind. I was nervous for few seconds with the kind of intention he threw at me, it wasn't that pretty. I didn't want to twist and turn the thoughts over my mind. Instead, I was always clear with every intention.

"I'm going to Virgin Island to find mom" I said without any hesitation.

He looked at me not smooth to watch at. His face unwilling to listen to what I needed to convey. He sipped his coffee and then turned with the unsatisfied expression to me.

"So, you contacted your mom right"

I shook my head without utter consent of dismay. There was the ardent fear that floated inside if dad would permit me to do so, but that's what I wanted to do.

"We got to save him dad" I added firmly.

"I do understand about your mom's safety Anna. It's not that easy for us to go. We could kill ourselves by many unwanted horror" he added.

"I do understand. I've some plan" I firmly said.

"I don't appreciate going you there. You broke my heart Anna" he said effusively.

I stared at the fire constantly, muttered nothing. He walked out of the fire place and walked to his room. He wasn't happy by me. But my desperate nature didn't bother about that. I stayed for a little while grasping the heat. I literally had no intention in hurting Adam. He had been a good dad to me for the last twenty years. I could barely stay without him. Since then, he was slightly upset with my decision. The whole day, he ignored to talk regarding my decision. Neither, he showed any sort of concerning care about me. I never could understand him. The day passed with the same climatic condition. Lexie had called me once but I skipped to meet her. And then Alyward made a call to me, he wanted to pick me up to his house for the dinner. He was always alone. I agreed to him, giving him the appropriate time by evening. It the worst kind of day I passed through, severe cold and heart throb anguish. Watching dad in such position made me even worst. By noon, I actually made an apology to him. Though the sky still covered with cold clouds and mist, there was no little sign of sunshine. The sudden change in the weather affected my inner sinus that troubled me in breathing. Dad was seated watching television. I picked a bowl of cornflakes with milk on it. I served him with one. I spent few more hours with dad before Alyward arrived.

"I don't want to lose you" his voice to soft to feel.

"Right dad" I ensured confidently.

He took his spoon and ate the milk cornflakes. He felt little confronted as I wasn't talking about going to Virgin Island anymore.

"You can go under one condition" he said finally.

"Are you sure about that?"

"You must bring back mom to complete our family"

"I promise dad" I said enthusiastically.

Just then the horn outside was audible.

"That's Alyward" I assured.

He shook and faced toward the television again. I went out to welcome him. When I opened the door for him, he was already standing right there.

"Hey" he embraced me and walked in.

He joined dad in companying him watching the NBA match.

"How have you been doing?" that came casually from dad.

"I'm doing fine sir" too fine to hear.

I prepared myself in the best attire I had. When I got down to catch him up, he was already outside at the front yard. I met dad for the last time before I parted for the evening. I made sure he doesn't get worry about me all the time. So, I had mentioned about him about my dinner visit to Alyward's home. He didn't mind of that.

"Have a good time" he said.

I walked out of the house, Alyward stood next to his car. He stared at my direction as I stepped toward him. It wasn't normal, he watched me but the blink of his eyes literally stopped.

"You look beautiful" he muttered.

I briefly smiled out as he opened the door for me. I got inside next to his driving seat. We passed the long silent empty road and as the evening fell the twilight rays shone from the forest end. It outshone into the clear sky, calling the end of the day. By the time we reached his house the day ended smoothly.

I returned home quite very late at night. He dropped me back. Dad was asleep by the time I was into my room. Only the glow of light at front yard was visible. As the deep night crawled in, the cold began to crap out into the air. Without further ado, I covered myself with quilt and went to bed early. It wasn't the best of night I had. I had a bad dream. When I woke up in the morning, the picture still hovered in my eye. Something really worst could take place. It frightened me more, even though I tried to withhold with a belief to be falsified just as dream. But often, I heard from people that dream in the early morning comes true. And it was one of those types. I got downstairs. Dad was busy preparing the breakfast for both. I joined him later in the kitchen.

"Dad, do you belief in dreams?"

He glanced at me, something that came out abruptly without his expectation. He smiled and took over the knife to piece the slices of carrots.

"Dreams are the pictures of your future" he said.

I didn't know what he meant by that. Who could be more eligible than to know it from Alyward. He was the right person who could explain me about dreams. I thought it.

"Give me the bowl" dad asked.

I handed him with careful act. I added to his preparations. I prepared finger chips for both. He took the loaf of bread which he fixed in the toaster. On the other side, milk was boiling. We sat for the breakfast together. That was quite after long time, I remembered we were sitting together to eat together. I felt the pleasant morning with joy. Nevertheless, the weather condition showed up to be fair enough at least for that moment of time. All I hoped it stays the same for the whole day.

"Planning to skip school"

I giggled and looked at him posing the unwanted sort of comment that came from him.

"I guess not" I said simply.

When we got over with the breakfast, dad was supposed to leave. He told me, he would go to Bakersfield. I remembered, I had visited the place more than once with Alyward. He didn't tell me the reason before he left. All he said was that it was important to go. He left home assuring he'd be late for the night. By that morning hour, it was all me alone at my home. I couldn't disobey dad or lie to him for skipping school. Moreover, everyone seemed to be busy preparing for the prom night. I had no passionate interest on that par. I thought about mom, or I could stay in fear about those obnoxious pirates who are on their way to Virgin Island. It couldn't be the best of thought I could think, which pulled me more into some kind of darkness where I see no ray of hopes. I'd visit the beach, I had the plan momentarily. It's been since the last meeting that I hadn't seen *Jimmy* and their groups. I got myself readied immediately and walked out of the house toward the beach. I wouldn't be receiving any call for today, I decided. I got myself fitted into truck. And as I moved out of the gate, I felt guilty about the fact that I was lying dad. *I skipped school hours*. But for my personal feeling, I couldn't hold on. I had to follow where my heart led me.

"I'm so sorry dad" I whispered inside as I drove through the way.

When I reached the spot, I undressed myself hidden from the rest. The beach began to get crowded as the day turned out to grow older. I dived in, and as my legs began to swim I followed into deep. I was into mermaid form. Deep in the ocean no one could possibly see me no matter how crystal clear the water was. Fortunately, the day hasn't turned bad with terrific coldness in the atmosphere. I searched for *Jimmy*. In their language, I began to call them out. Soon, in the direction of me, I saw him, approaching toward me. I felt peace whenever I was into my realistic form. This was who I actually born for.

It's the majority of my life I had lived as human but rarely, I felt the essence of being a mermaid, as though it wasn't that easy to live a dual life. The fact, that all of my kinds are away from me. It's the lonely girl who had been living in satanic world where cruelty was being manifested. It wasn't the choice of my life but it was the destiny that planned for me. I took the whole day to spend myself under the ocean. And the companion of dolphins was the splendid blessing I got till date.

The ship moved into the right direction. Nicholas Cook lengthened his binocular to look for any sight from across the Pacific mid Ocean.

"Guys, I can see some shelter" he muttered.

Zenna snatched the binocular from him to make sure. She smiled with hope and looked around the vast ocean.

"Do respect your Captain" Nicholas said regarding the snatch of binocular.

She looked at him, her face blatantly dull. She gestured nothing initially instead, her attitude toward him stayed hard and firm with ignorance.

"I'm not under anyone" she said strongly.

Nicholas made his face, though not annoying intention. She wasn't the kind of pirate girl who would be following others command. She headed toward the front deck.

"Listen to me all bastards" Nicholas began addressing his crew. At the front end, Zenna angrily looked at him. She then turned her face toward the ocean water. Jack Hammer at the other end was controlling the steering wheel.

"We're not to fear of fear. Look thy far land, that's going to be our shelter for few days. If you fear or misses home, you get the fuck out of this ship. We're pirates, we're the armies of sea.

No one can touch us. We worship the one who gives us power. So, my friend today is your day, when we hit that edging land we got to fight for our rights and snatch it by shedding blood, tear them into pieces, spill them into tiny fleshes, burnt them into ashes. Show them we're the real devil, the devil should fear us by our deeds. My friends imprint your name in their bloods. Be prepared" he ended.

That was a strong command from Nicholas Cook. All his armies drew their sword and shield, prepared to capture the tip end of Southern America. There ship just reached the tip end. It was the *Wollaston Island*, an Island under the governance of Chile. The ship reached the shore with a great thrust pushing it out through the sand dunes. Many of Nicholas's army jumped out of the ship before they anchored. However, the Island seemed to be out of danger. They were fortunate not to spill blood around to find their shelter. The ship was anchored. The rest stepped out of the board. Nicholas walked out of the ship and felt the sand dunes. The darkness almost covered the area. The last link of light was drooping down the horizon.

"Pull the tent" he shouted.

"All hail Captain, we won without losing our men" Jack Hammer patted him.

"Did you see Zenna?" Nicholas inquired.

"No" he said and walked to the rest.

Within no time the barren beach had turned into years of inhabitant lives. Fires were made all around to light the area.

"Sire your camp is ready" an army informed Nicholas.

He shook his head and looked for Zenna. She was seated along the edge of the shore. After he got her sight, he walked passed through the rows of tents. The soldiers began to prepare for the night rest. Some with the strands of music. Some sat with their bottles to quench their thirst. Quench their thirst I mean, they sat to rejoice the night with alcoholic party.

"What you doing here?" Nicholas asked her solemnly.

"I'm summoning my life to whom it belongs"

"I'm sorry about the board thing"

She looked at him and gasped her breath. Then she looked onto the waves that hit out at the shore.

"You shouldn't be here. They're waiting for you" Nicholas muttered.

"I'll be right there" she replied.

Nicholas joined back his team at the tent. Few minutes later, Zenna showed up. There was the smoke of gas releasing out into the atmosphere from their cooking chambers. Out in the shore, the born fire was made to steal the night. The crew added together to celebrate the success of their journey to the Island.

"To the dreadful and courageous pirates, here I'm to salute you all, to make the toast" Nicholas Cook, with the glass of drink in his hand.

He then lifted it up in the air and like a king he made the toast and began their celebration. He saw Zenna indulging with the crowd.

"You must take one" he said.

She was offered with a glass of wine. She willfully took from him.

"Enjoy the party" he said and left to the rest.

She shook her head and keened to join the mob. The night felt calm and as the season had changed, the wind began to flow out from the deep Pacific. The night felt very silent after their celebration got over. The peaceful sleep was under way. The wind thrust the tents very hard. It hit with the strongest velocity that it carried. There was the chance to bring storm along the shore. Jack Hammer got out of his tent. He looked around the place. There were few fire woods still burning into ashes. He had the thick cigar in his hand. He walked on toward the fire place to burn. The beach shore stood vacant with the silent fall of the deep night. Few bottles were left along, but all in empty state. The bones of roasted animals left as the residue. The wind whined to and fro. He stared at the direction of the ocean. The darkness never gave the access to view along the vast ocean. Jack Hammer sat along the fire edge to warm himself. The cigar kept him engage to himself. The cold wind began to whirl around the shore. He felt there could be any sort of thunder storm. Coincidently, the sky was under the coverage of dark clouds. There were no stars or the moon above. He stood from the posture and moved ahead to warn the rest. When he reached Nicholas's tent, he found him awake. He entered and was welcomed by him.

"Did you see that?" he said.

Nicholas was sipping a glass of wine with a book in his hand. He was seated on a beaded chair.

"The storm"

Jack was offered a glass of wine too. He joined by his side. Then rest of their discussion followed to go on. In every sip of his wine, Nicholas grew worried about his men. If the storm hit them, they might not survive, provided if it was really the strongest one. Yet, they had hopes to see ahead.

"The storm can't reach us" Jack showed positivity.

"Warn everyone" he said.

Jack went out to inform everyone. There was the darkness prevailed, the wind blew roughly around. The moisture was felt in the air. When he reached Zenna's tent, she in an advanced came out of her tent. The chaos amongst people buzzed out.

"What's wrong?" she said.

"Everyone, listen up to me" Jack raised his voice "Do you see the angry ocean out there. Friends behold to withstand the most ferocious war against god. The storm, that's arriving at the shore soon may wipe us out but, my friends we're warriors, we don't know fear, we are not afraid of death. Let the current hit us with thy thrust and we shall reply back with the same. Be prepared to face".

The lightening sound reached the earth surface. The blow of thunder storm warned the land lives. Nicholas came out of his tent and looked around. Zenna caught up his side.

"Good to see you".

Jack Hammer arrived shortly warning their men.

"Ask them to light fires and wait for the time. You did a great job Jack" Nicholas complimented.

He moved out of the place and immediately the fire woods were burned. And as the mid night passed away the storm gradually hit with a blow of winds roared through the island. It was the oncoming of darkest hour for the rest of the crew. The rougher it got, the tougher it grew to withstand. The wild winds from the deep Pacific hit the Island, the moment it hit the shore it uprooted all the built tents. The tall trees from the edge of the shore were taken down to ground. The huge waves hit the crowd with heavy punches. Few of men were carried away, for several times the waves didn't stop. The heavy windy rains fell harshly without any mercy. But their ship still floated steady under the ferocious storm.

"You can't tear us" Jack screamed looking upward into the black sky.

Nicholas Cook stayed steady inside his tent. The tent almost broke down. The thrust of the wind hit the shore hard, gradually people were scattered more in numbers, no one could be found in a cluster. Dispersed by the strong currents of waves, it took away many lives under the deep ocean. The trouble continued for hours. By the time, it slowed down very few were found helplessly at the shore. Nicholas Cook's tent was thrown out. Gradually the wind died out, so the rain. The stormed stopped but the night wasn't yet over. Seeing the scars of devastation, it mentally killed Nicholas. He had lost men and food. He looked around the place in his wet cloth. Searched for Jack, but seemed there was no sight of him. He took for granted, *he must have got drowned by the heavy storm*. Zenna somehow managed to escape the disastrous event.

"Captain" she peeped out of his hidden place.

"Thank god you're alive" he felt relief.

"Where's Jack" she inquired.

There was no response for him. There was no surety that he could declare him as dead. But instead, he opted to search for him along the shore. The dawn was almost on its way to cast out from the horizon. One of the best thing about Nicholas, he doesn't give up so easily. They proceeded to search for him with the remaining men. The dead bodies of others floated in the water. Few came rushing into the shore with the smooth movement of those calmer waves. In course of their thorough search, the dawn was out with the flash of light falling on. It cleared the area with darkness. The ocean looked calm and silent. Even the roar of waves reduced to lesser extent. As they walked on along the shore, few meters away a body was seen along the edge of the shore. Nicholas rushed to the spot to examine the body. Well, fortunately it was Jack Hammer. He had drunk liters of water inside his body. He lay unconscious on the wet sand dunes.

"Jack" Zenna turned his body.

She pressed his chest for many times. She constantly pressurized to throw out the water from his struck throat.

When then he coughed out loud with the splash of water thrown out form his mouth. He gently opened his eyes and felt the sudden entry of light in his eyes.

"Are you okay?" Zenna concerned.

He got on his feet and inquired about Nicholas. He was right before him. He was glad to have him back. He looked at the ocean, and the calmness literally felt peace around. The only thing that stood with steady motion was their ship. So fortunate, that their ship seemed to be the strongest amongst all other things they had.

"We have lost many men and food, before we move out of this place we got to recover few. So, we shall be stopping for few more days" Nicholas declared.

Everyone gathered at a place, took the responsibility to rebuild all the losses. With the remaining men, they began to build their tents all over again. Some with Zenna went to hunt for foods in the forest. The Island was never inhabited by any one. The sun shone out bright with sort of calmer bless. There was no sign of danger that signaled. Up in the sky, the White Sea Gulls restore their habits to fly. Nicholas Cook was in the ship, searching for the map. There were few liquor left behind under the deck. He brought them down. By noon, the place was back to normal. The sand dunes were dried. The heat of the sun kept the atmosphere burning. Under the influence of soft breeze from the ocean it kept however balance with the temperature.

"How long we're gonna stay?" Jack conversed.

"We need to restore with food. We can't go hungry the whole way. We've long way to reach" Nicholas said, as he opened the map route.

Jack shook his head and joined his mob in helping to fix the tents. By sunset, Zenna returned with her crew from hunt. They mostly had dead animals carried by each one of them.

Their night wouldn't go wasted that means, they would likely to spent the night with the mixed feeling of losing the rest and rejoice for those who survived. They began to prepare fire to roast the animals. The day ended with no sign of warning. But as the climatic condition suggested it wasn't the same again. It was pretty much clear sky with no whined of drastic winds. Nicholas arrived with the cases of liquor. He joined with the rest. He looked at everyone, it was countable number. He lamented over the loss of his men. The pain could be visible on his face.

"Are you okay?" Jack proceeded.

Nicholas took the glass of his liquor from his hand. Everyone had their glass of drinks in their hand.

"To this day, we mourn for those who gave their lives and we rejoice for those who survived" Jack made the toast.

The whole of the shore smelled out of those roasted meat. There was the clear night sky with stars twinkling. Nicholas looked up to feel the notion of being in solitude.

"There couldn't be any better than our survival" Zenna muttered.

She added by his side. There was no response from Nicholas for at least a minute. He kept gazing at the starlit night. When he was satisfied with his hearty attributes, he turned to look at her.

"My dad used to pick a shape for me when I was a kid. I never knew, how he did that with those stars. It's been long time I haven't remembered him. You know I was a bad kid" he said very effusively.

She breathed out and had the affectionate look at him. The silence stood for moment of time. The small waves touched them.

"Captain, the roast is ready sire" said one of the crew.

"C'mon let's join them" Zenna squinted.

They walked back to join the rest of the people. The music, dances, and rum were all out in one show. Such part of life could only be lived in one life of time. All looked severely happy to survive the storm but to those who couldn't make it made them felt insecure about it. The past couldn't be undone.

The party ended at deep midnight when their liquor finished consuming. However, the night stayed silent and peaceful along the Island. No sort of destructive arrival was felt. The crew had the best night of survival with peaceful dreams. In the next morning, it's the change of time. Nicholas Cook along the shore watched at the vast ocean. He had the old fashioned binocular in his hand. He stretched it out to look for the distance ocean. By far, miles away he found no object. It was only their herd along the Island. He collapsed it back.

"Did you get any sight" from behind said Zenna.

"Nope" he said and pulled his cigar.

"What do we do now?"

"Take some men and hunt. Fill the ship with foods." he ordered.

"Right"

Zenna followed out on her way, collecting few men for hunting in the forest. They climbed up through the clip reaching the other side of the Island. It's just the opposite on the other. Seeing the area, they were over drown with the captivating site, it made them spell bound with magical assert to let their mind in delusion. They got the belief there must be treasure hidden in the Island. The white sand dunes even made more comfortable to walk around the place. It was most captivating site they had been under. The fact, that was readable they actually had forgotten they were on hunt in the forest. Instead, they began to explore the site with greatest mystery.

"There must be treasure hidden on the Island" Zenna muttered.

The rest of her mob shook their heads. It's been after an hour that the realization had come on her mind about the hunting job. While the rest still under the influence of holographic dream.

"Let's move out of this place" she commanded.

They followed the path toward the deep forest. There was nothing that she could think about then. All it had to do was the treasure that she had realized. Somehow they did the hunting job. By sunset, they returned back. Nicholas was right at the edge of the water puffing his cigar in. The twilight was sinking below the horizon. He watched it deeply from his corner of his eye. It seemed fascinating with those kinds of colors that came out from the edge of the setting sun. He was intricately interrupted by her.

"So, you're back" he said.

Zenna shook her head wanting to say much more than what she had seen along the other side of the Island.

"I believe there's something more than what we observe on this Island" she said, intrigue voice.

"What do you mean?"

"I mean we should go look out for it. The other side it's just the opposite of this side" she seemed provocative.

"Oh! C'mon Zenna what could be more else here on this isolated Island, where you find no human settlements".

She wasn't able to bring that intrigued urge into him. Yet, she hasn't felt bad about it because somehow she was quite sure about the secrecy about the Island.

"There's a treasure out there?" she said with surety.

The fuzzy confused looked expelled out of Nicholas's face. He wasn't to believe; *could that be really true*. However, his face could be read with the evolved interest upon it. He wanted to be appropriate about the site. So, Nicholas finally merged with a thought to hunt for the treasure. He decided, he along with his men would visit the site the next morning.

Chapter Thirteen

I had toured the little of the town with dad on the early week Sunday. Over the whole week, there was constant call from Lexie and Jessy regarding the prom preparations. The prom was just a week away from then. Neither, Alyward did actually ask me for. I wasn't expecting so, stayed silent for the whole preparations week. On early Wednesday morning, he came to pick me up for the school. It's been almost a week, after I was actually going back to class.

"Hey, my mermaid queen" he addressed.

"Please don't" I chuckled.

He opened the door. I sat by his side and drove along the way. After a minute silence, he broke the quietness around.

"So, are you ready for the prom?"

I giggled "Are you serious?"

"I guess I'm"

"I'm not sure" I added.

"I'll pick you up on the event day" he said flawlessly.

I gave my desperate keen look toward him. We reached the parking lot. I had the sight of the rest. At the main building entrance, Lexie and Jessy were with the mob, discussing about the event. When we reached the spot, Lexie was the first to notice us. She called us to join them, but Alyward's intention wasn't that favorable toward them. He ignored instead, he moved straight forward to the class. Somehow with gesture, I had to mention sorry to them. She quite understood well, as she observed Alyward's disapproval face. She gave a brief smile to me. I followed him toward the section. We had Nash Billy's class the morning. After attending the session, we opted to move out of the premise toward the beach. We haven't visited anyone before we left the school campus. Thereby we skipped the rest of the period. Not because we intended to do so, I was in great need to heal up myself from my weakness that I was going through for the last few weeks. I needed to feel the water under and transform myself with my will to gather more powerful life than ever before. It's the only thing that gave me ocean of mind and healing ability to process myself with emotions and feelings. He never knew that transforming myself into mermaid gave me strength. The parking lot stood isolated, fortunately we weren't seen by anyone around. He drove the car quickly out of the school premise. We were on the damp road running toward the open space of meadows that led toward the beach road. The last night there were small drops of dew fallen but the cold was stable with its firm temperature. The whole way stood empty and the morning born out from the east. It just took half an hour to reach the beach shore. But the belief couldn't stand upon us. The thought never came up to witness something unusual today. As Alyward parked his car, there was the feel of something devastating approach from the edge of the shore. The wind began to blow wildly around the beach. It sprayed the sand into the air with great speed.

"I guess we should go back. This storm won't let you" he mumbled.

I wasn't sure if that was really a storm to hit the shore. I gave a thought to my conscious perhaps, I would like to check it out by going. Somehow, I felt the courage inside me to take the step out of the car. Before I did that, I looked at him once, with sudden fury of miscalculation on my face. The doubt roused in me it couldn't be storm, it was something else that was playing the shore.

"I need to get out" I urged firmly.

"You gonna hurt yourself, Anna" he said being cautious.

I didn't wind up with him instead, I followed out of the car and began to shuffle ahead. After few steps, Alwyard followed me. I waited for him until we got together. The splash of water along the edge, hit the shoreline with greater force than even before. Even winds, syopped us back from moving forward. After witnessing the dramatic natural phenomena, the waves along the ocean began to rise higher. Alyward saw it first. He was stunned by the scene. He disbelieved about what he was witnessing. I began to realized, the beach was empty. It could only be Tyler, the lone person, who was involved. After few more steps, the waves were actually rose higher by now. It fell on the water surface with thrust bringing the huge splash of water outside. It hit us with force but we could withstand. My sight grew more effective in course of time. Due to the spray of sands in the air, we couldn't able to view the way clearly. But as we marched ahead, I had the figure reflected before my eyes. And then there was Tyler along the edge of the shore. He was creating the huge monster waves, and those the sea creatures began to fierce with fear to save their lives. He was playing with his power or I could read out the intention about his action that he was up to. He built the ice sheet of bridge over the ocean surface and took his step to walk on that. He could control the whole ocean in his hand. He could destroy it with no mercy.

"This is insane" Alyward whispered behind me.

"We should go back" I focused at him.

I held his hand pulled out of the place toward the car. He couldn't believe what he saw.

"Who is he?"

"I'll tell you later. Let's get out"

He started the car. The engine sound reached to Tyler's ear. He turned to look toward our direction. He saw us, yet there was no such reaction of fury from his side. We rushed to vacant the place without further ado. I felt guilty about the fact that Alyward was with me. *I shouldn't have come along with him.* Now that long explanation would have to be provided. He knew that was Tyler. He saw his face with utter amazed.

"Man, this is gross. I don't know what I'm seeing but…"

"Everything will be clear" I assured.

He drove at very high speed. There was no chance that I could go back home. I needed to halt at Alyward's home for few hours. We swept away very quickly to reach his home.

"Now will you explain me; what's Tyler is kind of?" he demanded.

He opened the door and got inside. I followed behind him. He opened up the curtains of the window and let the light penetrate in.

"He's a *Demi God*" I said.

He looked at me with unsure face. But he was frightened to know that. He felt little disregarded with the kind of people he was with. He drank a glass of water to quench his dry throat.

"Is he always like that?"

"No…I don't know" I answered.

He came toward me and leaned against the window frame. He wasn't in state to talk about the stuff anymore. There was no kind of curiosity that emerged from him. I glanced at him briefly and looked out of the window to view the outside atmosphere.

"I'm sorry I lied to you about him" I spoke softly.

He shook his head and looked in my direction outside the window. There the coverage of silence for long time. Because, he never knew what he could do or what else could have done.

"He's got lot of power".

"Yeah!!! But he learned to control them" I ensured.

"I can't believe the whole damn thing. Firstly, you're a mermaid and then him, a *Demi God. Am I the only human here*?"

I got close to him and stared in his eyes. He looked startled and subtle with unfocussed mind and thought. I could read the chained fear that took birth on his face.

"You don't have to fear about him" I encouraged.

"What am I supposed to do now?"

"You have more power than him. You can control him; you can take over his mind"

"We're not enemy neither we're friend. But the truth is we don't like each other"

I stayed silent for seconds. I felt the breeze that slit in through the window. There was the sign of a bad day that pictured out of my mind.

"And I believe the days ahead are going to be the worst days ever. I can see that, there will be battle of bloods and savior" he said again.

"I won't let that happen" I sighed

"You can't Anna. You can't stop what's going to happen" Alyward was too firm in his words.

"I should leave home" I urged.

He shook his head and agreed to drop me back. The whole

way we haven't talked about anything. What rumbled in my head was how I shall have to deal with both? In an abrupt notion the phone rang up. I rummaged in my bag. It was a call from dad. I took it and informed about my return. The daylight was still outshining. He stopped the car at the gate.

"I'll see you later" I said and got out.

He watched me going in. Dad was early at home. I gave a brief smile before I went to my room. I felt exhausted with terrible day I had. I needed to meet up Tyler. For he knew it was me at the beach. He might have that false thought regarding me, which I wouldn't want to stir with no cause. The truth was he was in love with me, I knew that. He could go to any extent if that was the case. But I don't want to lose him for he had been my best friend in the whole town. The day ended with me, seated on the chair with those grueling thought in my mind. I closed the window to avoid the incoming of cold winds. Dad was in the kitchen. I decided to join him at least to compensate and free out my tired mind. I never said dad, about Alyward much. He just knew him as a gentle guy. But his nature as Clairvoyant wasn't revealed to him. No matter what could be the truth someday, it had to be out before him. And about Tyler perhaps, he knew them very well. Amongst us, dad was only the pure human who had associated with us all. I saw him grinding the pieces of onion to curve for gravy.

"Dad, aren't you afraid of Burney Gaige?"

He looked at me with sudden surprise face. Something, he wasn't expecting to hear. He took a breath, before he spoke about it.

"You mean to say I know nothing about them"

Dad knew about them. He knew they were *Demi Gods*. But, he never opened the topic regarding them. He sat on the chair.

"Why didn't you tell me before?" I inquired.

"I just wanted you to discover it"

"Why so?"

"That's because you wouldn't believe me, if I said that. But now you do"

The dinner was made and he served on the table. I helped him with few of his kitchen stuff. Gradually, I learned about the kitchen management. We sat for dinner together. I wanted to tell him about the incident that occurred at the beach. But I wasn't sure if I should say that. Without further thought of issue, I burst out to talk about the incident. But before that I wanted that dad should know about Alyward's real nature.

"Does Alyward got parents?" that came suddenly from dad.

"Huhh!!!!!... he lives alone" I muttered.

Dad found it curious to know that. He smiled a bit looking at me. He grabbed the spoon and began to eat the dinner.

"It must have been hard for him" he said again.

"He's different dad. I need you to know one thing about him".

"Yeah…go ahead" he said.

"He's a Clairvoyant"

He stared at me and took his soup. He shook his head a little and turned to looked at me again.

"Why you making it sound odd. That's the ability. Something unique in human" he added.

That kind of quest indeed made me happy to hear. There was nothing problem from him indeed he made it sound quite common of such people. I began to add my dinner with him. I wanted to burst out the incident that happened. Likewise, I needed to know how should I let him know about that.

"Dad, you know there's a lot of trouble these days going on at the beach"

"Yeah I heard about that"

"Well, today, we witnessed something that shouldn't be"

"What you mean by that?" he stressed.

"I mean, Alyward and I saw Tyler there. He was ferocious and danger too"

Dad gave up a thought on that. He wasn't in state to hear any further more. So realizing the situation, I stopped narrating. After the dinner, he was inside his working room. Through the clit of the door, I saw his desk cluttered with files. It was the last time I had seen the same way. I went to my room. I never thought so about Tyler that he would appear to be such someday. Something I wouldn't much appreciate if he was doing just to show out his frustration. That wouldn't be appropriate if he ever liked me as one of his own. The whole damn thing began only to protect me from Alyward. Well, to me Alyward wasn't the hell of monster but in truth the softest part that I ever felt in my life was from him. Considering Tyler, as the best friend had grown something more big into an issue of heart. That it turned into love. *When did it happen to him, I wasn't aware about.* But things have changed now, and it had become more complicated than ever before. Solving would be a bigger problem than to find the solutions. Instead, I opted it should be the same without any further amendment between us.

Tyler would never hurt me. But the bond between both will stay detached however the subject of concern would be the same. I being the subject in their life had lot of importance for both. I couldn't break any one of their hearts. I wouldn't want them to dismay though. But choices will lead me the way. At the end, what would matter will be my heart to listen. I slept the night without giving much thought over the rest part of my troubled life. I felt relax when morning broke in. I tried to forget about the past day. I walked toward the window and pulled the curtain letting the sunny light penetrate in. And as I did the same, to my utter clearance, I found Tyler right at the front yard. He was in conversation with dad. I opted to climb down to catch them up. I wouldn't be going to school until the day of prom. But I remembered Alyward would come to pick me up. I would disagree if he did that.

"Hey" I signaled at them.

Tyler flashed a smile and came forward to me. He embraced me tightly.

"I missed you so much" he said.

Dad was ready to leave the home. He got inside his car. He looked great in his uniform.

"You kids enjoy your day" he said and drove out.

"Thanks dad, take care"

We walked in and, took the sofa. I switched on the television with a program. The news channels happen to broadcast about the hurricane that slashed away the whole of town in Southern America.

"That's too pathetic to watch people dying" I said and changed the channel.

Tyler added with me by my side. He looked refreshed with his same eye color. But something had changed about him which I didn't notice. He had his hair cut in short. It matched on him very smartly.

"How's your school going?" he asked.

"Pretty good" I said and went to get the breakfast for both.

"Who's your partner for the prom?"

I wasn't expecting that, it troubled me to answer that accurately. I stayed silence for seconds. I handled the plates out from the kitchen and joined him back.

"Aren't you going to prom?" he asked again.

"I don't know" I said casually.

I offered him with the breakfast plate which he calmly took from me. He retrieved back to watch the television. There was no process of talking activity for a while, engrossed with the movie ahead on the screen.

"Didn't he ask you?"

Tyler never stopped asking question about that. I saw his envious face that flashed out. He wasn't that easy to look at. *Perhaps, my kind nature toward him may end very soon.* I didn't say anything though. My patience seemed yet acceptable.

"You both saw me the other day"

"We weren't expecting you there. Coincidently you happen to be at the right place in our right time" I said.

"We can't be friends anymore Anna; you know that" he uttered.

"Don't say that"

He stood from his posture and went out of the room. I followed him the way. He stopped in the middle of the yard.

"What's wrong?" I intended to know.

He turned toward me. His face gave the incoherent expression. He seemed to have lost his inner touch of his mind. He looked angry though it was feasible to find out. He seemed unsatisfied and desolate.

"What's wrong…everything's wrong here" he raised his voice.

"What do you want?" I demanded hard.

"Just because you're being nice to me, it won't mean you like me. He's right for you, right. The Clairvoyant guy"

I felt it harsh and insecure. The silence whirled for a moment.

There was no excerpt of words to be spoken about. It melted me inside with great endurance and pathetic feeling.

"We can't be friends anymore" he said, and speeded out fast.

"Tyler, Tyler……" I called.

He didn't look back. I felt guilty about it. I didn't mean to hurt him. I had no choice whom to listen. It made me feel discomfort and isolated without a friend. I broke on my knee at the same place with my hand regretting on my head. It wasn't that easy to explain him. The complicacy was difficult to make him understand. He wouldn't come back, I knew that. He was firm and dedicated in whatever he said. I walked in with some guilt of bad feeling. I switch off the television and went up to my room. I tried calling Lexie, but from the other end I had no choice then to leave a message for her. I wanted her to visit my home the evening. Everything began to get messed up. All appeared unsettled and cluttered like the desk of my dad.

By evening dad was back at home. I was waiting for him at the front yard. I made fire as the winter cold caught roughly within these few weeks. He stopped the car and parked inside the garage. I had the glass of wine on the table. I carried few books out of my room to spend the time in much better condition. The morning wasn't that good. Tyler was gone. And I didn't want any more to mess up things for bad at least.

"Are you okay?" dad joined me.

He placed few more woods into the fire to turn it more vigorous. I handed him the wine. He saw me reading the book without muttering any word even his thorough concern. He poured the wine for himself and opened his gloves to warm his palms. Then he shook me with some regard of response from me.

"I'm fine dad" I said and closed the book.

The smoke rose higher into the sky but the mist often blocked their way up. I looked up, there were no stars or moon seen above.

"How was your day?" I asked.

"It's the same, nothing new" he said sipping his wine.

I wanted to spend the week with dad. The prom was arriving this weekend. So till then I would spend the time with my dad. I only hoped that Alyward would show me up on that day. After spending about an hour outside, we ultimately got inside the house. Dad talked about his last visit to Bakersfield. I heard him saying about the people out there. We shared the dinner together. Straight after that he went to sleep. I thought to watch television but it pushed me out of interest. I went up to my room and grabbed the book I was reading. I pretty much grew to be a book worm within the week. Lexie called me up. She was very excited about the upcoming prom night. She told me, she had found a guy who would love to come with her. Precisely, she found boyfriend I assumed. We talked for long minutes. I asked about Jessy, she was coming with Peter Pho. That surprised me. I wondered how they had gotten so closed. But that was good to know. We hung the phone with that long conversation. I couldn't even surf the internet for the last one month. I needed a new modem. I had told the services to get me a new one. I got back on my bed with the book. I resumed from the page. After reading up to fifty pages, I was finally asleep.

I wanted to join dad the next morning. He wasn't willing to take me with him.

"What you gonna do there?" he asked.

"I'll just watch and read books"

"Oh!! dear you gonna get bore. I'll have to be busy with my work" he replied.

"I'll be fine dad"

"Really" he smiled "get yourself ready".

I got myself readied and prepared with my attire to come along with him.

"Any new adventures today?" I asked being intrigued.

"Well, I'll have to look for it"

 I got inside his police car. Of course, being in a police car it had different kind of feeling. I enjoyed riding with my dad. It made me feel very important person. We drove through the town area. We came across the beach too. I keenly looked at the sides. People began to crowd in. I gazed through the window as we passed through the way.

"It never looked empty" I said.

"Yeah!!…it's always crowded"

The spot where the ship was anchored was passed behind. I turned to look back through the glass. I carried few water bottles in my bag and few pancakes that wrapped in paper. I brought few for dad too.

"Where are we going?" I happened to ask.

"Bakersfield"

That gave me the joy of mind inside. He really made my day. I was lucky to join him. That's why I love the service of being a police. We get to visit new places.

"Really"

"Yup!!…I've a friend there" he said steering the wheel.

The day was yet to bloom out in bright light. The constant coverage of fog along the way made it even more exciting for the long drive. But, as we moved more interior toward the state the cold grew severe. It took us hours to reach Bakersfield. I had no watch in my wrist so basically I had no idea about the time. I tried to make out seeing the day. The cold caught me in an instant. I covered myself with the fur that I had carried with me. Dad was on his thick jacket. After travelling for an hour, we halted at roadside inn. The very moment I got outside the car, I felt the sudden blow of cold breeze that shivered my spines. *It's damn cold to walk outside* I felt the cramp on my body. I followed dad.

"You can take some hot tea" he said.

"Yeah!!!" I said plainly.

I looked around the place. Few meters away there was bunker I noticed. I gazed at it with lots of interest.

"What's that?" I intended to ask.

"That's a bunker. It's for the soldiers" dad replied.

But I could see no soldier out there. I ignored the rest to know instead, I followed dad inside the inn. We were served with ginger red hot tea. The smell obviously had a strong effect on nose. Under such phenomenal condition of weather, it was hard to chase with the kind of menu to be taken. I wasn't in position to take anything apart from the tea. Dad asked for himself few toast and French fries. I just had the intention to consume little less than him. So for me the French fires were enough.

"So, are you enjoying the weather?" dad talked, he sprayed the sauce on his plate.

"You're talking about the cold" I squished.

"I guess I'm" he said taking a bite of his toast.

"I don't fantasize cold very much, slightly allergic to the weather" I said sipping the tea.

I felt the warmth and the taste of ginger in my throat. It relaxed me for a bit but it wasn't that to beat the cold outside. However, it refreshed me with strong content of energy that emerged out. After the breakfast, we moved out of the place shortly. The last thing that I could carry from the inn was water bottle. My dad was driving again.

"What your friend does?"

"He's just like me. He works in a private security firm"

I shook my head and looked out through the window. The weather wouldn't change much I realized that, above the clouds hovered with cold of mist carried in the air. And I could barely bear the cold so smoothly. I never knew, how dad did that. The way stretched over the long line of coverage of tall trees. I could slightly hint to remember about my last visit with Alwyard. It wasn't the same situation, of course it's the last summer. After sitting in the damn car for at least about six hours we were finally in the town. We passed the restaurant, the same restaurant where Alyward once had brought me. We headed to dad's friend home. It's small town, in lesser population. He finally stopped the car and blew the horn. From the gate, a man came out to welcome. He wasn't like dad, much older than his age and looked yet strong. His hair almost gone only remaining portion along the edges of his head, those too were turned white. He seemed pleased to have us. He cluttered his voice in welcoming tone. Dad got out of the car and they both hugged each other in much like giving the impression they were school friends. I got out of the car after dad.

"Wiley, that's my daughter, Annabell"

He gave the same welcome gesture. We walked in to the house. The house seemed to be well furnished with the most specific design. Floors were very much reflective of light that fell on it. But it cramped me up with the cold. I shouldn't be like a hot creature. I barely have the ability of being a polar people to withstand freezing temperature. I should be able to face the cold being a mermaid. But that wasn't the case. My skin seemed to be sensitive with the outside atmosphere.

Often it troubled me, most of the time I had to be careful enough to be outside. That's why I loved covering myself with thick clothes. It protected the allergic feel on me. We had spent the whole day in the same town. I got to know lot about the town's people from Wiley. He lived alone deprived of any children. I felt pity on him. *How could an old man stay alone in such a big house*? It logically struck my mind. But then it seemed good, for he had no trouble that would surely to come in a family. We had the dinner with him before our returned. Even though I felt the time lazy, I couldn't complain of being in boredom, for it was my choice that I had come here with dad. I tried to enjoy myself in whatever way I could. It seemed it was just the smallest party that ever held on earth. Just the three of us, confined in a huge room with windows opened. Never felt it was a day even though after the windows were open. Only the feeling of cold breeze blowing inside could be felt. The constant coverage of fog around the area even made it more damped to hang around the town. I ignored to go out myself, although I knew dad would have given the key. We were supposed to return on that very day. Wiley prepared the dinner for us. It seemed the day passed away without any notice. Gradually, the darkness fell on. By the time we were on the dinner table it was half past eight. Returning back means another six hours of drive. That would be really exhaustible drive for me. And as the night slipped in, the chillness in the air grew much deeper. I felt the cold even more bitter and hard to bear. After the dinner was over, dad sat for few minutes with him to talk. I was outside, exploring the lawn. And I could see the neighbor's light glowing. I intended to look out through the window if I saw any human figure. Indeed, with much anticipation I found a middle aged lady coming out of the door. She had seen me, I figured that out.

"Hey there…. Is that your car?" she said looking at dad's car.

"Yeah!!...it's ours" I said

"Are you a cop?" she asked again leaning her hand on the railings of her veranda.

"No…my dad is" I gestured.

"So you're the Wiley's daughter" she said suspiciously.

"No…. I'm his visitor" I mumbled.

"Are you new in this town?"

"Yeah!!! Yeah" she never stopped querying.

However, it gave me little enthusiasm to talk to such middle aged lady. Dad and Wiley came out of the room. They saw me in conversation with the lady. Wiley had been her neighbor for the last twenty years.

"Hey Wiley…how you doing?" she asked.

"I'm doing good Helen" he said aloud.

So, accidently I've come to know her name. I was supposed to leave. They waited me at the car.

"It was nice to talk to you" I said.

"It was nice meeting you" Helen said.

"I'll have to go" I said and bade her bye.

She watched us from her veranda spreading the wet clothes to dry. So, finally we were moving out of the town. Wiley hugged me once and we parted once and for all. The weather hasn't changed and it will not until the next morning.

"Are you okay?" dad inquired controlling the steering wheel.

I looked at him and shook my head and leaned back to support my head. We drove along the lonely empty road. Up ahead no vehicle. It completely soaked with mist and fog. The visibility situation was not clear to watch front. I observed dad was having difficulty in driving the car. His vision slightly lacked.

"I can help you out" I said.

"No, that's fine. You go to sleep"

"Are you sure?" I said being more concern.

"Yeah" he said maintaining the speed under the fog light.

By the time, we reached home it was half past one. I slept for an hour in the car so there occurred a little chance I would be back to sleep again. Dad looked tired. Without waiting more time, he went to sleep. There was no call from any of my friends. I switched on the light and opened the window of my room. I let the chill breeze blow in. The room was exhausted with impure air. I let the fresh air come in. After I settled up the things, I grabbed a book and got myself up on my bed. It was 2:00am, I looked at the time. I pulled the table lamp close to read the book. By 3:00 am I fell asleep. Dad was out of the world, he seemed to be lost in his peaceful sleep. There was no noise of television downstairs. Even the howling of wolfs from the nearby forest had stopped. The silence of peaceful night prevailed all around the town. Outside, the freezing cold cramped the atmosphere almost the feel of an ice sheet cold smeared out. It was one of the bitter cold that the town had been experiencing over the past few years. I missed the heat for the last few months. But was helpless, couldn't go back to Arizona just to visit my old house. I never knew why dad sold the house else there would be an alternative to spend the winter. I knew the moment was gone for us to have the time of life back there. There was no reason going back to Arizona. The thought never came up on mind. And perhaps, it's just because the winter was too harsh on us. But the best thing that ever happened to me in this little town; I found the truth what love's all about. I felt it, I was living on it. That's one reason that gave me the meaning to my life. I got the real perspective what I was going to do with my life, and that I was never the like the others. I got the sole purpose to bring back mom in the family. Her protection of our kind was my first destined task I got. I never knew, if every morning would bring me the happiness around but with just the flow of hopes and feelings I got to move on. On the other hand, dad was my sole mighty purpose who always showed the way of motivation to be strong. We girls are very emotional and soft from inside. Further, being a mermaid, I had very different feel of my heart. Perhaps, it's even hard for any human mind to understand us. We mermaid are much more kind and emotional with feelings inside heart than any human. We get hurt very easily, we get dominated. Our kind need only care and love, pampered with hope and loving heart gives us the strength. Maybe, that's why dad never got angry on me. Alyward, I never saw him getting angry or frustrated. He seemed cool, calm and composed in his life. That nature got me more engrossed into him. *He knew how to love me.*

Chapter Fourteen

Nicholas Cook and his team couldn't find much about the treasure on their first attempt although they ought to go for the second time. The sun doomed below the edge of the ocean line. The fire woods were burnt and all gathered around them. The Island had been silent since the last storm. Nicholas Cook came out from his tent. He joined the crowd. Jack was seen busy roasting the leg piece of deer.

"That looks very mouth watering" Nicholas Cook uttered.

He walked toward the shore edge where Zenna stood watching the vast ocean under the moonlit night sky. She saw him beside her standing as he did.

"How are you Captain?" she initiated.

"We just have one day more" he added.

"I'm sure we will succeed tomorrow" she added firmly.

He shook his head "C'mon, they are waiting for the celebration".

She followed him adding up to the crowd. She was handed a glass of drink.

"We must not falter tomorrow. We're gonna make it. No matter, whatever we find in the Island, we carry with us. Enjoy" Nicholas Cook raised his glass.

The rest shouted showing the clouds of enthusiasm over the night.

"I fear we've to join the Caribbean Pirates" said Jack.

"If needed we will" said Nicholas, as they walked on.

"With these numbers of men we can't fight the mermaids" he added.

"You know nothing about them. They are magical creature, defeating them wouldn't be that easy I know that. But I've a plan, because every enemy does have some weak points in them".

"How will you do that?" Jack sounded keen.

"You the know Chief of Police daughter, we met at the bar".

"Well, I haven't met but just saw him" he interrupted.

"It doesn't matter. His daughter is one of such kind" Nicholas said sipping his glass "Get me another".

"So, then what's your plan"

"I'm sure she'll be there" Nicholas said.

The night passed on however, the brightness of the night sky kept glowing brighter. Nicholas Cook followed his way inside the tent. By midnight, they were all inside their respective tents. When the morning filtered out, they prepared to go for the venture to fulfill in finding the treasure.

The other side of the Island seemed to be pretty opposite than that of their side. After walking for miles through the cliffs and hills, Nicholas Cook along with his men planted their feet on the white sand dunes. All were given the best specific work in particular direction. Following out in different direction to find whatever they could. Zenna happened to lead her own team. Jack stayed back with Nicholas. The whole day was gone until by sunset, they rejoined back to club together. All in great despair and empty hand returned back. But it's after long wait, Zenna along with her team mates returned back to the shore. The day light ended by the time they showed up. And the ambience was allured with cool breeze that blew from the deep pacific. The swells of waves hit the shore edge. The gradual rise of moon was unleashing out from the clouds. The faint light began to cover the area. The patience seemed to get out of Nicholas's head. He wanted to leave without them. Momentarily, the voice interrupted them.

"We're sorry, we got late" said Zenna.

Seeing them carrying the iron boxes, there was the rise of some auspicious judgmental hope regarding the treasure. Nicholas keenly looked at them, his greed for the treasure slithered out on his face.

"We found these" said Zenna.

They dropped the boxes and gathered at one place.

"We carry them. There we shall reveal out" commanded Nicholas.

When they returned to their base shore, there was chant of joy amongst them. Fires were lighted all around to light the place. Above, the moon hovered with its milky glow. The iron boxes were held together at one place. It seemed the boxes were very strong and heavy to carry. It wasn't made just to store things but it was the hardest metal ever that it was made of. The boxes looked older than centuries.

"How old these could be?" Jack muttered.

"I never checked that" Zenna replied being very unconcerned.

Nicholas arrived to unseal the boxes. He ordered his men to break the locks. The hammers were strongly dropped with force on the locks. To break the safe, it wasn't the task of one man. When they opened up the four boxes, inside there was nothing more than black rust and dust that blew out. It wasn't the treasure inside that waited for them to unconcealed. The men cleaned up the surface and gradually it appeared with some content in it. They pulled them out of the huge metallic trunk. It looked heavy and strong. When they unsealed the bags, the display about the content was made. They found no treasure. No gold, no diamond or ruby that waited for them. Even ocean pearl wasn't the part of that trunk. All looked upset yet they explored the rests of the bags with hope to find something valuable. As they placed all the bags in row, they opened up in the open space. The moon light fell brightly on the Island. Although, it looked some kind of illegal activity was going there, they proceeded with other bags. There were few metallic shields and swords that were the part of their hunt.

"Gosh, these are weapons" Jack howled.

Nicholas Cook took a thorough look to the things. Zenna explored the rest. She found guns and bullets in the others. She was astonished. The guns weren't like the modern warfare types. It was modeled around in the nineteenth century.

"This looks too old to use" she said.

"We carry them along with us" Nicholas Cook blurted.

The crew was supposed to leave by next morning. Within the stay of a week in the Island, they have filled with the necessities that needed to survive for the rest of their final journey toward Virgin Island. At the edge to break the dawn, the horn blew in the ship. It's the alarm that warned them to prepare to leave toward the next destination. The tents were cropped down and packed and things were ultimately inside the ship by the rise of sun. Fortunately, the sign of storm wasn't the part of their willful journey. The havoc over the natural calamities stayed silent presenting them the best day to begin with their long term wish. The pirates boarded in the ship, it stood strong against those heavy weights of metal trunks.

"From here on, we aim at our destiny that's lying before us.

We'll follow the way that omen shall give us. Whatever evil we did, we leave them back on this Island. Be prepared to join the army. Be prepared to fight for our pride and strength" Nicholas Cook addressed.

"Turn the wheel and pull up the wind direction" shouted Jack.

They began to move out of the Island, running toward deep east from *Wollaston.* The sunlight spread out its bright day in the farthest part of the ocean. The rising of it from the horizon signified with the rise of hope into one's another mind. Nicholas Cook pulled out his old fashioned metallic binocular to look at the distant. He asked for the map to look at the direction. He stretched to look at the farthest point over the vast Ocean. He pointed few of his point over the map sheet. The *Falkland Island* stood few miles away from their location.

"Will we be stopping there?" Zenna claimed to know.

"No" he replied

The rest of the crew members were asked to mend the guns and the weapons they found. Everyone was specified with task on the ship to prepare themselves before anything disaster would arrive. Jack as always stood at the tip of the front deck of the ship. His vision stayed clear with focus over the stretching Ocean. The clear sky above with the glittering sunlight made their way very easy to move ahead toward east. The still waters in the middle of the ocean led them safely. Gradually, the atmosphere of the new incoming nature was felt. They were in the Atlantic by noon. That was good thing to them. They sailed smoothly without any obstacle.

"Captain, you said something about the girl" Jack walked off the deck.

"A girl" Zenna intruded her voice.

"Well, I didn't tell you all. Yes, the daughter of Chief of Police is not a pure human".

"Oh Gosh!!!" exclaimed Zenna.

She looked amazed and startled to believe the truth but she handled it with sense.

"We could have end her" she said again.

"Ending her along wouldn't bring anything to us. We need to destroy their whole kingdom under water" Nicholas sounded too determined.

Jack shook his head on his words, demanding to be realized his mission. The story was told to them. The plan was made, only they had to wait to execute.

"How this girl gonna help us to find them?" Jack squinted

"She don't know us we're their lives, she doesn't know we're the killer" said Nicholas.

Zenna was abducted by her thought. She had her opinion to be shared. After pausing for seconds, she muttered out with her decision regarding the plan.

"I'm not sure she's going to be in the Virgin Island" she added.

"She'll arrive to protect her mother"

"Mother, now what's the story" she needed explanation.

Nicholas took a deep breath before he opened up the long story of the past. The story kept them engaged and never knew they covered miles away from the Island. When they looked back there was no sign of land, the still water of the ocean influenced under the windy breeze. After he completed the story, Nicholas again pulled out his binocular to look for the direction. The ship speeded up with the flow of wind along the direction. Far across the horizon the ending twilight was visible. It's the arrival of end of day. The last intention to them was to cross the *Falkland Island* by sunset. After travelling through waters for hours, they felt the arrival of cold wind from deep Atlantic. Atlantic had histories about its weather nature. It's being considered one of the coldest Ocean on earth. Indeed, it was true to feel. At the darkest hour of the night, they finally got the sight of the Island. Few lights glowed as they passed along the edge of the shore. The Island had very few settlements.

"You can enjoy the rest until morning, provided no one shall be out of the ship" Nicholas Cook commanded.

They halted along the edge of the Island, some few meters away in deep section of the ocean. The ship was anchored with thick rope that kept it steady and stiff.

"These guns can bring us fortune" Jack said.

He had the gun displayed to Nicholas. He handed him to feel it. Nicholas looked at it carefully. He was obliged to have it in his hand.

"The Island wasn't a waste. These weapons will give us victory".

"Right Captain"

"Well, the dinner is ready" Zenna called for them.

Mom was seated in the dining table. The lunch was being served by Keren. She wasn't in great joy to feel about her life. She had the despair thought on her mind. She looked at the glass of water more in an inappropriate manner. Her eyes told more about fear than victory. Keren joined by her side with her plate with steak.

"Are you okay?"

"Yeah!!" she mumbled.

She pretended to take up the lunch with her. However, she seemed worried.

"You don't have to worry about Annabell. She'll be strictly fine and safe; I promise you" Keren filled with hope.

Mom shook her head and began to consume her lunch willfully. The silence fiddled in, there was only the sound of clunking spoon with the plates.

"What would you do if you were in my place?" mom asked.

"I never had a daughter Dora, and I suppose I may not be as strong as you are" she said.

After the lunch was over, mom was watching the news. The weather about the North Atlantic was depicted. As the scientist researched there could be tremendous storm arriving along the Islands in the ocean.

"I believe they would be here very soon!!" Keren spoke from behind.

"Oh! You scared me, Keren"

She joined and accompanied her. By sunset, they reserved to go to the beach. There couldn't be any better place than to spend around the beaches. Keren drove his antique Mercedes toward the beach. It wasn't full like any other day. And as the day was on its way to end, its obvious the beach was getting empty slowly. But, by the shore the beach bar and diners were open till late night. As the night would turn on, it wouldn't be a place for any families to hang around. It had the strict rule for all but during night young people were seen the most, especially teenage couples, who usually hang around through the shore. They were inside the bar. Mom ordered a drink. Keren had her favorite vodka shot. The music buzzed around. Everyone got out into the shore to shake their feet and hips.

"He looks hot. Why don't you just get to know him" Keren said.

"C'mon, I'm a mother for god sake".

She grinned. She walked off the bar, out into the shore to take part in crowded dance. Few minutes later mom joined her. They began the conversation as they moved feet.

"He's staring at you Dora" Keren said as she did her favorite step.

"Are you provoking me to hook up with that man?" mom grinned.

"No…I just asked you to get to know him" Keren added.

The music went louder and the beach wasn't anymore the empty place. As the show continued, crowd began to gather in numbers. Mom finally opted to talk to that man. Of course, he was stranger to her. But with due respect about Keren, she was willing to know him.

"Hi" said mom.

"Hello, I'm Shaun" he said.

"I'm Dora"

They both began to get engaged in conversation. Keren watched at them from the other corner of the crowd. Shaun had mom, held her hand to beat the music on the dancing sand floor. It was after an hour they both joined Keren, who was inside the open bar. She saw them approached toward her table. She smiled at them, as they walked in.

"Would you mind if we join?" said mom.

Keren shook her head willingly accepting their company. Mom gestured at her, thinking that she would add something in her words. She broadened her eyes at Keren, gesturing her face in some notion to continue with the conversation.

"Well Shaun, this is my friend, Keren" mom broke the silence.

"Hi" she said too quickly.

"Its' nice to meet you" he said.

"Would you like to have some drinks?" Keren added.

"Sure why not" said Shaun.

The night was at its deep time. Gradually, the crowd dispersed to get lesser in number. It was just the three of them still inside the bar. Realizing a lot later, Keren finally felt the need to get back home. Mom wasn't in complete sense. She drank too much. Somehow, Keren would have to carry her till the car.

"Well, I can drive you all" Shaun sounded too humble.

"No, thanks we'll be fine. I've my own car" Keren said.

It's the time to say goodbye to him. He was still there watching them both. Keren, did somehow carried mom till the car. She made her lay at the back seat, then searched for Shaun. He still waited for them to leave.

"It was nice to meet you Shaun. You're a good man. Goodnight" Keren applauded loud.

He gestured out through his eyes and smiled briefly. Keren drove the car out of the beach. Finally, they were back home through the lonely road. To say, mom was under controlled when she reached back home. She managed to get herself out of the car till the front door.

"Are you okay?" Keren concerned.

"Yes...indeed".

She opened the front door to get inside. Right at the couch she fell off her body helplessly. Keren sighed with a breath. She looked at her for seconds and escalated to help her out to take to her room.

"Oh! Gosh...what's your weight?"

Mom giggled and laughed out. Her eyes, browsed in drowsiness and the intoxicated effect still appeared on her face. Somehow, she managed to hold on her weight and placed on her bed.

"Goodnight Keren...and thanks for bringing me in" that was the last word mom said before she fell asleep.

Keren waded to her room. Its 1:00am when she entered her room. She glanced at the time once before she got herself settled in. Without giving further thought, she plunged in to her bed.

The silence in the morning could be one more reason that got them lazy on bed. Mom woke up, she began to walk out through the yard. She looked fine with last night hangover. Keren from the window noticed her. She added her up few minutes later. She had a cup of relaxing coffee held in her hand. She had carried for Dora.

"The morning is crystal clear" said mom.

She was handed by the coffee cup. Keren gazed up into the sky and saw the clouds clearing away from their position.

"Indeed...the light has reached us" she added.

"So, what do you think about Shaun?"

"What" mom giggled.

"Yeah" Keren raised her eye brows.

"No... way. I never gave such thought. For god sake, I'm a mother of a daughter".

"It's not what I meant. I mean to say you need someone to stay around you. It's just you could share few moments with him and feel the joy of being in a company" Keren sipped her coffee.

They reached the gate as they walked on the open yard. Then pull to turn back through the same way.

"Can't you stop discussing about him" mom ensured firmly.

Keren grinned and crooked a sound. She agreed not to do so. They walked back inside the house. Thinking to get the breakfast prepared. Mom switched on the television. She was watching the news headlines.

"Will you be okay with the milk?" said Keren from the kitchen.

"Yeah, sweetheart" said mom that was one way she addressed her to show affectionate feeling for her.

The day bloomed out, grazing the bright light through the yard. It's obvious they stayed away from human sight. So, basically they were miles away from human settlements. Adjacent to their home, the lake gave them ample of time to spend their afternoon. No one would be there to watch them. They could easily turn themselves into their original form. Likewise, that following noon, they had followed the same routine to spend the heat under the water. Keren got first into the water, she transformed into her mermaid form.

"C'mon jump in"

"Your tail looks very attractive" mom complimented on her.

Keren on joy of being in solitude life somersaulted on the water. I've never seen mermaid somersault. To be honest, I never thought about that. I never did, but I'd try once. It needed lot of strength at the tail to push yourself, high in the air. I lacked that strength yet. Mom undressed herself, she stood naked aside. Keren sighted her from the surface of the water.

"Wow…I'm sure Shaun wouldn't say no to you"

"Well, I don't give a damn on that" she said and jumped into the lake. And as she swam through the water she was on her marvelous form into a mermaid. She examined her fine body and added the company with her. Keren brought few drinks to hang around the place. They began to play around the confined area of lake, somersaulting and swimming cross the whole lake. Romancing around the water could be the multiple effects that would give the strength to them. Mom swam through the still water to get the drink. Just next to the lake the small uphill gave the panoramic view to withstand the heat of the day. However, the water in the lake was warm to apprehend the cold to control their body. Usually mermaids love to swim better in cold water. But, the mystery of the lake had something more to do. It gave the genuine effect that it meant for. During cold, it felt warm to be inside. The same goes during the summer giving the cold feeling.

Keren swam, splashing her tail smoothly on the water surface. She looked divine and marvelous on her appearance. Mom took the sip of the energy drink to regain her strength. She was asked by her to hand.

"What a beautiful day?" said mom.

"Someday, we shall climb the uphill to view the other side of it" Keren spoke.

She released her hand to swim again into the water. She asked Dora to join her again. The playful game began all over. The deeper they swam under water the more exotic they looked. The sun light reflected from their body that fell through the pores of water. It gave the shimmering effect like watching two mermaids playful and making the glow of love charmed amongst them. They whirled around forming the shape of ring, and the tails were the best part of it. It never looked it could be those two mermaids who lived with fear but it happened to be more cautious when they live on land. Under water, they seemed to be the most peaceful aquatic life, living the life of being in a heaven. But as we know, every creature does have life spam. Sometime, it's just the way they die or get victimized to their death. Often the fear would be from human. Like every sea creature, they are afraid of human, as like the mermaids are meant to be the same. The difference lies they have the power to transform to save themselves. It's the same method for all.

"Let's move up the surface" mom signaled.

Keren swam steadily so fast that the speed was tremendous to catch her. Mom followed her behind. She grabbed the drink and sipped in. When she got out on the surface, she found the gradual change in the weather. Perhaps, it's the call of strong current from the Caribbean. She noticed it with strong sight the wind arriving from the end of the uphill.

"I think we should get back" she uttered.

"Why?" that came from Keren.

"Look high up in the sky, the dark clouds began to cover the region"

"Alright" Keren agreed to do so.

She managed to scrawl out of the lake, and as she reached the land surface, her tail transformed back to human legs. Her body lost the shinning scales of coverage, and stood naked next to her clothes. She wrapped herself and completely dressed. That was quick. Mom got out of the lake.

"That wasn't pretty" said Keren in the direction of the harsh wind.

"It's gonna rain hard" mom added.

They walked back to home. Minutes later before they could settle their things, the whined of wind vigorously brought rain to the surface.

"This one bad thing living alongside coastal areas, we can't go out" Keren said, in dissatisfied manner.

Mom smiled and looked at her. They wrapped up themselves in warm clothes. Keren switched on the television and watched at the news.

"That's what I was talking in the morning" said mom.

She jerked up abruptly. It shook her spines with the sudden shock motion.

"You scared me" she admitted.

Mom was right behind her holding hot tea cup. She then gave another to her. Both sat up together cozily up the couch with warm quilts and began to wait for the end of the day, watching the television. The channel was changed and saddest movie was being played. The devastating storm arrived with strong force. It hit the roof with tremendous thrust. As they continued,

Keren moistened out in her most happy moment not because she was sad but the movie made her even more emotional.

"Are you crying?" mom said.

That was pathetic to see her cry, just because of the stupid love story. Mom gave the tissue paper to wipe her moistened eyes.

"You must be very emotional girl" mom said playfully.

She shook her head and looked at the direction to watch the movie. The rain hasn't stopped. And out through the window, the end of the day was clinching in with fresh air. The weather turned bitter cold with every single drop of heavy rains. Mom went in to prepare for the dinner. Later, Keren added herself in the company. The rain hadn't stopped the whole night. There was the influence of freezing cold outside. It wasn't easy to hold on only with those furs to keep warm. By nine, they sat together for the dinner. The hiss of wind was audible through the crack of the window. Keren escaped out to close the window. The storm didn't halt for the whole night. It couldn't be any other night to be well spent but in severe cold to held on with strong endurance.

Early next morning, the arrival of bright light through the fissure of the window brought hope to walk out of the room. Mom did the same, seeing the sunny side of the day. The silent and cool weather intently caught the intention of her. She felt good to be outside. The storm hasn't done any devastating destruction to the surroundings. All it changed out the weather to be more appropriately acceptable. Keren, joined later. Watching at their lake site, the water lever increased many inches. It was good observance to them. Indeed, it was the best thing they could receive naturally. They took a walk around the lake site that early morning. The uphill stood silent with smooth breeze passing through its edges. However, its steep edges looked smoother with fine slated floor. The last night rain washed away all the rough edges and stones that were hinged on it.

"The uphill looks smoother" Keren said in the direction of it.

Mom turned to look at the site. She was fascinated by the fact that she wanted to hike on the uphill on any holiday. She flashed a small pinch of satisfaction below her face.

"Wanna go hiking this weekend?" she added.

"Are you sure about that" Keren intrigued.

Mom shook her head and resumed to look at the uphill. The greenery flashed like the scattered pioneered color from heaven. It was best sight they could glance at early morning. The joy was felt with enthused mind and hope to watch at the open space of the nature. To be sure with the truth, mermaids loved open space than any confined and congested area. There was no sign of any vigilance that keenly observed. The safe and protected imbibe was felt with secure sense. Hence, to them it was always the best out of things they could hire to get on. It's been long term of their life, to stay in a secret spot. It wasn't known to any of human kind nor of their own. Living in isolation, away from all danger could be one motive that mermaid always felt secure among the rest of human kinds. We as mermaids crave for protection and safety. But if the case appeared to be opposite they could take any devastating step to fulfill their vengeance. When it comes to love and romance, we our kind seemed to specialized naturally. *We don't hurt the language of heart.* It's plainly understood in our nature. We, as soft kinds love to be hail and pampered with love and secure.

Just before the night of prom, Tyler showed up. That evening I wasn't planning exactly what I would look like at the show. But left undecided on whatever it could be. He joined us for the dinner. There was no serious conversation that I added with him. Frankly, I didn't want that too. On the dining table, we felt the silence for a while until dad broke his words.

"Are you ready with the prom?" dad sighted at me.

I gasped my breath, for I wasn't hoping the same. I hesitated. I smiled briefly before I pointed out with certainty.

"I don't know" I pressed my lips.

Tyler cornered his eyes toward me and passed the silent look in killer way. He had that unbeatable expression on his face.

"What are you thinking?" dad shook him.

"Nothing" he shrugged.

I felt the doubt that roused in him. That was observable through his eyes. He wouldn't like to watch me with Alyward. I didn't begin to say anything on par. I silently kept my spoon dealing with the dinner. After the dinner was over, there was the slight concern that grew on him. Dad went back to his working room. He got busy with his cluttered table. Tyler waited outside for my company. The weather outside was frenzy and cold. We walked the open yard for a while, feeling the brush of breeze over the skin.

"Are you coming tomorrow?" I asked.

"No…I guess I'm not" that was plainly direct from him.

"Is there any reason?"

"Do you think I would feel good watching you with your boyfriend?" he straightened.

The breeze violently patterned my hair. I browse through my hair, and settled them through the side of my ear. I considered for a second thought about what he meant by that.

"How does that supposed to make me feel?" I sounded soft.

"End of discussion…. I think I should go" Tyler in dispute thought.

I could read his face the jealousy and the arrogant hatred toward Alyward. Yet, it was something I couldn't able to hold on to bring the regardless solution. I can't be in love with two guys at one time. Neither the fact, that I could hate them both. They stood right in their own place. But somehow, my heart gave more weight toward Alyward. Nor I could ignore the crest of feeling for Tyler. I saw him walked away without any response of concern. He was heartbroken, I felt that. Most of the time, he visits the beach when something troubles him. He made the beach his second home where he plays with water and the huge swells of waves. I never knew, how it felt to be part of *Demi God's* life. It was more of a kind of having future with Alwyard.

I knew, where Tyler would be by tomorrow, hoping that he wouldn't be that violent with the world. He could do anything with his power. The beach would be empty except that he would be the one to control the ocean water. People who would witness would really sound like a freak. I felt guilty about the fact that I was still hiding my truth to him. Maybe I shouldn't anymore. It feared me about future option. I walked in to the house. I peeked through the door, dad was asleep by then. Without indulging to wake him up, I went upstairs. It was eleven past thirty minutes, I got back the modem few days earlier. I opted to serve the internet for a while. There was one message left from Alyward. He just ensured, he'd be here by evening the next day for the event to pick me up. After staying awake for a while I wasn't able to control myself. I slept the night. I rendered with a hope to bring the best day with exotic weather the next morning.

The air was enveloped with the smell of wintry fragrance. When I walked to watch outside through the window, the mist was gone and sunny side had fallen on the front yard. It brought smile on my face. Dad was shorting the long grasses with the machine, he waved at me happily. It's the kind of morning I always wanted to feel. I prepared to get down. I had seen the coffee mug on the table. I held it for myself. I walked through the smooth grasses through the yard and joined dad's company. He smiled at me at first point.

"Good morning".

"Morning dad…how was the night" I walked along his side, as he trimmed the grasses.

"Well, as usual. So, it's a special day for you" he added.

"I guess; it does become" I breathed out.

The shape of my breath air floated in the air as I watched coming out of my mouth. It's the effect of cold. I glanced to look outside the wall.

"When he's coming?"

"I guess by six" I added.

We continued with the conversation. I never talked to dad about the Virgin Island thing since the last time we had a conflict. I just had the heroic deed inside of me. And I needed the hand of Tyler for that. If I did that, at first let him know about my spectacular features of being a mermaid. Now that Alyward was aware about him, it could be easy to handle the situation regarding that. But when it comes to strength Tyler was far more superior then us. It would be unwise to go against him. To be honest, I never wanted to do so. All I needed to win his faith and trust. Knowing that he wouldn't go against me, but the rival between them would sometime be the agony to resolve. I gave a thought over that.

Chapter Fifteen

After dad completed trimming, we headed back inside. The breakfast was prepared beforehand. He wasn't going anywhere the day. We sat together for the breakfast. It was always the great feeling to have with him. But the saddest part it stood empty by mom. There was nothing, I could do to make things undo about the past. All about the day, I only had to wait till it was six. I spent the day watching movie alongside dad who kept himself busy on his cluttered table. The day bloomed bright as the time passed on. It was peace to be outside the bright sun. The yard looked even more fascinating to hang around. I received call from Lexie. We talked for an hour regarding the prom night. She found her partner. She was the kind of girl who seemed to be most excited about the event. I realized, the day was descending down toward the west. I looked the sinking rays that fell on the open yard. Dad has gone out to meet up his colleagues. Left alone was me at home. I'd be gone by the time he would return back home. I waited for him. In course of that, I received the message from Alyward. I felt the gleam on my face and hurried upstairs to be prepared.

And when the clock stroke six, right on time, I heard the bell rang. I prepared, I don't know how I looked, for the last time gave a glance to myself at the mirror. I was on blue, and it matched me with the color of my skin. I've never wore high heels that lifted me above the ground. I pondered if I would fit to walk on that, but gesture and intentions showed positive. And when I opened the door, there he stood on his black suit and bow on his shirt collar. I blinked my eyes ample times watching him decent and fashioned in that attire. I smiled at him, so soft to be felt that the same was from his side. He gave his hand. I placed gently on it, he grasped smoothly and we proceeded toward the car.

"You look graciously beautiful" he added.

"Thanks" I felt shy.

I've never wore such dress before. It was all my tight jeans and tops that were very much familiar to me. Shorts were my favorite ones. He opened the door for me. I gently got inside and sat gentle. Alyward from the other side took his way inside next to me. He geared the car and we moved out of the place. I could figure out the ending of the day, as the sky lining turned faint yellow from the twilight that covered the zone. I couldn't stop looking at him. He looked gorgeous and his eyes spoke diligently. I wasn't in state to believe to be in love with him. His golden blue eyes shimmer endlessly that captivated my sight.

"Why you looking at me like that?" he muttered.

It made me feel nervous for a while, so much alike to say an angel like guy would be asking me such.

"Nothing" I said seemingly.

He looked forward driving ahead. When we were at the front entrance of the parking lot, it wasn't something to be empty. It's literally crowded. It took few minutes to find space to park. I couldn't figure what the numbers could be inside. Everybody showed up. He gave his hand, I held his arm and gently walked on toward the entrance. The carpet way led us to the hall. Right at front way, the welcome gate was exquisitely decorated. We entered through the gate, it felt like the great welcome of important person. Inside the crowd was maintained. The music buzzed, and the floor was empty instantly. From the counter, Lexie roused her voice. I searched to look at. She came down to meet us.

"You look amazing" she said.

"You too" I added.

"Hi Alyward" she said.

"You look gorgeous" he complimented.

"Why don't you come around and see at the other things" she said.

I didn't know what she meant by those other things. We followed her that led to other side of open space. There in the green lit meadow, couples streaming out to dance with jazz.

"Would you like?" Alyward forwarded his hand.

Lexie left us after she showed the event. She had gone to join her man. I watched her going away with that flashy smile that threw on us. On the other hand, Alyward tending to persuade to get me on the dance floor.

"I'm not good at dance" I admitted.

He gestured too friendly I couldn't even bother to deny him. I placed my palm on his. He caught me and brought to the open side. The music was softly introduced. He caught me by my waist and the other firmly held. Our feet began to move in slow movement of steps. He was never the kind of fast dancer.

"I never knew mermaid would be so serene to look at" he fiddled.

"So, what special about Clairvoyant?" I reverted.

He smiled and felt our soul met each other so closely, that I couldn't even feel the cold breeze that was prevailed around. However, in that attire he looked in the kindest fashion.

"We aren't that good to people...they avoid" he glimpsed his eye toward me.

"I don't feel the same with you. In fact, I can't avoid you"

Our movement of feet continued as the music had changed. Within time few more couples were added to the group. From the other end, I had the sight of Lexie and his man approaching to the place. They joined along with us. As the time passed on the atmosphere allured in with the fresh peel of life that began to be felt. In his arm, I always felt the essence of existing in lively hood. And that majority of eye focused at him. He was flawless.

Love to me has grown over the years. Experiencing it in much hopeful way or to deserve to get what life supposed to give. For long time, we spent there, and the night gleamed bright with all kind of flooding lights from all side. I felt the warming cold, though the breeze blew smoothly brushing us. There was nothing that I would want to change about my life, *expect the unexpected* was the best that I could get from my life. Lexie and his man seemed very close to us. I smiled out over Alyward's shoulder peeking at them. She gave the friendly response in same manner. I could see his eyes glittered under the focus of light. And the more excited thing was I loved watching at his golden blue eyes. It had the magic of love in it. It wasn't a stare but a glimpse of light that I could possibly let go. When the music ended, we tend to stop and sit on the table that lay around. We walked out of the wooden floor and occupied by the side, watched the other couple's movement. The waiter arrived. He served us with the wine. Inside the hall, the buzz of dance music was heard, and even the noise level seemed high. That sort of gathering let everyone to get recognize and find new people to meet. That moment of time gave me the rebuilt thoughts; I was indulged for seconds, thinking about Tyler. I've seen his face the last day, he was truly broken from inside.

"What are you thinking at?" his voice shrilled softly.

There was the perplexed mixed of emotion that out surfaced on my face. I was still with no idea of where I was.

"Nothing" I stammered.

I sipped the whole glass of wine in once. That was absurd I knew. He looked shocked, his eyes stunned to see me.

"Are you okay? Do you want another?" he said.

I shook my head "yes".

The waiter arrived with another glass. He placed it before my eye. This time I tried to control my inner emotions. I picked the glass after long time. I knew I was silent. Alyward never mind that side of mine after all he talked less. When the dance was over, Lexie escorted us to the dining site. I was slightly controlled by the wine effect. I remembered five glasses of wine in my count. Never knew what for I did that. Yet, I pretended I was in sense. Alyward understood the fragile condition of mine. He, somehow supported me from all sides.

"You shouldn't be drinking much" He suggested, as we walked in to the dining hall.

"I'm sorry… you hate me right" I said, not serious but playfully.

He peeked at me and said nothing instead, he made me steady and occupied the table. We were served with the dinner. I could barely eat anything but the whole damn thing went wasted. After the dinner was over, we bade goodnight part to Lexie. I haven't seen Jessy and Peter's pair. They weren't available on our sight. We walked out through the open porch until the parking lot flashed before. It's flooded with varieties of car that one couldn't even imagine to look at the brands. Alyward clunk the door and let me inside. He was silent the whole way. What else he could have said. He wasn't the kind of guy who would get angry so easily. He flashed the headlights on and vacant the place immediately.

"I shouldn't have brought you here" he said, quite serious.

"Hey, I'm sorry, I ruined your evening" I admitted.

He said nothing instead, he pulled the gear and accelerated faster. Gradually, I was regaining my sense back out of the wine effect. I never drank so much before. At home, dad allowed me only just with one half-glass to intake with dinner. It's not daily basis just on certain occasional mood. Alyward braked the car at sudden motion. The whole way there was silence. I didn't realize, we were right at my front gate.

"Why you stopped?" I intended to know.

Then I glanced out of the glass. I got out of the car, and stood focused at him.

"Goodnight" he said softly.

He moved out quickly. He felt bad. I realized. I ruined his evening. That wasn't what I intended to do. I was lost in my got damn emotive thoughts and feelings. I made the gradual move toward the door. Dad saw me up, through the door glass. He opened the door. I tried to put the disinterest in talking about the event. He got the smell of wine rupturing out of me but avoided to comment on that. Instead, he allowed me to go upstairs in my room. He looked at me and breathed out.

"Get some rest" he sounded caring.

When I reached my bed, I sat thinking about the bad deeds in the event I committed. Somehow, I managed to pull out my clothes and changed into night dress. Beyond that I couldn't think of doing anything that night. I simply went to sleep without giving a thought about the day. When the next morning dawn arrived something was different in the nature. I glanced out through the window just to witness something I had been expecting. Tyler was with dad at the front yard. Seemed more involved with the garage repairing talk. I came down to join in their discussion. Tyler saw me at his first sight.

Dad turned just to know if I had a good sleep.

"I'm fine dad" I reassured.

"You look great" Tyler squinted.

"Would you mind if I join to help you all" I claimed.

"You want to work with us in the garage" dad simply said.

I shrugged and made my friendly face. We had breakfast before we could move on to the work. I skipped the school day, or more appropriately I wasn't sure if the school was open. I just remembered a week earlier that Lexie reminded me about it. The school would stand off for a week after the prom night. We began with the work. I learned few of the machinery parts about car from Tyler. I nearly forgot about the bike ride I had learnt. It's been long time I hadn't taken a ride of bike. Tyler felt comfortable with me though the reality of him was known to me. He never questioned about that. Neither, I did want to. But, underneath my heart I knew, I was lying to him about my nature in true of being a mermaid. But, he never had that single bit of raising doubt about me. He just knew me as plain human girl. We completed most of sore parts in cleaning dad's car and wearing out the torn ones. I had my truck needed with few of its part to repair. We decided to go after lunch. We halted to rest until the noon was overhead upon us. The weather had a clumsy feel of warm breeze that brushed through us. It was bearable with the cold thing, at least that day it was safe enough to walk around without fur.

At noon, we got inside the house for lunch. We had wonderful preparation on the table. The steak tempted me more than any other recipe that was laid. Dad poured wine to every glass, as Tyler opted to sit beside me. The clunking of spoon began to fiddle around, and in course of the process, there was the humming of sweet music that arrived from dad's working room. I loved the song and even if the silence prevailed at least the music kept us wondering.

"Thank you for coming by Tyler" dad solemnly said.

I looked up, out from the direction of plate. He shook his head, I saw him. He shyly glanced at me, flashed a brief smile. In regard to that, I attempted to stay silent. He understood that. After the lunch was over, we decided to halt for a bit. After half an hour, we were again at the garage. This time we were working on my Chevy. Gradually, the day drove toward West, I could watch the slanted shadow that fell on the ground. The twilight ended very soon, its winter and evening receive the hardest cold in the nature. After the work was over, we made bonfire. Dad from inside got the bottle of wine. For Tyler, he got a beer can. He joined by my side. The closeness that I felt with dad could never be expressed with my words. Indeed, he was the best dad I've ever got in life. Understanding the fact that he too worried about mom but he never flashed that out in open. After he handed the beer can to Tyler, he poured the wine for himself. He gestured me if I would like to try.

"We had a great day" he added.

I peeked at Tyler, for seconds he struggled to open the can. There was the silent blow of cold breeze that lingered around.

"How does beer taste?" I chuckled.

"Well, it's not sweet to taste. But it's hard to feel" he seemed kidding.

I didn't know what Tyler meant by saying hard, as I never wanted to taste though. We spent an hour and half with various talk. When the dinner was ready, we went inside escaping the wintry night. After the dinner was over, dad overtook his time in spending sometime inside his own den. Meanwhile, Tyler accompanied me with the fire outside that was still there. The thought struck me if I would try to reveal my truth. But, I was beeping in fear inside, *I might lose him if I say who am I.* The warm surrounding was felt, as the bonfire kept it pretty much accustomed. Tyler was just opposite to me seated on the ground. His hands wrapped his folded knee. For moment, I knew we wouldn't be talking.

"So, how's your dad health?" I said.

"He's doing well since last week".

Apart from the area where the bonfire stood burning, the darkness enveloped the area. I saw his bike parked at the entrance of the gate.

"Will you be going back?" I applied to know.

He shook his head "My dad will need me".

He turned more of a kind of saint silent type. Yet, he looked cherished with the kind of life he was living on. I didn't know our relation was more than that. It's more than we're friends.

"Hey, I've something to tell you" I struggled with the words.

"Yeah" he sounded cool.

I gave a thought momentarily whether it was right to let him know, what I was. Of course he deserved to know, I can't hide with a lie. He meant to me just like Alyward. He waited with a gaze at my face. I was lost into the sight of fire trending hard to look at it.

"You said, you're going to share something to me" he reminded.

I felt the jerk in sudden notion and turned to face him again. I gestured nodding my head.

"You have to believe me Tyler. I know, I lied to you but, I thought it's the right time that I should tell you now" I hindered.

He looked at me in conspicuous manner. I wasn't even ready to speak out. But seeing his eagerness, I felt comfortable with the situation. He made it easy for me.

"I'm not a human" I began.

He looked dazzled and startled yet prompted nothing. He sounded silent.

"Then who you are?" he murmured.

"I'm a mermaid"

He looked at me like he failed to believe the fact. His face soared out with undisputed controversial phenomena hearing the real truth about my life. He breathed out and gazed at me. It seemed, it made him discomfort with the truth that he bore to hear. Yet, there was no choice of prompt argument from him.

"So, it's all the crazy things been going on for the last few months" he said.

"You have to believe me Tyler" I ingested.

"Why did you lie to me?" he seemed to be yelling.

"Because, I didn't want to lose you"

"Does he know about it?" Tyler hopped his voice.

I shook my head "He was the first one to know about it".

"I can't believe you messed up the things, Anna".

"It's getting hard to trust you" he said again in dejecting tone.

"I was supposed to tell you" I incorporated.

"How am I gonna believe you that you are for real a mermaid girl?" his frisky angry tone.

I stayed without conveying the method to do so. However, I knew he would appreciate my legal action if I could really show him my real nature. He wanted a reply but under the current condition I could only assure him with my faith.

"You can come tomorrow at the beach" I prompted.

He breathed out, looked relax and shook his head remorsefully. Maybe, he was convinced by that.

"I should be going then; I'll see you around tomorrow" he promised.

I saw him walked toward his bike. He pulled the stand away and took his position to ride. When the headlight flashed out in great power momentarily it fell on me, as he turned the handle. For seconds, it made me go blind. Somehow, after the dilation of my pupil I was able to see him.

"Goodnight Tyler"

He once threw his glance at me and shook his head. He moved at quick speed. I threw the debris left into the fire and waited for it to get over. I looked at dad's room. The bulb was still glowing. But, I suspected he was asleep, as I could hear no sound of him cluttering on his table. Neither, he came out to add us. After the woods were over I got inside. I was right dad was asleep on the couch. I pulled the blanket to cover his body. I didn't bother to shift him on bed. He gleamed serenely and I least bother to disturb his sleep. I switched off the bulb and placed few of his files and pen on the table and walked upstairs. I tried surfing the internet searching for few books that I opted online. I had a tiresome day. Without further ado, I decided to go to bed. My bed seemed to be untidy. I tucked the bed sheets along the edges and folded all the unnecessary clothes. I was finally feeling the warmth of my blanket by 12:00 midnight. The last thing I remembered about the day, I revealed the truth to Tyler. To some extent, it gave me relaxation knowing that I wasn't hiding myself from any one now. It ensured me with secure feeling and trust on each other.

Dad was early when I heard him calling me down.

"Anna" he shouted.

"I'm up dad" I felt like yelling, for I felt the need of more sleep.

I hurried down and looked for him. He was in the kitchen preparing the breakfast. I grabbed the smell of toast and the bacon that being fired.

"What happen?"

"There's a letter for you on my table" dad pointed.

"Letter" unexpectedly I said.

I walked to his room, and yes it was for me. I saw my name on it but was wondering from whom it came. I flipped the envelope and read the name *Dora*. Dad didn't notice that. I held the letter and walked out of the room toward the front yard.

"From where did it come?" dad keened to know.

I ignored on his interest and followed out of the door. I unsealed the envelope. I took a seat on the log that was plainly kept unused.

Dear Annabell,

I know, I've hurt you both. But believe me my daughter, I wasn't to do so. Life kept me separated from you all and perhaps, I'm scared now if I'll ever be able to return to you all. Please understand my circumstances. I know I'm not even liable to ask you for forgiveness. I've just contacted you twice but please don't try to find me anymore. I'm doing this for you all. I don't want you and your dad should be victimized. All I'm concern is your safety and protection. I'll be the happiest mother on earth if I can sacrifice my life for my daughter and Husband. You were born to carry this legacy. Never think that I don't miss you all. It's because of you that I've been living my life, my daughter. Don't tell your dad he'll be heartbroken. He's softest person I've ever had in my life. He loves you very much. And I know he'll be very much in pain if he comes to know about me. I love your Dad, he's a good man, a good father and a wonderful husband. Please don't take my words too deep, all I wanted to convey and give my last word. Please don't come finding me. I love you both.

Yours Mom
Dora Cameron

I felt the tears rolling down through my cheek. I folded the letter back into the envelope. I was nervously stunned and felt the stiffness seated on the log. I only knew, what it felt like to get the cut in heart. My voice diminished, and I could speak none, all silent around and I knew, the worse phase clinching on me. Dad was calling loud from inside. He was done with the preparation of breakfast. I had the envelope held in my hand. When dad got fed up, he came out to look for me. Seeing me shedding with tears, he ran toward me.

"What's wrong?" he saw the letter in my hand.

He pulled out and began to read. After he was finished, he was dumbstruck or may be more than me. He stood helpless without strength on his body. I cared at that instant.

"Dad, are you okay?" I took position to hold him.

I took him inside. I felt his weight but more was the heaviness of his shattered heart. Somehow, I was trending to hold him tight and console. I made him seat on the couch. He looked dazzled and shattered perplexed with everything that came before him. Mom was right about him. Dad would be shattered into pieces. But, I tired myself in managing my traumatic feel to keep in control. The things wouldn't be the same again in our life, I could read the phase.

"Are you okay?" I concerned again.

This time he shook his head. But didn't speak instead, he rose from the couch and walked toward the dining table. He sat quietly, and he tried to learn the truth by now. I joined by his side. I poured the mango squash for him.

"You'll feel little better" I said.

He gleamed at me not in pure utterance to talk but his silence, showed much more than he would want to say. He took the glass gently from my hand and sipped in few amount. He felt his dry throat wetted by it.

"You can take your breakfast" he said lastly.

Saying so, he went to his room, I heard him closing the door. The letter was kept on the table, I collected back to keep it in a secret manner. I took a glass of the squash and headed upstairs to my room. I remembered the last night talk with Tyler. He would be expecting me any time. There were no messages from anyone I knew. I thought to skip the school all over again. It frightened me about dad. I needed to be at home at least for him. I knew, my grades would go down. I've never been that kind of studious student. I've always had my grades just above the passing level. Not the kind of brilliance opting for any higher university studies. I exactly had planned what my life was meant to be. When noon arrived, I went down. Dad was still inside, I forethought perhaps, he was doing well by then. I glanced at him through the crack of the door. He was working on his files all over again. It gave me sigh of relief for moment. I walked into the other room, and took the couch. I got the bowl of cornflakes mixed with the hot milk from the kitchen and began to watch reality show. When it was quarter past three, I heard the sound of whining bike. I looked out of the window pulling aside the curtain. Tyler was here. He pressed the door bell. I opened for him.

"Hey" he said.

"Come in"

He joined me. I offered him with soft drink that was left in the refrigerator. He wasn't the same alike like the last night. He seemed much more in willingness to know me better.

"So you skipped school"

"Yeah…I needed too" I said plainly.

"Where's your dad?" he inquired.

"Oh!!! He's inside with his files"

"Did you try your Chevy?"

"No…no…. not yet" I mumbled.

Dad came out from the room. I turned to look at him. He looked soared and there was the existence of rash spots on his skin. He slowly moved by an inch and took the sofa.

"Are you okay, dad?" I keened.

He nodded his head. I got off the couch and went to the kitchen to get something for him. He looked pale and disappointed.

"Are you ill, Sir?" Tyler asked.

"Yeah!!" dad's voice too weak.

I gave him the bowl of milk cornflakes along with the mango squash. The day was gradually moving to end. Tyler and I were supposed to leave for the beach. But what concerned me more was about dad.

"Dad will you be okay?" I made sure about it.

"Yeah!!! You both can go. I'll be fine here" he added confidently.

We moved out before the day ended. We took the ride toward the beach. My hand clasped him tightly as Tyler speeded the bike. That was long after I was actually riding bike. He was a great rider, I admitted as the air rushed through us. When were nearly at the beach. He braked and turned the wheel. I felt, I would fall on the ground as he made the drift. Fortunately, he was under control.

"Were you afraid?" he said.

"No"

He smiled and held me by my hand and walked on through the sand dunes. I could observe the twilight's end. Gradually, the shore appeared to be dispersed with people. We stopped at spot where he usually tests his power.

"How do you do that?" that came suddenly from him.

"What?"

"I mean; how do you turn into a mermaid?" his eagerness flashed out.

I grinned at him and looked at the ambience. It's silent, except that the swells were reaching the shore. It's calm weather and the waves roared very smoothly with the wind winnowing from the east.

"I trust you"

He shook his head. I felt reliable and secretive. He stood watching me with vigor mind set. I was undressed, naked and I could realize his throat dried off. He swallowed to handle himself. I walked toward the water and gradually into the deep. I turned to him before I plunged in the water. I swam deeper, my legs transformed and slowly my body took its shape. After reaching the distance, I moved out to the water surface. Tyler sighted me. He waved his hand at first. I called him once.

"You look amazing Anna" he shouted on his loud tone.

"Do you want to come in" I asked willfully.

He prepared himself as he began to outflow the water through his power. The waves began to grow at its height. I watched him like a scene of unrealistic phenomena. No human would believe he's a *God of Sea*. As the waves rose higher, he solidified and turned the form of bridge over the vast ocean. He stepped up. Like a surfing board, he began to slide his feet. As he moved, he pulled out the water from the surface, turning them to ice. That was how the path he created to skid over the rock ice sheets from the ocean water.

"Let's explore" he said.

I shook my head sighting at him from beneath. I plunged under water and began swimming. My tail had the fine movement, directing me all where. I seldom used my hand, everything I could manage using my body strength. He followed me in parallel. When the darkness began to crawl we were returning back to the shore from deep Ocean. The moon was edging out from the slit of mountains, and gradually the silver light began to focus on us. On reaching the shore, I dressed myself back. Tyler released his strength and the whole ocean was back to its original.

"You're truly different, and I'm sorry that I judged you wrong. It's crazy I know; I've never known the heart of a mermaid but with you I can feel everything" his voice engrossed effusively.

I breathed out directing into his eye. That brief smile flashed out of me. For no reason, I felt the moment great and memorable. I stayed silent browsing no thoughts.

"You know the truth now. Could we go?" I held his hand.

We walked on toward the bike.

"You get healed by water, do you?"

"Yeah!!..... I just have one treatment…that's water" he said.

He started the bike. I took my position behind him. And we galloped away from the site. Up above the silver glow followed us. It was the perfect moonlit night. And I reminisced over old moments as we speeded through the forest area. Half way through, dad called me. I assured him perfectly. As we neared to the house, from the gate I saw dad's room glowing. He must have been waiting for us. Tyler parked his bike inside.

"Hey! dad how was your evening" I asked.

He was seated watching television. Minutes later Tyler joined. I could smell the dinner he set for us on the table. He rose from the couch and joined for the dinner. After the dinner was over, Tyler left us early the night. I planned the next day to visit school. It's after long gap of vacation a week, I would be going back for education. I had seen Alyward on the prom night, the last time. Since that moment we weren't touch. Maybe, he had forgotten about the incident, I believed.

It's Monday morning. The beginning of new week always made me felt enthused about my days. I conceived about the whole weekend. I drove toward the parking lot of school premise. Alyward, as usual leaning his back on his car. He waited for someone. Of course, I didn't hope for me. And when I came out of my Chevy, he followed toward me. I clink the door, and right there he stood before me.

"I'm sorry about the prom night" he sounded apologetic.

There was nothing that I meant to say. It crumpled me with no hint of words what I shall express to him right then. But instead, I asked the favor from him.

"Could you do me a favor?"

We began to walk toward the section. Just so close to each other that, he almost brushed his white skin through my arm. At the main entrance, I found Lexie who seemed busy reading the winter schedule. She turned and casted glance on us.

"Hey!!! How was your weekend?"

"I had to work with dad in the garage" I added.

Alyward stood right behind me stiff, calm and composed. He pretended to be quiet. Lastly, he felt the need to join in our talk.

"How have you been Lexie?" he quested in.

"I'm good…. how are you Aly?" she talked.

"I'm fine"

"Well, meet you later" she said and walked to her direction.

"What favor you talking about?"

We reached the math section and stepped in to attend Nash Billy's class. He took his seat just next to me. I looked at him for once, foreseeing what could be the next in the process to attain my main objective.

"You know about my mother; she isn't here" I spoke.

He shook his head listening to me. Just then Nash arrived in the class. For an hour, we stopped discussing about the matter. When class got over, we spaced for time to ourselves. We arrived at the open space, the school garden. Under the shade of a tree we opted to rest as the warm day gave the feel of being in harmony of joy.

"I want you to help me to protect my mother" I added solemnly.

"How can I do that?"

Not sure but, he seemed very much obliged to know about it. Indeed, he felt privilege in doing so.

"I promise. I shall dispense my strength for the good cause" he added energetically.

We moved out of the place, headed toward the cafeteria. Lexie promised, she would join us for the lunch. Few minutes later, she joined us along. We had her order too. She looked greasy and slothful fashioned. She posted her smile as she walked through the door. She gently joined us, flavoring the silent quest.

"Any plan this weekend" she sounded too jolly.

"I guess not" my humble tone protruded.

She looked at Alyward. Almost shy, he was. He made a soft gesture to her. It looked indigestible to watch. He had always been famous secretly among the girls. He knew, what they are up to therefore, he never melted himself to be that friendly among the rest. When the lunch was over, we sought to return back home. We headed toward the parking lot. The day signed to end and as the evening engulfed in, the cold breeze slithered through the air. Lexie wanted to hitch with me. I never meant to be so mean. I began to feel the cold damping upon me. Alyward, stood right before his car.

"I'm sorry too about the prom night, I shouldn't have drunk too much" my voice soughed.

"That's fine" his catchy voice again.

He clunked the door and took control of the steering wheel. I waited for him.

"I'll see you around" he said and drove out of the place.

Lexie waited for me near the Chevy. She was busy on phone. She cut the call on my approach.

"Is he gone?"

"Yeah" I said.

I opened the door and fixed the key. She sat alongside me at the front seat. That was the first time she sat in my Chevy. Her face gleamed out under gloomy wintry light. We moved on through the lengthy forest covered area. The mist began to frozen out in the air as the darkness blanketed the atmosphere.

"It's comfortable Chevy" Lexie muttered.

"Dad's friend gave me as present"

She stopped by in our home that night. Dad was happy to see her back. Like always, we had a helping hand in preparing the dinner. The wintry night seemed absolutely unbearable. So unfortunate, it's the sudden change in the climate that led to the downfall of temperature below freezing point. And I could feel my feet hard enough to crouch on the floor. Maybe, it was the coldest night ever. I still had no thought, how the remaining days would pass. I waited for summer to arrive, in between I would feel the spring. Dad called when the dinner was prepared on the table. I was glad that Lexie was here with us. At least her presence never made dad feel lonely. Since the receipt of mom's letter, he always had been down. He hasn't gone to his work. Even I've never seen him on his cluttered table. He stopped working. And it did brought pain to him. I still had mom's letter with me. I've never opened since then.

I managed to pour out the wine to everyone. Dad limited himself to talk with people. Even his colleagues began to worry about him, as he remained absent for the whole week. But, he didn't mind for not working. He needed some space for himself. He never responded even the phone calls. Lexie sat beside him. She flashed a brief smile looking at him. I thought it lightened him for a while.

"Are you okay Mr. Cameron?" she said.

He shook his head improvising right to her. Then he approached to fiddle with the spoon. I cared to put forward the glass of wine to him. Dad willfully held the glass and sipped in. He felt the wetness of his throat which led him feel quite comfortable with the surrounding. He began to talk and like always, he tried forgetting about the past although in memory it haunted. After the dinner was over, we ought to walk out in the front yard. Somewhere at the corner of open space, we made fire to safe the winter cold. Dad looked very effusive at his outlook. Perhaps, he had something to tell. He gathered us around the fire. It's quarter past nine. And as usual the deep night would scribble, the cold would be bitter to withstand. The breeze soughed from west. As it passed the nature, it threw the wintry shadow. I made myself warm with heat.

"Do you want to listen to a story?" dad sounded interesting.

"Yeah" said Lexie, with keen interest reflecting on her face.

Dad began. We kept silent as the story began in horror. I've always heard mom telling the story but to me I began to feel the same with him. In fact, I started to like my life. *Sometimes, it may happen things may not turn in your favor yet to fulfill our needs we must keep the strength of hope and believe with us*. May be dad felt the same then. I realized a lot later that he had suffered a lot in bringing me up. And having mom in his life, it changed him in many ways. Perhaps, he never felt he was living with mermaid. But he seldom talked about those. Lexie seemed engrossingly interested in the story. I ignored to interrupt in between instead, I showed the same keenness. I saw dad how happy he was to share the story with us. As you know, I've grown listening to stories, so I could hold on to my patience. After an hour, I looked at the time. Its quarter past ten and, I could still smell the wet sand dunes that arrived with the winds. The fire still had the vigorous color to keep warm. And when dad suddenly ended the story there was momentarily a silence in the air. The winnowing of breeze could only be perceived.

"It was great" Lexie added slowly.

"I should go to bed" dad said.

He went inside. We waited for few more minutes. When the fire was almost over, we followed upstairs. Dad was asleep by the time we were inside the house. The next morning, I decided to go to the beach. Maybe I had the plan to call up Alyward. It wasn't my final routine though. In more like, I wanted his company at least to see his face. I would skip school for sure. I didn't want the rest to know about me in detail. The truth was supposed to conceal yet my destiny pulled with two guys. To them, I couldn't hide the reality. It was meant to share with them. And sharing means, it brought love to me. When morning dashingly arrived, the light focused on me. The curtains were aside. Lexie wasn't in the room. I floored my feet out of the bed and shuffled toward the window witnessing the gleaming yellow light reflecting from the front glass of my Chevy. I saw a shadow steady on the ground. The interest pulled me who could be that. From behind, dad flashed out of nowhere. I was still stiff watching out through the window. I saw a figure it's Lexie I was sure. I assumed may be Tyler was the shadow. I moved down to get myself clarified with the situation. I was right, Tyler was the shadow. He saw me from that distance coming toward them. His face gleamed hazily under the faint mist. I saw the friendly gesture talk that was carrying away between them.

"Hey!! Anna" he said.

Lexie turned to me, and flashed a brief smile. I felt the bright warm beginning of the day. I marched to them.

"Great to see you" I commented.

"You look great huh!!!"

Dad walked inside. He mentioned about the breakfast. So, we would be joining together at one table.

"So, you talked with him" I said cornering my eye to Lexie.

"Yeah!!! Your dad made it easy for us"

Tyler grinned "Well, his absence wouldn't have mattered though".

We had few conversations until dad called us inside. He had the breakfast prepared on the table. For some reason, he looked enthused. He told me he would love to join back to his duty. That was a good sign, I felt. He wouldn't have the time anymore to think about mom. That would probably give him the peace of mind. The table was well decorated with kind of food stuffs that I rarely found on the table. The plates of grapes, along with that had few green leafy vegetables.

The jug of mango shake looked tempting. At dad's end, the toast looked visibly hard with fried cheese upon it. Dad got out of the chair to get the cooked bacon. He placed it in the center of the table. Beside me was Lexie. I poured the mango shake for her. She had the sandwich untouched yet. Opposite to my side, Tyler whose plate was stocked with only French fries. Dad gave him the bread toast. It was the best homemade breakfast I ever tasted.

After breakfast was over, dad prepared himself to get to his office. He would be leaving us soon. Lexie, she would go to school but I decided to stay firm on my plan. I skipped going anywhere. Perhaps, I thought I would try to get the company from Tyler. When the day was almost on its edge to grow older, Lexie had left us for school. Tyler stayed behind. I haven't yet shared the plan with him.

"Would you like to go to the beach with me?" I said gesturing friendly.

He threw a local glimpse at me and smiled widened out.

"Okay" he agreed.

It's ten by then. We prepared to leave out. I had winter semester papers coming up. Within few weeks, the finals would be held. And here I was avoiding myself going to school rather, I took up the plan to visit the beach most of the time. Now that Tyler had no problem about me. Quite comfortable enough with a mermaid girl, his chivalry showed right. The next thing I had was to meet up *Jimmy*. Long time since I wasn't in touch with them. Of course, without them I wouldn't be able to execute my way to reach Virgin Island. Mom's letter brought me to halt in engaging myself in building my team. She didn't want us to find her. But, the zest will always stay with me to protect her at any cause.

It was just me under water that following noon. Tyler pretended to relax a bit along the shore. I had the chance to meet up *Jimmy*. We spent our time into deep side where the welcoming gala of dolphin's event was being held. The reason that human could train dolphin was because they are sensible enough to understand human language. We had the engaging time amongst us. And when I got out of the ocean water, along the shore, I found the wet sand dunes covering the whole area. There was outbreak of storm that easily caught up the place. Tyler was wet, under the tree waited for me. He screamed at my direction. I barely could hear what he was shouting. I marched in the direction and the winds rushed against me.

"We must go" he screamed again.

This time he was audible as I was closer to him.

"Right" I suggested.

He prepared to strike his bike. I took the position behind him and we galloped away through the heavy rain. Dad wasn't at home. The day began to slide down toward the west zone. However, the rain hasn't stopped yet. The chill cold began to slug in, catching hard on skin. We made fire inside the kitchen that kept us warm. I was on short with the transparent top. But the shawl covered me well. Tyler still could withstand the winter cold. He wasn't the kind of guy who would complain about weather. I was seated very close to the fire. He appeared from behind. I turned and took hold on my feet.

"Why don't you warm yourself?" I said.

He gleamed under the white light. His deep green eye seductively announced something desirable. As he shuffled on toward me, my breath began to take hold. I wasn't having anyone on my mind. It's just him before me. There was no sign of Alyward's name that came into my memory. I just knew his approach toward me took me closer to him. For the first time, the silence roared out in the stormy weather. And I felt his hand on my waist. Just the gesture followed on that talked between us. I was very close to his body. His shirt wide open, I placed my hand on his hard chest. I felt the touch of his nose on mine, as we desired to kiss one another. When I felt his lips met mine, we were out of the world for moment of time. It lasted longer than we expected. Maybe, we were going further away from that too. He began kissing my neck with wild calling heart. I knew, the pleasure wouldn't deny to me. He lifted me up and my legs keyed his body and that pushed us back with enormous jerk. The things around fell on the floor, but bothering those wouldn't be the right thing to do then. Though the floor felt cold it wasn't something to avoid. He constantly kissed me everywhere he could reach. It grew harder, and I never realized it was happening. My shawl was dropped on the floor. I began kissing him more than likely before. He tasted seductive and I wanted him strongly. Tyler's half naked body exposed. He grabbed me down under him. He was nearly upon me. But his lips never left mine brushing through each part of my body. I felt his hand on my breast. Even the touch of his soft lips on my navel left me on mood. Suddenly, I was hit with realization out of my brain.

"We shouldn't do this" I tried ignoring.

I breathed out and released myself from his hold. He forcefully paddled to settle on the floor. I walked out of the room. Just then, dad happened to knock at the door. The storm was still heavily falling. When Tyler sneaked out of the room, he was decently dressed with his shirt on. He passed the unsatisfactorily glance at me. He meant something by that, I read it on his face. Inside, the kitchen, the fallen things were left the same. Dad emerged into his room instead. I felt relief. Meanwhile, I opted to settle up the things. Tyler provided his helping hand. When dad fizzed out of his room, the first thing he could ask was about the preparation of dinner. We ignited with zest to prepare a handful of cheesy dinner. The work paced faster as we seemed to be hungry. Dad turned out to be a good chef. It's been many years that he had been doing the kitchen stuff all alone. I've just began to take myself look into the kitchen sometime. The dinner was ready within no time and, we all sat up together in the table to grace the food. The stormy rain still prevailed all throughout the town. Indeed, the cold was wilder enough to make any healthy man ill. But I sought to warm myself with the shawl I had.

After the dinner was over, I received the call from Alyward. His voice too exempted to be heard. I went to my room to deliver my conversation. He was on a scary mood. Perhaps, he had something to tell me.

"I want to meet you" he said.

I accepted the cause that he had. Maybe the next day could be the better day to see each other I explained. He meant it was an urgent deal to be notice. But, he didn't force to come up with thought to meet each other that night. The night was horrible as the rain and the winds never intended to stop. I wondered if Tyler would probably leave for home. But he's *God of Sea*, he could manage the water with his strength. Poseidon wouldn't be happy to watch doing something wrong against his will. I stepped down from my room. He waited in the hall way. Dad was inside, back to his cluttered table.

"I should be going" Tyler signaled.

"It's scary rain outside"

"I don't bother about it" he seemed very incoherent.

"Would you want my Chevy?" I felt the concern.

"No thanks…I'll ride" he straightened.

He walked out of the room. I saw him through the glass, wet by the heavy pour of rain. He didn't turn back to look at. *Love, it's always the hardest feeling to express to someone.* He speeded like the fire bolt of light. Within no time, he vanished out of my sight. I straightened my feet toward my room. As I proceeded, the scene browsed before my eyes about the kiss in the kitchen. I was right I halted myself. It would have been hard if we moved on with the love making feeling. Of course, it would make us feel guilty for sure and that the relation would come to halt no matter even if we tried hard to work upon it. I went to bed without giving much pressure on it.

The shower of rain was gone. I found myself to be a part of a dream. Dad knocked once at my door I sensed that. But I ignored as I wasn't completely awake. It was the second knock when it was almost nine past thirty. The knocked kept disturbing my head. I angrily woke out of my bed to look for. When I opened the door, there he stood gently with much sober style. I wasn't expecting him. Alyward looked very much heavy with information on his head.

"I needed to come" he explained.

I shook my head and let him inside. He took the edge of the bed to comfort himself. He looked around for a while and turned his face at me.

"You know they have reached the Caribbean Island" he began.

I kept with interest to hear what he was up to. Indeed, it shook me with little fear. I felt the petrified emotion inside of me.

"They have joined hands with rest of the pirates from the Island" he said.

"What am I supposed to do?" I said painfully.

I looked into his eyes if he would provide me with the solution. He began to think for a bit and looked out of the window. The morning was clear with the fresh breath of air that surrounded the environment. He shuffled slowly toward the window and pulled aside the curtains.

"We can make a plan to stop the war" he said after the silence.

"It's about my mother's life. We need Tyler by our side" I demanded.

As his name came up, he turned his face away, ignored the cause of his participation. He looked disinterested with the proposal that he was meant to bring up.

"Aly, you can't stay enemy to each other just because of me. I need you both. Why don't you both just settle among yourself" I sounded furious.

He stood quiet posing for nothing. His face almost over headed with anger. There was nothing he could talk about. Indeed, I knew getting them both together at one place wouldn't be that easy task. However, I needed to bring them both at one side. He began to feel discomfort as I continued to talk about Tyler. It would be the same argumentative from both side. The conflict of mind wouldn't be that easy to handle. It needed to be cured, and *the possibility was only to bring them together in whatever way.*

"You shouldn't be talking about him before me" he added.

I pressed my lips wondering about what he had about him inside his mind. The tool he wouldn't open up, I knew. There was nothing that could be sorted out them both. Yet, the hindrance has to be done to pull out the conflict of war against each other. I didn't utter for minutes. Alyward looked consciously nervous in matter of him.

"What's your problem with him?" I urged forcefully.

I wasn't even dressed up properly just to hear him say all those stupid things. Dad was gone. I heard the hissing sound of his car. And back in my room, I was arguing with the man I love. It wasn't to be appreciated, I found it very guilty. That's not the kind of morning I hoped for the last night. Of course, he did the right thing letting me know about the pirates plan but it wasn't a complete mission without Tyler in the team.

"You want to know, what's my problem with him? I just hate him" he said ferociously.

His stared maintained at me more like an angry man; he stood steady without movement. He then loosened himself to comfort himself with the ambience. It heated up both.

"I should get going" he said and walked out of the door, dissatisfied.

"Alyward…listen to me…just wait" I hurried down.

But he ignored to wait or to listen. He walked fast and got inside the car. By the time, I was nearly out in the front yard he was gone. There was nothing that I could stop him. Even if I disclose the matter to Tyler, *making them into friends they wouldn't find it logical*. The outside temperature was slowing down as the sun didn't show up. The cloudy sky with coverage of mystified fog damped the day. I needed to meet up Lexie to know about the curriculum of winter finals. I still lacked the idea about any subject that I've attended till date. I had only weeks in my hand to prepare for. Of course, I wouldn't want to let down dad. He was once called up by the principal because of my performance. It's not the second time that I would want to embarrass him. It's the final exam that I would be sitting for the freshman year. And then things would change up by the next year. I visited Lexie that day. She skipped her school hours. We studied for hours solving Nash Billy's math. In between that course, I received a call from dad. The weather didn't bother to change. The coldness crapped up on my body and felt it breaking away my bones. Dad wasn't in the town. He drove to Bakersfield, to Wiley's home. I responded about his caring process.

"Take care" I said and hung up the call.

He wouldn't be returning the night so he asked me to stay back at Lexie's house. I agreed to his consent concern. It's the second time that I was staying at Lexie's house. The last time

I stayed was before the prom night. The reason, I got stuck up due to my punctured tire. We sat for another hour to study. Of course, Lexie was better than me in math but I crossed with huge margin in English. Lexie had a music player in her room which I don't. The only desktop computer was the only company for me. After an hour study she hit on the music system. I looked out of the window and found the silence in the nature. At the front yard the beaded chair laid empty with no use.

"I'm going down" I stammered.

"It's cold outside" she warned.

"I know"

"Wait, I'm coming with you" she hurried and readied herself.

We walked along the open yard. I felt the drop of airy mist fallen onto me. The smoky breath indicated the cold that caught me. We decided to make fire at the front lawn. Just then, her dad and mom arrived from the service. Her mom got out of the car first. Felt my presence, she waved her hand at us.

"Hey!!...How you doing dear?" she embraced me.

The faint rays fell on the ground calling the end of the day. I gestured with ease at her. She joined us along the fire. Her dad came up few minutes later after he settled up the car. We spent an hour outside and gradually I could observe the end of the day. We walked in. I felt the sudden blow of warmness as we hopped inside. Her mother ordered us to be prepared to help her. I wondered what she was asking for. She was talking about the dinner stuff. When she came down, she groped for our company. Her dad in the living room. He had the television switched on. Lexie and I got busy in the kitchen. Very soon the dinner was ready on the table. Lexie's mom brought out a bottle of wine from the refrigerator. Lexie decorated the table for dinner.

"Mom, its cold outside" she said.

I looked at them, as they began to debate over it. She wanted to sip a glass. Lastly, Lexie had to give up over the silly debate. We sat together for the dinner. Her mother poured a glass for everyone. The dinner was fantastic, I hinted on my mind. Almost a week passed, I realized, I wasn't dining with dad each night. May be he felt bad about it that even we were two, we seldom sat together for dinner.

"What about your plan to Wisconsin this Christmas?" Lexie's mother asked her.

I almost forgot about the Christmas. I've never gifted dad till date. So, that's the only chance I would have to give him something worthy. I gave a thought on that as I fiddle with my spoon.

"Are you okay?"

"Yeah" I mumbled being shy.

"You can spend here. It's better here with all your friends. What do you say?" Lexie's dad suggested.

I gave a glance at her face. She made her face funny. I quietly smiled out. Then, I looked on my plate.

"Anna's here. You both can have great time" her mother added.

"So, you don't want me to go. Alright" Lexie sounded friendly.

After the dinner got over, we moved up to the room.

"I don't understand why my parents care about me so much" she sat on her bed.

I sat on the couch placed right in her direction. I was browsing what she had said. She was a lucky girl, I had to admit that. And when I realized the depriving love of mom, I felt really low and disappointed on Lexie's words.

"That's because they love you" I told her finally.

She stared at me with her rare sight. May be she felt I talked right. She pressed her lips and gestured smoothly.

"Would you like to join me?" she seemed very humble.

I abandon the chair and joined her on the bed. We had spent the night watching a television series. By midnight, she was already asleep. I was still engrossed with the series show. I couldn't leave it in the half way. So, I opted to spend the night little more late. When I was done with the show, I hopped to sleep the night. When the next morning blinked out, I found the whoop of feeling something good in the air. Lexie was still on her bed. I pulled the curtain aside looked out of the window. The fog was gone and the bright daylight resembled much like the golden shadow covered in. I decided to climb down to take a walk out in the front lawn. There I met her mother. We had a good chit chat with the rush of fresh air that touched us softly. After an hour walk, we followed inside. Lexie was already dressed up.

"Where were you?" she inquired.

"Just down there with your mom" I said.

"Get ready" her mom pointed at me.

"Hey mom!!!!" Lexie closed her up.

I took a little time to get myself ready to join them. The forethought picture browsed before my eyes. I nearly had forgotten about dad. Its quarter past nine now. I needed to be handful of responsible daughter to him. I tried calling him before I got down to the rest. But every time I did, there was no sound of response from the other end. I felt petrified and worried about him. It began to heckle my mind with great loss of strength and disappointment. I tried consoling myself with hope and faith upon lord. I got down getting myself ready. Maybe, I finalized to leave back home. I joined with Lexie's family for the breakfast. I was interrupted by a phone call. It wasn't an expected call. The moment I picked up the call, the voice attempted to withdraw me in. I couldn't hang up just like that without any confirming conversation. It shook me with sudden vibration that sprouted in my spines.

"Where are you?" Alyward asked, too concern.

My dad met with an accident on his return from Bakersfield. I felt nervous and feared with terror of lost hope and strength instantly.

"We're in the town's hospital" he added.

Momentarily my voice slowed down and for once in a moment, I actually felt how hard it was to bear sorrow and pain for someone you care about. I stood numb wondering at the plates on the table. It wasn't something that I could share. I just gave up the thought *I should leave immediately*.

"I need to go. I'm sorry" I said.

I plunged out of the table and straight went to my truck. I didn't care about anything but the panic thought about dad's accident controlled on me. Lexie followed me behind, she called me. But I didn't listen to care her that moment. My face doomed of expression and turned dull with heap of unwanted feeling that rose within me. I started the truck and galloped out of the place. I saw Lexie watched me go. Then I turned the rear view mirror to avoid the scene to me more pathetic. When I reached hospital, Alyward was already there at the ward room. Dad was equipped with pipes and tubes from all around. Somehow, I could notice his eyes were open to view around. He gave me a way to reach dad.

"Dad" I shuddered.

He just blinked his eyes ensuring that he was still okay. I held his hand and sat by his side for few minutes. The doctor came in to examine him. Alyward stood behind me, giving the touch of consolation.

"He'll be fine" he muttered.

He placed his hand on my shoulder and tried to comfort me. I waited for the doctor's final words. After he examined, he searched for me.

"He's absolutely fine. There's nothing to worry about" the doctor sounded very positive.

I felt slight relief by hearing those comforting words from him. He left us. Alyward had few fruits to eat. He offered me with an apple. Then he managed a stool for himself and sat by my side. The day was gradually sprouting out from the new horizon. We watched dad very closely. He could gesture his motion through his eyes. The rest body parts seemed equipped with tubes. The oxygen tube was fixed on his mouth so hearing him talk was not acceptable. Alyward, somehow made the time spent go well. We talked lots about our life. I knew, dad was happy to see us together. He would never disagree with my decision about him. For the first time, I felt I did something right in my life. Having Alyward was something to get a blessing from god. And that I knew however things went wrong, we somehow had maintained our relation against those odds. There was nothing that I would want to be new. He was perfect from all sides. It felt good to be with him. I felt protective and hopeful in his arms. Maybe, my world was more in him then to spend with the rest. Such feeling would only arrive only in the case if his presence made me felt around. Like every girl wish her man to treat her right, I was among one of them. He would never do me wrong. The fact that we knew, we were unconditionally in love with each other. In quest of searching friend in my new world I found him, like the light of an angel that simply meant for me. Just then, Tyler happened to show up. His breath pumping hard as it seemed he was hurry to reach the hospital.

"Anna" he said.

"Tyler" I said.

"How's your dad?" he seemed very caring.

He embraced me. He walked on to sight dad. I knew the situation could turn inappropriate. Tyler shared few words with him. I accompanied by his side. At one corner side of the room, Alyward stood grumbling with his breath. His eyes corner at us not very much welcoming though. In protest to that Tyler threw his glance with heavy hindrance look. There was nothing that both had common in them. Dad was asleep by then. Both overlooked at each other. I didn't want both to exchange words because that would lead an ill environment instantly. I walked out with Tyler out of the room.

"What is he doing here?" Tyler sounded very rough.

"He came to see dad" I said plainly.

We walked on through the length of corridor. The main entrance was ahead few meters away. We proceeded toward that way. Alyward stayed behind. I turned back to make sure he wasn't there right behind us. We were at the front porch of the hospital surrounding.

"So, how's your work going on at your garage?"

He grinned and laughed for seconds "It's not garage anymore Anna".

"Yeah!!! I remembered that" I fumbled.

"When the discharge date?"

"By 5:00 tomorrow" I added.

I never thought the worse thing about him. He was always helpful and charming guy. And the fact that kept us bind together was the secret that we held both for each other. But now the things were quite open between the three of us. There would be complicacy provided, if they both come together things would turn out to be different then.

"Anna, we must get back"

The voice interrupted us. I turned back. Alyward was really fast. I wasn't expecting him there.

"We must go" he said again.

His voice sounded serious to pull me back. His innocent eyes gestured too tempting that I found the need to hold back. I realized, dad was alone in the room. He tried to hold me. Just then the act of violence occurred before my eyes. Tyler with his full strength pushed him away. Alyward was thrown into the air, yards away from us he fell crushing onto the window glass. He received cuts and bruises. The streams of blood immediately began to flow out. I saw the real avatar appearing out from Tyler. He was in form to destroy.

"Tyler what you doing…. Just go away" I screamed angrily at him.

I ran to Alyward. He was helplessly fallen with cuts on the ground.

"You better don't touch her" that came aggressively from Tyler.

Their eyes both met each other. Of course, the line of enmity was seen on both. Tyler left the place. Immediate treatment came up.

"I'm so sorry" I said apologetically.

"It's not your fault" he said.

Alyward shared the same ward room with dad. Just few bruises and cuts that he needed to heal up. He was given the bandage to cover the cuts. The doctor gave him few tablets for the night. Dad woke up after long hours of sleep. He was amazed to see Alyward under that condition. His oxygen pipe was taken out. He could talk. I shifted closer to him.

"How you feeling?" I concerned.

"Slightly better" he spoke very softly.

Chapter Sixteen

The evening scrolled in and the night hour would picture like the longest time on earth. I ensured that I shouldn't go bore between this two medic people. I went to get a book near the lobby. When I returned to the ward room, the nurses began to take care of dad. He was given the dinner, even Alyward tried helping himself. I had to spend the night with them at least for 12 hours, I assumed. I've never been so familiar with medical stuff. I could never bear the smell that usually prevailed in every hospital. Instead it would make me feel like sick. But somehow, that night we had the air conditioning room which at least would fresh us inside. After the dinner got over, dad had talked to us for a while, until he was back to sleep. I noticed he was severely injured. May be it pained him to stay awake for long time. I slept by Alyward's side on the same bed. His warm breath kept me safe under the freezing night. At midnight, the nurse once came to give her last survey.

When the next morning froze out, I was still stuck up with my dream. Alyward kept me warm with the shawl. He went out, gleamed the first ray of the sun. When my feet touched the cold floor it took little time to withstand. Gradually I moved forward, I gave a glance at my dad. So peaceful, he looked, I hoped I could sleep like him. I walked out of the room searching for the soul whom I meant to be. Out in the open porch stood Alyward shimmering like the marvel rock, the bright sunlight even made him more watchful. He was healed with those bruises and cuts. I was amazed to see him like that. *What was he made up of?* I wondered sighting the view in the direction, his shirt wide open flipping by the touch of breeze that brought the fresh air around. He realized my presence and turned toward me. I hesitated and pulled my step back. Perhaps he wanted privacy, I couldn't get that. Instead, he stayed where he was. When he was done he followed toward me. I reminisced the scene back on my mind.

"How's your dad doing?" he questioned.

"Fine" I stammered.

He didn't feel like to know more instead, he set that smile on his face and walked toward the ward room. I followed him behind.

"How you healed yourself?" I interjected to know.

He grinned at me then he sat on the bed. He seemed to be playful.

"I mean so fast" I added.

"I never told you one thing about my healing power. I don't get healed by any medication. It's natural in me, the power of light provides me" he said.

By noon, dad was given the order to get discharged. He seemed pretty okay. Quite energized to handle by own. He was given the wheel chair. When it was five by evening all the necessary formalities were done. We could take back dad home. But, he was advised to stay on wheel chair at least for a month until his legs regained full strength. We reached home before the twilight sought to end the day. Alyward stayed for a while. He helped me out in preparing the dinner. Dad was seated in the living hall with the television on.

"I was scared of you at the hospital"

He chuckled and looked at me. The dinner table was prepared by then. I went to get dad out of the room. I had to roll the wheel chair for him. After the completion of the dinner, Alward was supposed to go back. It's been almost long months I haven't visited his house. Moreover, the finals were coming up. It's the beginning of December and I haven't yet planned for the Christmas.

"I'm so grateful to you for saving dad" I said.

Anytime" he said.

He kissed me on my forehead before he got himself inside the car. I waved at him once for the last time of the day. I knew the guilty feel that Lexie must have been enduring these many hours. I tried calling her out. At the first try there was response from her.

"What was wrong with you?" she blurted out.

"I'm so sorry Lexie, I know I shouldn't have done like that. I was in trouble"

"What you mean by that?" she insisted.

"My dad met with an accident"

"Oh!!...So sorry about that" her voice lowered down.

"How's he now?' she added.

"He's doing well" I answered.

We talked for more another half hour before I could go to bed. She confirmed me about her visit to me. Of course, we would be doing the study stuff. The winter finals were on the way. So, as far the situation appeared to me I would be spending most of the time at home studying and taking care of my dad.

For the first time, I had the feeling of disgrace toward Tyler. His violent act wasn't something to be hailed for. I disliked the matter, the fact that he shouldn't have touched Alyward. I knew, he was short tempered but that doesn't mean he had every right on me. Sometimes, one should know to control their emotions. It's not always the role of heart or feelings, we must give chance to think with our brains too. Often, we get what we feel but we must preserve for the best time. When it comes to love we seldom think with our minds. The blind folded heart and the emotions provoke to do whatever the case may be. That shouldn't be the case always. I thought about his angry nature. Maybe, next time I would be more careful with him.

It's December and the cold winter was at its height. Lexie showed up the next day. She met dad. They had a wonderful time spending together. The day was doomed with frost all around. There was no sight of sunlight that could warm the earth. Till noon, we studied for the finals.

"What would you do this Christmas?" Lexie asked.

We were out in the front lawn seated on beaded chair. Dad showed rapid improvement since the time he was brought to home. Few of his colleagues came to meet him up.

"I would like to spend with dad" I smiled.

Dad was along with us. The fire kept us warm. I haven't been to the beach at least a week. There was some sort of weakness that I began to feel. Somehow, I sought to maintain until the end of the week. I had a lovely end of the week by that part of time. Moreover, I had covered almost seventy percent of my final preparation. Neither Alyward showed up the whole week. He just like me was busy preparing for the final. The freshman year would be over within few days and I would have those memories spent around the school campus.

It's Saturday morning when I woke up with the zest to show up myself at the beach. The cold caught the surrounding very hard. I managed to keep myself warm with as many as woolen clothes. Gradually within the week, I turned weaker. I couldn't have the fresh breath of air filling into my lungs. That was one problem being a mermaid. We can't stay longer on earth surface with full energy. We needed refreshment and to gain our soul back from deep water. The oxygen that we breathe under water gave us the immense strength to bear pain and courage. I lied to dad about visiting Lexie instead, I drove to the beach. No one visits to the beach at this season of time. It's final exams and the preparation of Christmas all around keep them busy. The frost covered the whole area. Even the fog didn't give any access to view ahead. It's completely dense and white, chilling. No sign of people around. I undressed myself and stood naked before I could dive. I looked around. I felt the silence and peace around. Then I determined myself to dive in with the feel of strongest cold. I dived under water. The long shore line stood empty. And as I went deep under water, I began to feel the recreation of my body. My body gradually transformed into a mermaid. I felt the pearl of my heart glowing brighter and stronger. It reformed me into something new. I swam across the whole ocean wandering about deeper and deeper. I had new scales and fin on my body. My tail made better movement with the water and had efficient direction ability. I avoided *Jimmy*, however I didn't forget him. I looked more beautiful than ever before. It reflected before my eyes. And the reflection showered from the water surface. I came up onto the water surface and glanced around at the vast ocean stretching over the large part of the earth surface. It's amazing to look at the blue. But on that very day, the dampness was still there in the air and fog never recovered from their way. I spent hours till noon was seen slightly out of foggy day. I restored myself with great strength and ability. That's how we aquatic people live through their lives. When I returned home, dad had a visitor. I saw Burney Gaige.

"Hey…It's good to see you" I muttered.

I was on my short and the blue loosely fitted top. He rose from his seat and embraced me.

"I heard about your dad that brought me here" he said.

"Thanks for coming" I said.

I went upstairs to change myself. They got back again. They had been a well known good friend since the time we moved here. I got down back to catch them up. I had covered myself with woolen clothes to warm myself. And as the day faced toward west, I witnessed the memento of yellow light that fell on the yard surface. It's the sign, end of the day. I still had the summer memory pictured on my mind about Arizona days. It's the only recapitulating souvenir that I had on my mind. I miss the summer of the place. When the darkness engulfed around, we sat together out in front yard. Like always we had something fire in between. Burney opted to get some fine wine from the South. He had them brought with him. Somehow, dad could manage to stand up on his own feet by now. That was an encouraging sign of him. After an hour, we attempted to take dinner. It was almost half past nine when everything got over. Burney left us by ten. I felt good for that hour spent together. Dad as usual got back to his den. I went back to study. My preparations were almost done. But once for the last time, I persuaded Lexie to come over. She agreed happily.

The next day, she was here with me. We spent the whole morning discussing about the study materials. Likewise, a week passed away. I've never seen Alyward since the last time. Though I felt like visiting him, it wasn't that easy to do so at that hour of time. Or maybe the truth, I didn't want him to get disturb in his preparations. Under the strong coverage of frost and dew, I began my days so leisurely that it began to haunt me more about my mom. I found her letter under the drawer table. I glanced at it once but ignored to open up. It wasn't meant to read again. Lexie left me before the sunset. I wanted to stroll down the beach for that hour of time. Dad was doing some work in his room. He could walk by now holding a walking stick. He showed rapid improvement on his health. It gave me lot of relief. Without concerning him, I followed out toward the beach. But my intention wasn't to get down in the water. I just wanted to spent time alone. I sat on the dunes and watched at the slow descent of the sun. I found it enchanting with the chirping of sea gulls all around. Indeed, my loneliness felt much better to be with the nature's phenomena. And when the edges of the twilight sunk below the horizon, I marched to feel the fresh air through the shoreline. It felt good to be outside with the worry behind. And I never gave up a thought to think back about all those. I felt the determination roused within me. Inside, I still spoke of getting stronger but as days passed by I was still the same. Nevertheless, I always hoped for better change. I was enveloped by the darkness as the bright moonlit night began to rise out. I wasn't even in aware about my home that dad would be waiting for me. I just took every step ahead following the shoreline. I witnessed the rise of crescent moon above the horizon. It's milky glow edging over the surface. When then it was almost higher, I suddenly remembered about dad and his sickness. I turned back in an instance and followed to my truck. I drove through the lonely road experiencing the kind of drive through the deep forest that looked almost invisible before my eyes. The area doomed with dampness covered with fog and mist of frost. It felt difficult to reach back home. When I reached home, dad was actually in the kitchen preparing the dinner. He saw me buzzing in hurry.

"I thought you were at Lexie's house" he added calmly.

I browsed out a smile and shuffled toward him. I could see his body weight being supported on the stick.

"I was just out viewing the local side" I added.

I helped him take the chair. I wanted him to rest. However, he gave his company to me in preparing the dinner.

"I noticed you seemed to be busy with the finals" dad muttered.

"Kind of"

I placed the dinner on the table. We sat to begin with. There was nothing that I could talk with the words. So, for long time we had silence in the table. The clunking of spoons were the fiddling noises that came from the plates.

"I know it's been hard for you. I could never be like your mom" dad spoke in sudden.

I was amazed to hear. It wasn't something I would mean to listen. I looked at him. I had no thought what I could tell him for doing so much for me. Yet, he blamed himself that wasn't justified. He shouldn't feel bad about it just because I was deprived of mom's love.

"You did your best dad" I said.

He glanced at me once and flashed a short smile and got out of the chair. I washed and rinse all the dishes before I packed up myself. I saw dad once through the crack of the door. He was working on some files. He felt my presence out of the door. Incidentally, he turned back and saw me.

"Come in"

I moved my feet sloppy. I looked around. That was after long period of time I entered into his room. I remembered the last time when I did, I entered to fix his table lamp. The couch was next to piled bed. I sat upon it.

"When's your finals"

"Just a week away" I answered.

"Do you want to go for vacation this Christmas?"

It interested me to hear that but I wasn't sure if I actually wanted to. I pressed my lips, dad glanced at me and threw his warmly smile at me. He was too kind.

"I don't have any plan dad" I said plainly.

I helped him in compiling all his files together. But, we never talked about mom though; we had lots to talk about other things. By midnight, he was almost done. I waited for him to go to bed.

"Think about the vacation" he said.

"Alright dad, goodnight" I said and went upstairs.

I've never seen Tyler again since the last fight he had. But every time I tried to forget about the incident, it often appeared in my mind. I couldn't stop to neglect the scene. It wasn't that easy for me to watch Alyward weaker than him. However, I wanted to keep him away. But right now, all I could devote was to end my finals well. Lexie had her last meeting with me before the beginning of finals. Within the week, I had made all my revision and helped dad in all his file handling. He always kept asking about the vacation. Yet, I haven't come up with certain decision about it. Maybe, I should take up with him to go around the globe at least once in a life time.

"Where would we go?" I asked dad.

"Anywhere that wishes you to take" he said reading a file.

The last thing that I wouldn't want to do on earth was to become a cop. Dad always seemed with old files going through past records of criminals. It's the grittiest job I've ever found. Yet, he loved his job. I thought it wasn't necessary to tell him right now. He wouldn't mind, I don't know why he was up to that.

"Why the sort of vacation?" I asked.

He peeked at me and looked thoroughly. He came closer with the file in his hand. At the window end the table lamp brightly glowed focusing the entire room.

"I just want you to get some distance from this place. I know, you've been confined for the last few months at the same place. And I've seen you getting uncomfortable with the people around. You can get a chance to meet new people make new friends" dad added.

I breathed out and stood stable wondering around my mind. May be dad was right I gave a thought. I shook my head showing the vibes of pleasant agreement. He patted me at my back before I left his room.

"Good night dad" I said.

He gestured with his warm love of smile. I happily went to my room gave the last thought about my next day exam.

It's the beginning of my finals. I was early at school the morning. Lexie just reached minutes late. I haven't seen Alyward yet. I waited for him at the parking lot. Lexie showed her patience with me. Just then the hiss of his car sounded uttering. He parked his car with grand show of style drifting from right. That was amazing to watch at. I've never seen him so playful before. He walked out of the car and followed toward me.

"Hey!!!" he said and kissed me.

We moved in following the length of corridor. Each one of us then slopped in to respective classes to write the finals. After almost spending hours, we met once again.

"They have made an alliance with rest of the pirates" Alwyard said.

"How do you know that?" I keened.

"Last night I saw it, I looked into our lives"

"So, what did you see about us?" I was intrigued.

He pulled his face away and looked in the direction of empty yard. The cafeteria began to get filled up. I observed him in silence, he then turned again to face me.

"It's not easy. There's no such guarantee we would be together in future" he added being cautious.

I felt slight discouraged with those words. I shook my head in cause of sorrow although I tried to cover it with my casual expression.

"You mean, we won't be in love in near future, right" I sighed.

"You don't understand Anna there's lot of complicacy"

"What complicacy" my voiced rose louder.

"I think we should walk out from here" he said.

At the parking lot, we stopped at one corner. He breathed out and glanced at me. I wasn't in state to feel good about the incident. It truly disappointed me.

"You know what Tyler can do to me?"

"So, it's about him" I frowned.

He stood silent muttering no words. He looked around and again back to me. That unsettled mind inside began to kill me surging the cause of pain about being in love to a man who would be destroy by *Demi God.*

"You're far more powerful than him, Aly. You got to believe me" I said.

He hugged me. I felt his heart beat close to my ear. There was nothing that I would want to come between us. No matter even if it caused to die for, it was worth doing. Back at home, dad had a visitor. I was surprised to see him. His friend Wiley visited him from Bakersfield. It made me felt overwhelmed about his presence.

"Do you remember Wiley?" dad said.

 I shook. "Hey!!!.." I said.

He embraced me.

"How you doing?" said Wiley.

"I'm good. what about you?"

He was the same with that friendly nature. With short talk I went upstairs to change myself. I wondered dad refused to asked about my exam that was peculiar. I sat on the edge of the bed. The reverting thought handled my mind. I was frightened with the case that Alyward told me about. I knew, Tyler could go to any extent to harm him. *But I wouldn't let that happen.* I came down to catch up the rest. I had few more written exams to be completed. There was no certain plan that I yet inculcated to go for. But watching at the condition I felt the need to do so. I was finally ready to go for vacation after the finals. Somewhere down to Alaska. So this winter, I decided, I would end up settling with a cause to free up my mind from worries.

It's dinner time when Wiley had said about Alaska. Actually it was dad who had brought the topic. But coincidently it came out to be the place I had kept for the vacation.

"So what you think about Alaska?" dad came up with it.

I fumbled and the water sprouted out of my mouth as I tried to drink a glass of water. That wasn't good right, I hinged at my conscious, but the sudden talk about Alaska made it happen.

"Are you okay?" dad concerned.

"Yeah, I'm right" I snorted.

Then we began with the usual conversation. Of course, I agreed about the Alaska trip after the finals. I still had many more days to go. So for now, I was sure I would be spending my Christmas in Alaska. After the dinner was over, I didn't want to waste my time. So, I left them both for my study. I began to feel studious about myself although that's not my nature in true sense. I saw them both at the front yard, made fire and sat to spend the night all along. I watched them for minute through the window, as I felt the wintry breeze swiping in. I pulled the curtain to avoid the same and began to look at the book for my next written exam. I even stopped to serve the internet for a while. There was no sort of connection that I had kept with cyber world. While people used lot about social sites, I rarely opened or even registered my name. So, basically one could tell me I might be socially awkward. It's not that I don't like people but having my own time, I preferred the most. In most basic sense, I spend my time for myself then for the others. When the next day stroke out of the clear sky, I felt the realm of being in nurture environment, as the day seemed brighter and prettier than the past days. The sun shone out bright delivering its pure energy rays and nowhere the fog or frozen mist was seen. It all wiped out dryly out of the bright light. Wiley prepared to leave back home. I watched them through the window. I got downstairs to join them. Dad helped him with the bag to place inside the car. Gradually, showed improvement and now he wasn't anymore on his wheel chair.

"Hey!!! dad, where are you up to?" I asked.

"Morning dear" he said.

Wiley buzzed out from the other side of his car. He smiled and greeted me morning.

"Thanks" he said as I helped Wiley with his other bag.

When he was done with all his stuffs, he was ready to go. I held dad's hand and watched him get settled inside the car. He looked at us once. He started the engine.

"I had a great time" he said humbly.

"It was nice to see you too" dad uttered.

He drove out of the gate and we watched him fade away in the distance. I spent the rest of my time in studying for the next. After a week's final, it was finally over. Alyward had showed to our house at the end of the final day. Along with him Lexie too added. Dad wasn't at home. He had rejoined his job. By evening, he returned back. We had the dinner prepared for all. He was happy to see all of us being together. The days are off now and I had no idea about the remaining days to spend. We had the discussion about the vacation trip to Alaska. Alyward found it interesting too. Maybe, it could be the best thing that we had thought about the winter to end up. Lexie needed the permission from her parents. However, dad hadn't included himself for the trip. I don't know why. After all it was his idea about the winter break.

"Someone has to be here at home to look after" dad said pouring wine in his glass.

"It would be great if you could come along with us" Lexie concerned.

Dad smiled out and sipped his wine. I glanced at him and realized to understand his need to stay back. It wasn't what he meant for himself but all he wanted to do for me.

"He would be fine" I added.

We had a charismatic evening spending all together. I felt the great relief out of stress after the completion of the finals. Dad and Lexie joined together to watched a movie in the room while I walked with Alyward outside to gaze at the frozen night sky. I covered myself with woolen fur. There was no need of such for him, as for I knew he could heal or stay away from cold through his natural ability.

"There's nothing that I would want to stay away from you Anna. Every time of my breath, I think about you more than I could bear to stay away from you" that came effusively from his voice.

"You don't have to stay away from me anymore" I ensured.

He smiled and kissed me on my forehead. I felt the softness

inside his warm hand that made me feel safe. After a while, we walked in. Lexie was still on with the television screen. Dad had gone to sleep. He had the duty next morning to wake up early. Lexie would be taking the living room for the night. Alyward stepped upstairs with me.

"Are you comfortable with this?"

"Yeah!!!" I said.

He sat on the edge of the bed and gazed at me in deeper sense of moral vibes. The excruciating weather outside stumbled the window with the running wind that blew from north. I pulled the curtain and closed the window. Behind me he stood, so close to my body that inch wasn't the right unit to express. His hand ran through my body and then reached the hip level where he held me firmly. I felt his breath that smoothly brushed my skin at my back. I turned to face him and looked deeply into his eyes. There was the common thing we both wanted desperately. When his lips were closer to mine, I felt the reverie of his warm love. His lips finally met mine. We kissed each other like the first kiss of our love. It lasted for minutes and wasn't aware when we had stumbled onto the bed. His eyes deeply sensed me and the golden vibes in his eye color ensured the protective soul he had about me. I wasn't good at reading minds of people.

"I wanted to see you again in real" he whispered.

His fingers softly ran through my face. The he reached to my lips. I pretended the cause of feeling the tickling sense. Meanwhile, I looked at him engrossingly that perceived the florescent mind that he carried. I tried to smile and unfolded from his arm and gently postured to sit on the bed.

"You've to wait till morning comes in" I said slyly.

He joined by me side resting his back on the bed head. With the other hand he fiddled with my fingers. In between, he spoke about his past stories. He lamented the way he lost his parents in a tragic incident. He was just ten then, no strength to withhold those pains and sorrow. Yet, by growing years, he had shown bravery and proved to be responsible guy. As the night was in the mid, I began to feel the drowsiness crawled on me. My eyes blinked in a low light wanting to dream the night in his arm. He snuggled me with his arm and felt the sleep calling me. He gazed at my sleeping beauty of eyes and hazily I saw him, smiled out. Then I was off for the dreamy night.

Lexie helped dad to wash his car. I saw them spraying the pipe water over the vehicle. I watched them from the window of my floor. Alyward added by my side. His eye shimmered bright under the color of yellow bright rays. I still had the dizziness on my body. Maybe, I wanted more sleep. That was enough though. He placed his hand upon my shoulder and added himself in the direction to my view.

"I hope you had a wonderful sleep last night" he whispered.

I nodded and maintained in the direction. I turned back and saw his charming face that glittered brightly. He looked calm and composed expressed with the true value of lives.

"We should go down" I hinted.

He shook his head gently and followed me downstairs. There was nothing that I could silently complain about the day. Within a week time, the weather had shown better improvement. The fogs were gone and the breezy warm environment once again hovered. I heard the chirping of birds around and felt nostalgic about Arizona. Gradually, I began to forget most of it now, as I had spent too much time here at the *Sonoma County*. I had learned that with time we must try to leave what it used to be. Such was the thing for me trying to forget about Arizona as possibly as I could. Alternatively, I managed to consider the place with whole heart to accept. I got new friends and lovely people around me. But the best thing that happened to me was Alyward. That's the gift I received here. Dad saw us approached toward them. Lexie flashed a smile and rushed to me giving her usual type of welcome hug.

"How was the night?" she said.

Beside me stood Alyward, who hid to smile out, threw his sudden glance at her. There was shyness that floated on his face. Dad dried his hand with the towel as he walked to us.

"So, what's the plan for today?" he asked.

"It's a warm day, we drive to the beach" I shrugged.

"Alright, just be careful, just be cautious" he added.

We opted to take breakfast together. The plan was to move out soon after it got over. Dad wouldn't be available at home. He would be patrolling the town. Lexie had some concern call from her home so, she decided she would leave too. That session of time, we spent the hour in piling at the breakfast table. Soon dad was gone giving his latest therapy again. Lexie left us after hour dad had gone. It's just two of us, hereby tortured with the heckling thought to reach at the beach. I prepared myself as soon as possible before the day would come to an end. There at the gate end, Alyward snorted his horn in loud tone. He chugged his car as I heard him doing that. I looked once out through the window before I finally ready to set down. I waved at him, there was fake smile that came brushing through the air. He made his face at me. I ignored the rest and hurried down. I joined along his side, and we moved out in speed. At the beach it's quite sunny and people wouldn't leave the chance to hang out. At far shore distance, we halted after a long walk along the dunes. It seemed safe and silent with no sign of people loitered around. It made us feel the isolation from the rest but that's what we needed, a privacy to be more precise.

"Do you really want to know me more?" I whispered.

He gleamed at me and flashed a short smile. His lips pressed and shimmered in bright light. He shrugged. With slow motion, I began to open up my clothes. When I was out in bikini, the generosity of his behavior pictured out. He pretended to turn his face away.

"You don't need" I assured.

"Are you sure you're comfortable with it".

He turned gently toward me and maintained his steadiness. I unhooked my bra and reaching below to strip my panty down. I stood naked before him, and as the swells reached up the shore, I could feel the glow of mind enchanting out of the nature's gift. He swallowed in and exhaled a breath out. The intensity that screened in his eyes bothered me. I gave him my last glance before I dived into the water. He waited out in the shore dunes. With the deeper site under water, I finally found myself again. Transformed my whole body and legs into what real me. I haven't gone that far away from the site, but deep in the vast north where the swells were greater to swim. I avoided thinking about him. I resurfaced on the shore edge. I felt the push of small waves that passed by.

"You're the most incredible creature in the universe" he complimented.

Creature well, I didn't mind that word referring to me. He rested his knee on the dunes by my side. My legs in tailed form and that appeared awkward to me in the day light. Gracefully, there was no one to witness us. He gently sat down by the wet dunes along the edge of the shore. The swells kept coming and left into the deep. I tried sitting into a posture but never knew I couldn't do that. So, I lay with one of my hand supporting my head. We had spent the day watching at the vast ocean. And I like the fact that Alyward was very much supportive to me.

He had accepted me in whatever way I was, it mattered me more than anything else. The day gradually began to descend down the west. The twilight appeared, darkened yellow across the horizon. It's the sign of holy night, I grasped that feeling. He peeked at me and his eyes glowed like the rising sun of ending day.

"I'm glad you're here with me" I said.

He inched closer to me and caught by his arm. I felt his breath reaching to me, so close it tasted the intimate feel of being in one another's arm. He gazed deeply into my eyes, uttered nothing. That shivered me with nervousness. I felt the rise of height from the level. He lifted me in his arms, walked along the edge of the shore in that fashion. I was still the mermaid girl clasping my hand through his shoulder.

"Am I heavy?" I smirked.

He smiled and gestured his silent eyes. There was no hint of utterance on his face but there was the shine of truth that revealed. We turned back as the day slid to end with the slight coverage of darkness around. He dropped me on the dunes before we got inside the car. And felt the retransformation of myself into human. He kissed me with immense touch of love and pleasure. Something I was yearning for too long. We turned back home. By then the darkness engulfed around. I felt the whirled of wind that thrashed my body. I slid up the window. When we reached, dad was already there at the front lawn. Seemed he was searching for something important that dropped on the grasses.

"Are you okay?" I hinted my tone.

He felt the sudden steady voice of mine. He wasn't expecting though.

"Oh!!! You scared me" he rubbed his forehead.

"What are you searching?" I said.

Alyward came up, stood up by my side.

"I lost a coin, it's very old, very old" he repeated that word many times.

"Maybe we could help you out" Alyward shrugged.

Dad shook his head. I saw the light lit in his room. It seemed, he was busy with something else. The files weren't there on his table. He had settled them inside the cupboard. That was something new to look at, an unexpected formation. I walked inside.

"Is this the one?" I heard Alyward.

"Yeah!!! That's the one" dad said in relief.

I turned to look at them before I took up the last step inside the house. They followed in. The living room cluttered with dad's materials.

"What have you been doing?" I asked.

"It's classified" he wriggled.

Alyward chuckled and smiled out in slow motion. He felt it quite strange, it's the same feeling I had.

"Dad you're acting like FBI agent now" I muttered.

"It's none of your business" he said.

Well, he was right. There was nothing to do with those things to me. Instead, I began to ask him about the dinner. We had to prepare it until it was really ready. After the dinner, Alyward decided to leave back home. Its half past ten and the stillness in the air showed much of alluring emotion that blew off the rushing sound of dragnet fear that prevailed. I whispered him to stay back, maybe he could read up my mind, but I barely remember about his inability to penetrate my mind. I wanted him so bad to spend another night with me. Maybe, we could call it love with satisfied pleasurable feelings to share with emotions and patriotic love for one another. I escorted him till the gate. He kissed me once for the last goodnight kiss. I felt dad was watching us from the window, it sensed me. Indeed, he was, I was sure after we unlocked. He left for his home back under the shades of darkness night. I watched him until the car light faded away from my sight.

I hadn't talked to Tyler in like two weeks. Nor he showed up after the last incident. The thought often came up in my mind to seek him. I never knew, what could be his state of mind toward me. His hatred against Alyward still churned to stay strong. No able way could bring them together perhaps, it was destined with them. Ahead of me, I saw nothing more than a mere world of fire bolt causing huge traumatic damage. The chase had actually begun, blinded with the real force that erupted strongly molding every heart beat that kept me alive. The night crawled up on my shoulder squeezing me with killing cold that crapped on my body. Somehow, I could bear the night's sentiment to go to sleep.

The week was left only for us to be prepared to leave for Alaska. And I wanted Tyler should know about it. Of course the possibility, I had always wanted to believe to have him with us. But then it could never be perfect way to end up things. When the intense penetrating rays entered into my room, it smeared on my face that led me to break out of my bed. I was excited about the Alaska trip. It would mean different kind of experience. Dad was out in the yard. I slid down to catch him up. He seemed busy with piles of jumbled clothes that he had to dry up.

"Hey…" I said.

He glanced back as he pegged his last piece of cloth.

"I was wondering if you could take a tour of the town with Tyler"

"Did he come here?" I shuddered.

It's been about two weeks; he hadn't shown up. Nor dad had anything to do which would require him. Burney once visited last week. I wasn't at home, faintly I could recall I was with Alyward out in the town. By the time I returned he was about to leave, barely I could talk to him. There was no sign of cause that would deliberately let me ask about his son. I just had little bit of concern to wish him goodnight before he left us.

Chapter Seventeen

Things had changed so much into my life that looking back at it, I failed to realize how much my life meant to me. And then there was dad, who had been demolishing all his life just to support for both of us. It wasn't an adequate state to observe with great austerity. Yet, it made me felt good about the way we had come up since these years to live up with the people here. Furthermore, what would one seek of getting more than the love of life. The unconditional feeling for Alyward enthused me with hope and liberated the kind of life I wanted to live. I found the love which came from nowhere, unexpected but in good form. Initially, it was hard to endure the absence of mom in the family but with gradual time I managed to deal with it. There's nothing right even though I try not to remember her but sometimes, it haunted me over the night. I still felt the deprived heart of her within us. It's isn't a legacy but everyone of my kind had to come across such situation. Generally, our kind they never lose their father but it's something common that mom would leave the house for the sake of family protection. It never caught with true idea to stick with hierarchy ladder that mother had to go away from all. It wasn't the best of thing that our kind had been following. It needed a change and that change would be when every single mother would stay protected under the same roof amongst the family. That one generation of human kind would witness the culture of other life being fanatically it would raise the bar in the society to mix with the other kinds. In my case maybe it was happening to me. And the only hope that kept me get going was my mother. I knew, she couldn't get the life she dreamt about. To her, we always have been a mere soul of god's gift. Her sacrifice wouldn't be going in vain. I determined that she would deserve to get what she expected. Maybe that was one reason why I wanted to get back mom to us. Above all, there was vacancy of her in the family. The ardent feel of emptiness forecasted without ensuring about the perfection in the family, and the void stayed empty for long. The only longing thought that I was excited about, had she been here with us, she would feel aura of her daughter being in love with a kind guy. And of course Alyward, would be treated with love by her. But I missed those things.

Even though it seemed pretty good but deep inside we both knew, it wasn't the best of it. Thinking it to be a new beginning, new life, the road had led us steady till date. But I persisted to continue with hope and running ahead to throw the best out of me. Dad had done a lot for me. He brought the change in our living by shifting to Sonoma and that was right idea. Though at first I felt it awkward but as Alyward entered into my life, I began to feel the aura of living with him. I'd rather multiply my life with him as years passed by. Maybe, someday it would only mean between us. The only hope that stayed behind with my life could be more of him. Hadn't he been here with me, the cause of living my life wouldn't be served with better meaning. All I ever wanted to feel was the truth that could disclose what it would be like the future. The reason by now began to clear out, even if it was hard at the beginning, it worth waiting for. Dad had been the most patience man I had seen and that assured he would never fail in whatever task he looked on.

It was always the first time feel with Alyward. That gave me always the new reason to hope for the welcoming future. The faith and the understanding lined in the heart of our orientation. He had faith in me, so do I on him. When dad knew about him, he never put forward with the disagreement. The acceptance came up naturally to him as he had married the love of his life, my mother. So, he was never against love, to be more precise not against Alyward. Few things always stayed hidden within my heart, we haven't talked about mom since the letter was dropped to us. It wasn't like we had given up but we respected her ideology. In her letter, she clearly mentioned not to chase her, maybe she wanted to be left alone. It wasn't what we thought to get as feedback. I was scared then, even now it made me uncomfortable. I knew, she was in trouble not because she had called for it, but our kinds always thought for one another, just like I always thought about my mother. Even though it seemed crazy to me, I barely understood till date about her nature. Dad seldom said about her, what kind of woman she had been, all I knew was that she's kind and good woman and a wonderful mother and wife to my dad. *Facing the toughest situation may lead you to learn the absolute courage that one has to go through.* All through these years, I've faced it bravely and now I could feel the courage that blossomed to take any sort of risk. The tangled thoughts loaded my mind, as I looked out of the window watching at the blink of faded light that spread into the air. The night partially edged to mid section while I still failed to sleep hopping with mental stability. The night fell very silent. The bizarre noise from crickets weren't heard only the winnowing of breeze flapped the curtains.

Captain Nicholas received a grand welcome reaching the Caribbean Island. His fellow friend Henry Wardo, gave a warm greeting on his return. The next step they forged was to move toward Virgin Island specifically to Cruz Bay. They both had been a long time associative partners about the pirating business. Their army had grown stronger than ever before. It tripled their size with weapons and harpoons. The night was grazing with flashy buzz of dim light, as their mob gathered around the beach shore. The pirates never settled for permanent home. It could be anywhere they resided but in greater part the lonely beach shore becomes their business hub. In such synapse of time, the only factor that could build their partnership strong was the war against us, *the mermaids*. Both the sides had the motive in equal sense. Their cruelty of nature to destroy our kinds fed them with greediness and pride. The stories of war against pirates would remain immortals throughout the centuries. In coming ages of time, the victorious shall rise again. The difference between us and the sea goon could only be one. We have the human heart inside us but them being human they reside with evil inside. It's always been the same throughout the centuries. Our strongest enemies were none than the pirates. However, we have other evil forms against us, though they were lesser mortals. The dim light faded away as the bitterness of deep night rose up.

"You know the deal" Henry Wardo assured.

"There was no deal between us" Nicholas disagreed.

The two were inside their base tent. Probably, one had the wine glass in his hand. The fluffy smoke from the cigar blurred into the air as Nicholas Cook puffed.

"My Men will give their lives for you and in return you say no. That's wrong my brother" Henry sipped his wine.

"Why don't we share?"

"What you mean?" Henry intrigued.

The argument went on pleasurably in persuading gesture to one another. At that junction of time, they couldn't weak themselves by going against each other. The sharing word did troubled Henry. In glimpse of a thought, he felt like knowing what Nicholas talked about.

"We had come across an Island at the tip of Southern America. It's the *Wollaston Island*"

"What's the special about that place?"

"It's a bank of treasure, I assure you" said Nicholas interestingly.

"What makes you think I would trust you?" Henry rolled his eyes.

"Well, I never asked you but if you want the deal, you got to" Nicholas walked off the place toward his crew.

Henry looked on him not indulging much about the words of that man but stood in dilemma if he was right then, would he be able to give his word on that par. He sipped his last portion of wine left in his glass and watched at the vast ocean lying ahead. Probably, the two men wouldn't let go off things so easily. Each needed something or the otherwise they defy each other breaking their long term relation. They wouldn't even think of committing such blunder hilarious mistake under such circumstances where they seemed to be gaining from both side.

The dawn shone over the breaking tide of sea waves that clasped over the island. And there at one side of the shore quite away from the tent settlements, Zenna was mastering her sword skills. She had few of her attendants taking part along with her. The atmosphere stayed silent except that the roars of swells that reached the wet shore. Her breath exhausted with every move of her sword skill portrayed out in defensive method. She was indeed a great fighter with skilled movement of her hand against the wind. As they were involved with the activity, a young lad watched at them very closely. He wasn't a familiar face to them. Not to say much but he looked muscular and stiff, attitude with sharp jaw to get the prettiest outlook. Zeena sensed him. She stopped her practice session. Out in the long horizon of Atlantic line, the sun was streaming out with bright glow. The flow of tide reduced to much extent and while the chirping of birds from the nearby forest zone flew out in cluster to cheer the morning.

"Who are you?" she demanded.

He widened to smile out, a friendly gesture that showed like he knew her for long time.

"I'm Alvyn Wardo, younger brother of Henry Wardo" he said.

"You have a great mastery in sword fight" Alvyn complimented.

"Thanks" She made her face.

"I'm sorry…. I distracted you from the practice" he apologized.

"That's okay" she responded humbly.

"Yeah, go ahead" he said and left the place.

Zenna watched him go, then she resumed to hold her sword. By then the Island was wholly awaken up. The morning bloomed in ecstatic influence over the wind from the long vast ocean. When she was done, her fondness over diving into water pulled her toward the shore. She swam for few minutes until she felt the juvenile morning to hold on for the day to outshine over the blue sky. While walking out through the dunes toward the crew tent, the picture of him flashed in her mind imaging something had happened within that flick of time. She smiled hiding within herself. She went inside and dressed herself to get ready with the rest for the framing of their new plan in order to move ahead. At noon, she encountered Captain Nicholas Cook, just an hour before they would proceed for lunch.

"So, Henry Wardo has a brother" she said.

They walked on along the shore dunes proceeding toward the ship. The crew unloaded few of the remaining things as they would be staying for a week until they finalized with the plan.

"So you met him huh!!!" Nicholas heckled.

"Well, it wasn't a meeting, it happened accidently" she explained.

He laughed at her words and peeked at her with certain intention of kindness. There was the reflection of her inner core of heart about that man that read on her face. Nicholas perceived to be right that their meeting would cost him a lot of wealth and people.

"Well, just stay safe" he blurted in friendly gesture.

"I know you must be thinking what I'm not"

He smiled and commanded a member of his crew to put up the ladder. He climbed up. She followed behind as they reach the ship deck.

"So, did he accept the deal?"

"He will" Nicholas looked around the ship.

They got few left up things cleaned up and loaded with new. So, for a week stay they had enough food and water with them. In case of anything short they wouldn't hesitate to wish from their friend Henry Wardo. They returned within shortly for the lunch. At their base tent they had a visitor. The shore actually pictured as the small town of pirates. Henry and Alvyn had joined along with them for the lunch.

"Who is he?" Alvyn muttered.

"Oh!!! That's Nicholas the Captain, I was talking about and she's Zenna, I guess I'm right" Henry said.

Alvyn looked at her given the hidden glimpse of lightly lifted eye glance. There was the contact of sight between both, however it seemed pretty gross as it wasn't too kind to look at.

"So you both have met" Henry said.

"Yes brother, we did".

"Why not we proceed with the lunch" it came from Nicholas.

They sat up together. Zenna faced Alvyn straight in direction to his eyes. For minutes, there was silence amongst them except that Henry and Nicholas were seemed to blurt out with discussions.

"You shouldn't be looking at me that way" Zenna whispered softly.

Alvyn flashed a smile "Don't make me feel embarrass".

"Maybe you both should spend little time" Henry suggested.

"Are you sure, brother?"

They both walked out of the tent heading toward the dunes. The heat fell right above their head. The rusty influence of the wintry breeze from the deep ocean somehow maintained the temperature. And as they neared to the shore, the swells perceived to grow bigger. It touched their feet with the wet sand that pasted on their feet.

"I'm sorry being awkward to you" Alvyn said.

Both positioned to sit on the dunes. She looked at him in seconds of lightening glow. Her face smeared with the kindness that flagged to lay upon with crust of soft feelings that mounted on her. There was audacity of expression that flashed on her face. However, they felt the comfort being in the company of each other.

"I usually avoid talking to strangers" Zenna muttered gazing in the direction of vast lying ocean.

"That's reasonable" sounded friendly.

"So, how you got into the business?"

Alvyn gave a thought for seconds before he could break out

his story. He made a floppy face peeking at her. The smile arrived from her side. It wasn't resistible to avoid but gladly it was shimmered under the blue sky. He widened his lips and pressed giving his second thought to utter out the story in his connection.

"It's kind of boring thing you want to hear" he added.

"I enjoy the boring thing" Zenna grinned.

He began to pour out the long back connection with his brother and then into the business. In time, the color of the ocean began to change from bluish gray to yellow. The sign of ending day was visible right at the horizon. Gradually, he could wind up in short. The area shortly enveloped with the faint darkness around. The home going seagulls cried in the sky as they flew away. The scattering faint light spread into the air among them the airy breeze came collecting moisture from the deep ocean. Each looked at one another probably for the first time. Their eyes met with strong contact unleashing what they had felt the evening, spending together. They walked off the shore toward the crowd. Only the gesturing notion could be read between them, maybe the slight shyness occurred within their face. It wasn't something to be felt more from the other side of human heart. In all consideration it wasn't so call falling at first sight. Just the connection of acquaintance it could only be meant. When they nearly reached the crowd, they well sort to part each other. Alvyn had to go back to his crowd on the other side of the shore.

"It was nice talking to you" he added humbly.

She responded in flashy smile "It was good to be with you"

The night passed away, when the next bright light fell on the shore, the dawn glimmered in an array of faint light that withheld the shower of morning breeze. Zenna was on her way to training.

"Hey!!!! Would you mind if I come along with you?" the voice came from the other end.

She looked in the directed voice and found Alvyn walking toward her.

"Since when did you get interest in sword fight?"

"It just came randomly" he added, as they walked on.

"You shouldn't be here"

"I know, I'm sorry about your little lack of privacy" he winced.

When they reached the spot her attendants waited for her. Zenna got herself ready in position to get trained. She completed her first round. While Alvyn spotted her from every angle as he observed her from deeper point of sense. Hee was lost in her that he felt the evolving call of inner sense from his heart.

"Do you need a sword?" Zenna said loudly.

"Oh!!!! Yeah!!" he mumbled.

He was given few of the tips in handling sword fight. After an hour they stopped with the show. The rest of the hired went away to their respective crew.

"You never handled a sword ever before right".

"How do you know that?" Alvyn gestured his face.

"Well, it reads in your hand"

He widened his face and looked ahead toward the water. They spent few more time along the shore till the final rise of the sun fell wholly on the island. The greenery of the island shone with the glitters of freshly called nature. All in a while the peace engulfed the coast with purity of nurtured gift.

Chapter Eighteen

Henry agreed with the deal to join Nicholas to combat the mermaids. And that fresh morning brought them even closer than before, as they were seen together taking a walk along the shore. Heading toward the direction they had encountered Alvyn and Zenna. It was meant to be understood. The thought to grasp with the words didn't mutter out, as they knew the reason behind their both relations. No questioned arose from them instead all four headed toward the peace of silence and marched to the coast. After examining the ship, they returned back to join the crowd for their welcoming breakfast. The coast was brightened with the glimmering rays that reflected from ocean water, and that was truly exquisite to watch in the open. Alvyn and Zenna joined along with them. Like always they faced each other directly. Later when they were about to leave, they received the invitation of dinner the evening on the other side of the island. That flashed the hidden smile on Zenna's face.

Henry and Alvyn left the place with an invitation leaving behind. When noon scrolled in, the rest of the crew members already seemed to be exhausted. Rather the cause of their heavy loading of food items and weapons in the ship led them to expel their energy tiredly. When Nicholas looked out from the tent, he found the shore to be deserted, lost with none for his assist to be answered.

"You should let them take rest" Zenna buzzed out from the other side.

"Where's Jack?"

"At your service Captain" he stepped out.

"Find how long, will it take more to fill the ship?" he commanded.

Jack moved on toward the crew person. She stayed behind with Nicholas, they opted to sit down by the tree and discuss the situation to be preplanned before they move out toward Cruz Bay. There was the slightest fear that wriggled on his face. It wasn't shown however, it pretended to be read on his face. He began to get sweat under the calmly nature of cool breeze that lightly touched the coast.

"Are you okay captain?" Zenna concerned.

"Yeah!!! I'm right" he acted.

She offered him the wine glass with the artificial aroma of Caribbean flavor. He sipped in an instant gazing dreadfully at the swells that reached the edge.

"I'm afraid if he betrays me" he spoke gloomily.

She gave a thought on that until Zenna had come up with the boastful idea to enthuse with an affirmative boost. The connection of betraying and the price to be paid was supposed to be well served if that's the case.

"You know the price of it?" she added.

He shook his head and poured another drop of wine onto his glass and felt greasy about the time. His face however attempted to spread the right expression over those biased thoughts. And as the sun settled west they prepared to visit as far the invitation. On the other half of the island, the vicinity had the other kind of untouched surrounding. The air emerged to be bitterly catchy with moisture of cold. They received a warm greeting from the host. And as they mixed with the crowd they were perceived by Henry Wardo, who came out of his wooden tent holding the glass of wine. In the meanwhile, Zeena, busy stalking people in the crowd trying to witness the sight of Alvyn. Under the moonlit sky, the shore on the other half had the gray line that grazed spreading the occasional flavor of ocean smell. Just then from behind, Alvyn happened to hop on them.

"Great to see you guys" he added.

"Alvyn, she needs company" Henry added.

Nicholas and he walked on inside the wooden tent. Of course, it wasn't just an invitation but to make sure the deal was in perfect acceptance. His men all seemed to be pretty stronger than he expected.

"How do you manage these guys?" the questioned arrived from Nicholas.

He laughed and grinned and then sipped his wine glass. He exhaled out his breath and unfolded what he does for them. Nicholas carefully listened to him for the fact that he had been losing men each day who, either died of hunger or diseases. The priority of them he couldn't keep with higher concern.

"I've lost fifty of my men in storm and that counts in favor to receive from you" Nicholas added firmly.

"I sense the pity within me brother and with word I shall not set back at least for your sake" he poured another round in his glass.

Under the lamp light it glowed, red and yellow, and their shadow casted on the floor with scattered shape.

"I've reign the Island for twelve years and I know what defeat is all about. We shall not return empty handed but victory shall be our crown" Henry turned to look at him.

"I expect it true".

Out along the coastline, the crowded people jumbled up around a bonfire where rejoice of romance was gathered to witness. Amongst them Zeena and Alvyn added up to fill with joy.

"This is how you celebrate" Zeena talked.

Her voice sounded too low to be heard within the crowd. While the music kept beating the Island with soothing tune. All around the only kind of show that could be seen were the drunkard pirates who looked pretty much like a ghost under the faint light.

"Yeah!!! The real thing is about to begin".

People surrounded the bonfire in circle. All the strong muscles were the one to play the game. They placed their shield holding upon their shoulder forming the circular bridge.

"What they are doing?"

"They gonna choose two people. It's a game to chase around one another" Alvyn grinned.

The host made a loud noise and screamed with great voice. It all began where he chose the person. In an attempt to do so, his finger pointed toward Alvyn. The game turned utterly interesting as the crew began to fill the place more interestingly. In opponent to him another member was chosen.

"Alvyn, you're the man" a man shouted.

"Give me a bottle" he asked for.

Someone from the crowd gave him the drink. He swallowed within no time. He proceeded toward the circle.

"Watch out" he said pointing at her.

He got on his feet on top of those shields. Somehow, he balanced to stay steady until the game would begin. Ahead of him few shields apart stood the next. The chase would only begin if the host person would blow the trumpet.

"Hold me tight brother" he said to his shield man.

The trumpet was blown and the chase began. All around the circle, crowd began to shout in support for both. They followed through the shields. And as the game turned watchful it all pulled the attention of the rest. In that course of time, the coast was seemed more like a show ground. Yes, that's how people with no fear rejoice their lives. And among them was Alvyn the guy *who's in secret love with Zeena*. From the crowd, Zeena raised her voice, screamed in support of Alvyn. The show continued, it appeared hard to chase the other guy. Both maintained their balance on top of the shields. Meanwhile, Henry walked out with his partner Nicholas out in the dunes.

"What's going on there?" Nicholas keened.

"Oh! It's a game for the young men" he answered.

They walked toward the site, began to witness the panoramic exciting show. Alvyn was nearly close to the man with one shield difference. Within few minutes of chase, he grabbed the person, and on the last attempt to do so both tumbled down on the dunes. The applause came from all sides.

"That was pretty good" Henry praised him.

"Brother, I wasn't expecting you" he embraced.

"Good to see you Captain" he added.

They followed back to set up the dinner.

"I liked it" Zenna whispered.

The dunes smeared in the air as the breeze slithered along the coast. Inside the wooden tent, they caught up the table where the dinner was prepared for them.

"I'm glad you've come to us" Henry said.

The cluttered sound of spoon and fork began to fiddle. Out along the coast, the crowd gradually began to disperse. After the dinner got over, it was time for them to leave back.

"So when am I gonna see you again?" Alvyn spoke under the dark faint light.

"I guess the same place" she replied being very modest.

Alvyn stood upright right before her and with no sign of cause and bothering, he kissed her. There appeared no sign of rejection from her point. They were in love by now it was clear. Seconds turned to minutes still the positioned locked them against their lips. Nicholas, few meters away waited for her. Up above the grey shades of light began to hover around the island. The silent touch of sea breeze gave the effect of being in lone solitude. But more than that the peace around was felt with hopes of dreams coming alive.

"It's time we should leave" Nicholas muttered.

He released her safely from his arm. That gladly bonded them with that long kiss of touch. They walked along the edge of the shore until they could see the other half on their side. The fire burnt and few of crew members still awake to fetch them safely. When they reached their side, the glow of moon was faintly visible with scent of frozen breeze that came from the deep ocean.

"Goodnight Captain" Zeena said.

He shook his head and marched toward his tent. There was silence that resembled the night on his face. In a while Jack showed up. He stood unparallel against his body leaned on his shoulder over the wood.

"So, how was the other side?"

"You scared me Jack" she shivered.

"I heard something about you" Jack didn't stop talking.

She glanced and made her face on him. That utterly was a show of disappointment that flashed on her face.

"You never stop stalking me, do you?".

She walked on to her base camp. Jack watched her go, maybe in saddened stage. But that didn't bother him much. Of course, he was one reason that people around stayed happy. He never sought to reason, why she always had the ignorance feel toward him. Or maybe that she never liked him, no matter how strong like giant he was, woman don't give their importance much to guys like him. They don't like guys with heavy muscles and thick skin. He waited for a while along the dunes and then moved toward his tent. Of course, he didn't like the way Zeena had behaved like she never respected him. When the next morning broke out, the cry of seagulls was buzzing in the sky. It happened that Alvyn showed up that early.

It was their first meet. And he had not seen such huge gigantic man ever before on the Island. In search of Zeena, he coincidently happened to get encountered with Jack Hammer.

"You must be Henry's brother?"

"Yeah!!!!…you got it. Look I'm here to look for Zeena"

"That way" he pointed helpfully.

"Thanks. I'm Alvyn"

"Jack" he introduced.

"Nice meeting you" Alvyn said and left in the direction.

When he reached the spot he found her with the sword training. For minutes, he watched her. She hasn't realized his presence though. After few rounds of movement, she felt exhausted and opted to recreate.

"So, you showed up…huh!!!"

He walked closer toward her. She released her sword on the ground and took a seat on the dunes. She searched for a bottle of water to quench her thirst. She gently offered him for a sip. Few yards away, the ship stood firm and steady that anchored it from all sides. She watched at it with great vision to be withheld strongly.

"There's something I need to tell you" she quests for a space.

Alvyn thoroughly put on his ears and showed the gesture to make her feel comfortable "Yeah, go ahead".

"I've never lived a life what I dreamt of. I was all alone since twelve. I still do feel lonely when I watch at the sunset each evening. It's always been hard for me, struggling to survive whatever came. I wasn't a part of this crew but life landed me with them. There was no one to help me. You know why Nicholas Cook treats me that humble, because he was the one who gave me shelter and food to grow. I never saw my parents since they left me, and I still miss them but I can't let go myself. There was no one with whom I could share my feelings. I was wholly a lone world, it made me felt bad or sometime the worst phase of life" she sighed deeply.

Alvyn gave an effusive version of glance. His eyes read in emotive seasoning words that followed to be felt what she had recited about her painful life. He slightly managed to withdraw the situation from such effective saddening moment.

"Why don't you make me learn how to fight like you?"

She wriggled and grinned, with the softness in her eyes. She grabbed the strength out of her body and stood firmly on the dunes. She smiled with shallow zest on her face.

"Give him a sword" she asked the attendant.

She began to notch him in every motion of his movement. In time, she could feel the gradual improvement that he proved in less time. When the sun was rising out from the level, they stopped to rest. The practice was over.

"Why do you think you want to learn sword fight?" she handed him a bottle of water.

He looked extremely exhausted with drops of sweat water falling out from his body. He sipped the whole bottle and sat on the dunes witnessing the bright glow of rising sun from the edge.

"That's because I never felt like a warrior. I wanted to have that feeling" he smiled.

"It pretty much shows you never handled a sword before".

"You got it right at the first spot. I had a shrimping business earlier. My brother would help me out sometime. So, I rarely knew the mastery of sword until I began to work with him" he added soulfully.

They walked along the edge of the shore, as the brightening day evolved out in the warm form to suck out the dew on the wet sand dunes. The swells reached to touch their feet as they headed toward the long stretching north of the Island.

"How long have you been on this Island?"

"Quite a long, maybe five years till date" he said calmly.

She smiled at his humble gesture and, knowing that, gradually their inner attachment began to handle them more appropriately. At a quicker rate both got acquainted amongst them. But from either of them, walled to confess about their feelings. However, both inside knew what had been going between them. And that form of their love stayed silent no matter it didn't seem in need to speak out. It all understood within their hearts. Far beyond the coast, the birds fledge high up in the clear sky, they attended the scene of view to witness with the loved ones. Alvyn held her hand and stopped in mid way.

"I believe that it's getting hard for me to stay away from you anymore" he said softly.

Her eyes glimmered under the fallen light, below which the darken shadow casted on the ground. Her eyes imbibed in some notion to maintain the cause of being in one moment together.

"You can't fall in love with me Alvyn, it's not the sword fight" she urged.

He felt the sentimental touch of disagreement that caused him hard to swallow the truth of her words. She meant it honestly though the reality seemed something that eagerly read on her eyes. She turned her face toward the direction of vast ocean. It didn't have much to do with any of the rest except that she wasn't ready for it.

"It's already too late Zeena. Trust me when I say, believe me when I show and I promise you, I shall abide by with whatever cause to keep you happy" he added.

"I know, you're good man Alvyn. I think you should go back now. We'll talk later" she added firmly.

He flashed a shallow smile and gestured friendly in cool motion. He left with the imprint of captivated glance at her. She watched him go back along the route. From the mob a voice called her name. She turned back to answer the call. When she reached the spot, she found Jack indulged in some fight with his crew man. That wasn't pretty to sort at. He had blown his face and the blood split out of his mouth. Zeena rushed to the spot seeing the man bleeding.

'You're rude, cruel and merciless obnoxious dumb headed" she frowned at Jack.

The ferocious flattered on his face. He rushed to response to that.

"You don't talk to me that way, you slutty bitch".

"You have no right to say her that" Captain Nicholas in anger tone.

Jack saw him approached from behind. He didn't wait to hear the rest instead, he walked off the place without bothering about the rest. That wasn't an easy scene to take control of. Captain ordered the rest to take hold of the man to treat him.

'What's wrong with him?" Zeena squinted.

"I don't know. He's getting hard for me".

At noon the atmosphere allured with heavy wind. The sign of heavy rain was forecasted, as the moistened breeze began to blow in the coast. Maybe, it could turn into wild storm.

"Urge people to firm their position with strong hold the night. I can see the disaster approaching" Captain Nicholas ordered.

Zeena broke the news to all, as by evening all were prepared to face the heavy storm in case it arrived with furious intention. When the dark, marched in with the frozen air the storm welcomed in along the coast. However, it wasn't that distractive to waste people live. Nor it caused any damaged to the living lives on the Island. It arrived softly and went away smoothly. So fortunate with their cast of luck that nothing occurred to happen.

When the morning rose from the horizon, Nicholas buzzed out from the tent. In concern with the ship, he marched on to inspect if there came any disability by the mild storm of last night. Gladly, he felt relief that nothing had occurred that would go waste or caused them hard times.

"Seemed fortunate about the last night" Zeena squinted from behind.

"I wasn't expecting you" he said.

"When they gave you the word to move ahead?"

"Probably by next few days" Nicholas stared at the ocean.

They both walked back along the edges of the dunes. The water hit along the shore with small swells of tide reaching the Island. Just by his side, Zeena's company added the companion with more chords of tune to swing the early morning.

"So, do you like the guy?"

She felt amazed, wasn't in state to answer the question or precisely she wasn't hoping that question from him. However, she tried to maintain the cumulative smile on her face to outcast that she actually expected someday she would be raised about that.

"I mean, we're just friends" she added.

He chuckled and knocked his feet on the dunes to drain his wet feet. They reached the shore where the crowd gradually began to fill up the space. By now they had done all things about filling up the ship. He took one last glance before he addressed his men. Zeena stood by his side, paying her ears to listen up to what he had to say to their team. Nicholas began addressing his men in a way that would boost their moral feelings inside, rise the death from coffins. As the proceeding continued, meters away from their zone, Alvyn stood watching the parade. Zeena in coincident fashioned turned toward the other side. His presence was felt, she made her face and eyes shrunk throwing the glimpse of surprise outlook at him. Alvyn stood that meter away, ignored to step forward.

"Are you okay?" Nicholas keened.

"No!!!" she turned her face away.

Nicholas felt his presence, in fact he saw him that away. Somehow, he ended the speech soon. When he completed, he followed toward his tent with last word to her about being cautious with people. Alvyn arrived to meet her.

"I'm sorry, I interfered into your business" he said politely.

She smiled at him and notched his sensed behavior. While the morning allured with the fresh air after the mild storm, it had the aroma from the forest that located nearby. And they ensured to take a walk along the edges of the shore. Few distance away from the crowd, they spotted rock dunes that endlessly gave the access of view over the long shore that grazed with sands and mud. Up ahead to their sight they could watch those small tents that stood scattered firmly over the barren Island.

"My brother decided we would be leaving this weekend"

"Cruz Bay wouldn't be that easy for us" she breathed out.

And as the day burst out from its nest, the warmth of its breeze began to influence over the shore. It carried moisture with it. Alvyn looked at her sternly with some vibes of words that he glued inside him. So, to break out he wasn't in state to do so. However, the comfort he needed seemed less to willingly expel in true words.

"Why do you want to fight the mermaids?" he finally stroked.

"It's a long story, you'll gradually know when the time comes" she ended shortly.

Jack came up with news on the noon day. The other side, he meant Henry was forging to cheat him. However, he wasn't that sure about the outbreak of the hearing. He immediately thought to discuss the matter with Nicholas to warn him to stay alert. When he took the information to him, his first belief wasn't to accept it from Jack. He had never been so truthful in his words till date. His impression however kept fluctuating before Nicholas. When he said for second time, it sounded serious. Captain realized to respond to him.

"Are you sure about that?"

"I'm more than sure in what I heard Captain"

"He can't cheat me" Nicholas felt greasy about it.

He gave a thought to investigate if the words proved to be right. The indulging moment of sunset seemed to fade away from every viewer. And then there was Alvyn, who in strong state of confessing his feelings of love to Zeena had been strongly involved by now. They looked good as a couple. When the sun was finally set, they walked out of the site.

"You shouldn't be here all the time" she said firmly.

"You don't know him yet"

"Your Captain?" he giggled.

"You shouldn't underestimate his caliber"

"You don't know my brother and that's why they formed this alliance with us. Do you have any clue about it?"

Zeena looked startled and confused with his words. She instantly began to browse her inner conscious if this was conspiracy game between them. Alvyn left with that sort of decisive words that kept haunting her mind with fearful set. It wasn't something that she could make out, dirigible herself to Captain's tent. Where she found Jack in conversation with him.

"Is is right what I heard?" she strongly incorporated her voice.

That strangely focused their face in surprise note. May be they weren't expecting her to know about it. The rumor wasn't yet clear until they sort to talk with Henry. If that's the case the situation would probably be against them.

"We'll go seek him" the angry demand came from Captain.

By night, they strolled down to the other side. Henry who was on board, miles away in the deep ocean went to examine the way for their movement. They found his brother, Alvyn who was seated on a log with the rest of their crew with fire in the middle. Saw them approach, he stood on his feet and marched toward them.

"I didn't expect you all"

"We're here to meet your brother" Nicholas claimed.

Next to him Zeena stood with firm and stern look at him. It read on her face, she wasn't in state to show her innocent feel for him. Instead, she began to reciprocate her abhorrent behavior toward him. He understood her repulsive gesture and there was no sign of concern from his point. He paid his interest toward Nicholas although in some fashioned he cornered his eye at her.

"He's on board. Soon he'll be here. You can come inside" he escorted to wooden tent.

Outside, the babbling of crowd seemed pretty noisy. The hissing of tide ensured the swells were largely approaching toward the shore. Maybe the sign of tortured wind explored the land. The minutes turned to hour and yet there was no sign of return of Henry Wardo. Few moments later, a voice felt to reach nearer the tent area. Nicholas flipped the curtain to look at. Henry was in argumentative conversation with Alvyn, as they headed toward the wooden tent. When he stepped inside, he was amazed to see Nicholas Cook.

"I'm sorry, I made you wait longer"

With slow and silent movement, Alvyn slithered away from them. The exasperate face of Nicholas hinted the misunderstanding verse of conflict between them. The sense to realize arrived on him rather, Henry walked toward the table and prepared three glasses of drink.

"You heard wrong" Henry offered him the drink.

"What made you think I would falsify you, Captain" he added.

Zeena wasn't in state to hold her erupting disputes. She broke the silence of her long term shut mouth. She pointed out the reason that led them approach here. Moreover, the truth expelled by his brother to some extent may come true to them. She explained him with thorough detail. It took long time to settle down the wrong rumors. After hours of private discussion, they finally stepped out of the tent. Alvyn from crowd, turned to look at them. They followed on to their route.

There was desperate flash of eye from him in order to hold back Zeena for a while. But he knew, she was angry at him. The last imprint he could give to her was a smile that he let shine out as they passed the crowd. From her side, she paid no point of ardent interest although she saw him with the smile at her.

Chapter Nineteen

After longing weeks of loneliness, I finally took the step out of my house. I spent whole of a week in my cluttered room. And the reason that nobody showed was the freezing winter. It's December and Christmas carols were around. Lots seemed to be busy for the preparations. Few days ago, dad had bought a Christmas tree to begin with that. He decorated it on the front veranda that glowed red at night. Just a week away, we would be leaving for Alaska. What traumatized me was Tyler, never showed up for so long. I couldn't stay longer enough without concerning about him. When I reached his home, I saw him with few of his friends at the front yard. I felt the steering of my truck after along dealt of time. He heard me approached. Without any clue he skipped out of his posture and marched toward me. He had that intense notion to see me. He grabbed me high and embraced me tightly, moaned with happiness.

"I missed you a lot" his frenzy tone flashed.

"I'm so sorry for being rude" he added again.

He escorted me to meet up his friends. There were four in all. I've never seen them or in bulk male guys together. None were familiar. They introduced to me, in response I did the same.

"We'll see you later" said one of them, mentioning to Tyler.

They left us in understanding the privacy to be secured. Tyler's dad stepped out of the house. He seemed busy with his tools, like he was repairing some wooden window. He flashed a gentle smile. I waved hand at him.

"How's your dad?" he said from the distant.

"He's doing good!!" I added aloud.

Then he retrieved back to his work. Tyler came back after he escorted his friends till the gate. He looked eagerly in want of doing something or maybe he was very surprise to see me. I could read on his face. Indeed, he was glad to see me. We walked toward the garage. That was no more the same. It's after pretty gap of time I've come to his house. He did a great job by turning it into farm house extending with few rooms to study. I strolled inside as I felt the empty hollow blank room with no objects still kept. I flashed a smile as I inspected through the way. He stood and followed behind me. I turned the window opened and saw on the other side with the hammer being hit on the nail by Burney Gaige.

"Wonderful job" I appreciated.

"Look, I don't know I just got the sudden interest in books, and I decided to make into something else" he said.

When we approached to the other room, there were music instruments and guitars that were laid on the floor. Few posters and pictures stuck on the walls, pretty seemed it was like a room of an artist.

"Is this your room?" I claimed to know.

He shook his head and walked inch toward the window. He pulled the curtain aside and out the green meadow of the front yard was visible. It had the panoramic zest of feel to stay around. I saw his bike kept parked along the edge of the sloppy side of the yard. We walked out from the house. He wore a black leather jacket that terribly fitted on his muscular body. And his shimmering deep green eyes pelted with strong gaze at me.

"So, what's new with you this Christmas?" he talked.

I threw a short glance with big regard of cost and then walked on along his side. I wanted to let him know about the Alaska visit. But, before I began there's something I felt like knowing in deep from him. Maybe I should try or ignore, I was on dilemmatic thought. But I felt it important to unleash it out. After we reached the front porch of the house, I stopped for a bit before I marched to take the step ahead. It's noon and the day was flashing in bright light. It wouldn't be right if I leave without any clue to him. I never wanted to be selfish. After all, he had feelings for me. He turned back and gazed at me. I sorted to admit what I had inside. His stare gave me the zest to confess out. I didn't wait for time to be taken instead just few seconds of courage I gathered and uttered out.

"I'm going to Alaska with Alyward"

He dazzled at once and his face succumbed to fall low. Something, he wasn't ready to hear even though he pretended he wasn't envying about the situation.

"That's great" he said.

I could read the sense of regret in him yet doomed inside with heavy crust of anger and agony. He couldn't do anything to harm me. Nor he would think of doing such. He took up the step and asked me to follow him inside. I gradually took the initiative to march ahead. Inside, the television buzzed, out from the kitchen Tyler got a glass of drink. That was plenty to look at that huge size. He offered me one from his hand. I dimly glanced at the squash, and tried to take a sip. He took the couch and changed the channel. I quietly maintain to sit alongside him. He wasn't in his state to share even a little. I focused to understand what he was riding through his mind.

"I know; you don't find it appropriate me going with him" I shuddered.

He turned and followed to look at me with an unusual intention. His eyes read more than he could talk. And that enviousness floated on the surface. He sighed and turned to look at the television. I felt the hiss of wintry haze that followed in through the window. I looked at the site once and expected to hear from him. Until then, he remained silent.

"Why don't we walk out for a while?" I said again.

He shook his head uttering nothing but intention showed clear. He switched off the television. I followed him behind through the door. Burney Gaige was still at his fixing site. He waved at us, as we walked out of the porch area.

"So, when are you leaving?" he finally broke his silence.

I smiled before I muttered the word "Maybe, next week".

We strolled down through the street that led us to one of the finest site in the town. I still remember the lake we once visited and the stories about the mermaids who perished away. Meanwhile, I watched at the ranch that followed the green meadow down the road. We halted at the street café that cherished the aroma of coffee in the air. The freezing winter ensured it would be more drastically inclined to suppress the weather below normal temperature. We were served with the hot coffee. Few meters away, I sighted the group of young teenagers who were actually hitting their way back to home. I watched at them from the distant, wondering my old aged days. I haven't yet sipped the coffee that stood ideally.

"Would you be back soon?"

Momentarily, I felt the voice on me. I wasn't open with the surrounding nor was I on conscious state, in illusion swing about Tyler's presence.

"Yeah!!! Very soon" I mumbled.

We spent the hours in the self confined state. The minutes turned into an hour. And as the day was shutting to end, the real show of freezing winter engulfed over the area. We headed back, and while the ranch laid empty with the mist of frost that began to sparkle around the air. I saw few numbers of horses grazing. But they were under watch. Through the way, we talked about the evenings and the days to come. There was nothing that we discussed about more but both knew weren't suppose to talk about one another. After reaching the gate, I felt the need to return back home. The soothing smooth wintry breeze touched the empty air around.

"I should go back" I said.

He peeked at me and shook his head. The frozen smile flashed out unexpectedly and he acted cool with commendable heart. Lately, I felt good to have the day spent with him. The faded light began to doom out from the area, and as it did, the cold emerged to be stronger.

"When am I going to see you back?"

"I'll give a visit to you. Have a great Christmas" I added.

I clunk the door and settled inside the truck. I pushed the bottom and the engine was ready. With one last glance at him, I drove out of the place. On the mid way dad made a call to me and that he was asking about my decision over the holidays. When I reached home, I found him on the internet.

"Are you sure about the Alaska?"

"Yeah!!" I shrugged.

"No…I mean there are better place and you know it's winter" he added.

"Its fine dad" I said and headed upstairs.

"Oh!!! The dinner is ready" he said aloud.

When the next morning evolved out, Alyward was right at the front porch. Through the window, I had seen him glittering out in that sudden mist of cloudy weather. There was no sign of sunny light that fell on the surface. It's tremendously cold as the Christmas neared to its door. Dad was along with him. From behind Lexie added up. I strolled down and caught them up.

"What's the hot topic?" I said.

Alyward cornered his eye and threw his innocent flashy glance. He couldn't kiss me in front of dad. That was reasonable to behave appropriately before him. He smiled with shallow expression that engulfed him to stay silent for a while. And then after the hard course of talk dad left us. He drove out to his office. Waiting for the moment to happen, he caught me in an instant desire and kissed me without bothering about the rest. Lexie somehow had to room herself away from us and walked inside the house.

"You guys need to come in" she insisted.

"Let's go in" I said.

He wasn't to rescue his hand from binding me tightly from his arm. Rather another kiss came from him that touched my lips. And then we headed inside. I felt the traumatic coldness around. So, I wrapped around with another woolen jacket to combat the frosty weather.

By evening, we were out in the town to witness the hilarious sense of decoration that was put up around. I felt the real incoming of Father Santa around. And as we walked through the street, I had my hand hinged around Alyward. It's been after long time that I actually came out from the house. The aroma of the winter festival emerged to be great. Or to be precise I could genuinely say I found it much better than Arizona. Each house was ready to welcome the birth of Christ. But I knew, no matter what could be reason there I missed myself in real for the last few weeks. It could be, I might turn weak if I not visit the beach. Being living the human life and craving to see the real flesh out of my body it wasn't easy to program with the nature's rules. I was bound with normal people and just like them the limitations were upon me. The thoughts rumbled on my head, to that evening I wasn't aware if I was facing something awkward to be noticed.

"Are you alright?" Alyward pulled the chair for me.

With sudden browse of immature thought I pretended to be right although, I felt the weakness of my inner vibes responding. The fragility endured around to such part that I felt the rescue of my intuition was needed. I halted for the second gaze at him. Under the shaky motion, my feet braced me strongly on the floor before I took the chair. From the serving end arrived Lexie with the cups. I read the label of self service that was marked in red. Outside, the way stood empty and as those passersby showed their glimpse at us, there happened to be no cause of intriguing urge about the place. There were very few of us inside the restaurant. Lexie again came up with the plate of Italian Pizza.

"It's the best in the town" she giggled.

She took her chair. I was still at halt analyzing the denial thought out of my mind. From the side bar, I watched at the climate as the day drooped to end out. It might be the strength in my body gradually damping me away. How so ever, I tried to control hard to stay steady with the ongoing situation. I hadn't uttered even a single word since the last few minutes. On the other hand, Alyward tried to get me comforted with his alluring nature. I couldn't disclose the fact that I needed an immediate assistance. I was in great need to visit the sea, which I couldn't disclose openly to him. Lexie's presence slightly made it non executable. Alyward figured me out, for the fact, he remembered that water gave me strength to sustain as human.

"I think we should leave" he squirmed.

"But we haven't yet finished our food" Lexie claimed.

"It's urgent"

"What's the matter with you both?" she demanded again.

She began to feel the wrong of something that clutched amongst us. However, she didn't disapprove returning back. We walked back through the same path. Dad wasn't at home yet. I felt the complete loss of my strength by the time we reached the front door. I began to feel the loss of consciousness around me. The images of darkness appeared before me.

"Anna, are you okay?" Lexie concerned.

Somehow the support came from Alyward.

"Take me for medication" I muttered.

Alyward rushed me into his car immediately. He made it quick. Lexie watched, wondering what was going on.

"I'm coming with you" she demanded.

"No" Alyward said.

"No…I'm coming"

"No, you're not coming with us" he frowned.

I heard their fading voice in argumentative verse, as I lost my consciousness. Alyward drove me out of the place soon. She stood watching us, as we disappeared. I knew, Lexie wouldn't forgive for this but my hands are tied, I cannot unleash the truth to her. We rode toward the beach. Alyward pulled me out and gently placed me on the dunes. He patted on my cheek and tried to call me out. Then he sprayed water on my face that helped me to regain my sense back.

"We're here" he assured.

I gently got up on my feet "I'll be back".

I asked him to wait. As I proceeded toward the water, I undressed myself. He stared at my back. I dived into the water and swam deep into the depth of oceanic monuments. I was finally into mermaid. Gradually, I felt the bonding of my body with the aquatic period of life. The strength gave me hopes and energy to fight the outer world. I floated on the surface and then retrieved back into the depth. There was some charm to be into real form. I was born with this and, I couldn't throw it out. Even if I gave a thought, the nature wouldn't have allowed me to do so. My tail had the smooth movement with the finest fin that regenerated. I passed across the coral reefs that were sloppy on the sea bed. For that instant, I could follow my instinct what it directed me. *Jimmy* wasn't forgotten, I couldn't take the chance at least for that night. I needed to heal more than meeting up other creatures. Day by day, I was growing in size. Since the last I found lots of difference in me. I felt like a grown up lady mermaid by then. The enthralling feeling of being a part of one such kind enthuse me up. The difference between human and the rest of my kind didn't bother me anymore. Indeed, there was no point to ill human feeling that I could bear again. I was happy for who I was. After streaming through the waters for about an hour, I realized that Alyward had been waiting for me up there. But I felt the engrossing task to be in that form, for it was more tempting and realistic to stay such. I never felt such before, every time I found in my tailed form. But that night, I was eagerly willing to stay back forever in the ocean. But I couldn't, I had to justify both form of my life. And that I had fallen in love with a human, who seemed to be a futuristic guy. I encoded with that feeling and finally emerged out of the water after having the throughput of regaining my strength. As I floated out into the shore, the dunes covered with dew felt wet. I walked out toward him and the gentle breeze smothered through the easy environment. I covered again in my clothes. The frost in the air blocked the sight to get through the way. It took away the visibility of one's view. I approached toward him slowly. His reflexes yet didn't respond to him about my presence. And when I finally got there, he turned his back and faced me. He took in immediate unexpected state.

"Are you feeling fine?"

"Yeah!!!!" I shook my head.

It was too late and the night had grown old. Something we weren't supposed to be outside. At home, dad and Lexie waited for us impatiently. When they heard the sound of car's engine, they immediately flashed out of the room. There was no point he could argue on the matter; Adam knew the cause of all. Lexie however yet seemed to be unsettled with the fact that she hasn't even got a clue about the incident. However, it meant to stay silent for her. Lucky are those who willingly summons themselves upon the hands of almighty to grab the best of their life, and maybe that's what I was going through. Or perhaps, it's just the opposite happening with me. But regardless of all those intuitive intentions, I least bothered to indulge upon those acts, I only knew I had a mission plan to bring back my mother. And for that I could cause anything to do if I needed. The motive grew stronger than ever before. For me, it's always been the other way around with dad. But all through these years, I found the best in him. He's kind and generous father. After the dinner, Alyward joined upstairs with me. He stayed back the night. We talked about the planning of the next semester. Also the upcoming Christmas celebration and vacation trip to Alaska. There was no sign to say about my mother. All within few last week, it was doomed for a moment. I needed a gap to research for the exact way to reach mom. She hasn't come to my dream anymore nor her telepathy connection worked to talk to her. I couldn't search her. Since the last letter, she never wrote to us again. But I didn't forget her words that imprinted on my mind. Alyward gently joined by my side. He pulled the woolen blanket and covered me up. Then he stared at my face for long like he had never seen me in years.

"Why you looking at me like that?"

"You look different" he said.

I snuggled into his arm and finally I felt the calmness in the air. I fell asleep without anymore cause of wasting sorrow. When the morning broke out the shimmering rays of blessing fell on my face. The interrupted dream shattered into fragments as I opened my eyes. I found his arm still held me tight. I gently took aside of myself and released. He looked fragile with his eyes closed and that face sparkled with the glitters of happiness that showered on his face. So mesmerizing and soft, calm that screened. It wasn't easy to keep away from watching him. The serenity involved kept me strongly under watch. I looked peacefully at him just to feel he was there for me all night. I opened the window and pulled the curtain aside. The focus fell sharply on him and he struggled to keep continuing his sleep. He slowly opened his eyes and marked at me. The smile flashed out of him. His feet touched the cold floor and stepped ahead toward me. We watched outside through the slicking slit of the window and then gradually the frost happened to disappear as the day grew young.

After a week gone, the early Saturday morning there was the eagerness of being carried away by the soothing sense of vibrant nature. The day we were supposed to leave for Alaska for winter break. The Christmas was three days away since then. Alyward showed up by early morning. By noon, Lexie joined us. The trio would be indulging together for a week. It seemed hard at the beginning for Lexie to get acquainted with Alyward but in time both could be openly free and friendly.

Dad dropped us to the airport by evening. The flight timed at eight. In between we would be landing, I had no idea where could that be, I just knew we needed to exchange another flight. I had few books carried with me to keep myself engaged during the flight hour. The last moment appeared to be little sad as I would be missing dad for a week. However, it seemed great, I had the two along with me. Even though it was his plan, he skipped to join us. Dad kissed me on my forehead before we left for. *Love isn't just a feeling but it's like an art in life that needs to be constantly looked after*. That was how it meant to be, as I turned to look at Alyward, who was seated next to me in the flight.

Chapter Twenty

Dora was aware about the arrival of the pirates in trying to reach the Island. However, the news wasn't fallen to everyone. Within few weeks after the news, they were called by the head, Duncan, the only merman. They made a visit to him. There was nothing that they had planned for. Instead, they waited for their arrival until then they had decided they would plan out in their execution to be undertaken. Deep down under the Caribbean Sea they sort to look at one another.

"You both disappointed me" Duncan said in anger tone.

"We were about to tell you" Keren incorporated her voice.

"That's not the choice" he frowned.

That triggered with little insertion of fear within them. They had never seen his aggressive avatar. His tailed strongly twirled around his body and swam toward them. On his account, they could only float and listen to his insisting command. After an hour of thorough case of research of angering vibes, they returned back to shore.

"He shouldn't have been so disrupting in his conduct" mom said.

As they walked on through the dunes toward their car, Keren glanced back their way.

"I've never seen him getting so angry" Keren added.

They drove back to home. The television buzzed with the authentic Caribbean Salsa. From the kitchen, Keren held a plate of green salads added by her side.

"Did they reply you back?"

"No" mom said.

"Dora, I think you should give them a chance to meet you. They're your family" Keren sounded too generous.

"Adam won't forgive me" Dora sighed.

She took a bite of a leafy spinach and continued at the television. Keren arrived with a bottle of wine. She joined her seat back beside her. She poured in both the glasses. She watched the boring damn thing with her. Nor she insisted her to change the channel. The frozen breeze from the far deep ocean blew in rolling over the shore. Keren rose from her posture to shut the window down.

"Are you feeling cold?" Dora muttered.

She shook her head and calmly sat beside her. She breathed out and keenly looked at her face.

"You don't worry about them right"

"We shouldn't be talking about it" Dora felt discomfort.

"I can see the regret in your face Dora"

She nudged and rose from her seat and walked out of the room. The rule of frustration emerged out on her face. Keren watched her. She switched off the television and looked out for her. At the backyard, she found her seated lonely in desperate rate of sadness. Keren walked slowly toward her. She turned back and settled herself well. Beside her, Keren gently sat on the log. She exhaled her breath and looked at her. She realized with the sort of sentimental conversation they had inside. It wasn't something which Dora would appreciate all time. However, in many cases she reminded about us to her.

"I'm sorry, I got carried away" Keren released her breath.

Dora managed to look at her in notion of sudden emotive support. She shook her head uttering none of her voice. She sighed and glanced straight looking toward the forest.

"It's not that I don't want to go back. But what's more important is to keep them safe" she added.

"It's understandable" Keren showed support.

Both walked in, thereby the vacant in the air laid hollow with the incoming shackles of cool breeze. The night felt calm as the time redeemed to cast away the bad frost over the frozen sky. When the next day churned out, both took the chance to walk down the little town of bay house. The streets were in mood of celebration as the Christmas would be wonderful show over the whole Island. They had entered into a store, the Home Depot to collect the necessary requirements for the Christmas. When done with the shopping occupation they visited their all time Rene's corner, a cafe that popularly known for its aromatic Brazilian Cocoa. Both handled to grab a chair at one's corner. They were received with the host of welcoming presence at the entrance. It's Christmas and all visitors were sent back with a gift from the cafe. The owner met them once before they had left the place.

"It's a great pleasure to have you here Keren" said Rene Paul.

She had been the owner of the place since the last five years. That's how they put the name of the place on her name as *Rene's corner,* quite a familiar lady to Keren. They returned back by evening. There was the silence in the air and the weather began to get fragile as the windy shore attempted to get wilder, molder over the bay. This could bring the winter rain on the whole Island which wouldn't be that profitable for the people on the Island. But to our kind, it could bring the triumph on us, if the case showed to be positive. The ocean will have to turn brutal for sea explorer who had been trying to reach the Island. The ways would have to be severely blocked with hurricanes and disaster.

The dinner was ready on the table as both began to handle the fork and the spoon.

"So, did you think about inviting Shaun on Christmas night?" Keren said sipping her glass of wine.

"Yeah!!! I might"

After the dinner got over, they decided to take a walk out in the lawn. But the little windy breezy night got them stuck in the house. They declined the idea of strolling down the lawn instead, afterward they thought to spend the night in decorating the house. Till midnight the weather pretended to be silent but as the minute passed the sudden stroke of hurricane hit the Island. The terrific and the roar of winds blew from all directions. Dora struggled to close all the windows of the house. But the wind kept them in fear, no matter how strong the house stood steady there was always the chance to break out.

When the next morning glimpsed out, the angry wind seemed to have calmed down. There was no sort of home casualties around. Above all the clear sky stood humble with streams of blue color of the ocean. The nature of the free environment changed to be much favorable for sea surfers.

"I think we should walk down the beach" said Dora intricately.

The idea intrigued Keren and opted to grab the chance. By noon, they drove toward the beach. It wasn't the empty place it used to be. The reflection of clear light from the deep ocean blanketed the ambience with pleasurable notion to be. As they hit the shore side, the influence of winter breeze noted the incoming of extravagant winter festive moment. They walked toward the nearby restaurant. It wasn't the day to be wasted. Instead, lots were seen along the beach. Just a day away from real celebration of Christmas evening that would bring the enlightenment in the town. Dora reminisced about her past. She narrated the story how she would decorate her home at Arizona. She misses all those things. Above all, she thought about us. The waiter came by with the tray of sandwich and the cups of coffee. She gently placed and skipped off for other duty. For a moment, there occurred a silence between them but as the day brightened they strolled out heading through the edges of the shore line toward west where the day was setting down.

The reminiscing thought still hovered on her mind, Dora however related back herself with the past. In contribution to that Keren kept giving the company to the journey. The twilight still visible, and the cry of seagulls pulled them back way. After the splendid moment of time spent, they sought to return back home. The enthused for the one-time celebration caught them high as it was the only two in the lonely Island of human. Most often, the lake gave them the solitude feeling to have themselves up in their divine form of mermaid. And that they could spend the whole day in their original transformation. Of course, they gain their strength each day visiting the lake along the hill side. Under the prolific truth of life, the enormous hope of courage was being heaped upon them. It was until they had told Duncan about the arrival of the pirates on the Island that they could live fearlessly. However, the motive strengthened them.

Keren was settling her closet just few hours away from the break of Christmas night. She had the old pictures of her framed alongside the rack. Her mother held her with the sweetest smile that she could feel. Her past memory looked steadily on the pictures. That gave her little blow of sentimental acquisition to accumulate that she missed her mother. In doing so, Dora slowly walked in, while she wasn't in aware about her presence. Keren placed the frame back to where it belonged.

"You look beautiful" said Dora sighting at the picture frame.

"That's my mother" she sighed.

The clock ticked twelve and the divine day arrived to witness the birth of Christ. Lately, the night stayed charming. The remaining hours they could only view the outside world with the blow of lightening design all around the Island. The sky above glittered with the faded stars as the backdrop of winter cast to display its fragrance of frozen smell over the air. They could share their inner depth of heart that hour of the night. While both had the ardent expectation, they would have a visitor the next morning to celebrate the unending divinity. When the sun rose from the east, the freshly air from the south gave a blow of divine day to upheld the purity of nature. Other than witnessing the phenomenal serve of Christmas package, the Island happened to be one of the most visited tourist place.

The door bell rang up. Maybe many times, until it was intolerable to accept anymore. Not because it was too fussy to respond but both seemed to be busy in their task. Dora somehow managed to make her shower quick and headed to show up. She just wrapped herself in towel, knee level. When she opened, her expectation wasn't that much that she was taken aback by his presence. Shaun showed up.

"Who's there?" Keren glimpsed her face.

"It's Shaun"

Keren came out and received him inside. Shaun came for the first time and the way he actually thought it was far more than he could really think off. He looked around the house as he stepped inside and turned aside to gaze about all the things.

"I'm happy you came" Dora said, she buzzed out in complete dress.

"Well, Shaun it's great to see you" Keren greeted him.

He took the chair and Dora decided to comfort herself in the couch. Keren joined them. There was little shyness that delivered from both the sides.

"It's quite a big house" he said.

"Yeah….it is" Keren replied.

The day began to line along the shades of canopy that fixed the warmth of the winter day in pleasurable mood. It was just the expected meeting they had wished for. For Dora, it claimed to be more special. It had turned to be farthest case of better day to spend with Shaun. They had decided to take the route to the beach to witness the spectacular born of new beginning of the year. After they finished the little talk they drove to the beach. The truth still kept hidden from the people. In no chance of mistake, Dora would likely to trust Shaun. No matter they wouldn't unleash who they are. It's just the human nature part they had played their role on the land surface. When under water, they're no more the one with heart of human kind. In other words, the world to them is different from the world they come into. A sudden flurry of activity began to initiate at the other side of the beach. It's the young crowd that seemed to be indulged in their fancy way to be celebrated. However, it's the one way that the Island always had the gleam of real joy.

The evening gray line shaded along the horizon. The charm brought the essence of enormous rounds of happiness. Altogether, the time rhymed with soulful art of love. When the sun was covered with no more life, they turned back.

Shaun left after the well spent evening. Maybe for Dora it was more emotional moment to spend at least after years though she missed her family. Yet then, the visible act of being confronted was notable. For them it always took more to listen to their heart. With Keren by her side, she could possibly feel the life to look ahead with hope. Days passed on, the knock of the beginning of new day would be seen within time. *When the moment to realize about the past reads before your mind it's always hard to examine the fault that we come across.* Even then we self satisfy ourselves enduring to stay with those mistakes in life. Maybe the case could always be opposite if we don't look back. But somewhere in point of our life, we tend to reflect back once. That's one thing that our life teaches us about what we've done since beginning. Beyond that, we're either in state of happiness or sadness that gives us the reason to keep surviving. *A choice always gives us a way to hunt for that possible call us to stay firm with our hopes.* And a chance shows us the way why we shouldn't try to look for. *If choices aren't made by us, it is belief that choices make us.* There may not be time when our life would lead you to the right path, but our instinct always shows us the basic needs, it's the second chance that makes us belief. The best could be brought out of those hopes and faith. *Steps that we take may not lead us to the right path but our hopes, believe, faith, trust can show us the bright side of every tough way.*

I may be more tendering and soft within my inner core. My mother Dora, always showed her courage and I respected for her valor. Such inspiration was always commendable from her. I never knew since she left how she could be looking now. I only saw once last time when she had left us at Arizona. Later, she had just showed her apparent vision before my eyes. I belief, she was always watching us.

Chapter Twenty-one

Dad had few guest and colleague invited to home during the Christmas. He made a call to us, while we were at Alaska. Just few more days we had with the whole package. The chill winter sored us with terrific breathless cold Alaska. It was the first time that I actually had seen real Alaska, although I've heard a lot about the place in papers and television. By the time we returned back the year ended. It's the New Year evening when dad was already waiting for us. Alyward and Lexie added to us. The winter of past year was gone and I felt very relief by the fact that we were no more in Alaska.

Dad served the hot soup of tomatoes. Meanwhile, he had been quite busy on his phone. Just after we left for Alaska, a man died. The responsibility was given to dad to investigate about the case. He was seen inside his room. I threw a glance at him. When I sensed he was almost done with the talk, I called him out to join us.

"So, how was the vacation?"

Alyward peeked at me before he felt the comfort zone. Just then, I heard the sound of bike arriving closer. I wasn't to imagine it to be Tyler. For sure, it was him. And with no further ado, I just got out of the chair and walked out of the room. He parked his bike inside. I walked fast. He hurriedly followed toward me. He gave strong blow of hug and lifted me from the ground.

"I missed you so much" he sighed out.

"I missed you too" I added.

We walked in to join the rest. I didn't want anything wrong to happen. Somehow the situation must stay stable, I gestured. Tyler saw him and his fist gripped stronger. I ensured him to calm down within his control. He sat by my side. Alyward looked at me, his intention however stayed clear to me. He faced me to the other side of the table. Dad could follow the inner conflict that was prevailed in short time. He maintained the smile on all of us. After the dinner got over, I decided to spend few time with Tyler. Alyward and Lexie came up with dad in the living room.

In the front yard, I felt the airy silent blow through my skin. Tyler walked alongside me, indulged much more in sensitive gesture. He had been kind to me since the time we knew each other.

"I know, I should have told you about his presence" I said, hesitantly.

"It's not your fault" he peeked at me.

We followed few more steps ahead until the fire was burnt. We settled for a while feeling the warmth of its heat. The silence in the air added much of nervousness and that in between I felt, I was fumbling with my words. It showed clearly the other guy was just sitting next to me knowing the truth that he had his heart given to me. Now considering the reality, choices weren't the right things for me. I never needed to know, who would be my choices. I left the chance to my fate and choices must play the game for me. The beginning of this New Year showered my life in no different manner but it's pretty much clear, I got what I desired for.

"You look beautiful" he whispered.

I glanced at him, the reflection of the reddish ash fire painted on him. He looked brighter under the florescent effect of the bright fire light. I made a smile for him before I felt the word to tell.

"I could never thank you. You've always been the best friend of mine" I said intricately.

He seemingly looked at me and gestured slow with a smile on his face. His hand followed closer to me. I could smell the perfume of his jacket. I felt his palm ran on my cheek. The elusive touch of attachment sprouted out and that the whole world at once seemed to slow down. I felt the touch of his lips on mine, something I was suppose to set back. But some kind of feeling fixed me up and the thought of courage to move away never followed the instinct. The night stood calm and peaceful. We walked in looking for the rest. The protest arrived from Alyward who was willing to return back to home. He walked out of the room, saw me with Tyler. Dad watched the dramatic scene without indulging much into it. Lexie felt discomfort with the melodramatic scenario.

"Are you guys oaky?" she threw her voice.

"Yeah!!! We're good" I said showing no wrong.

Tyler stood by my side in no utterance of gesture and words. I followed out Alyward. He looked angry and unsettled. The fuzzy expression sorely indicated toward me. He wasn't in state to talk with the situation but in intense motion, he doped himself with rage and anger. When I had gone to fetch him, he was already in state to leave. I called him and pleaded to stop him.

"You should know what you've done. I'm sorry, I was wrong about you" he in firm voice and drove out.

"Alyward, Alyward......listen to me" I followed toward the gate.

Tyler watched us from the veranda. I turned to face inside. I followed the way. Tyler walked out to the front yard.

"He shouldn't have been here" Tyler said.

I endured the intensity of such words from him. Instead, I went inside. Lexie had been waiting me upstairs. Tyler tried to stop me. He held my hand. I frowned in gesture.

"You should get going. I'm not in mood right now to talk about the issue" I added firmly.

He sensibly withdrew himself and followed in the direction toward the bike. He galloped like the speed of shooting stars. Watched me in doodle mood, Lexie tried to cheer me up. The need to recreate myself was the only way that I could handle the game of frustration and relationship. The vision that I could picture showed me the only way to know what I was. The only source that gave me the real meaning to myself was the beach. That following night I decided maybe I shouldn't hide anymore. Though knowing that I shouldn't be that hurry letting people know about my reality. It's isn't human, we're way more different in our world.

"What's wrong with you?" said Lexie pulling the curtains.

The breeze was really thrusting the body with cold. And the crappy climate outside even made it worse. I could still here the sound of television downstairs. Dad wasn't asleep. The night was deep and the howl of wolves came from nearby forest. It came long after many months. Lexie compelled to break my silence.

"He shouldn't have come here?"

"Who?" Lexie plunged inside the blanket.

I turned toward her and intended to join her in the bed. I felt like not to disclose about the secrecy. She roomed for me and joined alongside her. I saw the new day arriving out of the window. Its late night and the effect of cold grew even stronger.

Lexie slept within no time. The only soul that remained awake was me who wandered watching at roof ceiling pretending to find out her image as she crawled inside the warmth of quilt. By the time, I tried to know, I was asleep the sun had already risen from the east. Lexie, initially tried to wake me up but the response of my intense sleepiness kept me holding. When I walked to the window, I found her out in the front yard. Dad was prepared to leave. I realized about the earlier day what we had gone through. It wasn't the best of start. I stepped aside and looped back at the edge of the bed and wondered about looking at those old pictures. The Freshman Year gone by and yet the period of the school days was intact. I wasn't in metal prepare to face all over again, going back to that same place with the same old Chevy. I tried to console myself until I prepared to step down. When I strolled out, Lexie saw me passionately. She was in preparation to go. I could read on her face the excitement that she carried for herself in wanting to go to school, meeting up the fellows.

"So, are you coming today?"

I looked around for a bit and then turned to her. She waited what I would tell or perhaps she was expecting the right answer. I gave brief thought over it to finalize if I was sure to go to school with her. It's the beginning and I'm not sure if I really wanted that to happen. I pondered. Alyward's presence would bring something new to me but not sure if he would show up after last night conflict.

"I guess not" I replied.

"Are you sure about it"

"Yeah!!!" I reassured.

She left me behind few minutes after her preparations. There was nothing to hold me back from doing the things but I needed some room for myself. There was no choice to be made, that I had been waiting for mom's connection for the last few weeks. Momentarily, I gave the thought toward the beach. I made the call to dad and let him know. I drove out immediately.

The beach stood isolated and I knew it was the best time that I could grab. I parked just next to the lobby area where people usually rest their cars. I moved ahead toward the water and slowly the dresses were fallen out of my body. As the tide welcomed me, I dived in and followed deeper inside. My legs and my body began to transform. And I gradually felt the need of being in happy state. I called with my voice on. *Jimmy* readily showed up very fast. We met after long months of gap. We swam through the tide and currents exploring the deeper side of the ocean. As we began to take the ocean tide, we passed through the ocean floor, the smell of those corals and the wreck of several ships that laid under. It began to be adventurous journey within the hour. *Jimmy* took me to their group. There I met their king again. I almost forgot about my mission toward the Island. But I haven't given the word yet *when we shall be moving ahead*. I was doomed with men on my sides. Persuading Tyler was really hard. On the other hand, the team to form between Alyward was yet lying suspended. I had no idea if they would really join to help me up. I had almost spent whole my days under the ocean. It gave me the real zest of being in real power of being a mermaid. Day by day the power on me generated rather stronger and steady. The sun doomed by the west when I looped out to the water surface. I needed to return back home. I gave a glance at my tail once the color seemed to have changed.

Dad was in the kitchen when I returned back. I heard him clunk with the kitchen stuff. I dropped the bag on the chair and looked for him inside.

"So, you skipped your school's first day"

"Dad, I found it really crappy under this cold winter day"

He gave a smile and flipped to get back to slice the carrots. I gently took the chair to sit beside, indulging with him in some kind of talk. The outside weather pretended to grow freezing and the frozen breeze came in through the window. I gazed at the outside darkness and felt the deep darkness with thorough call of certain humanity.

The morning stood calm by the sea side. Nicholas strolled out watching at those birds flying high. He had covered himself with long length woolen over coat. The gaze that followed out of his eyes stretched through the endless vast ocean. The wildest dream of historic memory flashed out of his brain. The reminiscing picture about his lost family rendered his heart with the frozen beat, he once used to hold for them. But on that sudden morning he felt even deeper about his lost. The step followed him behind. There was the sadness of his life that flashed on his face.

"What's wrong Captain?" Zeena said gazing at the rising sun.

He turned aside and looked at her. His eyes fiddled with little bit of sadness and frozen moisture. The swell began to lessen as it reached the shore.

"Sometime life teaches us more in an adventure way, in between the course I never knew, how much it meant to have lose something very precious in life. I realized that behind every loss of life, there's something that gives you to move on. No matter even your closest one goes away from you, they leave an impression that lead you to teach how to go on with life without them".

She breathed out and looked straight toward the ocean. By far, the days have gone and the wonders of living legend are buried with those memories.

"I believe you should talk with Henry Wardo about the latest concern about the Island"

"Perhaps, you should gather more information about their crew from Alvyn" he added.

There was the immediate silence from her side. Indeed, she felt slightly awkward which she wasn't expecting to hear from him. Nicholas walked out of the place meanwhile, Zeena stood watching at the horizon line from where the ending day was focused in great alignment. She withheld the feeling of being in isolated tool and gazed at the ocean water. Just then a voice arrived from behind. The huskiness stayed loomed in the air.

"It's isn't good when you know you're broken by your own"

She turned and looked at him. He joined by her side, had same line of sight watching at the vast ocean.

"What for you're here?"

He peeked at her and turned aside to look at the long shore. There the silence prevailed, the only that could be heard was the roar of swells that arrived smoothly. Alvyn looked at her once again pretending he had something to say. But the hindrance of words, stayed untold instead, the gesture began to operate more efficiently.

"I know; I'm not supposed to be here right now. I can understand you've been hurt" he added politely.

She looked at him and turned again to face the ocean. There was the fragrance of morning dew in the air. Listening to the vibrant sound in the air, they sought to take the long walk through the shore line. The whine of the frozen breeze touched them indulging more into the prosperity of being in lone solitude. When the day turned to noon they walked back to the same place. But this time, they had encountered with the Captain.

"You didn't show up" the voice utterly kind.

Alvyn at the first act intended to get a hand shake from him. There was the kind gesture from Nicholas.

"I know you've gone through very hardship of life" he added again.

His concerned grew much stronger for Zeena.

"Why don't you both join for the lunch; we have a big meal waiting" he called both.

Zeena somehow confronted herself without showing the expressed view of embarrassment. They walked into the tent where the rest waited for them.

"So, when your brother will give us the right day"

"Oh!!! Well, he has been giving a thought to that. Very soon, we'll move ahead toward Cruz Bay Captain" said Alvyn proceeding inside the tent.

He returned back to their crew by sunset. Back at their place, Henry had been longing to see him. His absence perhaps had the tormenting effect on him. The fact, that Henry always had been protective about his brother. Until his presence was felt within the time, he allegedly involved to crust out his anger on him. Which Alvyn didn't expect to receive on his return.

"You weren't supposed to visit them" the anger tone evolved out.

"I'm sorry brother, I disobeyed you" Alvyn put his head down.

"Sorry won't work. I've a task for you the next morning" he said.

He followed toward his tent. Alvyn stood numb watching at the flow of sea waves. Perhaps, that made him feel guilty about the way he had gotten treated. He walked on toward the edge of the beach line. When the night felt deeper into the open sky, he finally had his confronted mind to let go about his anger toward Henry. In his tent, before he oft to bed the last thought that he had in his mind was Zeena, that they had the whole day spent together. And the picture of shore line through the lengthy beach pictured before his eyes knowing that his love had crossed beyond any line of boundaries.

The morning brought out in an event that Alvyn was busy in piecing the woods through his sharp edge axe. The ambient sounded gloomy with the hiss of swells from the ocean water. The footsteps headed toward him. Alvyn sensed it was Henry who had come to look, if he was doing right with his punishment.

"I shouldn't have given you to work but you broke my heart kid" he said.

Alvyn shook his head and resumed to piece the woods.

"You can stop by the lunch time" Henry added again.

There was just a glitch of glance from him and watched Henry going toward the ship. The sound of cutting edge cracked the woods from Alvyn's axe. He began to wrap up as soon as possible.

He arrived to join his brother at lunch. He was done with the wood cutting. He was seated next to his mates. The wooden square table was served with the drinks and the meats that was obtain from hunt the last day.

"Do you love her?" that came from Henry.

"I don't know what you're talking about" Alvyn sipped his wine.

"Oh!!! C'mon don't make me fool".

Henry had never been so open about his brother's life. The zest to keep him away from danger was the first motive that he had always about him. But in time, now he began to realize that he had grown to be a man. He had every right to lead his own life but not to construe under anyone. Maybe that was last day that Alvyn would dine with his brother. After that he would be on his own. The response of such separation shouldn't give them set back. But in real heart Alvyn never wanted to happen such. No matter, what they had been through since kids both have done their best to grow up. And most importantly, he knew without Henry he wouldn't be no-where. The bond shouldn't' be broken just because of a girl. After that lunch, they met up again at dinner. This time it was seriously considered about their living condition of both being a brother. Henry gave the freedom to him in leading his own way of life. However, Alvyn didn't want to stay away from him instead, he showed that he cared for him. He would always likely to be with him in any kind of danger. To these words of him there was the ardent feeling of being the oneness between them. For the first time, Henry felt he did deserve to someone like a kind of person who really cared for others. And the words of his brother instilled him with hope that someone was always there behind him in every support of his life. Just before they would part for the night, Henry had the warmth of his heart for his brother, and that expression, that he was sorry for treating him wrong. It was after long time they both hugged each other.

The night felt calm as they parted to their respective tent. Henry watched him as he walked on to his tent. He sighed and felt the repression of being the cruel mind to his own people. That was a new reformed for Henry. He felt, he had grown much wiser than ever before. The thoughts rumbled in his head when he gently settled himself on his bed. He wandered watching at the perforated ceiling and then turned his body to let himself calmly down to sleep by the night.

Often, most people realize the meaning of life lately. Or that the freedom to elude for others stay doomed until the feeling of thought that usually tend to realize them. In certain way, *there are relations that would wholly depend on the freedom of each other.* Under those the source of manifesting human feelings and emotions would be freely depended on oneself rather than bounded to one another. And Alvyn deserved to have his own freedom of life to express and to fall in love with the girl he loved.

Chapter Twenty-Two

Keren still had the harsh feeling toward Duncan. Nonetheless, even if she tried to forget that part she couldn't. She knew, she felt very bad after they had informed him about the pirates' arrival on which they weren't given the appreciation instead, they were looked down upon their misleading situation. But that early morning of winter, there was some sort of rejuvenating feel around the yard. She was interrupted by her mate, Dora. At the front yard with lash green showcase the brightening yellow rays fell scattered around the yard. Dora walked through the way to her.

"What a welcoming greet" said Dora.

Keren had feeble smile and asked to join by her side. They began their conversation seated on the bench. And as the day began to rise from the east the soft feel of the ambience alluded around with the certain call of reminiscing past.

"Do you remember what exactly Duncan had told us" added Keren.

"You're still stuck with him. Let it go dear" she said pleasantly.

"I can't do that. He made us feel humiliated"

"How does that supposed to solve the problem?" Dora glimpsed at her.

There came no clue that they would likely to meet Duncan

again. Rather, they would seize themselves their fight by their own will against those sea pirates. For moment of time, the blink arrived from Keren, pretending that she had the solution to that. The fuzzy glance kept directed to her. Dora suspiciously looked at her. Maybe her mind could reveal out that something wicked was being handled.

"From now on, we're on our own. What do you say?" added Keren.

The rare raised eye brow expression flashed on Dora's face. She wasn't expecting to hear such sort of thing. Yet, she gave positive response to the concerning matter. Mom seemed to have agreed with her.

"Alright I'm in with you" she said.

"Let's get inside" Keren walked out.

By noon, they had visited the nearby water body just next to their hill slope. It's been long time after they had turned themselves into their form. Dora somehow had turned her body scales much weaker than ever before. Her tail couldn't get to enough strength to direct herself through the water. She was struggling as they swam deeper under water.

"Are you okay?" Keren concerned.

The voice feebly appeared to be audible and that mom was struggling hard to reach into the deep. Keren swam back to her and took control of her. She found her growing weak as her strength began to lose.

"Oh my god, you need to take rest"

Keren pulled her out of the deep water and managed to strike her out. At the slope side, she let her comfort and laid her down on the ground. By that time, she turned back to human. Keren still had the same glow over her whole body in mermaid form. With season they changed their color of their tail.

And the scales on her body still had the power to withstand strong currents of water and force over her. She carried Dora back to house from the lake site. Back at home, she made the comfortable suit for her. Dora's eyes were closed. In the process of losing her strength, she was unconsciously asleep. The petrified feeling indulged to take over Keren's mind. She began to feel the frightening cause in case if she doesn't make up to her life.

The night fell calm and it brought the shine of full moon over the dark sky and it was no more unlike any other nights. With Dora on bed, she kept gazing at her over the edge side and perceiving with belief that she might be able to keep things right for her in making her back as before. She headed gently and sat by her side. The eyes opened with struggle. And Keren met her sight.

"How're you feeling?"

The soft and lighted smile flashed on mom's face showing the relief over the pathetic pain.

"I'm good" she said.

Keren got out of the bed, moved downstairs and opted to get the bottle of fruit juice for her. When she returned, she found her toward the window. Watching at her she felt the need to offer quick assistance to her. She released the jug of juice on the table. Dora gazed at the full moon night and felt the soft breeze that blew in. By her side, stood Keren accompanied the gaze in the same direction. There was no sort of flaw about the night. And the best thing that clashed out was the peace that every other night didn't have.

"I got some fruit juice for you" Keren looked at her.

She peeked and showed the desire that she would like to accept the glass of juice from Keren. Dora walked toward the bed. The flapping window and curtains were pulled in. She picked up the glass of juice.

"You know distance has always been my friend. And I could never cover the gap between me and my family" she said effusively.

Keren shook her head and proceeded close to her. She sat just next to her on the edge. Passed a glimpse of sight to her and acquired a glass of juice for herself. She however, intended to keep the moment good for her. Their conversation turned even more insightful that took them away into their past and saddened over their deeds. They missed their family, friend and that counted their life. It wasn't until they discovered themselves that they were mermaid, their life had taken the turn away from the human world. When they figured out they weren't like one of them it barely let them feel in the group of human minds. Instead, they were naturally segregated from the rest of the world. Knowing they belonged from different species of life. It hurt the feeling at first but, with time they have developed the dual life to stay. Something everybody's not blessed with.

"You should go to bed now" Keren suggested.

Dora needed to visit the lake quite often from now on. She needed to regain herself into her real form. Keeping long time space between their synapse of being human and mermaid could perhaps, degrade their life span. In order to keep both in continued process, they usually needed to take over the water bodies that surrounded them. When the next morning broke, the first thing that came into her mind was to feed herself through the lake. Mom was taken to the lake.

"Are you ready?" Keren asked.

She shook her head watching at the hill side. Dora took her position to dive into the water. The splash of water fell on her as she saw Keren dived in. She followed her. With the flow of movement toward the deep, the transformation appeared to both. Their tail began to direct them according to their desired way. Dora followed Keren, she could make this time that she had regained few pulse of strength on her body. Her tail showed the smooth movement that she could control over herself. The bubbles of water ball opened out from Keren's mouth as she turned to look at her.

"You're doing good" she said.

They swam much deeper until they could see the lake floor. Feeling the whole aquatic world around them, they turned back to the surface. Keren was lying on the sloppy side of the lake bank.

"So what you think now?" Dora muttered.

"About what?"

Dora gave a shallow expression over that and sat next to her. She had something more relevant about the pirate's arrival.

"I can feel something danger to be taken place" she added again.

"We're safe here"

"I'm talking about the fight that we had undertaken with the pirates"

"We've a plan" Keren peeked at her.

The noon fell strangely on them, as the heat began to impulse out in more radiation. It wasn't like they were experiencing the winter end. But it had the welcoming notion about summer. When the noon day slanted toward its end they escaped back to home. And now, they had more implementing task to do for the future that the conflict of war had been on the rise.

It wasn't until the legendary stories that were being told from generations that inflicted with the vision into new generations who were born with such kinds. That led to the evolution of several alteration of human genome producing the avatars in life. Maybe the world needs them, and going against would somehow be the fall of guilty against them. Nothing would be spare if they come into power. In time, the humans would be dispersed from the living world and the expected scene of life would change providing it would be world for half bloods. The evolution would enhance the change of life and human beings wouldn't be considered as humans anymore from their genome. In contrast to that, the legends would be *Demi Gods*, *Mermaids* and many avatars that in future would come along with.

Dora was spotted at the lake the afternoon. She wasn't the fault of her life but agreed to let her go with the present condition that she had been facing in saving her daughter. There was nothing more than she could have done in protecting her family. She dived into the water thinking about me and dad. The thoughts still stayed intact that she tremendously missed us. But she had summoned herself with the kind of transforming life that she had been enduring where the danger is more prior to human life. As she began to move her hand and legs, she felt the toughest choice of her life path. Under water, she was resisting herself going against the transformation. She struggled and from all sides she felt the distortion over her. It brought the pain while she was enduring not to change. But it was natural and inevitable to escape the choice to stay as human. She screamed and felt the agony of being living the dual life which she never sensed to be a blessing. She couldn't compete and after long fight she was finally into mermaid. She turned to look at her tail, the color changed, her eyes in droplets of tears that mixed into the water.

Back in the house, Keren who was indulged with cup of coffee sensed something wrong that immediately shook her instinct. She felt the danger and was petrified to seek for. She looked for Dora in the house all around but seemed meaningless. The realization approved it was she, who hailed to be in trouble. Keren ran toward the lake and without waste of time she jumped into the water. She saw Dora struggling to withstand the change that transformed her into mermaid.

"Dora, what's wrong with you?" she yelled loud.

Keren pulled her out of the lake. She laid her aside on the bank.

"You can't go against the will of God, Dora. You've the gift, accept it" she said again.

Her moistened eyes spoke in no clue, Keren looked at her in more intensified way. She didn't like the way she had done to herself for it was something she was destined to be.

"You don't know what I feel inside Keren" she said.

Dora uplifted herself on the ground and sought to walk back to house.

"You know we're very close to our target and you can't let yourself do that. Think about your family and Annabell" Keren added as she walked alongside her.

Dora stopped suddenly in the midway. Her eye flashed the emotive cause of sudden dryness that revealed her the truth she was going through. She stared at Keren with great notion showing the rehabilitation. In such emotional content, she shook her head. Her eyes even deeper to stare that floated the current need to stay focused with her life. Both walked through the pathway that led them to home.

"I'm sorry, for being an insane woman"

"You don't. If I were in your place, I might have done the same too" consoled Keren.

When I woke up the morning the breeze was already dead. There was no content of zest in the air and that for the first time in the New Year, I had a dream about mom. I strolled downstairs searching for dad. He was out in the front yard examining his car.

"So, you're going to school right today" dad asked.

"I'll give a try" I added.

I've not been in contact with Alyward for the few weeks. After the end of Christmas, all have gone into their own rehab place to construe their living legend. I was left back being with dad to stay for the rest of the days. The school started. I hadn't showed up for two weeks since it began. I watched at dad splashing water on the roof top of the car. I glanced at my truck parked in the shed.

"Do you need any repair?"

"No dad, it's perfect" I assured.

I spent few more time with him talking about the Year's beginning. In the process of doing so, I told him the dream about mom. He wasn't that surprise to hear instead, somehow he showed that he was interested to know about. Just then the presence of Tyler altered in. We weren't expecting him that early day. He inwardly gave me a hug.

"How's your dad doing?" dad asked.

"He's doing good. He expected you today evening" Tyler added.

"What brought you here Tyler?" I questioned him.

He smiled at me and looked at dad's splashing water.

"I asked him to come, Anna" dad smiled.

"I'm done. I've school to go" I said and walked out.

Tyler looked at me. He joined dad in helping him in some sort of wooden construction. Few days back, dad told he would likely to have German Shepherd. The shed was meant for him.

When I got downstairs they were already involved in the making of the shed. I marched toward my truck and handled inside. The cornered eye from Tyler peeked at me with fluent version of gentle concern.

"Bye dad"

I ignored the rest of the companion. Back at school, I was expecting Lexie to be waiting for me at the entrance. I looked around until she called me. I marched toward her. There was no sign of Alyward that came by across the parking lot. I kept the inner question to myself. However, it trickled me all time during the class session. His absence began to indulge me more in worse way. I couldn't rely to attend more classes for the day.

At lunch I caught up Lexie, wondered about with the surety of asking her if she probably knew about Alyward. The lunch was kept on the table. But the gazing thought kept me indulged into something that I wasn't able to figure out.

"Are you okay?" she shook me.

"Have you seen Alyward?" I asked in no time.

"No... He's absent for the last few weeks" Lexie added.

She began to unfold the packet and fiddled with the spoon and fork. I avoided further to give the hinge over him rather, I joined to give the company at ease with Lexie.

"You look worried about him. Did something happen to him?" Lexie said, tearing the pieces of green leafy salad.

"No, it's fine" I ended shortly.

I returned home by the end of the day. Dad was in his den working up with the new files. I peeked at him through the slit of the door. He sensed about my return. I moved upstairs and relaxed myself for a little while. I began to miss about Alyward. Without any more hold unto my mind, I picked the number and dialed to him. From the other end there was no response. It said dead and the call got cut. It began to traumatize me with sadness and frustration that began to role on me. But somehow, I needed to stay calm. I gripped the strength over my emotional situation and pretended to stay soft without indulging in awkwardness. At dinner, dad called me down. Somehow, I could maintain the steadiness. There was no sort of thing that could grasp me inside with fulfillment of joy that moment. The dinner was served by dad. He poured me the glass of wine. I took a sip immediately to feel relax over my mind.

"How was your day?"

"Not as expected" I answered being dull.

I held the spoon and fork and began to cut the piece of bread. I applied the butter and cheese over it. Dad looked at me, perhaps he figured out something had been wrong to me. However, I presumed to stay settled with the ongoing talk without indulging much into him. The dinner got over early for me. I moved upstairs instantly. Dad watched me go, fiddled with unsettled mind. He realized that I needed to share what I had within me.

"Goodnight dad" I said, before I parted the night.

He shook his head in suspicious expulsion of his face. I looked at the phone if there was any response from Alyward. But the hope, doomed just next to me. I took up the bed silently. Out in the open air, the shine of moonlit night focused at the window. Neither, I could hold up myself to sleep nor could I keep my burning heart in peace. I grabbed a book from the nearby table and without listening to the outside world set the headphone into my ears with loudest of sound being played from the playlist. I held the book open right before me and began to read the story. The pages turned possibly at fast rate.

After a while, I glanced out through the window. I felt the winnowing of the cold breeze that blew inside. It thrashed like the icy temperate blow from the high mountain glaciers. My feet took the floor stepping toward the window. I pulled the window flap and the curtains and retreated back to my bed. For once I missed him next to me. When the morning rose from the east, I saw dad getting ready to get out as early as possible before the rising sun opened up. I hurried down to catch him up.

"Are going out?"

"Yeah!!!...I'll be back early today. Maybe by noon" dad said.

"You need to go to school" he added again.

"Don't worry, I'll"

He smiled and turned the steering wheel following out toward the gate. I watched him fade away from my sight. I prepared the breakfast for myself before I got ready to catch up the rest at school. I could still remember the first day during freshman year. Now that I was in sophomore, I gladly had done well till date. I moved out holding the insecure feel of missing the man that I had fallen for. It was the same scene when I reached the school parking lot. The space went empty without his presence. I felt the punch of unshielded outcome that pulled me down with sorrow which flashed on my eyes. The math class went empty without him next to me. It wasn't something that I ever expected to happen. I had no clue will that be the end between us, but there still had the chance that there might be something troubling him that kept him away from the rest of the world. I thought to seek for him at his house. Right after the class got over, I drove to Alyward's residence. Lexie saw me in hurry. We haven't met that day.

Chapter Twenty-three

At Alyward's home, I called for him. I saw everything shut from all around. I stepped though the stair proceeding toward the main door. The unlock door was opened and his name had me uttered out. There was no response from all sides. Moving upstairs toward his bedroom, found nothing but the empty vacant solitude around the room. I opened the window and viewed the panoramic site for once. It was never the same feeling as it used to be. With heavy heart, I moved downstairs heading back to my truck at roadside. While my feet loath heavy pulling me back to stay. The sorrow grounded me with more sadness and that I felt the cutting edge of knife running through me. It's very hard to accept when you know the person you love isn't anymore with you. Just in case, by fate's accident there might be a chance to bring back the life again. However, I never believed in such luck called the fate of luckiness. As I browsed through the ground floor, at the front table somewhere next to the front door, I had a glitch sight of an envelope kept upright. I marched to know for it. The letter was meant to me. He had some will of his heart to share his feeling no matter whatever way, he felt the need to convey to keep alive. Unfolding it, I shared the words within myself through great endurance and pain that thrashed me through open heart.

Anna, My love

Knowing that I've hurt you, it wasn't I supposed
to mean. Believe me what I had written here. There
are few things that I haven't told you about me.
You just know me as a Clairvoyant, and knowing that
I just want you to keep safe from cruel world.
I'll let you know everything on my return. But for
moment please forgive me for being an odd guy. Keep
the faith and I shall come back to you very soon. It
all happened without any knowledge of mine thereby
I couldn't inform you about my absence.

I knew you would come for me therefore I left this
letter to you. I'll always pray and have you in my
heart forever in my life.

Alyward Pyne

I couldn't resist but burst into rain of tears that endlessly fell
through my cheek. I felt on my knee on the cold floor. It lasted
for minutes under the same roof. After a while, I realized the
end of the day was nearly getting dark. I felt the vibrant shake
of my phone. Dad was trying to hold me on the line. I wiped out
my face getting it dry and moved out of the house following
toward my truck. I had the letter with me and, fearlessly I
drove through the road in speed. The darkness crawled on the
way somehow, I could visibly see the empty road with the
powerful headlights. All through the way the words made me
felt weaker and emotional turmoil took me under control. By
the time, I reached back home it was too late to be considered.

Dad wasn't settled with the talk done. I burst into anger without
concerning about him. I followed upstairs immediately without
giving the interest over his dinner. The unfair means of life
that bolted me kept me stitched with deep scar. I couldn't hold

anymore the phase of life I was going through. Just like the empty vessel, I began to lead out without any feel of outside world. The nights were turned into nightmare and painful to tackle. Often it gave me the fear and insecure pain inside to withstand the whole dark phase. Such feelings never could possibly be thrown away. The more I tried to calm the better it caught me with crapped teeth of pain.

At midnight dad knocked at my door. I dreamt about Alyward not necessarily a good one but it brought emotional pain into me. Hearing the scream of my voice dad ran to my door.

"Are you okay?" dad said.

Somehow, he cracked the hook of the door. Seeing me, he felt terrible about my condition. He saw me crushed and squeezed on bed with flow of painful strings of blood that terribly gave me the pain. He immediately took hold on me and began to console at ease. I felt his palm ran through my forehead. Few droplets of cold water, he smeared on my face.

"It's just a dream" his voice heard softly.

I gently opened my eyes and felt dad very close to me. That gave me little hope and regained through the bad nightmare. Dad spent an hour with me. He hasn't asked me anything about what I had been going through for the last few days. When the morning broke with the bright hope, I woke up feeling the cold floor beneath my feet. I walked toward the window and saw dad at the front yard. Tyler saw me at the window. The response was felt with a smile from him. I got down. They were still working on the dog shed. It was half built by now.

"Are you okay?" dad peeked at me as he pulled the wood to make the wall.

Tyler handed him the hammer and the nails to get it fixed.

"How have you been?" Tyler breathed out.

"I'm good. What about you?" I said.

"Nothing new" he smiled out.

The week passed on. By now, I could see the dog shed was made completely. Somehow with going days, I managed to complete the school hours. It mattered with the absence of Alyward. He seemed to appear all time but probably I knew, I wouldn't be able to see him. Gradually with the time, I inculcated to avoid in thinking about him. It needed to do else I was the victim of such haunting thoughts. However, I began to talk less or mingle with people. It didn't appear right to me. Lexie had always been the one who usually showed me the company anywhere. Sometime, I took time to find what it could be that Alyward had been hiding from me. At the time of loneliness, I read out his letter. His words didn't give the clue about his absence from the town. However, I concealed within myself with hope to see him back.

That night, Lexie companied me for dinner to my house. As usual dad was happy to see her. We had a great price of meal following with great steak from her side. Even Tyler was there to witness the dinner with all of us. They left us after we shared valuable time between us. I could gradually hold on to my heart and mind. Although, I couldn't completely forget about Alyward, I just learned to live without his presence.

That night for the first time after gap of months, I dreamt about mom. I felt it very real as if holding her next to me. It was truly the feel of overwhelming joy to sleep next to her. I felt the protective sheath covered on me. Next to her, there's no kind of sorrow and pain but the happiness that would fill into pouch with hope and integrity. She spoke to me with words of kindness and when I woke up from bed, I found myself in tears and she disappeared before my eyes.

The morning allured with fresh air and the chirping of bird. I had skipped school. Certainly, I hid the truth from dad that I was going to the beach. He was seen dodging with the heap of airbag trying to fit in his car.

"Are you moving out?"

"Yeah!!!" I answered.

I drove to the beach. There I found the vacant space that was prevailed within. I parked the truck at corner of the beach side. I followed to the edge of the shore wanting nothing more than to dive into the water. The last thought that struck me was Alyward who seemed to have made me feel like he had been watching me. Out of nowhere, I heard a silent voice that reached into my ears. It said to stay away from danger. However, I disobeyed the calling. The voice seemed to have been recognized as of Alyward's. I held myself stiff standing along the edge feeling the touch of freezing water from the coming tide. I slowly undressed and moved forward toward the water. Out from the horizon the sun rose in smooth manner giving the last glimpse of it, I followed under the water. Until then the voice still echoed into my head.

As I swam deeper, I transformed into a mermaid the real me. I found *Jimmy* who had been waiting for me. Flipping my tail across the water, we dodged with various sea creatures and the tour began with us. I realized my tail color had changed. I began to feel stronger and felt that I could handle myself regarding my relation with Alyward. The emotional turmoil mattered nothing more when I'm into form of my real life.

At dinner dad questioned suddenly about Alyward. From no expectation he did that. I explained, not much in detail making him belief everything was fine between us. There was no sort of serious talk we had the night but followed along with him to watch a movie after the dinner. For a while, dad companied me then he moved to his working room.

"I belief you should see Tyler" he smiled as he walked out.

"Alright" I shrugged "may be tomorrow".

At night, before I made myself into bed I had called Tyler for once. We talked for half an hour. I don't know, what we discussed but it continued for long. I assured him to see him the next day. He was glad to receive me. Perhaps, long time after I was visiting to his home. Moreover, I haven't seen Burney Gaige for months.

It's Sunday and dad wouldn't be going for his duty. But before I left home, I spent the morning breakfast with him. I ensured him about my return by sunset. I drove out with my truck through the long dense forest road that led me to Tyler's home. He was already waiting for me at the front yard. On my sight, he followed toward me. He showed the chivalry giving me a warm hug. I felt it hugely and the heart beats began to settle within me. We walked back to the house through the yard, I happen to notice his bike parked. It sensed something within and I felt it very close.

"Let's take a ride" I said gazing at his bike.

"Are you sure?"

"Yeah" I shrugged.

We rode through the longest way with densely covered forest path. Just in mid the road passed on and I could view the straight road that followed out in length endlessly. On both to our sides, the tall trees stood firm without any end. The breeze rushed through my body. And my hands clasped him tightly as we rode.

It felt good to be outside and somewhere inside my memory Alyward still existed knowing that he was gone. The cobblestones were still wet from the morning dew. *I felt little joy of happiness running through me. I didn't know why, but to me it seemed like the sweetest thing I've ever felt in my life.*